P9-EMN-805

Praise for *New York Times* bestselling author
FAYE KELLERMAN
and
MILK AND HONEY

"Faye Kellerman's best novel to date: deeper, richer,
more emotionally complex."
James Ellroy

"No one working in the crime genre is better."
Baltimore Sun

"She does for the American cop story what P.D. James
has done for the British mystery, lifting it beyond genre."
Richmond Times-Dispatch

"Compelling . . . Her characters are fully drawn and the
gritty story moves on relentlessly."
Indianapolis Star

"Reading a good thriller is very much like taking a great
vacation: half the fun is getting there. Faye Kellerman
is one heck of a tour guide."
Detroit Free Press

"Engrossing . . . horribly riveting."
Roanoke Times & World News

"A wonderful mystery . . . **MILK AND HONEY** is one of those books that leaves strong reminders long after the last page is turned. It is startling in its content and frightening in its execution."
Ocala Star-Banner

"Kellerman is a master of mystery."
St. Louis Post-Dispatch

"A believable, intricate mystery in which series hero Decker is revealed as even more complex, interesting, and sympathetic than in earlier appearances."
Publishers Weekly

"Kellerman does an excellent job . . . Her novels blend good police procedure with insights into a society cloistered from most of us."
Los Angeles Times

"She is a master storyteller."
Chattanooga Free Press

Also by Faye Kellerman

FAYE KELLERMAN

MILK
AND
HONEY

A PETER DECKER/RINA LAZARUS NOVEL

AVON BOOKS
An Imprint of HarperCollinsPublishers

AVON BOOKS
An Imprint of HarperCollins*Publishers*
10 East 53rd Street
New York, New York 10022-5299

Copyright © 1990 by Faye Kellerman
ISBN: 0-380-73268-8
www.avonbooks.com

First Avon Books paperback printing: January 2003
First William Morrow hardcover printing: April 1990

Avon Trademark Reg. U.S. Pat. Off. and in Other Countries, Marca Registrada, Hecho en U.S.A.
HarperCollins® is a registered trademark of HarperCollins Publishers Inc.

Printed in the U.S.A.

10 9 8 7 6 5 4 3 2 1

To the family—
Jonathan, Mom, and the kids.

And to my breakfast buddies:
Elyse Wolf, Lynn Rohatiner,
Debi Benaron, and Frieda Katz.

MILK

AND

HONEY

🌱1

The flutter of movement was so slight that had Decker not been a pro, he would have missed it. He yanked the wheel to the left and braked. The brown unmarked screeched, bucked, then rebelliously reversed directions in the middle of the empty intersection. Decker began to cruise down the vacant street, hoping for a second look at what had attracted his attention.

The Plymouth's alignment was off again, this time pulling to the right. If he had a spare minute, he'd check it out himself, haul her onto the lifts and probe her belly. The department mechanics were a joke. Overworked and underpaid, they'd fix one problem, cause another. The guys in the division were always laying odds on what would bust first when the vehicles were returned from service—six-to-one on a leaky radiator, four-to-one on a choked carburetor, three-to-one on the broken air-conditioning system, the odds improving to two-to-one if it was summertime.

Decker ran his fingers through thick ginger hair. The neighborhood was dead. Whatever he'd seen had probably been nothing significant. At one in the morning, the eyes played tricks. In the dark, parked cars looked like giant tortoises, spindly tree boughs became hanging skeletons. Even a well-populated housing development like this one seemed

1

like a ghost town. Rows of tan-colored stucco homes had gelled into a lump of oatmeal, illuminated by moonbeams and blue-white spotlights from corner street lamps.

He slowed the Plymouth to a crawl and threw the head-lights on high beam. Perhaps he'd seen nothing more than a cat, the light a reflection in the feline's eyes. But the ra-diancy had been less concentrated and more random, a rip-ple of flashes like silver fingernails running up a piano keyboard. Yet as he peered out the window, he saw nothing unusual.

The planned community was spanking new, the streets still smelling of recent blacktop, the curbside trees nothing more than saplings. It had been one of those compromises between the conservationists and the developers, the con-struction agreed upon by both parties while satisfying nei-ther. The two groups had been at each other's throats since the Northeast Valley had been gerrymandered. This project had been hastily erected to smooth ruffled feathers, but the war between the factions was far from over. Too much open land left to fight over.

Decker cranked open the window and repositioned his backside in the seat, trying to stretch. Someday the city would order an unmarked able to accommodate a person of his size, but for now it was knees-to-the-wheel time. The night was mild, the fog had yet to settle in. Visibility was still good.

What the hell had he seen?

If he had to work tomorrow, he would have quit and headed home. But nothing awaited him on his day off ex-cept a lunch date with a ghost. His stomach churned at the thought, and he tried to forget about it—him. Better to deal with the past in the light of day.

One more time around the block for good measure. If nothing popped up, he'd go home.

He was a tenacious son of a bitch, part of what made him a good cop. Anyway, he wasn't tired. He'd taken a catnap earlier in the evening, right before his weekly Bible session with Rabbi Schulman. The old man was in his seventies, yet had more energy than men half his age. The two of them had learned together for three hours straight. At midnight, when the rabbi still showed no signs of tiring, Decker announced he couldn't take any more.

The old man had smiled and closed his volume of the Talmud. They were studying civil laws of lost and found. After the lesson, they talked a bit, smoked some cigarettes—the first nicotine fix Decker'd had all day. Thirty minutes later, he departed with an armful of papers to study for next week.

But he was too hyped up to go home and sleep. His favorite method of coping with insomnia was to take long drives into the foothills of the San Gabriel Mountains—breathe in the beauty of unspoiled lands, knolls of wildflowers and scrub grass, gnarled oaks and honey-colored maples. The peace and solitude nestled him like a warm blanket, and within a short period of time he usually became relaxed enough to sleep. He'd been on his way home when he noticed the flash of light. Though he tried to convince himself it was nothing, something in his gut told him to keep going.

He circled the block, then reluctantly pulled over to the curb and killed the engine. He sat for a moment, smoothing his mustache, then slapped the steering wheel and opened the car door.

What the hell, the walk would do him good. Stretch out his legs. No one was awaiting his arrival at the ranch, anyway. The home fires had been put out a long time ago. Decker thought of his phone conversation with Rina earlier in the evening. She'd sounded *really* lonely, hinted about coming back to Los Angeles for a visit—just her and not the boys. Man, had he sounded eager—*overeager*. He'd been so damned excited, she'd probably seen his *horns* over the telephone wires. Decker wondered if he'd scared her off, and made a mental note to call her in the morning.

He hooked his hand-radio onto his belt, locked the car, and opened the trunk. The trunk light was busted, but he could see enough to rummage through the items—first-aid kit, packet of surgical gloves, evidence bags, rope, blanket, fire extinguisher—where had he put the flashlight? He picked up the blanket. Success! And miracle of miracles, the batteries still had juice in them.

A quick search on foot.

The early morning air felt good on his face. He heard his own footsteps reverberating in the quiet of the night and felt as if he were violating someone's privacy. Something darted in front of his feet. A small animal—a rat or a lizard. Scores of them roamed the developments, all of the suckers pissed off at being displaced by building foundation. But that wasn't what he'd seen before. That had been bigger, at least the size of a dog or cat. Yet its gait had been odd—staggering, as if drunk.

He walked a half-block to the north, shining his beam between the nearly identical houses. Not much space to illuminate; the homes almost abutted one another, separated only by a hedge of Eugenia saplings. The houses were cheaply built, the stucco barely dry but already beginning to crack. The front lawns were patches of green sod, and many of them held swing sets and aluminum lawn furniture. Some of the driveways were repositories for toys, bicycles, baby walkers, bats and balls. The uncluttered driveways housed vans and station wagons, and small motorboats as well. Lake Castaic was fifteen minutes away. The developers had advertised that, and had succeeded in their goal of attracting young families. Ten percent down and low-cost financing hadn't hurt, either.

He strolled to the end of the street—this one was called Pine Road—then crossed over and started back to the unmarked. Then he heard it—a faint whistling in the background. A familiar sound, one that he'd heard many times in the past but couldn't place at the moment.

He jogged in its direction. The sound grew a little louder, then stopped. He waited a minute.

Nothing.

Frustrated, he decided to head home, then heard the whistling again, farther in the distance. Whatever was making the noise was on the move, and it was a quick little bugger.

He sprinted two blocks down Pine Road and turned onto Ohio Avenue. Loads of imagination the developers had when naming the streets. The north-south roads were trees, east-west were states.

The noise became louder, one that Decker recognized immediately. His heart raced against his chest. The adrenaline surge. The sound was now clear—a high-pitched wail. Goddam wonder it didn't wake up the entire neighborhood.

He ran in the direction of the shriek, pulling out his radio and calling for backup—*screaming heard on Ohio and Sycamore*. He pulled out his gun.

"Police!" he shouted. "Freeze!"

His voice echoed in the darkness. The crying continued, softer than before.

"Police!" Decker yelled again.

A door opened.

"What's going on out there?" asked a deep male voice, heavy with sleep.

"Police," Decker answered. "Stay inside your house, sir."

The door slammed shut.

Across the street, a light brightened an upstairs window. A face peeked out between the curtains.

Again, the crying faded to nothing. Silence, then a chorus of crickets singing backup for a mockingbird.

The noise returned again, this time short sobs and gasps for air. Obviously a female, possibly a rape victim.

He would have received the call anyway.

"Police," Decker shouted in the direction of the crying. "Stay where you are, ma'am. I'm here to help you."

The sobbing stopped, but he could hear footsteps trudging through the Eugenias, followed by the creak of unoiled metal. Decker felt his fingers grip the butt of his Beretta. The sky held oyster-colored clouds, the smiling face of the man in the moon. Enough illumination to see pretty well even without the flashlight.

Then Decker saw it—the glint of metal!

He jumped out from the Eugenias and yelled, "Freeze!"

The reaction he received was a high-pitched tinkle of startled laughter.

The kid had to be under two, still retaining the chubby cheeks of a baby. It was impossible to tell whether it was a boy or girl, but whatever it was had a head full of ringlets and saucer-shaped eyes. It was swinging on the seesaw on somebody's front lawn, fragile little hands gripping the handlebars, eyes staring up in wonderment. Decker became aware of the gun in his hand, his finger wrapped around the trigger. Shakily, he returned the automatic to his shoulder harness and called off the backups on his wireless.

"Off," ordered a tiny voice.

"For heaven's sakes!" Decker stopped the seesaw. The toddler climbed off.

"Up," it said, raising its hands in the air.

Decker picked the child up. The toddler lay its head against Decker's chest. He stroked its silken curls.

"I'm calling the police out there," yelled a frightened voice from inside the house.

"I *am* the police," Decker answered. He walked up to the front door and displayed his badge to a peephole. The door opened a crack, the chain still fastened. Decker could make out unshaven skin, a dark, wary pupil.

Decker said, "I found this child on your front lawn."

"My God!" said a muffled female voice.

"Do you know who this child belongs to?" Decker asked.

"Know the kid, Jen?" the man asked gruffly.

The door opened all the way.

"You found him outside *my* house?" Jen said. She looked to be in her early thirties, her hair dark brown, pulled back into a knot. "Why he's just a *baby*!"

"Yes, ma'am," said Decker. "I found him or her on your swing set."

"I've never seen the kid before in my life," Jen answered.

"The neighborhood's crawling with rug rats," the unshaven man said. "All I know is he's not one of ours."

"There're lots of new families in the area," Jen said. She shrugged apologetically. "It's hard to keep track of all the kids."

Decker said, "No sense waking up the entire neighborhood. I'm sure we'll get a panic call in the morning. The baby will be at the Foothill station. Spread the word, huh?"

"Sure, Officer, we will," Jen said.

"I'm goin' upstairs," said the husband. "Back to sleep!"

"Goodness." Jen shook her head. "That little cutie was right outside *my* house?"

"Yes, ma'am."

Jen chucked the child's chin. "Hi there, sweetheart. Can I give you a cookie?"

Decker said, "I don't think we should feed the child right now. It's a little late."

"Oh yes," Jen said. "Of course, you're right. Can I offer you a cup of coffee?"

"Thank you but no, ma'am."

"What's a baby doing out in the middle of the night like that?" Jen chucked the child's chin again.

"I don't know, ma'am." Decker gave her his card. "Call me if you hear of anything."

"Oh, I will, I will. The community's still pretty manageable. It shouldn't be too hard to locate his parents."

"Jennn!" screamed the husband from upstairs. "C'mon! I gotta get up early."

"What will you do with him?" Jen asked quickly. "Or maybe it's a her. Looks like a little girl, don't you think?"

Decker smiled noncommittally.

"What do you do with stray kids like this, poor little thing?"

"He or she will be cared for until we can locate the parents."

"Will she be put in a foster home?"

"Jennn!"

"That man drives me nuts!" Jen whispered to Decker.

"Thanks for your time, ma'am," Decker said. The door closed behind him, the chain was refastened to the post.

Decker looked at the toddler and said, "Where the heck did you come from, buddy?"

The child smiled.

"Got some teeth there, huh? How many do you have? Ten maybe?"

The child stared at him, played with a button on his shirt.

"Well, as long as we're up so late how 'bout you coming to my place for a nightcap, huh?"

The child buried its head in Decker's shoulder.

"Rather sleep, huh? You must be a girl. It's the story of my life."

Decker headed toward the unmarked.

"Lord only knows how you escaped. Your mom is going to have a fit in the morning."

The toddler tucked its arm under its body.

"Snuggly little thing, aren't you? How the heck did I notice you in the first place? Must have been the shiny zipper on your PJs."

"Pee jehs," said the child.

"Yeah, PJs. What color are they? Red? Pinkish red, kind of. Bet you *are* a girl."

"A gull!" mimicked the toddler.

Decker's smile faded. Something in the air. He smelled it now—the stale odor on its hands, on the front of its pajamas. Clotted blood. He hadn't noticed it at first because it had blended with the color of the child's sleepwear.

"Jesus!" he whispered, his hands shaking. He clutched the toddler, ran back to the unmarked, and unlocked the door.

Where the hell was the kid bleeding from!

He placed the baby on the backseat and unzipped its pajama sleeper. He shined the flashlight on the little body, the skin as smooth and pink as a ripe nectarine. Not a scratch on the chest, back, or shoulders. The forearms and wrist were spotted with a small, dry rash, but the rest of the toddler's skin wasn't cut, cracked, or punctured. Decker turned the child over. The back was clear as well.

He held his breath, praying that this wasn't another ugly sexual-abuse case. He undid the diaper. It was soaked, but as far as he could tell, the child was unscathed. It *was* a she, and no blood was flowing from any of her orifices. He refastened the diaper as best as he could, then checked her throat, her head, her ears, her nose. The kid endured the impromptu examination with stoicism.

No signs of external or internal bleeding.

Decker exhaled forcibly. He swaddled her in a blanket, pulled out an evidence bag, and dropped the pajama sleeper inside. He buckled her in the backseat as tightly as he could, then drove to the station.

2

Marge Dunn hummed out loud as she walked into the detectives' squad room. Her cheerful mood was immediately silenced by a grunt and a sneer from Paul MacPherson. She frowned and brushed wisps of blond hair from her round, doelike eyes. A big woman, tough when she had to be, she didn't like crap first thing in the morning.

"What's eating your ass?" she asked him.

"One doesn't whistle at seven in the morning," answered MacPherson. "It's profane."

Marge sighed. MacPherson was the only black detective in Foothill, and all eyes were upon him. He was constantly forced to prove himself, and playing supercop got old very fast. Marge could understand that. Being the only woman detective was no picnic, either. MacPherson spent long hours at work. Made him good at the job, but gave him a problem 'tude. He was also constantly on the prowl.

"You been up all night, Paulie?"

"Gang shoot-out, two A.M., with bad-breath Fordebrand in Maui, guess who caught the call? Two DBs and a six-year-old in intensive care with a bullet in her brain—it made the headlines of all the morning papers, Marjorie. Don't you read?"

"Not if I can help it," Marge answered. "Paul, my man,

10

you're so pale you're starting to look white. Go home and get some sleep."

" 'To sleep, perchance to dream . . . ' " Paul raised his eyebrows. "I just got my season tickets to the Globe Theater in San Diego. First production's *All's Well That Ends Well*. Come with me, my sweet, and I promise you an extraordinary experience."

"Pass."

"Come on, Marjorie," Paul said. "Expose yourself to culture."

"I have culture." She reached inside her desk and pulled out her flute case. "This is culture."

"Culture is for yogurt," said Mike Hollander, lumbering in. He settled his meaty buttocks on a chair and pulled out a pile of papers from his desk drawer.

"Good morning, Michael," said Marge. "Did you get the invitation to my next recital?"

Hollander tugged on the ends of his drooping mustache and gave her a sick smile. "Mary and I will be there."

Marge gave him a pat atop his bald head. "For that, I'll serve you coffee."

Hollander smiled, genuinely this time. "You can toss me that old doughnut, Margie. No one else seems to be eating it."

"Righto." She aimed and fired. Hollander caught it in his right hand.

MacPherson said, "You're actually going to her recital."

Hollander whispered back, "The sacrifices one makes for friendship."

"You're an asshole," MacPherson said. "You listen to her produce squeaky noises and I ask, what's the payoff?"

"It makes her happy," Hollander said.

"Makes her *happy*?" MacPherson said. "I don't believe you said that, Michael."

"I heard that, Paul," Marge said.

"*Mea culpa*, madam," said MacPherson. "I apologize. I

don't pick fights with women who outweigh me by twenty-five pounds."

"Twenty," Marge said. "I lost some weight since I broke up with Carroll. God, what an appetite that man had. I never realized how much the two of us ate." She went over to the urn and poured two rounds of coffee, one in her unadorned mug, another in Hollander's—a ceramic cup fronted with two 3-D breasts, the nipples painted bright pink.

"Done with the paper work yet, Paulie?" Hollander asked. "Shit, that must have been bad."

MacPherson said, "I don't give a rat's ass about the DBs. Both of the punks were subhuman. It's the little sister that burns my butt."

"She get in the way of cross fire?" Marge asked, handing Hollander his cup.

MacPherson shook his head. "Get this. She was trying to protect her older brother—the punk. Such a sweet little thing. What a waste!"

"Where's Decker?" Hollander asked. "He's late this morning."

"He took the day off," Marge said.

"Oh, that's right," Hollander said. "He mentioned he was meeting some old army buddy that got himself in a jam."

MacPherson said. "Rabbi Pete's upstairs committing an immoral act with a minor."

Marge smiled and sipped.

"I shit you not," MacPherson continued. "He's in the dorm sleeping with a kid under two. As a matter of fact, Margie, you'd better wake him up. Some dumb social worker's going to see him and the kid together, and poor Pete'll be charged with sexual abuse."

"What happened?" Marge asked.

"The rabbi found the kid wandering the streets in that new development about one this morning. Brought her into the station house."

"Which development?" Hollander asked. "There's been a

bunch of them lately. Assholes gerrymander the district, and we've got all these rich boys coming in and building all over the place."

"Manfred and Associates," MacPherson said. "You know. The one where all the streets are trees or states."

"The one above the old lime quarry," Marge said.

"You got it," MacPherson answered.

"Decker call IDC yet?" Hollander asked.

"Nah," MacPherson said. "Too early for that. He just filled out the forms and placed her under protective custody. The kid probably climbed out of her crib and escaped through a doggy door. Pete's hoping for a frantic call any moment."

"I'll go wake him," Marge said. She placed her mug on her desktop. "Enjoy your coffee, Michael."

Hollander said, "Thanks. It's as close as I'll get to tit this morning."

She walked out of the squad room into the front reception area. A middle-aged Hispanic was gesticulating to the desk sergeant. He was beanpole-thin, his face etched with deep sun lines. The sergeant looked bored, his chin resting in the palm of his hand, his eyes looking over the head of the Hispanic to Marge.

"Yo, Detective Dunn."

Marge waved and said, "Sergeant Collins."

"Is Sergeant Decker around? I need someone who can speak Spanish."

Marge said, "I'll go find you someone bilingual, Sarge."

"Thanks." Collins turned to the Hispanic. "Down, boy. Over there." He pointed to a bench against the wall. It was occupied by a biker with bulging arms blued by tattooing, and a diminutive girl with stringy hair. "There, there!"

Marge said, *"Sientese aquí, por favor."*

The man began speaking to Marge in rapid Spanish.

"No hablo Español," Marge said. "Wait. *Un momento. Sientese.* On the bench."

The Hispanic nodded his head in comprehension and sat down between the woman and the biker.

Collins said, "These dingdongs speak more Spanish than English over here."

Marge asked, "Where'd you transfer from, Sarge?"

"Southeast," Collins answered. "Five years in that shit-hole. They don't speak English over there, either. Only fluent jive."

"Most of the people in this division are hardworking," Marge said.

"Yeah," Collins said. "Till they get their papers and apply for welfare. Seems like America is the land of opportunity as long as you aren't American."

Marge smiled, made a quick exit. Collins hadn't been in the division more than a week, and the SOB was already bitching and moaning. He probably hated women, too. Marge shrugged him off, figuring a five-year stint at Southeast could do strange things to anyone.

She climbed up the metal staircase and opened the door to the dorm.

Decker wasn't sleeping. He was wrestling with the kid on the floor, trying to change her diaper. From the looks of the struggle, the kid had the edge. The big redhead was so involved in the ordeal that he hadn't even heard the door open.

"C'mon, kiddo," Decker said. "Just onnnne more second—no. No, don't do that. Hold still. Shit. Excuse my language. Just hold—"

The kid kicked her legs with all her might.

"Happy? You just ripped the diaper again."

Decker tickled her ribs. The toddler broke into peals of laughter.

"Ticklish, huh?" Decker tickled her again. She spasmed with guffaws. "Now listen, buddy. I'm talkin' tough now. I've got to get you protected. Let me just get this . . . this damn tab—this tab over here. . . ."

The little girl ripped the diaper off and gave him a self-satisfied smile.

"God, you're rambunctious." He paused, then said, "And you're a cutey, too. Are you hungry?"

"Hungee," the kid repeated.

"Then how about we put on the diaper? Then old Pete will get you some milk while I try to wake up with a cup of coffee."

"Hot," the toddler said.

"What's hot?"

"Hot."

"Is something burning you?" Decker looked around, touched the floor. "I don't feel anything hot."

The baby smiled again.

"Yes, if old Pete don't get some coffee soon, he's going to drop on the spot."

"Hot," the child repeated.

"What's hot?" Decker asked, frustrated.

"Maybe she means coffee is hot," Marge suggested.

Decker whipped his head around.

"How long have you been standing there?" he said.

"About a minute."

"I don't suppose you'd like to help me."

"You're handling her very well, Pete."

"Get me another diaper," Decker said. "She keeps ripping them off. I think she's ready to be trained."

"Tell her mother that when she comes to pick her up," Marge said, throwing him a new diaper.

Wincing, Decker diapered the toddler, then picked her up. "This is Auntie Margie, pumpkin," he said. "Say hello."

"Well, hello there," Margie said, reaching out for the child. The girl jumped into Marge's arms. "Well, aren't you a friendly little thing." She smiled at the baby, then looked at Decker.

"What's on your mind, big buddy?" she asked him. "You've got a hinky expression on your face."

"What time is it?" Decker asked.

"Around seven-thirty, I guess."

Decker asked, "Have we received any phone calls yet about a missing child?"

"Not that I know of . . . It's still early, Pete."

"When Cindy was that age, she was up at six o'clock every morning. I remember it well because *I* was the one who was up with her. It's kind of late for a mother not to notice her child missing."

"Kids differ. My nephew used to sleep till nine. All of my sister's friends were green with envy."

"Just proves my point," Decker said. "Most kids aren't real late sleepers."

"But this one could be," Marge said.

Decker didn't answer her.

"What else is sticking in your craw?" Marge asked.

Decker said, "I found her in a pajama sleeper, Margie. I had it bagged. It had recent blood on it."

"A lot?"

"More than a nosebleed's worth. And none of it looks like it came from the kid. Her body was clean except for a little rash on both her arms."

"Blood on a pajama sleeper isn't an everyday occurrence," Marge admitted. "I don't like it, either."

There was a moment of silence. Marge broke it.

"Think her mother was whacked?"

"Maybe a suicide." Decker shrugged. "The kid's obviously been well cared for. No superficial signs of abuse. I figure I'll wait until nine. If no one calls in by then, we'll do a door-to-door search where I found her last night."

"MacPherson said she was wandering around the new development over the quarry."

"Yep. The newest Manfred job—a couple hundred houses. Looks like I got my work cut out for me."

Marge said, "It's your day off."

"Not anymore," Decker said. "It's okay. I don't mind doing my bit for this little thing. All I need is a couple of hours off in the afternoon. Do me a favor, Margie. Get the kid some juice and bread or something. She must be starved."

"Sure," Marge said. "Want some help canvassing the area?"

"You've read my mind." Decker reached for his cigarettes, then retracted his hand. "What time is it now? Eight?"

"Quarter to."

"I'd like to pull another hour of sleep before we begin talking to the good folk, if you don't mind."

"Go ahead. Maybe the situation will resolve itself with a frantic phone call."

"I sure as hell hope so. But I'm not overly optimistic."

"Want me to punch her description into the computer?" Marge asked.

"That's a little premature," Decker said. "Go ahead and snap Polaroids of her for ID purposes. And if you get a chance, print her feet, also. Maybe they will match some hospital newborn file."

"Want me to call IDC?"

Decker frowned. "Yeah, I guess someone should. If no one claims her, we're going to have to take her somewhere."

"I'll call up Richard Lui at MacClaren Hall. He's a nice guy with primo connections to the good foster homes. Did I ever tell you I went out with him?"

"Was this before or after Carroll?"

"After Carroll, before Kevin. We didn't last too long, but we had enough of a good time that he still does favors for me."

"Well, use the clout, woman. Ask him to call Sophi Rawlings. She's a great lady and happens to be in the area. I think she's licensed to handle them this young. If you

make yourself unusually charming, maybe we can circum-
vent MacClaren altogether and take her to Sophi's directly."

"No problem. Richard is wild about me." Marge smiled
at the little girl and said, "Let's get you some grub, honey."

"Honey!" the child shouted.

Marge laughed. "*You're* a honey."

"Honey!" the toddler echoed.

Decker waited until Marge and the kid were gone then
sank into his bunk. He fell asleep with a smile on his lips.
He dreamed of Rina—lost, lovely days that he hoped to re-
capture very soon.

❦3

Sweet dreams so real, yet like spun sugar, a touch and everything dissolves. The blast of incandescent light. Marge's voice.

"Wake up, Pete."

"I'm up," he grunted.

"Are you up as in paying attention?"

"What time is it?"

"Ten."

"Ten?" Decker sat up, almost hit his head on the top bunk. He rubbed his eyes. "Why'd you let me sleep so late?"

"Mike and I just came back from a two thirty-four."

"Need me for anything?"

"Nah," Marge said. "The woman's stable. Date rape. Happened last night. She finally got the courage to make the call this morning. Got a shitload of physical evidence— the girl was slapped around. Mike's filing for the warrant right now."

Decker yawned. "What's with the kid?"

"No one called to claim her. She's with Lucinda Alvarez right now. I just got off the phone with Richard Lui. He said if we fill out the necessary forms ASAP and bring them over to him, we can take the kid directly to Sophi Rawlings

19

and bypass MacClaren. If no one claims her in seventy-two hours, Richard'll set up an arraignment in Dependency Court."

"Great," Decker said. "If you fill out the forms, I'll take her to Sophi's."

"Fine."

"Still want to do a door-to-door with me afterward?"

"Why not? I've got nothing pressing until two in the afternoon." She started to walk away, then stopped. "Oh. Rina called. She said she's not working today. Asked for you to call her back when you get a chance."

"Thanks."

Marge took another step, then added, "Jan called, too."

Decker said, "What the hell did *she* want?"

"I didn't ask, Peter."

As soon as he was alone, Decker dialed the New York number. The line was full of static. Rina picked it up on the third ring.

"Hello there," Decker said.

"I was hoping it was you," Rina answered.

"Well, it's me," Decker answered. Her voice gave him a chill down his spine. He said, "Are you feeling all right?"

"Fine. Why do you ask?"

"You're not at work."

"Yes, I guess I'm not."

There was a pause.

"What's wrong, Rina?" Decker asked.

"I can't go into it over the phone. It'll take up too much of your time. You *are* calling from the station, aren't you?"

"Yeah."

"I can tell. Their phone system is very poor. I love you, Peter."

"I love you, too," Decker said. "Are you still thinking about coming out here?"

"How does Wednesday sound?"

Decker grinned. "It sounds terrific. I promise to keep my hands in my pockets when we're in public."

Silence on the other end.

Decker said, "Rina, doll, what is it?"

"Do you have time, Peter?"

Decker sighed. "Not a lot right now, unfortunately. How about if I call you back in a couple of hours?"

"Don't bother. It's nothing earth-shattering. We'll talk about it on Wednesday. I'm coming out by myself, leaving the boys here with their grandparents. . . . I need some time alone . . . to talk to you."

"I feel terrible cutting you off like this," Decker said.

"No," Rina said, "I'm cutting you off. Just have an open ear for me on Wednesday, okay?"

"Sooner," Decker said. "I'll call you tonight and we'll swap tales of woe."

Rina paused. "That will be difficult with the boys home."

"Why? Are the kids giving you a hard time?"

"Oh no. Not at all. It's just that . . . forget it. We'll talk about it when I come out. Are *you* okay?"

"I'm fine," Decker said. "Maybe a little sleep-deprived. Maybe a little hungry . . . a little horn—"

"I get the picture," Rina said. "Your drives need an overhauling. Unfortunately, I can't do anything on the phone."

"Promise you'll make it up to me on Wednesday."

"It's a deal."

"I love you, Rina."

"Love you, too."

She hung up.

Decker wondered for a moment what could be bothering her. Whatever had happened took place around a week ago. Since then, Rina had become withdrawn, almost melancholy.

Sudden homesickness?

Decker hoped so.

Now came the call he dreaded. Decker dialed the number
by rote. A moment later, his ex-wife's voice cackled
through the receiver.

"Hi, Jan," Decker said.

"Nice of you to return my call," she said.

Decker paused. After all this time, he still couldn't tell if
she was being sarcastic. He decided to play it innocent.

"No problem," he said. "Have you heard from Cindy?"

"That's why I called," Jan said. "I'm passing along her
message. She's fine."

"Thank God."

"You can say that again."

Another pause.

"Where is she?" Decker asked.

"Portugal."

"Is she having fun?"

"She seems to be having the time of her life."

"Good."

More silence.

Jan said, "This little European jaunt may be great for
Cindy's development, but it's turning me into a wreck. I
can't wait until she's home."

"Neither can I," Decker said.

"It was your idea."

"It was Cindy's idea."

"But you approved of it."

"And so did you."

"Only *after* you did. What could I do? It was two against
one . . . as usual."

"Oh for chrissakes, Jan," he said. "Look, Cindy asked you
to give me a message. I got the message. Anything else?"

"No."

She hung up.

Two women hanging up on him. More than any man
should have to take.

He dressed quickly, threw two quarters in the vending

machine, and pulled out a cup of black coffee. He sipped away the sour taste in his mouth and walked at the same time, the coffee sloshing over the rim of the paper cup and burning his hands.

They'd placed the kid in the conference room. She seemed to be enjoying herself, scrawling over the morning-watch blackboard with white chalk. The room was littered with scraps of paper, cookie wrappers, and broken pencils and crayons.

"Hello there," Decker said to the toddler. "Remember me?"

The kid ran around in circles and shrieked with unabashed joy. Someone had dressed her in makeshift clothes—baggy pants and a pullover sweater much too big for her. The cuffs were rolled up to her knees. Decker regarded the tot's baby-sitter. Officer Lucinda Alvarez was in her twenties—slender but muscular—in the peak of health. At this moment, slumped in a folding chair, she looked as energetic as an overcooked noodle.

Lucinda said, "I didn't bust my ass in the academy to do this kind of work."

"Kids take it out of you."

She stood up and frowned. "What really pisses me off is that they automatically assigned this to me 'cause I'm a woman."

"I'll take her now."

"I mean, why didn't Sarge assign this to O'Grady or Ramirez?"

"I don't know, Lucinda."

"Yeah, well, *I'm* going to find out."

"Does she have a bottle or anything like that?"

"Yeah. Somewhere. The kid thought it was great fun throwing it around the room."

Decker smiled.

Lucinda said, "Sure! Laugh! You haven't been baby-sitting."

"I had her all morning," Decker said.

Lucinda eyed him with doubt. "So what do you want for that? A medal or something?"

"All I want is the kid."

"Take her." Lucinda threw her purse over her shoulder. "Take her with my blessings."

She stormed out of the room. The kid giggled when she slammed the door.

The foster home was similar to the other houses on the block, built from whitewashed wood planks, the paint peeling around the window sashes, with a tarpaper roof and faded green awnings. The front yard was enclosed by a chain-link fence and held two swing sets and a climbing apparatus shaped like a geodesic dome. Several children, wearing shorts and T-shirts, were playing outside, supervised by a young black girl.

Decker curbed the Plymouth in front of the house, and unbuckled the little girl riding in a car seat. He took her out of the car, walked over and unlatched the gate, and showed his badge to the woman outside. She nodded and sent one of the children—a girl of around seven—into the house.

Sophi Rawlings came out a moment later. She was of indeterminate racial origin and could pass with equal ease as a light-skinned black, a Micronesian, a Hispanic, or a kinky-haired Asian. A bosomy woman, she was in her fifties, with a close-cropped salt-and-pepper Afro, round brown eyes, and a broad nose dappled with dark freckles. Her manner was reassuring, her voice held a soothing lilt. She clucked her tongue when she saw Decker holding the toddler.

"My oh my, Sergeant Decker," she said. "Where did this little one come from?"

"Believe it or not, I found her wandering the streets last night."

"Where?"

"In a new development right above the old lime quarry."

"Any leads?" Sophi asked.

"Not yet."

Sophi placed her hand on Decker's shoulder. "If there's leads to be found, you'll find them."

"Thanks." He handed the child to Sophi.

"Don't look so glum, Sergeant. She'll be in good hands."

"I know she will be, Ms. Rawlings."

Sophi smiled. Though neither one of them were formal people, for some reason they were always formal with each other.

"Have you taken her to a doctor yet, Sergeant?" Sophi asked.

"No."

"I'll take her this afternoon."

"Personally?"

"This young I take them personally."

"Thank you, Ms. Rawlings," Decker said. "And I'll need a blood sample."

"May I ask why?"

Decker said, "There was blood on her pajamas when I found her. So far as I could ascertain, her body is free from abuse or injury, so I don't think the blood is hers. But I want to be certain."

"Oh boy." Sophi paused. "Whose blood is it?"

Decker shrugged.

"Something's happened to her mother," Sophi stated.

"Maybe."

"Or father," Sophi added. "Don't rule out the possibility that she was abducted by her father and he turned her loose when he saw how much work babies can be."

"Good point," Decker said. "'Course, that still doesn't explain the blood."

Sophi looked at the child and said, "We're talking too freely. They understand a lot at this age."

Decker nodded.

"I'll take good care of her," Sophi said.

Decker smiled sadly, then said, "Ms. Rawlings, she has a little rash on both her arms. Have the doc check that out for me."

"Sure," Sophi said. "Did you name her, Sergeant Decker?"

"You name her, Ms. Rawlings."

"How 'bout Sally?"

"Sally," Decker said. "Sally's a good name." He stroked the silky little cheek. "Behave yourself, Sally. You hear?"

The toddler smiled at him, then burrowed her brow in Sophi's inviting bosom.

Decker walked back to the car.

"When are you meeting your scumbag friend?" Marge asked Decker.

"Around three."

She switched into the left lane of the freeway and floored the accelerator. The 210 was empty today, the mountains flanking the asphalt abloom with flowers and shimmering in the heat. It was already late June; summer had overslept this year, but the high temperatures this week had finally marked its awakening. The mercury was already past 90. Decker turned up the air-conditioning.

"And this scumbag was an army buddy of yours," Marge said.

"Yep. Stop calling him a scumbag."

"Hey, that's what we've always called rapists."

"Alleged rapist."

"Shit." Marge passed a big rig and rode the tail wind. "Now you're playing lawyer on me. What was his excuse? 'She asked for it,' or 'You've got the wrong guy'?"

"You've got the wrong guy."

"Figures." Marge shook her head. "He's a scumbag, Pete. Don't get sucked up by him because he once saved your life or something."

"He never saved my life." Decker took out a cigarette.

"You're smoking. I hit a nerve."

"Did you bring a map of the Manfred development?" Decker asked.

"It's in my purse. About two hundred and fifty houses. Hope you brought a comfortable pair of shoes."

"I'm starving," Decker said.

"Want to stop at a Seven-Eleven?"

"Not enough time," Decker said. "And that's why I'm smoking. Not because you hit any nerve, lady."

"Peace, bro."

Decker laughed.

The car exited at Deep Canyon Road—a main thoroughfare that traversed the mountain-pocket communities of the Foothill Division of the LAPD. The road was narrow and winding, but as it hit the business district, it spread into six lanes. The unmarked passed through the shopping district—discount dress outlets, fast-food drive-ins, a Suzuki dealership, Mexican cantinas, and bars built for drinking, not mating. The retail stores soon yielded to the wholesalers—lumberyards and brickyards, roofing supplies, warehouses. Beyond the warehouses was residential land—small wood-framed houses, and larger ranches. Churches stood like watchtowers every few miles.

Decker had bought empty acreage in the district years ago, right after his divorce. The land had appreciated, but not as much as property in the affluent parts of L.A. But he liked the open space—his ranch was zoned for horses— liked the mountains and the convenience of being fifteen minutes from work.

They passed the turnoff for Yeshivas Ohavei Torah, a religious college for Jewish men—Jewtown, the other cops called it. Women also lived on the premises, with their husbands or fathers. Rina Lazarus had been an anomaly—the sole widow. The first time Decker had ever stepped foot in the place had been two years ago. He'd been the cop assigned to a nasty rape case, Rina had been his star witness.

Two years ago, and such significant change had over-taken his life.

Rina. She was the kind of woman men would murder for. And there she'd been, locked up in that protective, religious environment, oblivious to her bewitching powers. Her lack of guile made her even more appealing to Decker, and he moved in where others had feared to tread. But there were trade-offs. Rina wanted not only a Jewish man, but a religious one.

Baptist-bred Decker, now a *frummie*—a religious Jew. He'd had lots of second thoughts about becoming Jewish, let alone Orthodox. The extent of his observance had been a major source of conflict between them. How *committed* was he? Rina had decided to find out. She left the yeshiva—left *him*—and moved to New York a year ago, claiming he needed to be alone to make his own personal choices.

Six months later, away from her, away from the pressure, Decker arrived at a decision. He liked Judaism—his own modified version. He'd be observant most of the time, but would bend the letter of the law when it seemed right to do so. He explained his convictions to Rina one night in a three-hour phone conversation. She said it was something she could live with.

Now all he needed to do was convince her to move back and pick up where they had left off.

Two days to go.

Decker stared out the window. Marge had turned left, cutting northeast. They passed a pit of huge boulders and sand deposits—rocks stripped of ore, leaving only dusty wasteland. A half-mile north was the Manfred development, two square miles of land cut from mountainside. Fifty yards down, workers were framing a convenience center. Marge parked the car on the first street, and they both got out.

"This is really the boonies, isn't it?" Marge said.

Decker said, "The land won't be empty forever. Much to the conservationists' displeasure."

"Well, I've got to agree with them on one account. These houses certainly don't blend in with the landscape. Kind of reminds me of the lost colony of Roanoke."

Decker smiled and said, "How do you want to divide up?"

Marge said, "Maple runs down the middle. I'll take the houses north of it between Louisiana and Washington."

"Roger," Decker said. "Keep a look out for unusual tire marks or tiny footprints. Maybe we can trace little Sally's late-night trek through the neighborhood."

"Ground's dry," Marge said kicking up dust.

"In the early morning, the air was full of dew. You never can tell."

"All right," Marge said. "Here's one of the sexy Polaroids I took this morning."

The snapshot showed the blond, curly-haired toddler grinning, her nose wrinkling.

"What a little doll," Decker said.

"Yeah," Marge agreed. "Meet you back here . . . when?"

"Two hours from now?"

"Two hours sounds about right."

"Good."

They split up.

Nada.

Two and a quarter hours of searching, and nothing but a pair of sore dogs. Decker radioed to Marge.

"The hour's getting late," he said. "How many houses do you have left?"

"About twenty," she said. "Why don't we call it quits? I'll get the ones I missed and pick up the ones that weren't home tomorrow or the next day."

"Meet you at the car," Decker said.

He walked back nursing a giant headache. Maybe it was

the lack of food and sleep, but some of it was caused by a sinking feeling that there was a corpse out there collecting flies.

He leaned against the Plymouth, waved to Marge as she approached.

"You've got a knowing gleam in your eye," Decker told her. "What did you find out?"

"That a lady on Pennsylvania is boffing a repairman from ABC Refrigeration." Marge consulted her notes. "There was this one woman, a Mrs. Patty Bingham on 1605 Oak Street. She denied ever seeing Sally, had no idea who she was, etc., etc. But something about her didn't feel right. Nothing I can put my finger on, but I suspect she's holding back."

Decker asked, "Why wouldn't she want to help identify a little kid?"

"It might implicate her in something nasty," Marge said.

Decker nodded. "I don't know about you, but whatever the story is with Sally, I don't think the kid lived in this development."

"I'll agree with you there," Marge said. "Too many people denied knowing her. And in a place with this many children, where the kids all play together, some of the neighborhood mothers would have recognized her . . . unless her parents kept her locked up and segregated."

"I don't think so," Decker said. "Sally's a sweet little girl—relates well to people, talks a little, smiles a lot. She doesn't seem like a socially isolated kid to me. Plus, in my interviewing, none of the moms I'd talked to mentioned a weird family on such-and-such street."

"Yeah," Marge said. "In a small neighborhood like this, a weird family would stick out." She furrowed her brow. "So that brings us back to the crucial question. Where the hell did Sally come from?"

"Sophi Rawlings made an interesting point. Maybe she was a pawn in a custody dispute. Maybe Dad kidnapped her, then discovered how much work she was and dropped her off here to be found."

"Here?"

"A nice family neighborhood," Decker said. "Someone was bound to notice her."

"Except no one did," Marge said.

"I did."

"But you weren't from the neighborhood," Marge answered. "And what about the blood?"

Decker shrugged.

Marge said, "How about this: Dad and Mom live close by. Dad whacks Mom in an argument, panics, and drops the kid here."

Decker said. "But where do Dad and Mom live if they don't live here?"

Marge said, "There're a few isolated ranches around here." She looked toward the mountains. "Probably more squatters than we'd care to admit in those hills."

Decker nodded and said, "In the meantime, start up a Missing Person file on Sally. I'll go to meet my buddy—"

"The rapist."

"Alleged rapist," Decker said. "You punch Sally's description and prints into the computer. Also, contact Barry Delferno."

Marge stuck out her tongue.

Decker said, "Want me to call him?"

"No, no, no," Marge insisted. "My past experience with the sleaze shall have no bearing on my professional duties."

Decker held back a smile and said, "I hear he's doing very well since he made the switch from bail jumpers to stolen children."

"His off-duty car is a 'sixty-four metallic-blue Rolls Silver Cloud," Marge said. "We're in the wrong field."

"Yeah, well, we already knew that."

"What do you want to do with my lady on Oak?"

"You want me to talk to her?"

"Yes, I do. Maybe a big guy like you can intimidate her into baring her soul."

Decker said, "I can do it now, or I can let her sit on it and come back tomorrow. My personal opinion is to leave her alone for the night. She may see the light in the morning."

Marge thought, then said, "Okay, let her sit on it. But not *too* long."

"You think she's planning a one-way trip somewhere?"

Marge shook her head. "No indication."

"Great," Decker said. "Let's go. You drive."

~4

Decker stood outside the Los Angeles County Jail. It was a lousy day to dig up bones—three o'clock and the sun was still blasting mercilessly. Sweat ran down his forehead, beaded above his mustache. Reaching into his back pocket, he pulled out a handkerchief and wiped his face, then sat down on the lone cement bench stranded on an island of scorched lawn. Although large and looming, the gray prison building in front of him cast only a couple feet worth of shadow. No relief there. He took off his suit jacket, and rechecked his watch.

C'mon, you son of a bitch. Let's get it over with.

He stood up. The bench was hot. Besides, he was too antsy to sit. A Khaki-clad sheriff's deputy walked past him and nodded. Decker nodded back, pulled out a cigarette from his shirt pocket, and began to peel the paper, letting the tobacco shavings fall to the ground. Thirty-seven out of forty cigarettes he handled per day ended up skinned, but better that than smoking the suckers.

Finally, the glass doors opened and Abel Atwater came out into the afternoon swelter. His former quarterback body had become emaciated—insubstantial under a blousy shirt. The top was faded stripes of orange and green, the weave of the fabric loose and speckled with moth holes. His jeans were frayed at the knees, and on his right foot was a rubbed-out suede Hush Puppy. The left pants leg, Decker knew, housed a Teflon prosthesis. His eyes were more deepset than Decker had remembered, almost sunken. His nose was longer and thinner. Limping along with surprising grace, he twirled his cane, Charlie Chaplin style. The loose-fitting shirt, the rhinestone-studded walking stick, the white bandage around his head, and the dark beard gave him the look of an Arab emir about to hold court.

He saw Decker and broke into a wide smile.

"Hey, hey, hey," he said, hobbling over, his arms spread out like two parentheses. "Yo, Doc. How goes it?"

Decker rebuffed the embrace and looked at him.

"We need to talk, Abel." He rolled up his shirtsleeves.

"Hey, Doc, why the long face? C'mon, what they're sayin' is shit." He got down on his knee—his good one—and imitated Al Jolson. "Don't you know me? I'm yo' baby." He laughed. "You remember me. Ole Honest Abe Atwater with the ten-inch prick."

"Your prick got you into big trouble, Abel."

Abel rose. "Lighten up, Pete. You don't think I really raped her, do you?"

"She was full of your semen."

Abel drawled out, "I didn't say I didn't fuck her. I said I didn't *rape* her."

Decker grabbed Abel's shirt and pulled the thin face close to his.

"She's got a five-inch cut running down her cheek with twenty stitches in it, three broken ribs, and a collapsed lung from a stab wound." He tightened his grip. "And your jism was inside of her. Now I'm going to ask you a question, *Honest Abe*, and I want the truth! Understand me well, I mean the *truth*! Did you rape her?"

"No."

"Did you cut her?" Decker screamed.

"NO!"

"You'd better not be shucking me, buddy, because if you are, you're gonna look back on our days crapped out in Da Nang as fond memories . . . catch my *drift*?"

"Jesus fucking Christ, Pete. I'm telling you the God's honest truth. I didn't rape her!"

Decker let go of him and stared at the broken face.

"You're in big trouble, buddy," he said.

"I know," Abel said weakly. "I know I am."

"You can't pretend that nothing happened, Abe."

"I know."

Decker placed his hand on Abe's shoulder and led him over to the bench.

"Let's sit down and talk about it."

Abel dabbed his brow with a tissue. Despite the long, untrimmed beard and the unkempt dress, he smelled freshly scrubbed. He'd always been meticulous about his hygiene, Decker remembered. Used to groom himself like a cat. When the rest of the platoon was covered with caked-on scum, Old Honest Abe Atwater would be spitting into his palm, trying to wash off the grime.

"Thanks, big man," Abel said. "Thanks for bailing me out."

"S'all right."

"I really mean it."

"I know you do."

Abel threw him a weak smile. Decker opened his arms, and they gave each other a bear hug.

"Good to see you, Doc." Abel broke away. "Though I wish the circumstances were a tad better."

"You have a lawyer?"

"I thought maybe you could help me out."

"I haven't practiced law in twelve years."

"Do you know anyone?"

"Not offhand," Decker said. "I do most of my work with district attorneys. Who's your PD?"

"Some incompetent with a perpetual allergy. Nose is running all the time." Abel pinched off a nostril and sniffed deeply with the other. "Know what I mean?"

"I'll ask around," Decker said. "We'll dig up someone."

"Appreciate it. Preferably someone without a habit."

"That's not so easy."

"I know. I wasn't being facetious." Abel looked at the sky and squinted. "Hot one, ain't it?"

Decker didn't answer.

"Not interested in the weather, huh?" Abel said. "Well, how 'bout them Dodgers?"

"Abel, have you eaten anything today?" Decker asked.

"Some swill for breakfast. Amorphous goop that doubles for Elmer's in a pinch."

"Let's get something to eat."

"I'll check my finances." Abel took out his wallet. "Damn. Forgot my platinum card. We'll have to forego Spago."

Decker looked at his watch. "Let's fill our bellies. It's late and some of us have a long drive home."

Decker swung the unmarked onto the Santa Monica Freeway west. When he hit the downtown interchange, the traffic coagulated. Vehicles burped noxious fumes into a smoggy sky. At least the air conditioner was working, sucking up stale hot air and turning it to stale cool air. They rode for a half hour in silence. When Decker exited on the Robertson off-ramp, Abel spoke up.

"Where are we going?"

"Does it matter?"

"Nope."

Ten minutes later, Decker pulled up in front of the Pico Kosher Deli, turned off the motor, and got out. Abel followed.

"You like corned beef?" Decker asked, popping dimes into the meter.

"At the moment, I'll take anything that's edible."

Decker placed a crocheted yarmulke atop his hair and secured it with a bobby pin.

"What's with the beany cap?" Abel asked.

"I've become a little religious in my old age."

"Religious I can understand," Abel said. "But since when have you become *Jewish*?"

"It's a long story. Best reserved for another time. Let's go."

The place was half full. Out of habit, Decker chose a back table that afforded privacy. Off to the left side was a refrigerator case loaded with smoked fish—metal trays piled high with lox, cod, and whitefish chubs. Decker looked at the plastic laminated menu.

"What's good?" Abel asked.

"Everything," Decker said. "One of the few haunts left that serves an honest meal."

A waitress came over. She was very young, wide-hipped, with blond hair tied back in a ponytail. Abel winked at her.

"What's the story, sugar?"

She smiled uncomfortably.

Decker said, "I'll have a pastrami on rye with a large orange juice."

"Make mine a salami and cheese on rye with a Bud. If you can't find a Bud, I'll take you."

Decker rolled his eyes. "You can't have cheese here, Abel. The place is kosher. They don't mix meat and dairy products."

Abel said to the girl, "Then just give me you, honey."

"Give him a salami on rye and a Heineken," Decker ordered.

The waitress nodded gratefully and left them. Abel bit his lower lip and drummed his fingers on the tabletop.

"Want to tell me about it?" Decker asked.

Abel rubbed his face with his hands. "She was a hooker, natch. She called herself Plum Pie. I don't know her real name—"

"Myra Steele," Decker interrupted. "She's eighteen, which makes her an adult. Thank God for small favors, otherwise you'd be in the can for statutory rape even if you didn't coerce her. She's from Detroit, has three priors for soliciting—two when she was still a juvenile, the last one three months ago. She used to work for a pimp named Letwoine Monroe—he was the one who posted bail for her after her last arrest—but I found out he bit the dust a month ago in a drug deal that went sour. I don't know who she's peddling her ass for now."

There was a brief silence.

Abel said, "Why didn't my lawyer *tell* me all of this?"

"He probably didn't know," Decker said. "It's all incidental to your case. I just like details."

"*Incidental?* The bitch is a hooker with *three* priors—"

"For God's sake. Lower your voice, Abe." Decker sighed. "What she does to earn a buck is irrelevant. If you forced her to have intercourse, it's rape."

"I didn't force her to do anything. It was a mutually agreed-upon *business* transaction. And I certainly didn't beat or slice her."

"Abe," Decker said, "if you've got to go to hookers, you go to hookers. But why didn't you wear a condom, for chrissakes? In case you haven't heard, there are nasty viruses floating around. What, Nam wasn't enough? You've got a death wish?"

"She didn't have AIDS."

"And how do you know that?"

"She's got one of those cards from a laboratory certifying her clean."

"Abel—"

"Yeah, cards can be forged." Abel broke in. "I'm well aware of that, Doc. But we believe what we want to believe. And condoms don't fit my fantasies."

"You're a first-class ass."

"Tell me something we both don't already know."

"Where'd you find this babe?" Decker asked.

"Strutting up the boulevard. My nest isn't too far from the garden spot."

"Go on."

"We made arrangements, and she took me up to her place. Jesus, what a sty! Place was redolent with foot odor and other rancid—"

"Get to the point, Abe."

"Okay, okay. We fucked. She was good, and I wanted more. So I paid for another round." His eyes narrowed as he concentrated on bringing back the memory. "I was feeling really virile. I hadn't felt like that in a long time, Pete. This one . . . I don't know . . . she was really good. I paid for a third time—"

"Where'd you get all this bread?"

"From good old red, white, and blue Uncle Sam. I'm part of the national debt, Pete. Sammy owes me forever for my leg." He wiped his forehead with his napkin. "Also, I pick up spare change from odd jobs. My needs are simple, and sex is cheap."

"All right. Go on."

"By the end of the third time, I was pretty wasted."

"Were you doping?"

"No. She was, but I wasn't. By wasted, I meant tired. I asked her if I could crash out at her place, and she agreed."

"For a fee."

"It's America," Abel said. "Everything has a price."

"Around what time was that?" Decker asked.

"About one, two in the morning. She told me she was through for the evening anyway. She'd made her quota, and her main man would be happy."

The waitress brought the sandwiches.

"I'll be right back," Decker said.

He got up and walked back toward the restaurant's kitchen, over to an industrial sink. Hanging over the lave was a two-handled brass stein and a roll of paper towels.

Decker took the chalice off the hook, filled it with water, and poured it over his hands twice. Shaking off the excess water, he dried his hands and said the blessing for the ritual washing. He walked back to the table, mumbled another blessing over bread, then chomped on his pastrami on rye.

Abel stared at him. "You're real serious about this."

Decker chewed, swallowed, and gulped down half his orange juice. He said, "My woman is religious."

"Your wife?"

"Not yet," Decker said. "But I hope to change that very soon."

"We're talking about marriage number two, right? Or is it more?"

"Only two."

"When did you divorce the first one? What was her name? Jean . . . no, Jan."

"Yeah. Jan. I don't want to talk about her."

"Didn't you two have a kid?"

"Still do. A daughter—"

"Cynthia."

Decker nodded. "She's going to be a freshman at Columbia this fall. The marriage was worth it for her."

"So she's what? Seventeen? Eighteen?"

"Seventeen."

"About the same age we were when we met," Abel said.

"Frightening," Decker said.

"Damn frightening," Abel said. "Did I ever tell you I got married?"

"No."

"I did. About seven years ago."

"What happened?"

"Nothing. We're still married, so far as I know. We don't live together. No one can live with me."

"Kids?"

"Not mine," Abel said. "She's got three from previous liaisons, none of them married her. I took pity—seventeen-year-old girl and three kids. Nice chicklet, cute, but stupid as shit. Just can't say no. So I got her fixed up with an IUD. I send her a little cash, see her when I go back home for Christmas. She's happy, I'm happy."

"It's great to be happy." Decker raised his eyebrows. "Let's get back to the rape."

"Where was I?"

"You paid to sleep over at her house."

Abel nodded. "That was the last thing I remember. Next thing I knew, I woke up—handcuffed. My skull is cracked open, and the bitch is screaming bloody murder. . . ."

"She said you held a shiv across her throat while you raped her. Then you went nuts. She knocked you out by cracking a lamp over your head, then called the police."

"I don't even own a shiv."

"You still get those blackouts?"

"Yeah. But not *this* time. I was *sleeping*, Doc. I heard someone screaming, woke up and saw blood." He shook his head, trying to clear his thoughts. "I thought I was having another routine nightmare. Man, I never stopped getting nightmares, you know. But this one seemed ordinary enough. So I said to myself, 'Abe, go back to sleep. It's just another nightmare.' Only it was *real*. God, was it real."

His eyes became pensive and moist. "I don't know what happened, Pete. All I know is, when I went to sleep, the girl was whole."

"Is it possible that you had a blackout, did something to her, and woke up without any memory of it?"

Abel swallowed hard.

"I swear to God I didn't rape or beat her."

"Okay," Decker said. "I believe you." He finished his sandwich and orange juice. "You didn't beat her up. But someone did. The report said there was no break-in or forced entry, but Myra often slept with the windows open.

She could have known the assailant—a john who got rough or her pimp—tried to cover for him, and you were a convenient scapegoat."

"I don't know how they can pinpoint my semen in her," Abel said. "The broad was a hooker. She must have been swimming in a sea of cum."

"She claims you were the only john who sodomized her last night. That's how the lab made the positive ID."

Abel looked down.

"I didn't rape her," he said tensely. "I paid for everything I took. And I didn't get rough with the lady, Pete. Goddammit, you know me! I don't do things like that. And it was *never* for lack of opportunity."

Decker knew that was true. They'd both seen their share of grunts on the rampage. An M-16 strapped to your back, you never had to pay for it—just went into the hooches and took whatever you wanted. Women, girls, even boys, it didn't matter. Screw them in front of Papa-san, it's only a gook. Came back to the squad a double vet—fucked 'em and wasted 'em. Abel had never signed up for that club.

Decker, more than anyone, had known him as a gentle and compassionate human being. Always the one sneaking orphans onto the base, only to have them kicked out by some shitfaced captain who said it was against the rules. Honest Abe Atwater, putting on puppet shows with empty IV bottles wearing grease-pencil smiles. Stealing rations to feed the homeless left in the gutted villages ripped apart by cross fire. Always trying to make nice. His downfall: He lost his leg because of his heart. Everything they'd been warned against. A friendly that had been VC. A fluke Decker had found him. Even flukier that Abel had lived.

"You'll get me out of this mess, won't you, Doc?"

"I'll do what I can. But it may take a while. You need a good lawyer who can buy you time."

"I don't have a hell of a lot of loot." Abel shrugged. "Matter of fact, I'm busted."

Decker frowned.

"Don't worry about it, Pete. I'll figure out something. And I intend to pay you back the bail money. Just as soon as I get my disability check."

"Forget it," Decker said. He glanced at the wall clock. "I've got to get home. But first I have to say grace after meals, so be quiet for about five minutes."

Decker prayed, then rose and slipped Abel a twenty. "This should get you back home by taxi. I'll call as soon as I have something to tell you."

Abel looked at him, a hound-dog expression on his face. "I'm really sorry about this, Pete. Seems I only call you when I'm fucked."

Decker said, "What else are friends for?"

❧5

Marge picked up the printout and frowned. Sally's description and footprints hadn't matched anything stored in the mainframe's data banks. Though it wasn't unusual for the computer to turn up a blank, because the kid was so young, she'd hoped for a break.

She looked up Barry Delferno's number. The first time she'd met the bounty hunter, she'd expected someone fat and swarthy with a bucket's worth of grease plastered on his hair. Instead, she found a tall, sandy-haired muscle man with dancing eyes. He'd asked her out and she'd accepted, only to find out a week later that he was married.

Bounty hunters. No matter what they looked like, they were all sleazeballs.

She punched Delferno's number into the phone, and a moment later a deep voice resonated inside the earpiece.

"It's Marge Dunn, Barry," she said.

"Detective Dunn," Delferno crooned. "How's the LAPD's finest?"

"Not bad."

"You know, I was gonna call you."

"Were you now?"

"No shit. I'm divorced, Margie. For real this time. Free and clear. You can check it out, if you don't believe me."

44

"I called for professional reasons, Barry. Got your current caseload in front of you?"

"Margie, Margie, Margie. What *is* the rush?"

"I don't chat when I'm on duty."

"So how 'bout if we chat over drinks?"

Marge ignored him. "We picked up a little girl—around two, curly blond hair, brown eyes, height thirty-two inches, weight twenty-six pounds. I've got Polaroids and footprints I'd like to fax over to you. See if we come up with a match."

"As long as the match is a *love* match between you and me, my Greek goddess."

"Knock it off."

Delferno said, "I love a woman who talks tough. It turns me on. Gets my blood boiling and my—"

"You're wasting your breath."

"All right. Be surly. I'll get you anyway. In the meantime, send me the pics and the prints."

Marge placed the information into the machine. She said, "Call me back when you've got them."

"How about dinner? Tonight, even. Wait, tonight's not good. How about tomor—"

"I'm hanging up now, Barry."

"It's not nice to alienate the hired help."

Marge laughed and placed the receiver in its cradle. She poured herself a cup of coffee and waited for Delferno to call back. A few minutes later, her phone rang.

"Dunn," she answered.

"Nothing," Delferno said.

"Sure?"

"Positive. Never seen the little tyke. Was she abused?"

"Nope. She seemed to be very well cared for."

"Foul play with the parents?"

"Could be," Marge said. "We found blood on her pajamas. Ask around for me, Barry."

"What do I get in return?"

"What do you want?"

"How about a weekend in Cabo San Lucas? We'll four-wheel it down to Baja, dip our toes in the gentle warm *oceano*, and fish for yellowtail."

"I don't fish."

"Then we can sunbathe on the white-sand beaches . . . no tan lines, Margie."

"I'm involved with someone else, Barry," Marge said.

Delferno paused. "I heard you broke up with Carroll."

"Well, you heard wrong," Marge lied. "You remember Carroll—six-six, two-sixty, hands as big as catchers' mitts."

"For chrissakes, why didn't you tell me in the first place, Margie?"

"It slipped my mind. Kinda like your wife slipped yours a while back."

Delferno paused, then said, "Was this whole thing a setup for revenge?"

Marge smiled. "Well, let me put it this way. If I'm ever interested, I'll give you a call. Until then, give me and the kid a break and pass on the photo to your buddies. Maybe they've seen her."

"If it means another chance at your body, Detective Dunn, I will do that. I like my women like my tales—long and tall."

"I like my men like my good-byes—short." She laughed and hung up the phone. Decker walked into the squad room.

"What's so amusing?" he asked. "I could use a few giggles."

"Delferno," she said. "Same old lech."

"Any luck with Sally?" inquired Decker.

"Zip. I told Barry to pass the picture along to his colleagues. I also tried the Missing Children Hotline. No one matching Sally's description has been reported recently."

Decker sighed. "Poor little kid. This has turned into a rotten day."

"Worse than most?"

"Yeah, when it involves a two-year-old, it's worse than most."

Marge turned and faced him. "Lunch with your rape-o friend didn't go so good?"

"Par for the course."

"Did he do it?"

"He says no."

"And you believe him?"

Decker paused, then nodded yes.

Marge said, "The friend in you says innocent, but the cop decrees guilty."

"No," Decker said. "I really don't believe he did it."

"Jesus," Marge said. "What's between you and that scumbag that's turning your brain to mush? *Did* he save your life?"

"I told you no."

"Then how do you owe him?"

"I'm not paying off a debt, Marge. I happen to think he's innocent—"

"Oh, give me a break, Pete," Marge said. "Fess up. Was he your illicit lover or something when all you men were dogged out in the combat zone?"

Decker laughed. "No."

"What are you going to do for him? Bribe the judge? Burn the files?"

Decker sat down at his desk and peeled another cigarette. "I'm going to find the man who raped and cut up the hooker."

"You already bailed the guilty party out of jail, my friend."

"Well, I don't think so."

Marge leaned back in her chair, shook her head. "A seasoned guy like yourself, falling for his shit . . . Let *me* look into it. At least I'm objective."

"Nope," Decker said. "I've got my eyes wide open, Marge. I can handle it."

"Sure you can."

Decker rubbed his eyes and said, "We can keep bickering like this, honey, or I can do something productive like go home and get some sleep."

"Pete!" Marge said. "You called me *honey*!"

"That's 'cause you're acting like a broad, Margie."

Marge grinned. "No, Decker, you're acting like a civilian."

Decker said, "I'm going home. Beep me if something comes up with Sally. I'm going down to Hollywood Division tonight and review the case files. Try to get a handle on this hooker. You can call me there if anything comes up."

Marge leaned back in her chair. "Colonel Dunn says that the attachments he made with his war buddies ran deeper than blood. That true with you?"

"Nope."

"Yeah, Colonel Dunn has been known to spout a lot of shit."

Decker smiled.

"You didn't get together with any of your buddies when you came back to civilian life?" Marge asked.

"Only once," Decker said. "Somewhere between the second and third hour, after we rehashed all the old nightmares, I discovered I didn't have a thing in common with any of them."

"And that was it?"

"That was it. You know, Margie, I worked *damn* hard at putting it all behind me. And it's especially hard because America has had a sudden change of heart and decided we weren't all baby-killers. Nam vets have become the darlings of Hollywood. Indochina has great box-office appeal—all those shirtless sweaty bodies crawling through the jungle. Leeches! Gooks! Grunts going nuts! Makes for exotic drama. And the producers? They're former hippies who now drive Mercedes instead of VW bugs. They want to

talk to us, make nice. Except I remember how they treated
me when I came back to the world. It don't wash, babe."

"Colonel Dunn was once asked to be a consultant on a
Nam film."

"What did your dad do?"

Marge blushed.

Decker said, "That bad?"

"Let's put it this way. The screenplay was long, and Mom
didn't have to buy toilet paper for a month."

Decker burst into laughter.

Marge asked, "So who's this guy who you're going the
distance for?"

"Abel Atwater," Decker said. "A hillbilly boy from the
Blue Ridge Mountains of Kentucky." Decker's voice had
taken on a nasal twang. "One of eleven chillun. His father
could barely read and write, his mother was completely il-
literate. Abel learned to read by sifting through mail-order
catalogs. He used to entertain us by reciting Sears, Roebuck
copy. Bright guy. The war messed him up."

"A lot of rape-os are intelligent."

"He doesn't fit the profile. He's not manipulative, he's
got great impulse control. He's not the kind of person who
goes around beating up hookers."

Marge didn't answer him.

Decker said, "All right. If I'd be brutally honest with myself, I'd say there was an off-chance that he freaked and did
it. But we were in combat together for a while. I never saw
him explode. Abel had a rep for being coolheaded. Type of
guy the COs chose for pointman—lead-off guy in foot patrol—because he was careful and didn't panic when things
got hot."

"Ever see him kill anybody?"

"You saw smoke, you busted some caps. Simple as that.
When everything cooled off and you went in for cleanup,
you'd see all these fucking bodies. Well, they didn't drop
dead from birdshit. You were shooting to kill, you killed. In

answer to your question, I never saw him waste anyone for the sake of killing, and there was plenty of that going around!"

Decker stopped, took a deep breath, and let it out slowly.

"Abel could have been something if the war hadn't left him paralyzed. Matter of fact, he wanted to be a *cop*, but Charlie blew off his leg and ended that dream."

He snapped a pencil in half.

"I'm his dream, Marge. Maybe I feel guilty because Abel had all the fantasies, and I wound up with his dream."

The phone was ringing when Decker opened the door. He raced over to the kitchen wall, his Irish setter, Ginger, nipping at his heels, and picked up the receiver.

"Did you just walk in?" Rina asked.

"Yeah," Decker said. "I didn't even close the front door. Hang on a sec."

"Sure."

He walked through his living room, Ginger following him, barking for attention. The room was comfortable, full of furniture made in his size—an overstuffed sofa, two buckskin chairs, and a leather recliner that sat in front of a picture window. In the heat, the room seemed alive, seemed to sweat. Decker quieted the dog and shut the front door. He drew open the front-window curtains, and a white square of sinking sun fell upon his Navajo rug.

He picked up the receiver and pulled out a kitchen chair with his foot. He sat down and petted Ginger's head.

"I've got all the time in the world for you now. Speak."

"That's why I called." She dropped her voice a notch. "The kids are home. I can't really talk. We've got to leave any moment for my brother-in-law's birthday party."

"You sound thrilled."

"I'm nearly faint with excitement."

"Don't go, if you don't want to."

"I can't get out of it. At least not without lying."

"Then be honest. Just say, 'I find all this family stuff boring—' "

"Boring is the least of it."

"Troubles with the family?"

"Something like that."

"They're giving you a hard time because they don't approve of me."

"Much more than that. Hold on."

Decker heard her quiet her younger son, Jacob. When she returned on the line, he said, "Boys want to talk to me?"

"Very much," Rina answered. "Look, can I call you back tonight?"

Decker paused.

"You're working?" Rina asked.

"Just tying up odds and ends. I'll put it off."

"Don't bother. I bought my ticket this afternoon, so I'll see you in two days. Want to take down all the flight information?"

"Yeah, let me get a pen." He rummaged through a junk drawer and came up with a red pen and the back of an old electric bill. He placed the paper on the wall and said, "Go ahead."

Rina stated all the pertinent data, then gave Jacob the telephone.

"Hi, Yonkel," Decker said. "How's it going?"

"Fine."

"How's school?"

"Fine."

"How's basketball?"

"Fine."

"How many lay-ups did you do yesterday?"

"Four."

"Terrific."

"Thanks."

"Are you taking good care of your *eema* for me?"

"Yes."

"Being good to your grandparents?"

"Yes."

"Great," Decker said. "I miss you, kiddo."

"Peter?"

"What, Jakie?"

"When can we come back to your ranch?"

Decker sighed, hesitated. The kid was a sweetie. Decker pictured him talking on the phone, big blue eyes wide with innocence. He said, "Honey, you're welcome here anytime your *eema* says it's okay."

"I miss the horses."

"They miss you, too."

"Okay, 'bye. Here's Shmuli."

Rina's elder son came on the line.

"I'm upset," Sammy said.

"What's wrong?" Decker asked.

"Why can't we come to L.A. with *Eema*? It's not fair!"

"Sammy, I'd love for you guys to come out here—"

"So why can't we come with *Eema* on Wednesday?"

"Because there're things that your *eema* and I have to discuss privately."

"So we'll wait in the other room while you guys talk."

"It's not that simple, honey."

"*Eema* just doesn't want us around."

"No, honey, that's not true."

"It is true. You're just defending her."

Decker paused a moment. The boy had to be handled carefully.

"Sammy, honey, try to understand this. I haven't seen your *eema* in six months. We're kind of like strangers, and it's going to take us a while to get to know each other again. Now, I want to know your *eema* real well before you and your brother and I get reacquainted. That way I can pay attention to you guys and not have to worry about your mother. Does that make sense to you?"

There was a long silence on the other end of the line.

"Are you and *Eema* fighting?" Sammy asked.

"No, Sam, not at all."

"I mean, you're not breaking up, are you?"

"No."

"Because if you are and you're just trying to protect me . . ."

"We're not breaking up."

"Well okay . . . Peter, can you talk her into taking us?"

"I don't think that would be a good idea now."

"Then *when* can we come out?"

"Before baseball season's over."

"*Baseball* season! That could take *three* more months."

"One thing at a time, Sammy," Decker said. "Let me talk to your *eema* first."

"You sure you're not hiding some bad news from me?"

"Sammy, I promise you, I'll see you before the summer's over," Decker said.

"Okay," Sammy answered sullenly. "Here's *Eema* again."

Decker felt tense. The kid always wore him out. Sammy was a typical firstborn—precocious, sharp as a tack. He'd been the light of his father's eye, Rina had told him. His father's death had hit him very hard, made him very suspicious of losing people he loved.

Rina came back on the line.

"They're angry I'm not bringing them home with me," she said. "Especially Shmuli."

"I heard," Decker said.

"They miss Los Angeles. They miss you. I miss you, too."

"Then come *home*!"

The line went quiet.

"You still with me?" Decker asked.

"I'm still here," she said. "We've got a lot to talk about. How are your studies with Rav Schulman?"

"Fine."

"What are you learning—oh darn! The doorbell's ringing. It's probably my sister-in-law. I'm not wearing a *shaytel*, and Esther's going to yell at me for answering the door with my hair uncovered."

"Tell her to shove it up—"

"Peter."

"She doesn't approve of me, I don't have to approve of her."

"Esther's not the problem, although she *has* problems. Dear God, I never realized the extent of her problems. Unfortunately, now they've become my problems and—now, she's banging at the door. Any moment one of my neighbors is going to stick a head out and ask what's wrong. Tiny apartments they have here. I feel like a laboratory rat. Things are really a mess. I've got to go."

"Wait. Don't send me off like that."

"Love you," she said.

"Love you, too."

Head pounding, Decker stretched, then filled the dog bowl with food. He opened the kitchen drawer and took out a vial of aspirin. He washed down two pills with a cold Dos Equis and looked at his watch. Six-fifteen—still plenty of daylight left to work out the horses. The temperature had dropped to a comfortable 82 degrees. An hour with the animals, another hour of study, a couple of hours of sleep, then a date with gumshoes from six over the mountains.

Hooray for Hollywood.

6

The Hollywood substation was a brick building—square and windowless—landscaped with three Monterey pines sprouting from a rectangular patch of dirt. Across the street were the requisite cheap motel—a place to spend the night when your man was in jail—and two bailbonds' storefronts whose doors never closed.

Decker climbed the front steps and entered the reception area. The room was walled with redbrick and yellow plaster, the front desk colored Day-Glo orange. The flooring was ancient yellow tile, the grout permanently blackened. In the center of the room, inlaid in the tile, was a red-and-black granite "Hollywood Boulevard" pavement star, the words LAPD HOLLYWOOD STATION #6 inlaid in brass. A hype was leaning against a coke machine, swaying on his feet to keep his balance. A fat man stood against the side wall, sipping coffee, checking his watch against the station's clock. Two teenage black girls, wearing shorts and tank tops, sat on the attached bench at the back of the room, their fingers twirling the cornrows of their hair, lips slightly parted, eyes fixed upon the star as if it represented a myriad of fallen dreams.

Decker showed his gold badge to the desk sergeant and went inside the detectives' reception room. The detective

manning the phones had an amoebic ink stain on the pocket
of his shirt. He was balding and needed a shave.

"Yeah?" he asked.

"Decker from Foothill," Decker said. "I'm looking for
George Andrick." He showed the detective his badge.

"I'm Rados," he said. He regarded the chalkboard duty
roster. "Andrick's on Robbery. He's in the field. Should be
back soon."

"Then I'll grab myself some coffee and wait at his desk."

Rados handed Decker an unused Styrofoam cup. "Help
yourself to the swill in the back."

"Thanks."

Cup in hand, Decker entered the squad room. It was bigger than Foothill's, carpeted, and had metal desks instead of
tables. Each unit was indicated by burnt-wood signs hanging from the ceiling. Robbery was in the back, left side,
sandwiched between the lockers and CAPS—crimes
against persons. Andrick's place of honor was in the
middle-left of a capital I-shaped arrangement of desks. A
supervising detective sat at the head of the *I*, reading a
memo, his lips curled into a sneer. He looked to be in his
late forties, his face scored with wrinkles, his shoulders
packed with muscle. He noticed Decker's badge and stood.
They were about the same height.

"Medino," he said. "What can I do for you?"

"Decker. I called earlier. I understand Andrick was the
field investigator for a rape case couple of days ago. Perp
was booked here, transferred downtown. His name was
Abel Atwater."

Medino said. "The gimp."

"That's him."

"Scrawny thing."

"I'd like to look over the file."

"Andrick has it locked, and I don't have the key."

"I'll wait."

Medino shrugged. "Suit yourself. Coffeepot's over to the right."

"Thanks."

Decker poured himself a cup—black mud. He sipped as he walked back to the desk. "You guys have gotten carpets and new desks."

"No thanks to the city. Some civilian donated them. Only thing the city's given us this past year was a few push-button phones. Their idea of state-of-the-art equipment."

"At least you got the phones."

"Yeah," Medino said. "But only one per unit. City doesn't want us to become too spoiled. The individual dicks still have rotaries. Just look at the crappy colors they give us—pinks and blues and reds. Now how can you have a professional image with a pink phone? Place looks like a nursery school."

"I noticed the playpen back there."

Medino nodded. "We get our share of kids dumped at the doorstep."

"I just got one of those," Decker said. "She wasn't dumped at the station. I found her wandering the streets. No one's claimed her."

"How old?"

"Two."

"Black?"

"White."

Medino shrugged.

Decker said, "Her pajamas had blood on them."

"That's unusual," Medino said. "Kid okay?"

"Appears to be fine," Decker said. "Can't say I'm feeling too optimistic about her mama, though."

"Another one bites the dust," Medino said. "What's your connection to the gimp? He wanted for something out there?"

"He's an old buddy of mine," Decker said.

Medino whistled. "You should start hunting for some new friends."

"How deep is his shit?"

"From what I remember, neck high and still rising."

"What do you know about the victim?" Decker said. "Besides the fact that she was a whore."

"Not much more than that," Medino said.

"Do you know if she had a rep for tricking with rough johns?"

"No idea," Medino said. "Why don't you go upstairs and try Vice?"

Decker asked, "Chris Beauchamps still work Vice here?"

"Baby-faced Beau?" Medino said. "You bet. One of our best undercover men. Looks so fucking sincere. I think he came in about an hour ago. Go up and talk to him. I'll buzz you when Andrick is back on my nifty new push-button intercom. LAPD goes high tech."

"Myra Steele," Beauchamps said. "Yeah, I've got a file on her somewhere."

Decker stared at the Vice detective, finding it hard to take the kid seriously. Surfer-blond hair, deep blue eyes, Malibu tan—the kind of looks that screamed party hardy, let's shoot the curl.

Beauchamps pulled out a folder and said, "Here we go. Old Myra Steele, aka Plum Pie, Cherry Pie, Brown Sugar— a lot of them use *that* moniker." He handed Decker a file. "The only thing I have on her was a bust three months ago."

"That bust happened when Letwoine Monroe was still her pimp," Decker said, scanning the papers. "Before he was whacked."

"Right," Beauchamps said.

Decker asked, "Was he whacked in Hollywood?"

"I don't know where he was whacked, but we found him here, stuffed in the trunk of a black Caddy stolen from North Hollywood."

Decker said. "Myra Steele doesn't look eighteen to me. She barely looks pubescent."

"Her birth certificate says eighteen," Beauchamps said. "And she's pubescent, believe me. I've seen her on the streets couple of times since, her tits are more than ample for the halters she wears. Those photos knock a couple of years off of her."

"Who's Myra's old man now?" Decker asked.

"Letwoine's ladies were divided by the other pimps in the area," Beauchamps said. "Some went to a Mideastern prick named Yusef Sabib, some went to Willy Black, a couple went to Clementine—"

Decker groaned.

"I thought he was your buddy," Beauchamps said, smiling.

Straight white teeth. Guy should be selling toothpaste instead of busting whores.

Decker said, "Everyone needs a pet maggot. Do you know who Steele went with?"

"No," Beauchamps said. "And she didn't volunteer his name when Andrick asked her. I know that 'cause Andrick asked me if I knew the name of her man. I put the word out, but so far have come up blank. There's some new dudes in town—Cubans. Marielitos. Meanest sons of bitches I've ever had the pleasure of dealing with. Into weird cult things—"

"Santeria?"

"You got it."

"I worked with Miami PD for two years," Decker said. "We had our fair share of Castro's rejects."

"So you know about the dudes," Beauchamps said. "They threaten grave bodily harm to women with loose lips. Might be one of them owns Myra."

"They have names?"

"I've crossed paths with only two. They actually weren't so bad, because they were really young. But their older brothers and father . . ." Beauchamps waved his hand in the air and pursed his lips into a whistle. "One called himself Conquistador, the other was El Cid."

Decker laughed.

"Yeah, real imaginative tags." Beauchamps paused, then said, "Why are you so interested in Ms. Steele's pimp?"

"I just want to know who he is," Decker said. "A friend of mine was accused of raping ole Plum Pie, and before I pass sentence on the sucker, I'd like to make sure he's really guilty of the crime."

"The hillbilly gimp," Beauchamps said.

Decker looked up. "Yeah, that's him."

"I was here when they booked him," Beauchamps said. "They say he fucked her up pretty bad."

"Well, he screwed her," Decker said. "No doubt about that. But I don't think he cut her."

"You're saying the pimp slashed her and she laid it on your friend?"

"It's a possibility," Decker said.

"Anything's a possibility. Just a matter of how much you want to play ostrich." Beauchamps paused. "I busted your buddy a while back."

Decker winced. "When?"

"A year, maybe two years ago."

"What for?"

"Soliciting an undercover police officer."

"Female officer?"

"Yeah," Beauchamps said, grinning. "She was female. I worked the van. He was hobbling around the mean streets, saw our lady, and took the bait. Didn't seem the least bit upset when he was arrested."

Decker said, "Know if he was ever arrested for anything else?"

"You haven't checked to see if he had priors?"

Decker shook his head. "I'd better stop acting like a dick and start acting like a dick."

Beauchamps burst into laughter. "Loser friends can take it out of you. I had this old high school buddy, a real rotten SOB, but at sixteen, I thought he was great fun. He's at Folsom now, and he keeps telling all his washed-out mutant relatives to contact me if they get into trouble. I don't think a week's gone by where one of those nut cases hasn't called me up and asked for a favor or free advice. God, that jerk has caused me nothing but grief."

"Did he give you a hard time?" Decker asked.

"Who? My loser buddy? Constantly."

"No," Decker said. "*My* loser buddy."

"Not while he was here," Beauchamps said. "Very cooperative. Served his time down here and that was it. He was a weird guy, Decker. Used to wash his hands about six times a day."

"An LB," Decker said.

"What?"

"A Lady Macbether," Decker said. "Some of the guys in the platoon had a hard time washing away the blood and guts."

"He was an army buddy of yours?"

"I hate that term—army buddy."

Beauchamps shrugged. "Want me to get his rap sheet?"

"Yeah."

Beauchamps punched Abel Atwater into the computer. A few minutes later, he handed the printout to Decker.

"Three priors," Beauchamps said. "All for trying to buy undercover pussy. Horny little bugger."

"It ain't nice, but not exactly sexual assault," Decker said. "Maybe Myra made him real mad."

Decker said, "Why would Myra Steele keep quiet about her pimp if he didn't have anything to do with the assault? You'd think she'd get in touch with him first thing."

"I don't know what was inside the lady's head, but I'll tell you this. Some of the ass-peddlers get real pissed at their ladies for getting beat up—treat them like damaged goods. Hers probably has a vile temper, and maybe she doesn't want any more pain."

"She still in the hospital?"

"For sure. Likely to be there a while."

"Where?"

Beauchamps shrugged ignorance.

"Know who's paying the bill?" Decker asked.

"Nope. But I suspect she's at County, and the city's footing the expenses." Beauchamps's phone rang. He answered the call and said, "Andrick's back."

"Super."

"Good luck."

"Thanks."

"Torres and Hoersch were the first unit to respond to the four-fifteen hotshot," Andrick said. He was in his late fifties, overweight, with a florid complexion. "There was a lot of commotion, a lot of blood, and they immediately called it in as an ambulance cutting. I got there about fifteen minutes later. The girl was being loaded onto the stretcher, your friend was cuffed, crying and bleeding from a huge gash across his head."

Andrick unlocked his file cabinet and loosened his tie. Decker noticed he was breathing heavily, sweat stained his armpits.

"You okay?" Decker asked.

Andrick said, "Yeah, I'm okay."

"You don't look so hot."

"I said I'm okay," Andrick answered tightly.

"Fine," Decker said. "You're okay. Can I see the file?"

Andrick tossed him the folder. Decker read a moment, then said, "The ambulance took the girl. Who took Atwater to the hospital?"

"I don't remember," Andrick said. "Someone must have called another, because they didn't put the two of them in the same wagon."

"Nobody was tending to Atwater's head wound all this time?" Decker asked.

"Look," Andrick said, unbuttoning his shirt, "you got a victim, you got a perp. One ambulance. You're gonna lose some sleep because some rape-o asshole bled to death?"

"No." Decker scanned the file. "You heard him say this? Or is this what the uniforms reported that he said?"

"Nope," Andrick said. "Everything I wrote down in my notes, I heard with my own ears. . . . What exactly did I write?"

Decker read, " 'I'm sorry, I'm sorry. I didn't mean it. Fuck, I didn't mean it. I'm sorry. I didn't mean to hurt anybody.' "

Andrick said, "Yeah, I heard him say that. Those kind of statements don't do much to clear your good name. Is it hot in here?"

"A little," Decker said absently. Lost in thought, he remembered Abel uttering similar words before. One particular memory suddenly flooded Decker's consciousness. Heavy fire. A gutted village. A little girl around six, her belly blown away. Abel standing over her, his eyes watering from all the smoke. He had whispered it:

I'm sorry. I'm so sorry. I never wanted to hurt anybody, honest to God, I didn't.

Ugly recollections. He pushed them away and looked up at Andrick. His coloring had become pale, his skin pasty, dripping with sweat.

"Jesus!" Decker whispered. "You're sure you're okay?"

"A minute." Andrick looked around. Medino had gone to the john. It was safe. He yanked open his desk drawer, and with shaking hands opened a vial of tablets. He placed a pill underneath his tongue.

A minute later, Decker said, "How long do you think you can hide your condition from the department?"

"What condition?" Andrick said. "I'm sucking on a peppermint."

"A peppermint?"

"Yeah, a fucking peppermint," Andrick said. "Keeps my breath fresh. . . . Look, Detective, I've got two more years before I cash in twenty-five big ones and a nice-size pension. We've got the condo in Murietta Hot Springs, two daughters in college, I need that extra ten percent to make ends meet, you know what I'm saying? So if you want to talk about the case, that's all right by me. If not, find the door."

Medino came back to his desk. Andrick cleared his throat. Decker understood the hint. He said, "Where's Myra Steele now?"

"Originally, they took her to Hollywood Pres, but her mom moved her to County because she didn't have any insurance."

Decker said, "Mind if I have a word with Myra?"

"Be my guest," Andrick said. "She should be there at least another week. Why all the interest in this case?"

Decker explained his involvement.

"And you think your scuzzbag friend is innocent?"

"I'm withholding judgment."

Andrick sat back in his chair and wiped his damp forehead with a handkerchief. He felt much better, was breathing easier. "So what are you gonna do with Myra Steele? Grill her until she retracts what she said?"

Decker said, "Hell no! If the sucker did it, I'll kill him for doing that to her and making an ass out of me. But for starters, I'd like to know who's pimping her."

"You won't get the name from her."

"I can try."

"Sure," Andrick said. "Try." He gave Decker a wary half-smile. "And if you get it from her, you'll give it to me, right?"

"Absolutely," Decker said. "I'm not playing hot dog."

"Just so you and I understand each other."

"It's your collar, Detective," Decker said. "I don't dance

with anyone else's woman,'cause I get pissed when someone dances with mine. I'd like to copy the file."

"Go ahead," Andrick said.

When Decker returned, Andrick said, "Your partner's on
the line."

Decker picked up the phone and said, "What's up?"

"I got a call from Delferno," Marge said. "One of his pals
says Sally looks like one of his kids. Mother's from Sacramento. She should be down maybe one, two in the morning.
Kid was grabbed by Dad about six months ago."

"How old would her kid be?"

"About two and a half."

"Sally's not two and a half."

"Delferno faxed me the picture of the missing kid—kid's
name is Heather Miller. She's supposed to be small for her
age, and there's a *strong* resemblance."

"Okay," Decker said. "I just hope Mama doesn't go into a
major depression if it's not hers."

"Well, that's a chance she's willing to take."

"I'll be at the station in a couple of hours," Decker said.
"Would you call Sophi Rawlings for me?"

"Already did, Pete. Where're you going now?"

"Gonna cruise for sugar."

Marge said, "Wear gloves."

It was nearly midnight, but Sunset Boulevard was still
teeming with bugs. Decker found three streetwalkers idling
at a corner gas station next to a Mideastern vender selling
huge stuffed animals at ridiculously low prices. The toys
were imports, and no doubt didn't meet American safety
standards. A month ago a batch had been seized at Foothill,
all the teddy bears and doggies stuffed with flammable rags
that combusted spontaneously in hot weather.

Decker parked on a side street and approached the streetwalkers. The first whore might have been a plump,
freckled-faced farm girl, except she was wearing fake

leopard-skin hot pants, a matching halter, and knee-high black boots. The other two were black. One had dyed her hair platinum blond and painted her clawish fingernails high-gloss black. The other girl had a short Afro, a fur choker around her neck, and seven earrings in each ear. As Decker neared, the one with the earrings nudged the one with the claws, and the trio began to disperse. Decker sprinted to them and yelled, "Wait!" The girls stopped. Fingernails spoke up:

"We're goin'."

"I suppose you ladies have some ID on you."

The girls began to reach into their purses.

Decker said, "Don't bother. I believe you. I'm a very trusting fellow."

The girls eyed each other. A black-and-white pulled up at the corner. Decker showed his badge and waved the cruiser away.

"Say what, Detective," said Fingernails. She was gazing at her feet. Her spiked heels gave her at least six inches of height. A wonder she didn't need a balancing rod to walk.

"What's your name, honey?" Decker asked.

"Anything you want," Fingernails answered. The other hookers laughed.

Decker's eyes bore into hers. "What's your name?" he asked again.

"Amanda."

Decker stared at her for another minute. He asked, "And how long have you and your girlfriends worked the area?"

"You gonna bust us, or what?" asked the plump white girl.

Decker said, "That all depends."

"On what?" asked Amanda.

Decker said, "On if you cooperate."

"Watchu want?" Amanda asked.

Decker smiled.

Amanda said, "C'mon. I'll do you in the back alley."

"Do what?"

"Do what you want," Amanda said.

"What do I want?" Decker said.

Amanda's eyes clouded. "I ain't saying no more."

"I'm not here for badge pussy, Amanda," Decker said.

"Then what do you want?" asked the white one.

"A little help."

The girls were silent.

Decker said, "Question number one: Any of you know a lady named Myra Steele?"

More silence.

"Aw, c'mon, girls," Decker said. "Where's your sense of civic duty? Besides, the longer I hang around, the more I drive away your business."

"Why you hassling us?" said the one with the earrings.

"'Cause you guys are the first streetwalkers I saw," Decker said. "And I love leopard skin." He eyed the white girl. "What's your name?"

"Chrissie," she said.

"Chrissie," Decker repeated. "Glad to know you, Chrissie. You know Myra Steele?"

"I might."

"You know she was beat up pretty badly?" Decker asked.

"I mighta heard something like that."

"Oh, and what else might you have heard?" Decker said.

"Don't say no more," Amanda whispered.

"You have something to share with us, Amanda?" Decker said.

"I didn't say nothing," Amanda answered.

"You know, Amanda, I hang around, it's your pockets that are goin' empty. Your man gets pissed off at you, not me. See, I've got time. I'm paid to do this."

"Bully for you," said Amanda.

Decker asked the girl with the earrings, "What's your name?"

"Maynona," she said.

"Maynona's a nice name. Can I call you May for short?" Decker asked.

"I don't give a shit."

"Good," Decker said. "I'll call you May. Did you know Myra Steele, May?"

"Maybe."

"And maybe you know she's still in the hospital?"

"Maybe."

"Maybe you also know who her pimp might be?"

"Maybe I don't."

"But maybe you do."

Maynona looked off to her right, stared at stuffed pink elephants and black-and-white pandas.

Chrissie said, "I think she was an independent since Letwoine got blowed away."

"Nice try," Decker said. "But you know and I know that no one is an independent here."

"Well, maybe she wasn't no independent," Chrissie said. She unknotted her halter strap and tied it tighter. The increased pressure flattened her round breasts and made them pop out of the sides of the garment. She gave Decker a sultry smile.

He remained stone-faced and said, "So if Myra Steele wasn't an independent, who was she working for?"

The girls were silent.

Decker took out a pack of cigarettes and offered one to each girl. He lit their smokes, then lit one for himself.

"There some new foreign businessmen around here that scare you gals?" he inquired.

"Maybe," Amanda said.

"Do they have names?"

"You ain't getting them from me," Amanda said.

Decker opened his jacket. He said, "See that gun?"

The girls didn't answer.

"It's a nine-millimeter automatic," he said. "We dicks are

finally beginning to get real, you know what I'm talking about. Mr. Foreign Businessman starts hassling you, you tell me. Mr. Beretta and I will take him out to lunch."

"Shit, that's puny against a sawed-off," Amanda said.

"You know, we can carry shotguns, too," Decker said. "But we're getting ahead of ourselves. Who's Myra's man?"

"I ain't' tellin' you nothin', 'cause I happen to know that the dude's crazier than shit," Amanda said.

Decker smiled, wondering, How crazy is *shit*? He said, "Mr. Foreign Businessman of the Hispanic persuasion?"

A faint flicker passed through Amanda's eyes. Decker went on.

"Happen to be spookin' you with some weirdo hexes?"

"My man's not Myra's," Amanda said defiantly.

"Sure about that?" Decker said.

"Yes."

"Does the name Conquistador ring a bell?"

Amanda sneered. "He's a wimp."

"El Cid?"

"Wimpo *dos*," Amanda replied.

"What can you tell me about Myra's man?"

The whore drew her finger across her lips.

"Think about it, honey," Decker said. "Give me something, or maybe your man will hear things you don't want him to hear."

"I'm real scared," Amanda said. But it was false bravado.

"Myra's man is suppose to have a tattoo on the back of his hand," Maynona volunteered. "Between his thumb and forefinger."

Chrissie spoke up. "A heart with a ribbon on it."

Decker nodded. A Mariel tattoo—traditionally, it meant an executioner. The guy was bad news. "Anything else?" he said.

"Swear to God, that's all I know," May said. "We keep away from them."

Decker believed her eyes if not her words.

"This is all stupid," Amanda said. "They said it was her john that cut her, not her pimp." She bit her lip, then said, "You know something different than that?"

Decker said, "Yeah, what about this bad-assed john? Any of you know him?"

The girls didn't answer, but exchanged knowing looks.

"Anyone of you ever service him?" Decker asked.

"Why you so interested in Myra Steele?" Chrissie asked. She scratched her cheek, still pocked with acne. "And her john?"

"Because rumor has it that this mean ole trick has been bailed out," Decker said. "Now we've got a pissed-off pimp and a psycho john running the streets. Shit, ladies, I'd hate to see one of you end up like Myra."

Maynona raised her eyebrows. Decker caught it.

"Ever service the man, May?" he asked.

She didn't answer.

"Boy, you gals are kind of quiet tonight," Decker said. "You know what I'm gonna do? I'm gonna fill in the blanks. I'm gonna say that all three of you have serviced him, 'cause this trick likes ladies of the evening, and he's been cruising the area for years."

"You can think what you want," said Amanda. Her eyes had returned to the ground.

"You ever see to his needs?" Decker asked.

She didn't answer.

"Did he ever get freaky with you?"

She stayed silent.

"Well, if you're going to be like that, just maybe I'll drop the word that you gals dig servicing John Q. Psycho."

"You don't scare me, Mr. Hot Shit Detective," said Amanda.

"I'm not trying to, Amanda."

"Yes, you are, and it ain't working," Amanda said. "I ain't afraid of Myra's john. Dude's a lame-o."

"A lame-o?" Decker said. "You mean he's stupid?"

"No," Maynona said. "He limps. That's 'cause he only got one leg."

Amanda said, "He tries anything, I'll bust his head open . . . like Myra did."

"That so?" Decker said.

"Yeah," Amanda said. "That's so. Besides, Mr. Lame-o Big Dick never done nothin' bad to me."

"Big Dick?" Decker asked.

"The dude is *hung*," Amanda said. "I mean to say he packs a wallop." She laughed. "But he always paid for what he took."

Decker said, "Was Big Dick kinky?"

"Not with me," Amanda answered.

"Sadistic?"

"Nope. Not once. I don't take shit from no one."

"I heard the guy's a vet," Decker said. "Knows how to shoot, knows how to handle knives."

There was a moment of silence. Amanda broke it.

"Don't bother me none," she said, her voice less convincing. "My old man takes good care of me."

Decker said, "I bet he does, as long as you make your quota. But when things get a little slow, I bet he's not too understanding."

Amanda didn't answer.

Decker paused, then said, "So the gimp never tossed you, eh?"

"Not even a little bit." Amanda smiled. "I was surprised when I heard it was Lame-o Big Dick. He never seemed like the type." She sighed and added, "But I been wrong before."

❧ 7

The woman looked composed from afar, but as Hollander got close, he noticed a spasm in her right lower eyelid. Her face was long, her complexion mottled with two pronounced bags under washed-out blue eyes. Her lips seemed almost bloodless, her tawny hair hung limply to her shoulders. At her side was a man in his fifties, medium build with gray wavy hair and brown eyes. Stubble was sprinkled over his fleshy cheeks and large chin. Must be the bounty hunter, Hollander thought. He escorted them into the squad room.

"Charlie Benko," the man said, holding out his hand.

Hollander shook hands and smiled at the woman. She had tears in her eyes. Hollander said, "You people want some coffee? You must be tired after flying in so late."

"Not for me, thanks," said Benko. "I'm already tanked up with caffeine. Dotty?"

The woman shook her head.

"Tea? Hot cocoa, maybe, Mrs. Miller?" Hollander offered.

"Nothing, thank you," she whispered.

"Have a seat," Hollander said.

"By the way, Detective," Benko said, "her name isn't Miller. She remarried. It's Palmer."

"Sorry about that," Hollander said. "Uh, you explained her the procedure—"

"Yeah, she knows she can't just waltz in there and take the kid. Paperwork right, Dotty?" Benko patted her hand. "We're hopeful on this one. The bastard ex was spotted in the area a couple of times before. Unfortunately, I still can't find him, but it doesn't mean the sunnabitch isn't hiding out somewhere."

"What's his name?" Hollander asked.

"Douglas Miller," Benko said. He opened his briefcase and pulled out a picture. "Appreciate it if you'd pass it around. Bastard's wanted for back alimony on their other three kids."

Hollander stared at the picture and said, "He just took one of the kids?"

"Yeah, the other kids are older and wouldn't go near the sunnabitch," Benko said. He threw his arm around Dotty. "Thank God for small favors, huh?"

Dotty started to smile, but her face crumpled. She buried her face in her hands.

"C'mon, Dotty." Benko hugged her. "Everything'll be all right, honey, just take my word for it."

Dotty continued to cry. Benko looked up at Hollander and shrugged. He said, "When can we see the kid?"

"I'm waiting for Detective Dunn. She's the one who'll accompany you to the foster home."

Dotty dried her eyes on the back of her sleeve and asked, "Is she okay?"

"The kid? Oh yeah," said Hollander. "Just fine."

"I mean she wasn't beaten up?" Dotty asked.

"No. Not at all."

"Doug drinks," Dotty said. "Don't have no control when he's drunk. That's why I left him."

"Smart move, Dotty," Benko said. "Smart move."

Dotty said, "Oh God, I want my little girl back!" She

broke into sobs. "He did it on purpose. He don't love her, he just did it to spite me, the bastard."

"We'll get him," Benko said. "I'll find him, Dotty. I always do. Something'll come up."

Hollander said, "How'd he snatch her?"

Benko said, "Just never returned with her on visiting day. Some asshole judge demanded the sunnabitch have parental visiting rights. Well, like I said, the other three wouldn't go with him. But a little two-year-old, what does she know? Friggin' judge. Letting a sunnabitch like him have visiting rights. Dotty tried to tell her about Doug, but the bitch wouldn't listen."

Hollander continued to stare at the photo. He asked, "How recent is this picture?"

Benko said, "Why? You know the sunnabitch?" He smiled at Dotty. "See? I told you something would come up. These guys are sharp. Where you know him from, Detective?"

"I don't know him under the name Doug Miller," Hollander said. "But the sucker looks familiar. Let me stew on it."

"Sure, take your time, take your time!" Benko checked his watch, then began to pace. "I got loads of pictures. I'll start showing them around here again, since you say he looks familiar. When's the girl coming?"

"Who?" asked Hollander.

"The girl who's taking us to the foster home."

Hollander smiled. "Detective Dunn is five-eleven, one-sixty. She's female, but she ain't no girl. She should be along any moment." Still focused on the picture, Hollander shook his head.

"Keep looking, Detective," Benko said. "It'll come to you."

"What did your ex do for a living, Mrs. Palmer?"

Benko said, "I don't know what he's doing now, but he was a roofer when Dotty was married to him, right?"

Dotty nodded yes.

"Well, we've got lots of laborers living in this area," Hollander said. "He'd blend in without a second glance. Ah, the detective cometh."

Marge gave a wave. They stood as Hollander made all the necessary introductions. Marge held Dotty's hand and said, "I'm sorry for all the pain you've suffered. I really hope we've found your little girl. But I'll tell you again what I told you over the phone, the child we found looks younger than two and a half."

"Heather's little. She looks young," Dotty managed to say. She brushed her hair away from her face.

"I hope she is your Heather," Marge said. "Has Sergeant Decker arrived yet?"

Hollander said, "He was called in on an emergency code seven. You can buzz him if you need him."

Marge shook her head no and smiled inwardly. Code seven meant a meal break, but when they used it in front of civilians, it meant getting tied up with something personal. In Pete's case, he'd probably gone home to catch up on sleep. No matter. Let the guy rest.

Hollander said, "Detective Dunn, take a look at this photo for me."

Marge studied Douglas Miller.

"He look familiar?" Hollander asked.

"Yeah, let me think, let me think," Marge said. She examined the picture, then handed it back to Hollander. "I'm blocking. It'll probably come to me when I'm showering." Marge turned to Dotty. "Are you ready?"

"As ready as I'll ever be," she answered.

It was nearly three in the morning when they reached Sophi Rawlings's home. Sophi was dressed in a short-sleeved white cotton shift and a lightweight shawl. She was standing outside the door as Marge pulled the unmarked up to the curve. A thin layer of mist lay suspended in the early morning air. As they came out of the car, Dotty's breathing became audible.

"I'm Detective Dunn, Ms. Rawlings," Marge said. "I spoke to you on the phone. This is Mrs. Palmer, the possible mother of Baby Sally, and this is Mr. Benko. He accompanied her down from the Bay area."

"Come on in," Sophi said. "The girl's asleep, but I left a night-light on next to the crib."

"Let's go," Marge said.

Dotty grabbed Benko's shoulder for support.

"Can you walk okay, Dotty?" Marge asked.

Dotty tried to answer yes, but the word wouldn't come. She nodded instead. Marge took her hand anyway. Flanked by Marge and Benko, Dotty slowly made her way to the nursery, the walk seemingly interminable.

The toddler roomed with three other children. The first was a black girl of four. She was sleeping atop her covers, dressed in Snoopy babydolls. Opposite her were two steel cots. Two girls, four and six, slept in undershirts and underpants. They both had long, thick hair that covered most of their backs. The crib was in the far end of the room. Benko led Dotty over to it. Building up courage, Dotty finally peered inside. Her eyes immediately watered, her fingertips brushed the curls off of the sleeping toddler's forehead.

Dotty stared at the baby for a long time. Benko cleared his throat, but Dotty didn't respond.

After a few minutes of silence, Sophi whispered, "It's not your daughter, is it Mrs. Palmer?"

Dotty paused, then shook her head no.

"Take your time," Benko said. "Don't rush it. Take another look—"

"It's not her, Charlie," Dotty said. "Oh, Charlie, she's missing Heather's dimples, and Heather had a little mole at the tip of her left ear. And Heather has thinner eyebrows . . . and longer lashes . . . and—oh, Charlie, what am I going to *do*!"

Dotty's eyelids fluttered, and she pitched forward. Marge caught her by the shoulders, and she and Benko carried her limp body into the living room and placed her on an old plaid sofa.

Sophi said, "I'll go get some water."

"And a towel, too, please," Marge said. She muttered "shit" under her breath. "Where do you go from here?" she said to Benko.

"I'm gonna keep searching." He poked his finger in Marge's shoulder. "You keep thinking who that sunnabitch looks like, lady."

Marge knocked his finger away. "Don't get in my face, kiddo."

Benko held his hands up. "Jesus! Sorry."

Marge sighed. "S'right. It's been a long night."

Sophi came back with the water, salts, and a moist towel. She broke open the capsule and held it under Dotty's nose. Dotty stirred, then opened her eyes.

"You're fine, baby," Sophi said. "Just fine." Gently, she dabbed Dotty's forehead.

"Hi, Dotty," Benko said. "You did just great, honey."

"It wasn't her," Dotty moaned.

"I'm sorry, Dotty," Benko said. "I'm truly sorry. I thought maybe we had a chance. . . . I'm sorry. This is just a little setback. We'll find the sunnabitch and your Heather."

"Oh, God," Dotty wailed.

"Take it easy, honey," Sophi said. "Drink this." She raised the cup of water to her lips. Dotty sipped slowly at first, then gulped the water down.

"I've got to get out of here," Dotty whispered.

Benko said, "You gotta rest a minute, Dotty."

"*Please*, Charlie," she begged. "Please get me out of here!"

"Okay, okay," Benko said. "I just don't want you to overexert yourself, you know? C'mon, Dot. I'll help you stand up."

"Thank you very much, Ms. Rawlings," Marge said. "I appreciate your help."

"You tell Detective Decker that I'm taking Baby Sally to

the doctor's tomorrow," Sophi said. "And I'll get what he asked for."

"I'll do that," Marge said. "Let me help you, Mrs. Palmer. Lean on me."

Benko whispered into Marge's ear, "Please, Detective. Please! Find me that sunnabitch!"

Decker woke up at six, let the dog out, showered, shaved, dressed, then said an abbreviated version of *Shacharit*—the morning prayers. He'd once recited the entire service and had even wore phylacteries, but lately that seemed like an awful lot of bother for very little spiritual enhancement. So he settled on saying the *Shema*—the essence of Judaism— and eighteen verses of silent devotion. When he finished, he put down his *siddur*, then studied himself in the mirror. He patted his flat stomach, flexed his biceps. The body wasn't the problem, it was the face. Those bags! It made him look like the big four-oh had stepped on his face years before. A pisser, since he just entered his fifth decade of life a year ago.

What would Rina think?

Shit.

Gorgeous Rina. Gorgeous *young* Rina. Not yet thirty, she could still pass for a high school student if she dressed simply. As Decker stared at his face, he knew he looked old enough to be her father.

"Fuck it," he said.

He went to the kitchen, slipped four pieces of bread into the toaster, and pulled out a quart of milk. The kitchen window faced his back acreage—flat dirt fields that disappeared into mountainside. The morning summer sun was strong, pouring its thick honey into the crags and rocky crevices. The window was open, the air was dry and dusty. As he drank from the carton, he heard Ginger yapping excitedly. The barking was followed by the steady blows of a hammer, and the noise was coming from his property. From his barn.

"What the hell?" Decker said. He went out the back door and stopped short at the entrance to the barn. Abel was in the middle of the room, kneeling on his prosthesis, ripping up a rotted plank of flooring. At his side were a tool chest and a box of nails.

Ginger barked at the sight of a stranger. Decker quieted the dog and said, "Abel, what are you doing?"

"Your barn and stable are a stack of cards, Doc," Abel said. "Floorboards warped, the stalls are coming apart at the seams. The beams weren't fit properly. Y'all put 'em up yourself?"

"As a matter of fact, I did," Decker said.

"Getting sloppy, Doc."

"Abel—"

"And your barn wall is Swiss cheese," Abel said. "Full of bullet holes. Shoot-out time at the O.K. Corral, Pete?"

Decker ignored the remark. "How'd you even *get* here?"

Abel pointed to a motorcycle leaning against the wall.

"You biked here?"

"No, Doc. I carried it on my shoulders."

"Don't be cute," Decker said. He petted Ginger and walked over to Abel, stood over him. "Let me see your driver's license."

Abel looked up. *"What?"*

"Let me see your driver's license."

"You're shittin' me."

"The license?"

Abel hesitated, then reached in his pocket and threw the license on the floor. Decker picked it up, looked at it, and handed it back to him. Abel pocketed the card.

He said, "You know, I once had a good friend, but he turned into a cop."

"Yeah, well, yesterday, you didn't call the friend, you called the cop."

"Well, maybe it was my mistake to call him at all."

Neither one spoke for a moment. Abel continued tugging up on the floorboard.

"Your ceiling don't look that hot, either," he said. "You can see daylight through the rafters."

"You're going to roof my barn, Abe?"

"All I have to do is screw my leg into a scaffold jack, and a tornado couldn't dislodge me."

"Abe, you don't have to do this. . . ."

"Yes, I do, Doc. Yes, I do indeed have to do this. It serves a right fine purpose for me."

"I never expected you to pay me back."

"Well, you see, Pete," Abel said, "that's where you and I differ. I always intended on payin' you back in one fashion or another. Ain't got no money on me. But I sure as hell have time."

"Let me ask you this, Abe," Decker said. "What if I find proof-positive evidence that you did what you're accused of doing?"

"What if?"

Decker chewed the corner of his mustache. He pulled out a pack of cigarettes from his shirt pocket and kneaded it. He said, "I'll nail you, buddy. I swear to God, I'll nail you."

"You find any evidence that I hurt that lady, and I'll give you the hammer. So do your job. It don't worry me any."

Ginger jumped onto Decker's chest again and panted.

"I think the critter's hungry," Abel said.

"Yeah," Decker said. "C'mon, girl. Let's eat breakfast. Are you hungry, Abe?"

"Nope."

"Look, don't be shy—"

"I ain't hungry."

"You want some coffee? I always make extra."

Abel said, "If you come back out, you can bring me a cup." He looked at Decker's cigarettes. "You gonna smoke them, or just giving the cellophane a massage?"

"Take the whole fucking pack," Decker said, tossing them over.

"No need for profanities," Abel said. "Got some matches, or should I eat them raw?"

Decker gave him a book. "Don't burn the place down."

"Depends how much it's insured for."

"Not enough," Decker said. He went inside and fed the dog. He fixed two more pieces of toast and brought them along with two cups of black coffee. "Just in case you changed your mind about being hungry."

"I said I wasn't," Abel said, a cigarette dangling from his lips.

"Fine." Decker sipped his coffee. "I'll toss 'em."

"I'll take 'em," Abel said. "You shouldn't be wasting good food." He stubbed out his smoke and devoured the first piece of toast in three bites.

Decker asked, "So what do you aim to do for me, Abe?"

"I figure I'll rebuild everything from the ground up. When I'm done with the barn, I'll move on to the stable. The whole thing shouldn't be costing more than a couple hundred worth of lumber, maybe another hundred for the hardware."

"I'll pay for the supplies," Decker said.

"All right," Abel said. "I'll feed and exercise your animals, if you want."

"Sure. That'll save me about an hour a day. If you want to take a pleasure ride, go ahead. Just do it in the morning or late afternoon. It's too hot otherwise."

"I hear you."

"Abe," Decker said, "how about if you start the job a week from now? I've got someone coming in from out of town this afternoon. I'm going to need some privacy."

"I'll be discreet."

"No offense, but I don't want you around," Decker said. "I don't want anyone around. The barn can wait."

Abel bit his lip and nodded.

Decker said, "It's nothing personal. . . ."

"I know."

"Call it quits around noon. It starts getting pretty hot out here anyway."

"I'll be gone."

Decker sighed and gave Abel a firm pat on his shoulder. "Be talking to you. Hey, you want a beer or anything for later on?"

"Only if it's dark and imported," Abel said. "I'm picky about my brews."

"I've got some Dos Equis. I'll bring you out a bottle."

"Thanks."

Decker waited a moment, wishing he could think of something to say. Once conversation with Abel had been as natural as a draw of breath. But that was many moons ago.

He went inside the house to fetch the beer.

Marge showed the picture of Douglas Miller to MacPherson.

"Know this one, Paulie?"

MacPherson glanced over his shoulder. "No. What's the piss-bucket done?"

"Kidnapped his daughter," Marge said. "Doesn't look familiar to you? He looked familiar to Mike and me."

"Never seen him," MacPherson said.

Marge rapped her knuckles on her head. "The *mug books*! Shit, my brain was mud last night. I should have made an appointment for the bounty hunter to come in and take a look. I hope he's still in town." She pocketed the picture and dialed the phone. Decker walked into the squad room.

"Ah, the man's big day," MacPherson said, with a leer on his face.

"You talking to me?" Decker asked.

"I believe I am, Rabbi. Correct me if I'm wrong, but is not this indeed the day that the fair Rina arrives?"

Decker stared at him. "You been *listening* in on my phone conversations, Paul?"

MacPherson shrugged. "I can't help it if you tie up the party line."

Decker said, "You amaze me, Paul. Every day you reach new heights of assholism."

"Admit it, Pete," MacPherson said. "We're all voyeurs and eavesdroppers. That's our field. Probing."

"You eavesdropped on my *personal* phone conversation. Paul, that's so . . . juvenile."

"I hope you find out what's troubling your lass."

Decker gave him a murderous look. MacPherson winked and went back to his paperwork.

Marge hung up the phone and said, "This scumbag look familiar to you?" She tossed Decker the photo. Decker studied it for a moment, then shook his head. "Who is he?"

"He's the asshole husband of the lady last night."

"Oh." Decker concentrated on the picture for a long time. "No. I don't know him. How's the lady doing? When you called last night, you said she was pretty upset."

"I just got off the phone with her bounty hunter. He said she'd calmed down. He sent her back this morning. He's still in L.A. and is going to look through our mug books. I *know* this joker lives in our area."

"I'll keep my eyes open," Decker said.

"What are you doing this morning?" Marge asked.

"I've got a court appearance at one-thirty. I have to go *downtown*, can you believe that noise? The Lessing case."

"Why aren't they arraigning him at Van Nuys?"

" 'Cause they've got him booked downtown. He was out

on bail, and raped a girl in Wilshire Division. Shit, what is the *matter* with these judges? I think Lessing's bail was only ten grand."

"Probably the same bail as your buddy's," Marge said.

"Dunn, don't start with me," Decker said.

"Just pointing out a certain irony."

Decker said, "Thank you, Detective Dunn, for that little lesson. I think I'll be useful and go back up to the Manfred development right now. Talk to Patty Bingham—the one you thought was hiding something. Maybe contact a few of the neighbors we missed yesterday. Want to come with me?"

"I've got a date with a twelve-year-old charged with vehicular manslaughter," Marge said.

"Tut, tut," MacPherson said, looking up from his paperwork. "What is this world coming to?"

"See you later," Decker said to Marge.

"Have a splendid time tonight, Peter," MacPherson said.

"Eat your heart out, Paulie."

A peroxide blonde opened the door until the chain stopped its advance. Her complexion was sallow, her eyes a strange shade of seawater green. Kids were screaming in the background.

"Yes?" she said.

"Police, Mrs. Bingham." Decker showed her his badge. "I'd like a few minutes of your time."

The green orbs began to dart in their sockets.

"What do you want?"

"It concerns a missing child." Decker took out the photo of Baby Sally and slipped it through the door. "We're trying to locate this little girl's parents—"

"I already talked to the police yesterday," the woman said. "I don't know who this kid is."

"Mommy . . ." said a tiny wail.

"Wait a minute!" the woman snapped.

Decker said, "If you'll just take your time . . ."

"I said I don't know who she is!"

Decker lied, "But I was told by a neighbor down the street that you might know—"

"Who told you that?"

"One of your neighbors."

"Which one?"

"Uh, let me look at my notes," Decker said, flipping through an empty notepad.

"Was it Jane?" she fired out. "Did Jane tell you I know this kid?"

Another kid screamed, "Mommy, Andrea hit me!"

"I said *wait* a minute!"

Decker squinted, trying to get a better look at Patty Bingham. They were still talking through the chain.

"Yeah, it was Jane," Decker said.

"Well, Jane is a liar!"

The door slammed in Decker's face. He thought the interview was over, until he heard the chain unlatch and the door opened all the way. Patty Bingham was wearing cutoff shorts and a T-shirt. She was a decent-looking woman and was tight in all the right places, but looked as if she'd traveled more than a few miles in her life. She seemed to be an angry woman, but her eyes gave Decker a quick once-over and her expression softened. She cocked her hip.

"Look, sir . . ." She let out a small laugh. "I don't know *what* Jane Hickey told you, but I don't know who that kid is. And I've got five of my own—"

"Five?"

"Well, three are from my husband's first marriage. They're visiting him for the summer. Ain't that a riot! What did you say your name was?"

The phone rang.

"Want me to get that, Patty?" yelled another voice.

"Yeah." She faced Decker. "Your name?"

Decker showed her his badge again.

"Jane has a kind of big mouth," Patty said. "Know what I mean?"

"But why would Jane say you knew this kid if you didn't?" Decker asked. "Please Mrs. Bingham, the kid's in a foster home, and we don't know who her parents are. If her parents don't want her—"

"Oh, I doubt that," Patty said. She turned red.

"Why?" Decker asked.

"I mean . . . who wouldn't want such a cute kid like that?"

"Some parents are very strange."

"Ain't that the truth. Want some coffee? We could drink in the backyard. Ain't so noisy back there."

"No thank you, Mrs. Bingham. So you have no idea who she belongs to?"

"No idea."

"Does she look like anyone you know around the neighborhood?"

"Nope. Sure you don't want to come in for a cup of coffee?"

"I'm afraid I'll have to pass," Decker said. "I still have quite a few more doors to knock on. Take one more look."

"It won't do any good."

"Humor me," Decker said.

Patty gave a cursory glance at the photo, then shook her head.

Decker said, "I just hate to see such a cute little kid like her in a foster home."

"I'm sure her parents will turn up," Patty said.

"I don't think so," Decker said.

Patty bit her thumbnail. "Well, it's not my problem if they don't. I'm not the savior of the world, you know."

Decker said. "Maybe you want to keep the photo, just in case—"

"Waste of time."

"Please. Just show it to your neighbors."

Patty bit her thumbnail again. "You're a stubborn man." She took the photo, looked at it, and stuck it in her hip pocket.

Decker said, "Thank you for your cooperation, Mrs. Bingham."

"Sure. And don't listen to Jane. She's got a big mouth."

Decker smiled and walked away. Once inside the unmarked, he radioed in a request for the address of a Mrs. Jane Hickey. She lived a block and a half away, one of the houses where no one had been home yesterday. This morning she was outside, watering her small patch of front lawn, wearing a sunsuit. Her hair was wrapped in a kerchief, her face was deeply tanned.

"Mrs. Hickey?" Decker said. "I'm Sergeant Peter Decker, LAPD. I was wondering if I could have a couple of words with you."

Jane looked at the badge. "What do you want?"

"I just spoke with one of your neighbors, Patty Bingham," Decker said. He pulled out another picture of Baby Sally. "I'm trying to identify this little girl and locate her parents. I showed the picture to Mrs. Bingham, and she said it looked familiar to her, but she couldn't place it. Do you have any idea who this child might be?"

Jane eyed the picture and laughed.

"What is it?" Decker asked.

"She looks a little like Patty's youngest," Jane said.

Decker's eyes widened.

Jane said, "Of course, it isn't Andrea."

"Do they look a lot alike?"

"Just a little around the eyes . . . and the hair." Jane handed the picture back to Decker. "All kids that age kinda look alike. Chubby little faces . . . you know. I don't know who this one is, though."

"Never saw her around the neighborhood?"

"No," Jane said.

"You're sure?"

"There's a lot of kids around here," Jane said. "I'm not *positive* that I've never seen her, but I don't know the kid personally."

Decker said, "Thank you for your time."

He drove back to the Bingham residence.

"You again?" Patty said, when she saw him at the door. But she was smiling.

"I think I will have that cup of coffee," Decker said.

Patty's smile turned to a grin. "Why don't you come around through the side? I'll meet you at the back."

"I don't mind drinking with all the noise," Decker said. "I like kids." He walked inside before Patty could object.

The house was center-hall plan—living room on the left, dining area to the right. The living room was sparsely furnished and sterile—a white velvet sofa and matching love seat, a glass coffee table, and a fireplace that had never been used. The dining area held a fake wood-grain Formica table and eight chairs. Through the dining room was a kitchen stocked with all the latest appliances, the countertops white Formica, one section already marred by a burn mark. The cabinets were new, but the finish was cheap and full of varnish bubbles. Right off the kitchen was the family room. It was piled high with kids and mess—laundry, toys, scraps of food. The TV was blaring. Three older children were slouched on a brown-and-white plaid sofa accented with Naugahyde straps. A four-year-old was sitting cross-legged on the wall-to-wall brown shag carpet.

"Sure you want to drink coffee with all this noise going on?"

"Where's the fifth?" Decker asked.

"Huh?"

"The fifth kid," Decker said. "I only count four."

"Oh," Patty looked around. "Brian, go find the baby."

"I'm watchin'—"

"I said, find the baby," Patty demanded. "Shit. I'm always looking for one of 'em."

A boy of around ten slipped off the couch, a perpetual sulk plastered on his face.

"Who's he?" asked one of the older girls. Her hair was cut short, and she had braces on her teeth.

"A cop," Patty said. "I'm giving him some coffee. You take cream?"

"Black."

"Cops can drink when they're on duty?" the girl asked skeptically.

"If it's coffee," Decker said.

"Mind your own business, Karen," Patty said.

"I was just asking," Karen whined. "Geez."

Brian walked in, carrying a two-year-old. She was wearing nothing but a diaper. Decker stared at the face. Old Jane had a good eye. There was a resemblance. It wasn't unusually strong, it wasn't uncanny, but both little girls shared a certain look.

"That's the little one?" Decker asked.

"My bundle of trouble," Patty said. "Here's your coffee."

"Thanks." Decker kept glancing at the baby as he drank. Maybe it was the playful look in the baby's eyes. Sally had playful eyes.

"So," Patty said. "How long have you been a cop?"

Decker gulped the coffee as fast as he could. "Too long."

"Seen it all, haven't you?"

"Yes, ma'am."

"So have I," Patty said.

"Give me a break," Brian muttered.

"Keep your damn thoughts to yourself," Patty said.

Decker put the mug on the countertop. "Thanks for the coffee, Mrs. Bingham. I've got to go now."

"You're a fast drinker." Patty nudged him in the ribs. "Hope you don't do everything that fast."

Decker groaned inwardly.

"How 'bout a refill?" Patty said.

"No thanks."

The air conditioner suddenly blasted cold air atop his head.

"Gotta go," Decker said.

Patty said, "Hey, maybe I'll see you around, huh?"

Karen rolled her eyes.

Decker said, "Maybe."

He left as quickly as he could.

❧ 8

"*How was Patty* Bingham?" Marge asked.

Decker loosened his tie and said, "Patty has strong, un-fulfilled sexual needs."

"What?" Hollander looked up from his paperwork. "What's this about unfulfilled sexual needs?"

Marge said, "Go back to sleep, Mike."

"A crime-lab report came in for you, Pete," Hollander said. "It's on your desk."

"Thanks," Decker said. He sat down, opened a bottle of aspirin, and swallowed a couple of tablets without water.

"Unfulfilled needs, huh?" said Marge.

"Can I get this woman's phone number?" Hollander asked.

"You wouldn't want it," Decker said. "She's a piece of work." To Marge, he said, "Her youngest kid looks a little like Sally."

"Is that significant?" Marge asked.

"No, not really," Decker said. "Just a point of observation. As far as Patty goes, maybe she does know who Sally is, maybe she doesn't. I had a hard time reading her, because she was coming on to me so strongly."

"Is she listed in the book?" Hollander said.

Decker said, "I talked to some more neighbors. No one knows Baby Sally by name."

Marge shrugged. Decker broke the seal on the manila envelope. He pulled out several sheets of paper and began to scan them.

"What did you order?" Marge asked.

"Lab report from the scene of my friend's crime."

"Still delusional," Marge said.

"A little delusion never hurt anyone." He read on. "They didn't lift any prints off the shiv. It was cleaned."

"Your friend wiped it," Marge said.

"Why would he wipe the shiv?" Decker said. "Supposedly it was his shiv, not hers. Of course it would have his prints on it. Seems to me he'd just stick it back in its sheath and leave."

"Decker," Marge said. "Watch TV. Criminals clean their weapons."

Decker said, "Let's reenact this. My friend rapes and cuts this girl. He wipes the shiv and puts it on the table. Now, presumably, he's getting ready to go and intends to take the shiv with him."

"Okay," Marge said.

"Now if you were cut like she was, you'd scream, right? You couldn't help yourself."

"I would think so."

"So say she screamed when he sliced her. Are you going to wipe your shiv calmly and lay it on the table, or are you going to get the hell out of there, figuring her screaming may have alerted someone?"

"He was cocky. Or he was a psycho who enjoyed watching her suffer."

"I can't buy that," Decker said. "Margie, he's seen it all—arms and legs and shit blasted all over the place, moaning lumps that used to be people. Some guys got off on torturing anything with slanted eyes. Blood lust or they just went nuts. Not Abel . . . not Abel."

Decker covered his mouth, felt himself breathing through his hands.

"You all right?" Marge said.

"Yeah," Decker said quietly. He wiped his forehead with his jacket sleeve. "Logic tells me that a true rape-o would leave as soon as he was done and worry about cleaning the knife another time. And consider this. His prints were found elsewhere—all over the apartment, as a matter of fact. But *not* on the weapon."

Marge said, "Maybe he intended to wipe the apartment clean, but she stopped him by clobbering him with the lamp."

"Yeah, that's another thing. The gal's dripping blood and has a collapsed lung, but she has enough strength to hit him with a lamp. And what's he doing while she's crawling on the floor and retrieving a lamp?"

"In the john?"

"She didn't bong him as he exited the john. If I were him, I would have noticed her and stopped her."

"He was too busy cleaning the shiv to notice."

"Which brings us back to the first point, do you calmly clean your weapon after all this commotion took place?"

"Maybe he had her terrified."

"Not too terrified. She bopped him with a lamp." Decker thought a moment. "I wonder who called the incident in?"

"The PR would be on the tape. Look up the incident number and give Hollywood a call."

Decker read further. He said, "There are gross inconsistencies here—the clean shiv, the statement of the whore, the time frame. . . . Hey, we've got a bloody footprint lifted from the kitchen floor that didn't match the shoe Abel was wearing. It was a size-nine left-foot, rubber-sole number."

"Maybe he changed shoes."

"Marge . . ."

"It's possible."

"Abel doesn't have a left foot," Decker said. "And he

rarely wears a shoe on his prosthesis. Someone else was in the room."

She didn't answer.

Decker said, "Sixty-forty a *good* lawyer could get him off right now, without any further investigation."

"Is that what you want?" Marge asked.

"No. What I want is to find the mother who did this and clear Abel's name altogether. But that may not be possible." Decker checked his watch, then locked the file in his desk. "I'll go over it later. Gotta go to court now."

His phone rang.

"Sergeant Decker? It's Ms. Rawlings."

"Hello, Ms. Rawlings," Decker said. "How's my baby Sally?"

"Fine, Sergeant. I just want to tell you that I'm taking her to the doctor's this afternoon. Would you like to come pick up the report around four o'clock?"

"Unfortunately, I'll be at the airport," Decker said. "How about if I come pick it up first thing tomorrow morning?"

"That would be fine, Sergeant."

"Thanks for phoning, Ms. Rawlings," Decker said. "Take good care of my baby girl."

Rina slipped her arms under Peter's jacket and hugged him tightly. She couldn't remember the last time she'd felt so happy, so *relieved*. Strong arms, something to *lean* on. She could feel her muscles loosen, her shoulders and jaw go wonderfully slack. Peter bent down and kissed her gently on the lips. She knew they had to move, that they were blocking the path of people deplaning, but she couldn't bring herself to break the embrace. Peter finally did it for her.

He looked at her at arms' length. Metallic blue eyes, creamy, smooth skin, pronounced cheekbones highlighted by a windswept stroke of blush. Her hair was long and loose—a beautiful ebony wave sheathing her back. She wore a navy shirtdress gathered at the waist, bisected by a white belt.

"You look gorgeous," Decker said.

"You do, too."

Decker laughed. "That's not true, but it's nice of you to say it." He picked up her carry-on and her wardrobe. "Did you bring a suitcase?"

Rina shook her head.

"Then let's get out of here."

The freeway was jammed rush-hour traffic in the afternoon heat. The unmarked's air conditioner tried desperately to cool off the sticky upholstery, but the temperature gauge's needle was grazing the red zone. Horns blasted, the sun reflected blindingly off chrome fenders, side mirrors, and rear windows. Decker shut off the air conditioner and cranked open the window.

"Car's going to overheat, honey," he explained.

Rina nodded, rolled down her window. A gust of exhaust fumes from a bus assaulted her nostrils.

"Welcome back," Decker said with a smile.

"This would be welcome weather in New York. I left one-hundred-degree heat and ninety-percent humidity. At least it's dry out here."

Decker took her hand. "Your hair's uncovered."

"You noticed."

"Is that a statement?"

"Sort of."

Decker took his suit jacket off, inched the car forward. "You want to talk about it?"

"First tell me how you've been," Rina said.

"Nothing changes around here. God, I've missed you."

"I've missed you, too." She took a tissue out of her purse and dabbed his forehead. "It's so good to see you, Peter. Sometimes I wonder why I left."

"I've been wondering about that, too."

"I think I wanted you to find God . . . or my concept of God . . . I don't know. How are you and God doing?"

"I can't speak for the Big Man, but I'm doing okay."

"How's Rav Schulman and the yeshiva?"

"Rav Schulman's fine."

"Did you spend Shabbos with him last week?"

"No, I changed my mind," Decker said. "I have a hard time staying in someone else's house. I'm better off spending Shabbos at home, davening by myself. I'm just not a group person, Rina."

She nodded. "How's Cindy's vacation coming?"

Decker grinned. "She's having a wonderful time. Jan's having problems with it. I think she's going to have a hard time letting go, and is going to dump on anyone who'll let her. I pity Allen."

"Is she giving *you* a hard time?"

"Nah. Not too bad considering that in four months my child-support payments will stop and Jan'll lose her last little leash on my life. Now, when my daughter needs me for money, I can send it to her directly."

"Is that an improvement?"

"I'm going to find out." He kissed her hand. "You're stalling."

"Oh, nothing's wrong with me, Peter," Rina said. "It seemed like a big deal over there. Now, it seems . . . silly. I just had to get out of New York."

"Are you planning on going back there?"

"That all depends."

"On what?"

"On if I have a home here." She faced him. "Do I?"

"As far as I'm concerned, you do."

"Then I guess I'm moving back."

Decker grinned.

"Great," he said.

*   *   *

Rina stepped out of the car and inhaled deeply. "Soil!" she said. "Land. Look at your citrus grove! The trees grow out of the ground instead of pots. It's so beautiful."

"Never thought of it quite like that," Decker said.

"Everything looks so green," Rina said.

"Actually, everything has been fried by the heat," Decker said. "Come on inside, I'll get you something to drink. I've even stocked my refrigerator for you."

"Peter, take me for a ride."

"We just got out of the car."

She threw her arms around his neck. "On horseback."

"Horseback? You?"

"Yes, me. You've always wanted to take me riding. Now, I'm giving you a chance."

"Right now?"

"Yes. Right now."

"You're not too tired?" he asked.

She shook her head no.

"It must be ninety-five degrees out here," Decker said.

"It'll cool off soon."

"I'm thirsty," Decker said. "Can I get a beer first?"

"Okay."

"Thank you."

"You're welcome."

Rina brought his mouth onto hers. She felt his hot breath, smelled his sweat, rubbed her fingers into his damp hair. He pulled her closer, undid the top button of her dress, and slipped his hand down the front. Her skin was warm and moist.

"Sure you want to go riding now?" he said.

She didn't answer, kissed him again. Sweet, long kisses.

"It stays light out for a long time," Decker said. He unsnapped the next button, she unknotted his tie. She kissed him again.

"Why don't we go inside?" Decker suggested.

Rina didn't move. She stroked his chin, traced his jawline with her fingertip.

"It's cool inside," Decker said.

Rina laced her arms around his waist.

"You know, I'm trying to be subtle here," Decker said.

"I can see that," Rina said. "You're doing a fine job."

"Yeah, but it isn't working," Decker said. "Well, since
Mr. Sensitivity ain't making any hay, I'm reverting back to
caveman style." He picked her up, unlocked the kitchen
door, and headed for the bedroom.

The early evening temperature settled in the mid-80's, the
sky was polished silver lined with rust and lavender. The
sun was a fiery disk of orange, sinking quickly behind
mammary swells of mountain. Decker pulled a brown stallion named Bear to the Left and followed the foothills,
trampling through gray-green shrubbery, hay-colored grass
and scrub brush. Wild flowers carpeted the rolling land—
orange California poppies, white and blue alyssum, tiny
white spring daisies.

Decker knew the trail by heart, but had taken a flashlight
for Rina's benefit. She sat, nestled in his arms, her dress
flowing down the sides of the saddle, eyes half-shut, lips
parted. She'd been more wonderful than he remembered—
soft and sensual—but distant, troubled. Decker knew that
she'd never let go completely until after they were married.
Rina could never shake her religious belief that sex outside
of marriage was wrong. Still, she had come to him will-
ingly. . . .

They rode for a half hour without speaking, rode until the
crickets began their foot-rubbing, and low-pitched hoots
from woodland animals echoed in the air. A sliver of
bleached-white moon peeked over the hilltop.

"This is beautiful," Rina said.

"I should take more time off," Decker said. "You're good

for me. You slow me down. If you weren't here, I'd be working."

"I can't believe I was battling the subway yesterday," Rina said.

"Are you ever going to tell me what's bothering you?" Decker asked.

"Don't spoil the moment."

"Stop stalling," Decker said.

Rina sighed. "It's my brother-in-law."

"Which one?"

"Pessy. Esther's husband. The one who owns the fur factory."

"The one you do the books for," Decker said.

"Yes."

"He came on to you," Decker said.

Rina sat up in the saddle. "How'd you know?"

"And you're shocked. Especially because he's *frum*."

She slumped back against him. "Obviously, you're not surprised."

"What'd he do to you?"

"Oh God . . ."

"What'd he do?"

"He backed me up into a corner a couple of weeks ago."

"And . . ."

"He was inappropriate," Rina groaned.

"How? Details."

"Stop acting like a detective."

Decker laughed. "Did he kiss you?"

"Yes."

"What'd you do?"

"I was so shocked, I didn't do anything."

"Nice move, Lazarus. Did he feel you up?"

"Peter, could you cool the blow-by-blow?"

Decker grew serious. "Did he get rough with you?"

"No," Rina said. "No, he didn't. As soon as I recovered

from my shock, I got out of there, and he didn't try to stop me. Oh, Peter, how could he have *done* that? Betrayed his wife as well as me. What gets into people like him?"

"He's horny with low impulse control."

"He wears a *gartel* for God's sake!"

"What's a *gartel*?"

"It's a sash that Hasidim wear to separate the clean from the unclean parts of their body. This is the man who always leads *Kol Nidre* on Yom Kippur, can you believe such hypocrisy?"

"Obviously, he has a lot to repent for," Decker said. "Is he still harassing you sexually?"

Rina sighed. "Well, he hasn't backed me into any more corners, but he's done other things."

"Like what?"

"Peter, he frequents massage parlors."

"How do you know that?"

"He gives me the receipts for the books and tells me to take them off as business expenses."

Decker burst into laughter.

Rina said, "What's so funny?"

"Forgive me, but only a Jew would be so brazen," Decker said.

"That is such an *anti-Semitic* thing to say!" Rina exclaimed. "Whose side are you on?"

Decker said, "No *goy* on earth would have the hutzpah to try something like that."

"*Ch*utzpah," Rina said, correcting his pronunciation. "*Ch, ch*. The sound is guttural. At least say the word right. And I don't believe that *goyim* are any less *chutzpahdic* than Jews."

"Maybe we Gentiles just don't think as creatively."

"We?" Rina said. "You're Jewish, remember?"

Decker hugged her. "Yes, I remember."

Rina paused, then said, "Are you happy being Jewish, Peter?"

"Very happy."

"Really?"

"Really," Decker said. "I wouldn't tell you yes if the answer was no, honey."

She sighed. "I wonder sometimes how we must appear to the outside world. All those guys accused of insider trading."

"White-collar criminals. At least they don't kill anyone."

"It's a *chillul Hashem*—disgraces God. I read about these rip-off schemes, embezzlement. I cringe whenever I see a Jewish name associated with it. Imagine how the blacks feel when they watch TV and see all these gang members being arrested."

"You're sensitive. Not all people take it to heart."

"And now my own brother-in-law."

Decker said, "So old Pessy likes a back rub."

"Old Pessy gets more than a back rub. . . . Peter, he leaves these pictures in the ledgers for me, pictures of his naked *kurvas* in obscene poses. They're all black. He loves black women. I guess he figures they're not Jewish. . . . I don't know." Rina covered her face. "I see him watching me, waiting for me to discover the pictures, then he laughs when I find them. He thinks it's just hysterical when I blush."

"The man is definitely an asshole."

"I don't know what to do. Sixty percent of the hookers in New York have AIDS or AIDS-related complex. I want to tell my sister-in-law, but I know what it will do to the family."

"Are you sure he sleeps with the whores? He may only take pictures of them."

Rina said, "I'm not positive he sleeps with them. I just assumed he did."

"Some men take pictures because they can't perform. Pessy may be one of those."

"The man is a pig—a complete and utter pig. And a pervert as well. Why is he torturing me? I tell you why! Because I'm safe! A perfect victim! He knows I won't tell his wife, because of what it would do to her. The pig! He wouldn't try stunts like these if you were around. But I'm alone, so what can poor little Rina do? And what *should* I do about my sister-in-law? She won't believe me. *I* wouldn't have believed me. Pessy appears so decent, so religious. How can I tell Esther what a swine her husband is? I love Esther. She was always good to *me*. I feel so *bad* for her."

"You want to know what I think?"

"I'm asking you, aren't I?"

"You're not going to like the answer."

"What?"

"Let it ride."

"What! I can't do that. He'll give her AIDS."

"Only if he's sleeping with the hookers."

"So I should wait?"

"Let it rest, honey. Otherwise, you're just going to be the villain, and who the hell needs that?"

"Maybe I can send her the picture and write an anonymous note."

"Rina, what's your sister-in-law like?"

"Esther's not a horse, if that's what you mean."

"No, I don't mean that," Decker said. "I mean is she able to get along without a husband? What does she have, four kids?"

"Five."

"Five kids. And she's how old?"

"Forty-four."

"A forty-four-year-old ultra-Orthodox woman with five kids. Where's she going to go if she divorces Pessy? Where's she going to live? Back home with her parents?"

Rina didn't answer.

"Does she have any skill to earn a living?"

"There's alimony."

"I'll bet you old Pess would fight her tooth and nail. Hell, he might even hold out on giving her a religious divorce unless she gives up everything. It's been known to happen, and this guy is scum to begin with."

"So I should just let the creep get away with it?"

"You quit your job, right?" Decker said.

"Yes, but—"

"You're moving back here."

"But—"

"*If* he pesters you when you return, let me know, and I'll take care of him."

"What'll you do?"

"Beat the stuffing out of him."

Rina laughed.

"I'm serious."

"He's five-nine, three hundred, Peter. Punches would just graze the fat."

Decker held back laughter. "You were felt up by a fat man?"

"He French-kissed me."

"That's disgusting."

"I washed my mouth out," Rina said. "Three times! I can't believe I let him do that. I feel like such a jerk. I should have slugged him, but I didn't. Why did I allow him to do that?"

"Because he took you by surprise. It was like date rape. You didn't do anything wrong. Rina, if it were anyone else other than family, I'd tell you to slap a sexual harassment and sexual misconduct on him. But your sister-in-law is the aunt of your children, her parents are the boys' grandparents. *If* he keeps leaving you pictures when you get home, tell him you're going to sic NYPD Vice on him. If he's a jerk and keeps doing it, we'll make good on our threat. I can get some names, a couple guys down to his office and scare him. If he backs away and stops pestering you, drop the whole thing. I know you want to help your sister-in-law, but I'm afraid by telling her, you'll be doing her more harm than good . . . but, it's your decision."

"Oh great. Thanks a lot."

They rode in silence. Decker held Rina tightly, thinking how logical her odd behavior seemed now. All of it—the uncovering of her hair, her eagerness to sleep with him—fit together. She'd become temporarily disillusioned with religion—or at least with religious people. Pessy had sexually harassed her, but his pestering had hurt her instead of making her angry.

"Forget about him," Decker said.

"Easier said than done."

Decker said, "I don't know how this is going to come out, but I'm going to say it anyway. Rina, assholes come in every shape and form. Don't throw the baby out with the bathwater."

"What do you mean?"

"Well, don't be upset with Judaism, because there are some religious Jews who are pigs."

"I know that," Rina said. "I'm not *that* naive."

"Yeah, but it's different when it's your relative."

"How can he do those things and daven in the morning, Peter? Yitzchak, *alav hasholom*, always looked up to Pessy because he was so learned."

"Your husband only knew that side of him. Unfortunately, you know another. God wouldn't have made laws against adultery if Jews didn't cheat. Don't let this slimeball ruin our time together."

Rina sighed. "I guess you're right."

"How are you holding up?"

"I'm a little tired."

"So am I. We'll head back." Decker pulled the reins, and the stallion reversed directions.

Rina looked up at the stars. Thousands of them, so clear and white, like grains of salt spilled upon black velvet. She said, "I wish we could sleep out here."

"You want to sleep outdoors, let's go back home and I'll set up some sleeping bags. This isn't really camp ground. Besides, I don't want you to go home with a bad case of poison oak . . . in an awkward place of your body."

Rina punched Decker in the shoulder.

The phone woke them at nine-thirty in the morning.

"Morning, Pete," Marge said.

"What's up?" Decker said.

"Who is it?" Rina asked sleepily.

"Marge," Decker whispered. He came back on the phone. "What's going on?"

"Sorry to disturb you."

Decker rubbed his eyes. "No sweat. What is it?"

"Are you listening?" Marge said. "As in fully awake?"

"Uh-oh."

"Prelim blood forensics on the kid's PJs. At first, it's just all ordinary O-positive blood. Same kind as the kid's. But the electophoresis of the blood enzymes shows we have an amalgam of blood typings. Almost as if someone mopped up the crime scene with the kid's PJ's."

"Oh boy. How many different groups are we talking about?"

"At least two, maybe even three or four. Forensics still has more tests to run."

Looking at Rina, Decker muttered the obscenity instead of saying it out loud. At least two bodies baking in the heat somewhere. The kid's parents?

Marge filled in the silences. "Not a good thing, partner. Also, there were tissue fibers mixed with the blood."

Decker turned away from Rina and whispered into the receiver, "Skin? Hair? What kind of tissue?"

"Not that kind of tissue," Marge said. "White facial tissue. Like in Kleenex. Like in someone tried to wipe the mess off the kid."

Decker said, "Clothes show up any prints or latents?"

"Dead end there, Pete. Nothing retrievable off of the clothes."

"Damn."

"Yeah, well . . . now for the good news," Marge said. "You can use a break, right?"

"Right."

"Sophi Rawlings called about the doctor report. I took the liberty of picking it up for you."

"Thanks."

"Ain't we a team," Marge said. "Do you remember telling Sophi to ask about a rash on Baby Sally's arm?"

"Sure."

"Well, she did. You know what the pediatrician said it was?"

"What?"

"Bee stings."

"Bee stings?"

"Bee stings. He thought it was unusual that such a small child would have so many bee stings on her forearms."

"How many were there?"

"About a half dozen on each arm."

"Anywhere else?"

"Nope."

"Kid must have stuck her hand in a hive."

"I just got off the phone with the doc—his name is Andrew Trapper. He said something else was unusual. The stings caused little, tiny bumps, but not much inflammation. That only happens, he said, when the child has been repeatedly exposed to stings."

Decker said, "Are there any bee farms around the Manfred area?"

"I called up the agricultural commission. They gave me the name of the bee commissioner. I'm waiting for him to call me back."

"Good thinking. I'll meet you at the station in about a half hour."

"You're coming in today?"

"Yeah, looks like I have to." Decker shook his head, knowing he wouldn't rest until he found those bodies. "Bees, huh? Well, at least it's a new lead. You know, bees would make sense. Remember how she reacted when you called her honey?"

"Yeah," Marge thought back. "Yeah, she sure said that word clearly."

Decker said, "If you have any time, see if you can pick up a bottle of Benadryl. It really cuts down the swelling if we happen to piss off the bees."

"Buzz, buzz," Marge said. "We get all the fun assignments. Coming in won't cause any problem for you with Rina?"

"I hope not."

After Decker hung up, Rina said, "You hope not what?"

"I hope you won't mind if I have to go to work. I've got this two-year-old kid, Rina, and I'm trying to locate her parents—"

"It's okay, Peter. I heard you whispering. It must be serious."

"I'm sorry."

"It's fine. I have to see my parents anyway. You didn't want to come with me to visit them, did you?"

"Definitely not."

"So it's no problem."

Decker crawled out of bed. "Sure?"

"Positive."

He smiled. "You're a doll."

"Peter?"

"What?"

"Uh, I don't have a car."

Decker froze.

Rina asked, "Could I borrow the Porsche?"

"The Porsche?"

"Yes. The Porsche. The shiny red car in your garage. Is it running?"

The shiny red car that had taken him five years to put together. Hundreds of hours, scouring through junk lots, garages, and ads in papers to find the perfect parts. Decker said, "Uh, the Jeep's running fine."

"I'm nervous about driving a four-wheeler on the freeway. It's so open and tips over too easily."

"It has a roll bar."

Rina pushed hair out of her eyes. "Well, all right. If you think it's safe. . . ."

"No," Decker said. "No, forget about the Jeep. . . . Sure, take the Porsche. I'll get you the keys."

"I'll be careful with it."

"It has a very delicate clutch."

"Okay."

"And be sure not to downshift too early. Use the tachometer."

"Okay."

"And don't yank it into gear—"

"Forget it, Peter, I'll take the Jeep."

"No, no, no. I insist."

"You're sure?"

"Yes, I'm sure."

"You know, if you run me past the cheapy rent-a-car lot, I could probably get something drivable. You remember my old Volvo. I'd feel at home in an old clunker."

"I won't hear of it, Rina. Take the Porsche. You want me to help you take the top off? Cruise in the open wind?"

"If it's all the same to you, I feel a lot safer in a locked car with the air-conditioning on. When we ride in it together, we'll take the top off. Okay?"

"Deal." Decker paused, then added, "I'll just back it out of the garage for you."

Rina broke into laughter.

9

MacPherson looked at Decker and said, "I hate fanatics."

Decker didn't respond. He poured himself a cup of coffee from the squad room's urn.

"Though I suppose it's not entirely your fault," MacPherson continued. "You're heavily under the influence of pussy."

Decker sipped coffee and said, "Some itty-bitty thought is germinating in that feeble brain of yours, Paulie. Want to tell me what it is?" He added, "Are you able to articulate what it is?"

Hollander said, "I think he's referring to your beany cap, Rabbi."

Decker's hand went to the crown of his head. He'd forgotten to take off his yarmulke. This morning, he'd recited all of *Shacharit* before he went to work. He'd even put on phylacteries for the first time in a month. Rina had seemed pleased, but Decker had wondered if he hadn't acted hypocritically. On the drive over to the station, he'd decided that there was nothing wrong with keeping the peace in the home front—*shalom bayis*. Besides, after the incidents with her brother-in-law, Rina needed a little restoration of faith. Decker pocketed the skullcap.

"Converts are the worst fanatics," MacPherson said. "Like reformed drunks, they have something to prove to themselves, so they have to prove it to everyone else."

"Stow it, Paul," Decker said. "I'm not in the mood for your dimestore philosophy."

"Marge'll be back in a minute," Hollander said.

"Do you know if the bee commissioner called her back?"

"I think she spoke to someone about bees," Hollander said.

"Pete," MacPherson said, with a sigh, "one day, when the nookie's worn off, you'll rediscover your balls, look in the mirror, and come to *grips* with yourself. No matter who you fuck, what you do, what you eat, or what you wear, you can't get away from the fact that you're a six-foot-four, two-hundred-thirty-pound, gun-toting, mean-assed cop. You're about as Jewish as ham and cheese. You're a *shiska*, Decker. Admit it and be at peace with your soul."

Decker said, "You mean *shiksa*, Paul, and that's used for Gentile *girls*. The word you're looking for is *shaigetz*. Or just plain *goy* will do."

Technically, he wasn't either, but MacPherson didn't know that. None of them did.

"You know what I'm talking about," MacPherson said.

"Paulie, if you weren't so full of shit, you'd be white," Decker said.

"Touché," Hollander said.

MacPherson growled.

Decker poured himself another cup of coffee and fingered his yarmulke through his shirt pocket, contemplating for the hundredth time how he would have turned out had his Jewish biological mother kept and raised him. He would have been the same physically—chromosomes didn't change—but all his life experiences, everything that made him the man he was today, would have been different.

Yet, forty-one years later, he was returning to his ancestral bloodline. Part of the reason was Rina; she wouldn't marry him unless he was Jewish *and* religious. But there was more than just her love that kept it going. Something inside had pulled him to Judaism, kept him tethered even though it meant long hours of biblical studies and added restrictions to his already harried life. Ask him what it was and Decker couldn't define it. Paul ribbed him about the transformation—all the guys at the station had at one time or another. They were baffled. How *did* you dismiss forty-one years of being a Gentile? Decker's answer: You didn't. He still considered himself the child of the parents who'd raised him, the offspring of a solid mother and a strong father who'd reared him Baptist.

He'd finished his second cup of coffee when Marge and a fifty-year-old pouchy-cheeked man walked into the squad room.

"Sergeant Decker," she said, "this is Charlie Benko—the bounty hunter who thought that Baby Sally might have been the kid he was looking for. He's going to look over our mug books and see if he can't recognize the scumbag kidnapper husband amongst our finest."

"Good idea," Decker said. "How's the mother doing?"

Charlie splayed the fingers of his right hand and rocked his wrist back and forth. "She'd be doing better with a better husband."

"Number two is a creep also?" Marge asked. "Some women just seem to pick all the winners."

"Ah, number two doesn't beat her or drink or anything like that," Benko said. "He just doesn't give her much of a shoulder to cry on. What the hell, he figures, it ain't his kid. But at least he should fake it better. Know what he told Dotty? Forget about this one, we'll make our own."

"Sensitive man," Marge said.

"Yeah, like the kid was a baseball lost in the bushes, lose one, buy another. Well, Charlie Benko finds all the fucking baseballs, even if he has to get down on his hands and knees and crawl through the bush himself, know what I'm talkin' about? That's why I'm givin' Dotty a hundred and ten percent. Hell, I'm not even charging her for half my time. In the end, it pays off. I can sleep at night, and if I need a future referral, Dotty's gonna tell them that Charlie Benko ran the extra mile for her."

"Here are the mug books," Marge said. "You can sit at my desk."

"I'll find that sunnabitch one way or t'other," Benko said. "Little Heather ain't gonna wind up another lost baseball, I'll tell you that."

"You want some coffee, Charlie?" Marge asked.

"Sure. Milk and three teaspoons of sugar. I used to drink it black, but life's too short. The big C took my wife three years ago. Since then, I say what the hell." He paused for a moment, shook his head, then opened the first mug book.

"You going to be around, Detective Hollander?" Marge asked.

"Why?"

"If Charlie finds the scumbag, he'll need someone to punch him into the computer."

"No problem," Hollander said. "I've got to take a quick run down to the nuthouse, but I should be back in an hour."

"Nuthouse?" Benko said. "You work with them psychos, Detective? Boy, I've met more than a few psychos in my time."

MacPherson said, "The nuthouse is San Fernando Valley Juvenile Hall. The building's located on Filbert Street."

"Filbert—ah, nuthouse, I get it," Benko said. "I like that."

"While Detective Hollander is absent, I'll be happy to help out Mr. Benko in any manner deemed necessary," MacPherson said.

"A rare burst of altruism from Detective MacPherson," Decker said.

"Yeah, thanks a lot, pal," Benko said. He turned another page.

Marge pulled out her notes and said to Decker, "This is

what I've got. Mitch Appleman, the bee commissioner, gave me some addresses of apiaries in the neighborhood. The big commercial ones are off the Antelope Valley Freeway near Canyon Country. A little far for Baby Sally to walk."

"About five miles too far."

"But," Marge said, "there's an area, a small valley called Sagebrush Canyon, right outside our jurisdiction. It runs between the mountains, starts right above Hansen Dam and Lakeview Terrace, and curves above the new Manfred development. Lots of pastures—alfalfa and clover fields. Appleman says there are a couple of independent bee farmers out there. I think that's our best bet."

"Who has jurisdiction?"

"It's an independent city in L.A. County. I wasn't able to find out if they have any local law. Maybe they import in time of need."

Decker said, "Let's take a look."

Marge steered the unmarked onto Foothill Boulevard, the division's main thoroughfare that hugged the base of the San Gabriel Mountains. The sun had burned away the smog and a dry wind was whipping through the air. The two-lane street had no sidewalks and was lined with an odd mixture of the industrial and agricultural—ramshackle ranches stuffed between two blocks' worth of building-supply wholesalers, brickyards next to specimen-tree nurseries. Marge drove past rows of potted trees laid out like tombstones, past a large stretch of dried-up spillway floored with smooth, chalky-gray boulders. A shirtless cowboy was riding a horse along the arid bed, one hand on the reins, the other gripping a leash attached to a black Labrador retriever.

The road crossed over the spillway, and a moment later, they whizzed past parkland. A half-dozen teenage boys were playing basketball on an asphalt court radiating heat waves. Off to the side was a shaded playground. Mothers, wearing short-sleeved shirts and pleated shorts, were pushing toddlers in swings, fanning themselves with the palms of their hands. Opposite the park were a K mart and a sheet-metal plant.

A TV jingle played through Marge's brain, an ad for a supermarket that claimed to cater to Middle America. She sang, " 'Don't have a big, foreign car . . . ' "

Decker looked at her.

" 'Don't have a mansion on a hill . . . ' "

"You could have fooled me," Decker said.

" 'But I'm an Amerricann . . . ' "

Decker said, "Know what I see when I look at those ersatz good old folks commercials? Card-carrying members of SAG, making union scale, hoping that the commercial's aired a hundred times a day so they can have a big, foreign car or a mansion on a hill."

"But look at this natural beauty, Pete," Marge said, pointing to a gravel yard. "Now would you really give this all up if . . . say, you hit the big spin in the lottery?"

Decker let go with a full laugh.

Marge said, "And what would *you* do with all of that free time on your hands?"

"Oh, I don't know. Lots of things come to mind," Decker said. He thought, Most of them have to do with Rina and a bedroom.

As if she read his thoughts, Marge asked, "How's Rina?"

"Hanging in there," Decker said. "She's moving back."

"No shit," Marge said. "What prompted that?"

"My prowess."

Marge smiled. "I'm happy for you, Pete."

"Thanks," Decker said. "I'm really happy myself."

"You two going to do it?"

"If she doesn't change her mind again, yes."

"You're not nervous about it?"

"No," Decker said. "Not at all."

"I'm petrified of marriage," Marge said. "What if it's the wrong one? Charlie Benko's right about one thing. People aren't baseballs. I'm not the type to just throw the bum out. Even if I realized I made a very baaaad mistake."

Decker said, "You know, Margie, the job dampens us emotionally. Has to be that way—otherwise, we'd be crying in our beer all the time. So the few times I react with my heart instead of my head, I don't really think about the consequences. I just enjoy the pleasure of feeling."

Marge furrowed her brow. "Know what I'm going to do? I'm gonna *think* like that."

Decker smiled, then stared out the window.

Turning left, Marge hooked the Plymouth behind a velvet green golf course and followed a small, winding road chiseled into the mountains. The foothills were mounds of sand-colored rock dotted with withered shrubbery, and tall grass parched straw yellow in the dazzling sunlight. Specks of color sprouted through the gravel—tiny blooms of white-purple, lemon-hued dandelions, orange poppies, giraffe-necked sunflowers. The unmarked's transmission bucked as the car ascended and as they reached the top of the first hill, a huge crater of stone and steel came into view. The concrete bowl had once been filled with millions of gallons of water. But deemed old and unsafe, Hansen Dam had been drained in the early eighties. Marge looked at the empty shell and sighed.

"Every time I see it, I can't help but think of the millions of dollars and work hours . . . just gone."

"It's rumored that Manfred wants the land," Decker said.

"You're kidding. I didn't hear that one."

"I think Mike told me," Decker said. "He's up on that kind of thing. Be nice if they filled it again. We could take our boats out here instead of going to Lake Castaic."

"Knowing Manfred, they'll probably fill it with toxic waste," Marge said. "There's going to be a big meeting at the municipal courthouse about their newest plans for a seven-story office building. On the twenty-seventh of this month. The ranchers are going to try to put a freeze on buildings over two stories. Interested?"

"Not really."

"What are you going to do? Wait until they invade your neighborhood?" Marge shook her head. "They're building right behind my house, beautiful piece of land that used to be cornfields. You know, I could accept the fact that maybe L.A. needs more houses than corn, but they haven't even sold out their last two developments. They're turning this place into tract-o-land."

Decker said, "Watch the curves, Marge."

"I see them." She mopped her sweaty forehead with the back of her hand. "All those tracts don't bother you?"

"I'd prefer to leave things status quo," Decker said. "But I'm not losing any sleep over it."

"Until they build behind you."

"No," Decker said, "I wouldn't like that."

Marge braked suddenly as she entered the next curve. Directly below lay the verdant floor of Sagebrush Canyon. She shifted the automatic into low gear as they descended into the valley. Thick red-adobe rocks and boulders framed long stretches of pink-white clover, lavender alfalfa, and the silvery-gray leaves of purple sagebrush. The fields had been recently irrigated, the water droplets still clinging to the flora, sparkling like shattered glass in the sunlight. The air seemed a bit cooler, but the winds were still warm and strong. The sky was iridescent blue.

Decker said, "Right around the corner and I never knew this place existed."

"Neither did I."

The Plymouth reached the mouth of the canyon and turned left. The first landmark they saw was a roofless barn, fronted with haystacks in the middle of a field of jersey cows. Five minutes later, they passed a one-story white-washed house. Tacked atop the doorway was a hand-

painted red-lettered sign, reading SAGEBRUSH CANYON GEN-
ERAL STORE. A half-mile farther was a stucco diner with an
EATS signpost carved in the shape of an arrow. Across the
road was an old-fashioned two-pump gas station, a phone
booth, and a wooden shack. The strong smell of uric acid
assaulted their nostrils.

"Something's cookin'," Decker said. "And it ain't moon-
shine."

Marge said, "Only one thing smells like that."

"Two things," Decker said. "You forgot about piss."

Marge laughed. "We got meth. Now where are the bikers?"

"Close," Decker said. "I guarantee you that."

The valley once again turned into glistening fields—cow
and sheep pastures. A mile later was a large wooden indoor-
outdoor structure shaded by tall eucalyptus and thick-
trunked olive trees. Souped-up Harleys, Honda GSMs, and
BMW choppers were chained to posts on a side gravel lot.
The front part of the building was an open patio set up with
tables and chairs. Dozens of tattooed, shirtless bikers
slumped lazily in their seats, shooting the breeze while they
smoked cigarettes and joints, and guzzled beer. Some were
completely naked from the waist up, others were shirtless
but had donned leather vests. Most had oversized bellies
and hair falling down their backs, the long strands tied away
from their foreheads with red bandannas. A few of the men
held skin-and-bone women on their laps, the girls looping
stringy arms around their fat men's necks.

"Our illustrious chemists," Decker said.

"Meth," Marge said. "Some things just go together—
love and marriages . . . horses and carriages . . . bikers and
uppers."

Decker said, "I know the song, but I missed that verse."

Marge said, "Just your old-fashioned cottage industry."

Decker said, "If this were a movie, you and I would

storm the place, crack open some heads, and demand some answers."

Marge said, "Well, that's the difference between Hollywood and reality. For one thing, Hollywood doesn't concern itself with the ACLU and search-and-seizure laws. Not to mention the fact that these beer-drinking gentlemen are packing."

"Don't tell me you're wary of a few motorcycle enthusiasts."

"I?" Marge replied. "Bite your tongue. But you know how these hick lawmen are. We go in and do their dirty work, they get all pissed off at us big-time dicks."

"True, true."

"So we'll let the bikers go this time."

"Just this once," Decker said.

"Of course," Marge said. "Next week, that shed's still standing, I'm going in and busting some chops."

Copses of eucalyptus lined the road, darkening the asphalt. The air-conditioning sucked in the scent of menthol. Riding another mile, the trees disappeared and they came upon open fields once more—acres and acres of purple alfalfa bloom filled with grazing livestock. In the middle of the area, a green signpost pointed to a dirt road. It read, TO L.A., ORANGE BLOSSOM DEVELOPMENTS.

"That's the official name of the Manfred tract," Decker said. "Someone wants to dump Sally, he takes a quick ride over the mountain and he's in civilization—somewhat."

"Well, it's better than leaving the kid at the biker bar. Did you catch its name?"

"Hell's Heaven," Decker said, turning the air-conditioning fan down a notch. "Cute."

They rode another mile. Marge nudged Decker in the ribs.

"Look up ahead," she said.

A burnt-wood sign read: HOWARD'S HONEY FARM—ROAD TO OFFICE ONE MILE DOWN. The turnoff was a loose gravel lane that wreaked havoc on the unmarked's tires, the office a greenpainted lean-to. Marge parked in front of the shack, and they both got out and stretched. The shed was surrounded by acres of sweet-smelling clover. In the distance was a two-story redwood farmhouse.

Decker knocked on the door to the office. When no one answered, he took out a glove, slipped it on his right hand, and turned the unlocked handle. Inside were a metal desk piled high with graph paper, a swivel chair, and a file cabinet. On the wall behind the desk were pinups—a blonde with her rear in the air and a brunette with the finger of her right hand in her mouth, the fingers on her left pulling up the lips of her vagina. Other wall decor included an out-of-date calendar from an auto-parts store, and a battery clock that said five after five. Decker checked his own watch. It was around eleven-thirty. A half-eaten pizza was falling out of a garbage can, flies covering the cheese like a topping of raisins. The air smelled rancid—garlicky and hot.

"Phhhew," Marge said.

Decker closed the door. "I have a bad feeling about this, Margie."

"If that pizza's any indication of what's to come, I don't like it either. Think we should check in with our khaki counterparts?"

"Not yet," Decker said. "Let's take a hike up to the farmhouse."

They started across the fields. Halfway to the house were a dozen rows of two-foot-long pine boxes resting six inches off the ground. A low-pitched hum filled the air. Marge and Decker exchanged watchful looks. They walked another ten feet, then froze.

A funnel-shaped black cloud exited one of the boxes. It came upon them so suddenly that they had no chance to go forward or retreat. The humming grew in intensity—a deep moan. Bees blanketed the sky, swirling like a tornado intent on uprooting them.

"What do we do?" Marge said, panicking.

"I'd say draw, but I think our weapons are useless," Decker said, talking out of the side of his mouth.

"Peter—"

"Just stand still," Decker said.

"I don't want to die this way," Marge said, as bees swarmed past her face.

"Calm," Decker said soothingly.

The buzzing became a maddening dirge. The space around them was thick with wings and cooler because of it—hundreds of tiny little fans moving the warm air upward. Decker kept his eyes open, saw gray shadows of fuzzy blips dart past him. Bugs in flight careening into him, falling in his coat pocket, touching his face and neck. He forced himself to breathe slowly, remembered reading about a contest in the papers—who could grow the biggest bee beard . . . contestants allowing thousands of bees to land on their faces and cheeks. Bees tickled the inside of Decker's nose. *Calm*, he repeated to himself. He felt as if he were drowning in the suckers.

After what seemed like hours, the funnel abruptly landed on a pine box three feet in front of them, covering the wood like a brown woolen tablecloth. A few strays buzzed around Decker. At last he felt safe shooing them away. Marge followed suit. She was shaking.

"You okay?" Decker said.

Marge nodded.

"I suggest we walk away from the boxes," Decker said.

"Slowly," Marge added. "What the hell was that?"

Decker said, "I don't know. I've never been around bees before."

A few minutes later, the boxes were nothing more than dots. But the acreage was filled with foraging bees—workers seeking pollen from the pink, white, and purple blooms.

"God, why couldn't MacPherson be assigned to this?" Marge said.

Decker didn't answer.

"Sometimes, Pete, I hate your stoicism."

Decker still didn't respond. Marge gave up. A minute later, a percussive pop broke through the air.

Decker halted his steps, brought his hands over his head. "Shotgun."

"Sweet Jesus, now what?" Marge said. "Police!" she shouted.

"Stay where you are!" commanded a voice. It came from behind them. Decker straightened up and turned around. A man wearing a wire-veil hat, thick gloves, and a leather apron was approaching them. He was tall with a sizable paunch, and held a long-barreled shotgun. Marge started to step forward.

"I said stay where you are!" the man said. "And Lord, I mean it!" He emphasized his point by shooting into the air again. Marge jumped.

"Police, sir," Marge said. Her voice was surprisingly strong.

The man seemed unimpressed.

"What the hell you doin' on my property?"

"No one was in the office," Decker said.

"Don't give you no right to come steamrolling over my fields. Scaring my bees."

"I'm sorry, sir," Decker said. "Truth is we just wanted to talk to the owner of this honey farm. He wasn't in the office. We figured we'd try the house."

"Don't bullshit me, slick," said the man. "Your plain-folk manner and southern drawl don't fool me none. You're one of them builders. My pappy told you we ain't interested."

"Mister," Decker said, "I'm going in my pocket and gonna pull out my badge. I'm a police detective, and I'm wearing a gun. I'm telling you what I'm doing, so don't let your finger get itchy on that trigger."

The man didn't answer. Decker moved deliberately, fishing into his pocket and finding the fold containing his badge and ID. He showed it to the man.

"Don't prove nothin'."

"Are you Mr. Howard?" Marge asked.

"One of 'em," Howard answered. He removed his veil hat, exposing a bald head and a leathery face colored nut brown. His eyes were close-set, his nose was fleshy and full of veins, his lips were cracked. "Who the hell are you?"

"A detective, also."

"Suppose you got a badge, too?"

Marge started to open her purse.

"Forget it," said Howard. "L.A. don't have enough crime that it's got to send two of its po-licemen to come up and bother us." Howard spit behind his shoulder. "Get off my pappy's land. This is swarming weather. Bees might decide they don't like you any better than I do."

Decker pulled out a picture of Baby Sally. "Know this little girl?"

Howard's face drained of its color. Marge started to say something, but Decker interrupted.

"*I* sure as heck don't know who she is. She's living in a foster home, mister. You know that's no place for kids. I don't know who her parents are, but I was kind of hoping they might live around here."

The men stared at each other for a minute or two. Howard's denuded head was coated with sweat. He stared upward, squinting in the sunlight, then put his veil hat back on. Decker licked salty sweat from his lips.

Howard said, "Whychu think she lives around here?"

"Because the poor little thing had bee stings on her arms—"

"City don't got no bees?" Howard asked.

"The doc we took her to thinks she has a whole lot more stings than a city girl should have."

Howard spit again. He said, "I got work to do."

"So do I," Decker answered.

Howard said, "And whachu mean by that, boy?"

"Just what I said," Decker said. "I mean to locate this kid's parents. Recognize her?"

Howard looked at his feet and kicked the ground absently. He said, "Go into the big house. The women are in the kitchen, jarring honey. Ask 'em 'bout the kid."

"Thank you, Mr. Howard," Decker said.

"Whenchu find her?" Howard asked.

"'Bout a day ago."

"Where?"

"Over the hill."

"In L.A.?"

"Yep."

"She okay?"

"Yep," said Decker.

Howard placed his hat back on his egg head. He said, "Tell Darlene to give you a piece of honey cake. Darlene's my wife. And tell her to get you a pitcher of *ice*-tea, too, boy. You're sweating like a chained bull."

Decker said, "It's hot out here."

"Specially in that suit," Howard said.

"You ain't kiddin'," Decker said.

"You ken take off your jacket," Howard said. "It don't impress me none."

"Then I think I will," Decker said. He removed his jacket.

Howard waved them away and headed in the direction of the pine boxes. A scented breeze perfumed the air. On top of the farmhouse, a Chinaman whirled furiously. A V-shaped formation of sparrows soared through the liquid sky.

"Let's go," Decker said.

"You shut me up," Marge said angrily.

"Yes, I did."

"He *knows* who she is," Marge said.

"Of course he knows who she is," Decker said. "And if he

wanted to tell us, he would have. Apparently, he finds it more acceptable for us to be informed by the womenfolk."

"I don't like to have my feet stepped on."

Decker slung his jacket over his shoulder and threw his free arm around Marge. "I'm sorry I shut you up, but I know these guys. They haven't heard of the women's movement."

"Where'd you learn how to drawl, Pete?"

"Gainesville has its share of southerners. I grew up with hundreds like our pal Mr. Howard. He's nothing more than a transplanted good ole boy. Lots of them in this area. Don't believe me, just step into the tack and grain shop off Foothill Boulevard and listen a while. You'd swear you were in rural America. We just don't come into contact with the farmers because they're usually good law-abidin' citizens. But just step on their toes, try pushing them around. You'll wind up with a butt full of buckshot."

Marge said, "Well, I'd certainly like to give Mr. Howard an enema with my thirty-eight."

Decker smiled, drew his arm away. "Don't let him get to you, Detective Dunn. These guys are a species unto themselves."

"Why wouldn't he tell us who the kid was?" Marge said.

"Because they're mules, Marge. They get ideas into their heads and nothing will budge them. My dad's that way. So is yours, from what you've told me. Ever say anything that changed his mind once it was set?"

Marge shook her head.

"Stubborn is their middle name," Decker said.

"Think Howard's hiding something?" Marge asked.

"He could be." Decker paused. "Or he's just a wary guy. Obviously, he hasn't had friendly exchanges with some developer—"

"Manfred?"

"Probably."

Marge said, "I wish he'd talk to us."

"That's the way these people work," Decker said. "They're stubborn and secretive. Howard's determined to keep his mouth shut, but he wants us to find Sally. So he sends us over to the women. And a little birdie's tweeting in my ear that we're going to discover important info over iced tea and honey cake."

❧10

Like a tackle, the woman blocked the front entrance of the farmhouse. Her body said, *Just try to get past the door, mister.* Thick arms were folded across a bosomy chest, feet stretched apart and planted solidly on the floor. Her face was round and flushed and held muddy blue eyes and an incongruously small button nose. Her hair was black streaked with silver and tied back into a braided knot. She wore a short-sleeved gingham dress, most of the green checkered print concealed by a white baker's apron. Cloyingly sweet air was pouring out through the threshold.

"Yes?" she said.

"I'm looking for Darlene Howard," Decker said.

"Yes," she repeated.

Decker said, "The mister told us we were welcome to some iced tea and honey cake."

"Who are you?"

"Police, ma'am," Decker said, showing his badge.

The woman studied the gold shield and ID card. "You're from the other side of the mountain."

"Yes, ma'am," Decker drawled.

"What are you doing here?"

"That's what I want to talk to you about," Decker said.

"And Byron sent you here?" the woman said.

"If Byron is Mr. Howard, he did, ma'am," Decker said.

The woman's eyes landed on Marge. "Who's she?"

Marge opened her purse to find her badge, but Decker gently placed his hand upon hers. "This is Detective Dunn."

"She like your partner?"

"Yes, ma'am," Decker said.

The stout woman stared at Marge.

"You married?" she asked.

"What?" Marge said.

"You married?" the woman repeated.

"To him?" Marge said, looking at Decker.

"To him, to anyone," the woman pressed.

Marge hesitated, then said, "No, ma'am."

The woman said. "An unmarried woman shouldn't be workin' with no man. Tempts the devil in him."

Decker said, "The city has lots of room for temptation, no doubt about that."

Marge turned around and rolled her eyes. What was the point of all this bullshit? Show the bitch the damn picture. But Pete acted as if he had all the time in the world.

"So what're you doin' working with her?" the woman asked.

"Detective Dunn's the best." Decker smiled at the middle-aged hausfrau and said, "C'mon. You know how it is with us men. If we didn't have you ladies to keep all our paperwork straight, we'd never get anything done."

Marge coughed. Decker's face remained impassive.

The woman smiled with thin, pale lips. "Ain't that the truth. Well, come on in. It's a hot one outside."

"You're Mrs. Howard?" Marge asked.

"Last time I checked, I was, Miss Detective." She stepped aside to let them in. "You can call me Darlene. Everybody calls me Darlene. That's my name."

"Thank you, Darlene," Decker said.

They followed her through a sunlit living room. The furniture was country pine, unstained, sanded as smooth as porcelain. By the color of the wood, the pieces looked to be at least fifty years old. Two six-foot sofas faced each other, both upholstered in a white-and-blue floral print. Doilies rested on the arms of the sofas, throw pillows stitched with petit point decorated the back. The fireplace had a wooden hearth; above it were elaborately embroidered samplers of fruits and vegetables.

Darlene's destination was the kitchen, which took up the back portion of the house. Twice the size of the living room, it was filled with the latest in modern cooking equipment—metal freezers, food processors, hanging copper pans, and a stainless-steel industrial oven and cooktop that ran the length of the entire rear wall. Atop the burners were steaming cauldrons. Even with all the windows open, the air was choked with the smell of honey. A reedy blonde was stirring a pot, her back to them. A radio was blasting out Randy Travis, who was wishing he was in 1982.

"Who was it, Darl?" the blonde asked loudly.

Darlene shouted, "Look and see for yourself."

The blonde whipped around. "My goodness, why didn't you tell me we have company?"

She was much younger than Darlene, with an oval, freckled face that was pink and moist from steam, and hazel eyes opened wide in surprise. She had on a long apron over jeans and a T-shirt. Her smile was crooked, but Marge liked it. She was the first friendly face Marge had seen down here.

"Well, sit on down," the blonde said, turning off the music. "I'm Annette."

"Please to meet you, ma'am," Decker said. "I'm Detective Decker, and this here is Detective Dunn."

Annette's face clouded.

"They're policemen," Darlene said.

"What's this all about?" Annette asked.

"Now, that ain't polite, Nettie," Darlene scolded. "Go get these people some *ice*-tea. Can't you see they're sweating?"

"Oh, yes," Annette said. She fiddled with her hair, which

was bunched into a net. "Of course. I'm sorry. Please sit." She motioned them to a round, cherrywood table at the entrance of the kitchen.

"Thank you, ma'am," Decker said.

"I'll get you some honey cake," Darlene said. Her fingers brushed against Decker's shoulder.

"Sure smells fine in here," Decker said.

"Bet you say that to all the people you visit," Darlene said.

Decker thought of his routine calls: women who'd been raped, often beaten as well, kids who'd been physically and sexually abused, underaged punks who, while flying high on Jim Jones or dust, had pumped Grandma full of lead.

"No, I don't say that to all the people I visit," he said, smoothing his mustache. "And that's no lie."

Darlene placed two slices of honey cake in front of them. Decker tasted a forkful of the mocha-colored wedge. He chewed slowly. Marge wondered how he could masticate for so long.

"Well?" Darlene asked.

"One problem with it, ma'am," Decker said.

"And what's that?" Darlene asked.

"The piece is too small."

"Oh, you," Darlene said, slapping his shoulder lightly. "I'll give you another piece. Just finish what you got first."

"Yes, ma'am," Decker said.

"And how do you like it?" Darlene asked Marge.

"Delicious," Marge said. It was the truth. The cake was almost too rich and moist to eat. Like drinking cream.

"Well, sit down and join us, ladies," Decker said. "Me and my partner don't like to eat alone."

"I suppose we could use a break," Darlene said. She wiped her forehead with a white cotton towel. "Though Lord knows, I'm tired of honey cake."

"We sell it," Annette said.

"I'm not surprised," Marge said. "It's terrific."

Darlene said, "We sell cakes, cupcakes, cookies, syrups, jellies . . . just about anything that you can make with honey."

"Who do you sell your products to?" Decker asked.

"Nobody too special," Darlene said. "Just a few people here and there." She paused and shrugged. "A few wholesale outlets."

Decker recognized the feigned nonchalant tone in Darlene's voice, knew instantly she was trying to downplay the business. Same breezy timber his father had adapted if you asked him about the state of his finances. Ask Lyle Decker about money, and his stock answer was "Can't complain." The hardware store had been good to him, netted him a few bucks in the bank. What Lyle wouldn't tell you was that the store had netted him enough money to buy up Florida land that was later sold to Disney Corporation. His few bucks in the bank were more like a few million bucks.

"What kind of wholesale outlets?" Decker pressed.

Annette washed her hands, dried them on her apron, and took a seat. "Oh, Karrol's restaurant decided they liked our muffins. And we just got lucky on an account with Tucker's Pancake House. I'm real proud of that one."

Marge looked at Decker, raised her brow. He knew what she was saying. Between the two chains, that was about twenty-five restaurants in the L.A. area alone. But neither one voiced the comment out loud. Annette kept talking.

"We're marketed under Howard's Honey Farms and Bakeries."

"You have any competition from the other honey farms?" Decker asked.

Annette said, "Well, there are the bigger honey farms down near Lancaster . . . and up in Ventura. But here in Sagebrush, it's just us and the Darcys now. They live 'bout two miles down the—"

"More cake, Mister Detective?" Darlene broke in. "You're almost done."

"Thank you, Darlene," Decker said. "And some tea, if you don't mind."

"'Course," Darlene said.

"The Darcys are good friends of yours?" Marge asked.

"No," Darlene answered. "At least *some* of them aren't."

"Now, Darl—" Annette said.

"Let's put it this way," Darlene said. "Pappy Darcy is a fine man. But he's had a lot of trouble from his children."

Annette looked down. Darlene squeezed her lips together until they disappeared into white lines. A moment later, she blurted out, "Pappy D.'s son has a wife that is pure devil, and I don't mean that lightly, I can tell you that."

"In what way?" Marge asked.

Darlene went deep red. Decker saw it and asked, "How 'bout that tea, Darlene?"

Darlene nodded, her hands were shaking. "Right away." She served them two frosted tumblers of tea. Decker drank his in six gulps.

"It sure is good tea, isn't it, Detective Dunn?" Decker said. "What's in here that makes it so special?"

"Honey," Annette said.

"Well, I know there's honey in it," Decker said. "But there's something else . . . ginger, maybe?"

"You've got a good palate, Mister Detective," Darlene said. "We sell our tea, also."

I bet you do, Decker thought. He said, "So you and Pappy Darcy are the only honey farms left, huh?"

"Only 'cause that greedy witch hasn't had her way," Darlene said. "She's been trying to get Pappy D to sell out those builders."

"Manfred?" Marge asked.

"Yeah," Annette said. "Those are the ones."

"They've been creating a lot of mischief around town," Marge added.

"They're building all over the place," Decker said. "Making lots of people mad."

"Well, I can tell you that Pappy H was fit to be tied when Pappy Willard sold out to them," Annette said. "Pappy H and Pappy D tried to talk him out of it, even offered to buy up his land, but they couldn't compete with the price that Manfred was offering them."

"What are they planning to build on the land?" Decker asked.

"I don't know," Darlene said. "No one does. Land's just sitting out there, doin' nothing. No cows, no sheep. The clover hasn't been turned over in a year. It's a mess." Darlene wiped her mouth. "Boy, when the witch found out the price Manfred paid Pappy Willard, she started working on poor Luke to get Pappy D to sell and hasn't let up since. Day in, day out—"

"Now how do you know that?" Annette said.

"Things get around," Darlene said. "Things get around."

"Darl, for being such a Christian, you sure don't turn the other cheek," Annette said.

"I'm a fine Christian," Darlene said. "I just know the Devil when I see him . . . or her."

Annette said, "You could at least call her Linda instead of the witch all the time. You know, it's gotten so that the kids call her the witch to her face."

"Well, that's what she is," Darlene said. "A refill, Mister Detective?"

Decker nodded.

"How 'bout you, miss?" she asked Marge.

Miss? "Thank you," Marge said.

"A witch is a witch," Darlene said. "And if it was you, you'd think she was a witch also."

"I'm not calling Linda an angel," Annette said. "She was wrong to do what she did."

"Darn right she was wrong." Darlene angrily poured tea

from a ribbed glass pitcher until the brown liquid sloshed over the rims of the tumblers. "She did what she did 'cause she's a witch. Can't get away from what you are."

"I just don't think it's a good Christian example for the kids to hear you carry on," Annette said, mopping up the spill with her napkin.

"And I mebbe don't care about what you think," Darlene said.

"Well, you might care, if only for the sake of the kids."

"The kids are just fine, thank you."

Darlene sat down stiffly and clasped her hands tightly. Annette bit her thumbnail. A moment later, Annette reached out for Darlene's hand.

"We bicker a lot," Annette said. "But that don't mean we don't love each other."

Decker smiled.

"More cake?" Darlene offered. Her voice was shaky.

Decker said, "No thank you."

Marge said, "It sure was delicious. Would you part with the recipe?"

It was Decker's turn to cough. Marge's idea of baking was microwaving a frozen coffee cake.

Marge added, "If it's not a family secret. My granny has a recipe for Christmas fruitcake that she wouldn't part with even if Jesus came down from heaven and asked her for it in person."

Darlene smiled tightly. "Well, you don't have to be Jesus to get the recipe here."

"Matter of fact," Decker said, "might be a good idea to give Detective Dunn some of your other favorite recipes. Her cooking could use it."

"This is true," Marge said.

"One of the reasons she can't find a man."

Marge covered her mouth with her hand. Pete was spreading it thick. But, as always, they were thinking along the same lines. Both of them wanted to split the women up.

She'd work over Darlene, while Decker pumped the young one. After the last interchange, the gals would remain muzzled as long as they were together.

Marge said, "Well, my cooking could stand a little help."

Darlene said, "I'd be delighted to share my cooking secrets with you."

"Why don't we go in another room where it's quiet and you can explain to me exactly how you make your dishes?" Marge said.

"What about the police business?" Darlene said.

"If it means an improvement in Detective Dunn's cooking, it can wait."

Marge threw him a mock dirty look.

Darlene said, "Then come on. I'll get us some pieces of paper."

As soon as they were out of earshot, Annette whispered, "Please don't judge Darl too harshly."

"I take it that Byron and Linda had a little something going," Decker said.

"It was awful," Annette said. "Just plain awful. The way Darl talks about it, you'd think it happened yesterday instead of four years ago. She still talks about going over there and pistol-whippin' Linda—" Annette stopped talking for a moment. "'Course, she don't mean it."

"Of course," Decker said. But he made a mental note in his head.

Annette said. "Darl just can't let go. It's not good for the kids to see her in such a state whenever Linda's name is mentioned." Annette took the net off her hair. "You know what really gets to me?"

"What?"

"Now I'm not condemning Linda—no, not condemning. What's the right word?"

"Condoning," Decker tried.

"Yeah, that's it," Annette said. "I'm not condoning her. But Byron was at that mo-tel same as Linda. Everyone talks about how bad Linda was. Pappy Howard rants against her, Pappy and Granny Darcy rant against her. Everything's her fault. But let's face it, Mister Detective, it takes two to tango. And no one says a word against Byron."

"Even Darlene?"

"Especially Darlene," Annette said. "She acts like it weren't his doing at all. That Linda bewitched him. But you know like I know that Linda didn't kidnap Byron and carry him off to the mo-tel all by her lonesome."

Decker sipped his tea. "Which motel was that?"

"A place in town called the Sleepy-Bi," Annette said. "Darlene found a matchbook in Byron's pocket and asked him about it. He hemmed and hawed, then broke down. My Lord, what a mess!"

"Linda and Byron still see each other?" Decker asked.

"No, sir," Annette said. She shook out her hair. The amber strands fell to her shoulders and framed her face. With her hair down, she looked younger, prettier. "They just did it the one time, four years ago."

"Just *one* time?"

"Well, that's what Byron told Darlene. And I believe him. I like to believe the best in people."

"Neither one of them divorced, huh?" Decker asked.

"Nope."

Figures, Decker thought. A woman like Darlene would never let her husband go. Just hang on to her resentment and make his life miserable. He said, "Yeah, Darlene doesn't seem like the divorcing type."

"You got it right about that, mister," Annette said.

Decker asked about Luke, did he seem like the divorcing type? Annette appeared to be wrestling with judgment. Just how *much* should she say, how much could this stranger be trusted? He stared at her for a few seconds, then gave her a disarming smile.

Again, Annette bit her thumbnail. "Well, Luke's mom, Granny D, she was ready to throw Linda out on her bottom.

You know, there's always a lot of problems between daughters-in-law and mothers-in-law. But this was more than your normal competition."

"I should say so," Decker said. "Any loyal parent would be furious."

"Well, they are very loyal to Luke, and they were pretty darn furious. I'll tell you that," Annette said. "Pappy and Granny D talked till they was blue in the face, but Luke wouldn't hear of divorce. He's a nice guy. Still talks kindly to Byron, treats Linda nice, too. Everybody would like to forget about the whole thing. That is, everybody 'cept Darlene."

"How old is Linda?"

"Oh, she won't say, but I reckon she's about forty."

"Quite a bit younger than Byron."

"Byron's fifty-two," Annette said. "I think that was part of the whole thing. A middle-aged fling, like they say."

"How old's Luke?"

"'Bout the same age as Linda. He looks young, though. Younger than Linda, that's for sure. I don't know, maybe he is. Lord knows what Linda saw in Byron. You met Byron?"

Decker said he did.

"Byron's a fine man, but no Magnum P.I. And Luke's a nice-looking man. No one could understand it." Annette shrugged. "Linda's a free spirit. Oh, she's settled down some since the baby was born, but before then she done some pretty wild things."

"Like what?"

"Like the affair." Annette collected her thoughts. "Linda just wasn't a homebody. She didn't like to sew or cook or bake, though she can whip up some fine food. I think that burns up Darlene, too. Linda's darn good in the kitchen. If she wants to be."

"A good baker, too?" Decker asked.

"Yes, sir."

Decker wondered about the extent of the competition. He

asked Annette if Linda ever tried to market her baked goods. The young woman burst into laughter and answered no, explaining that Linda wasn't the industrious kind.

"Then what'd Linda do with all her free time?" Decker asked.

"She spent hours over the mountain doing Lord knows what. And she liked to hang around the Heaven. Go out there in the afternoons with her sister-in-law, Carla, and drink with the boys. Innocent, I'm sure, but it didn't look nice."

Decker recalled the biker bar. His eyebrows raised a notch.

Annette caught the gesture. Quickly, she said, "I know it doesn't seem right for Linda to be goin' there to drink. But you gotta realize, sir, that it's the only show in town. Heck, the Heaven's not really a *bad* place, as long as you're not a nigger. They're not evil boys—a little rowdy, sure—but they leave us alone, and nobody messes with them or us because of it. For us, the place ain't more than a beer and pizza joint. Jeff's addicted to their pizzas. Buys the big ones, eats half of it, and throws the rest away. I keep telling him to buy the medium ones, but men don't listen to their wives much."

"Jeff is your husband?" Decker asked.

"Yeah. Darl and I are sisters-in-law."

Decker smoothed the corners of his mustache. He said, "You're much younger than Darlene."

"Twenty years younger. Darl's been like a mother to me. A good mother." Annette flicked hair off her face. "Byron's from Pappy H's first marriage. His mom died when he was fifteen. Jeffrey, my husband, is from Pappy H's second marriage. Jeff has a sister, also. She lives in Pomona, married to a real nice guy. They breed Dobies."

"Where's Jeff now?" Decker asked.

"With Pappy and Granny H, and Byron's oldest sons, at a

meeting—Western Beekeepers Association. They're gathering down in Fall Springs this year. Byron offered to watch the farm so they could all leave. I couldn't go with Jeff 'cause I couldn't leave Darl with all the jarring and baking and cooking. Not to mention the kids. There's eight between us. Three of mine, five of hers."

"Lots of kids."

"Well, it ain't that bad 'cause Darl's first two boys are big—twenty-one and nineteen. They eat like hogs. Golly, it seems that somebody's mouth is always chewing something."

"How old are your kids?" Decker asked.

"Nine, eight, and six. Two boys and a girl. Darl's kids help me a lot with them."

"Do Linda and Luke have lots of kids?"

"Just the one little girl. Guess she's 'bout two."

"Linda was thirty-eight when she gave birth," Decker remarked. "A little on the old side."

Annette's voice dropped to a whisper. "I think they had some problems. That might be one of the reasons that Linda was so wild before the kid. But a big belly slowed her down some."

Decker calmly took out the photo of Baby Sally and laid it on the table. He asked, "Is this Linda Darcy's little girl?"

Annette's eyes focused on the picture, then inched back to Decker. They had darkened with worry. "That's Katie, all right. Is she okay?"

"Katie's fine. When was the last time you spoke to Linda?"

" 'Bout a week ago. What's this—"

"Does Linda have a phone?" Decker interrupted.

"Of course she has a phone. They put the lines underground so the winds don't knock 'em out. Winds can get pretty fierce down here."

"Can you call up Linda Darcy for me?"

"What's this all about?" Annette asked.

"Call her up for me, please."

Annette stood, hesitated a moment, then walked over to the phone. After the thirteenth ring, she hung up.

"No one's home," she said. Her voice cracked.

Decker said, "Do you know if she and Luke went to that bee meeting in Fall Springs?"

Annette brightened. "Of course. They probably all went down together."

"Would Linda go without Katie? Maybe leave the girl with a baby-sitter?"

"Linda? Never. Katie is her third arm. Linda even takes her into the Heaven when she wants a quick brew. All the bikers know Katie by name."

Decker thought a moment.

"Who's your lawman around here, Mrs. Howard?" he asked.

"Lawman?"

"Yes, lawman. Is there a sheriff that lives in the neighborhood?"

"No," Annette said, shaking her head. "We're too small for that."

"Okay." Decker thought for a moment. It was premature to call the sheriff's station, because he had nothing to report except the identity of a lost child. But if he didn't, there was always the chance that some jerk would accuse him of grandstanding outside his jurisdiction. He decided to place a quick phone call to County to cover his butt. He said to Annette, "If you don't mind now, I'd like to use your phone for a moment."

"Sure," Annette whispered. "Is everything all right?"

Decker pretended not to hear and picked up the phone. "Why don't you go see what the other Mrs. Howard and Detective Dunn are doing?"

"You don't want me to overhear, do you?"

"No, I don't," he answered. "Go on. I'll fill you in later."

Annette didn't argue. A minute later, all three women were back in the kitchen. Decker whispered something into the receiver, then hung up.

To Marge, he said, "The toddler's name is Katie Darcy. I just placed a call to County Sheriff, told them what we were up to in a few sentences. I'm waiting for them to call back. Shouldn't be more than a few minutes."

"What's going on?" Darlene asked suspiciously.

"Detective Dunn and I are going to take a ride over to the Darcy ranch," Decker said. "Is it just straight down the road?"

"I can take you to the Darcys, if that's what you want," Annette said.

"I don't think that would be a good idea, ma'am," Marge said.

Darlene asked, "What's this all about, Nettie?"

"Well, I don't rightly know," Annette answered.

Decker said, "Katie Darcy was found two days ago wandering around a residential area just over the mountain. We've been trying to locate her parents. Now that we've found them, Detective Dunn and I are going to pay them a little visit. The both of you have been very helpful. Thank you."

Darlene glanced at Annette, then at Decker. "The witch is a witch. But she never leaves that kid out of her sight for a second."

"That's what your sister-in-law told me," Decker said.

"Then what's going on?" Darlene probed.

"That's what we're hoping to find out, Mrs. Howard," Marge said.

Darlene frowned.

The kitchen became silent. A minute passed. This time, Annette started to pick her nails. Darlene massaged her hands.

Decker said, "It might be better if we waited by another extension in the house. That way we won't disturb your work."

"I won't hear of it," Darlene insisted. "Sit down. I'll get you some more *ice*-tea."

Marge said, "Thank you, Mrs. Howard—"

"Darlene," she said. "Everyone calls me Darlene."

More silence. Annette fidgeted, then got up and turned on the radio. Don Williams was singing about Tulsa Time. Decker hummed along.

Annette smiled at him. "And here I thought you were faking the drawl and everything just to get us to talk."

Decker laughed.

Annette retied her hair. "I like Don Williams. Has such a pretty voice."

Decker nodded.

"Darlene met George Jones once," Annette said.

"Oh, Nettie!"

"Go ahead and tell them," Annette prodded.

"It was nothing," Darlene said. "It was twenty years ago."

"Tell them anyway," Annette said.

"Well," Darlene said, breathily, "Byron was playing backup guitar for an old act called the Pineridge Boys at the Palomino. You know 'bout the Palomino?"

"On Lankershim," Marge said.

"Yeah," Darlene said. "He used to play bluegrass. My Lord, this was a long time ago. Anyway, who should be in the audience but George Jones. Without Tammy, I might add. I thought I'd die when he came up to Byron and me afterward. He said Byron was a real fine picker." Darlene sighed. "But Byron's duty was to his pappy and the farm. Never even thought one minute about being anything else."

Darlene picked up a wooden spoon and stirred the cauldron. "It was a long time ago."

The quiet became noticeable again.

Darlene said, "This batch is done, Nettie. Give me a hand with it."

"Can I help?" Decker offered.

Darlene said, "You can pick up the other side and help me take it off the stove and onto that metal cooling pad."

Decker grabbed two pot holders and lifted the cauldron himself. "Where?"

"Right behind you," Annette said.

"Thank you, Mister Detective," Darlene said.

"What are you cooking?" Marge asked.

"Apple-honey syrup," Darlene said. "I gave you the recipe for it."

"Oh yeah," Marge said, "the one where you strain a half-dozen cooked Granny Smith apples."

The phone rang. Decker announced it was probably for him and picked up the receiver. He was silent for a moment, then turned his back to the women and whispered into the receiver. A minute later, he hung up and told Marge that Sheriff's gave them the go ahead.

Byron Howard lumbered into the kitchen, announcing he was thirsty. His bald head was beaded with rows of sweat. He took a callused hand and mowed the water down, wiping his wet palm on his pants leg. He didn't look any happier to see Decker than he had the first time.

"You still here?" he asked them.

"Looks that way," Decker said. "We're leaving right now, Mr. Howard."

"They're goin' to the Darcys, Byron," Annette said. "Katie Darcy was found on the other side of the mountain, and the detective thinks that don't look so good, considerin' how close Linda was to her and all."

"Thank you for your time, Mr. Howard," Decker said. "Sorry for the intrusion."

Byron faced Decker and blurted out, "I'll take you to the Darcys."

Darlene's face froze in shock.

Annette stammered out, "Now, Byron, I don't think that's a good idea—"

"I'm going," Byron insisted.

Darlene's look of surprise had turned to hatred. "Who's gonna mind the farm?" she asked.

"I weren't be more than ten minutes, Darlene," Byron said. "For God's sake, woman, I think you can last that long with me out of reach."

Darlene's mouth fell open.

Byron's eyes beseeched Decker's. "Please, mister. I won't get in your way."

Decker paused a second, then nodded for him to come along.

"Let's go," Marge repeated.

"Ten minutes, Darlene," Byron said. "I swear it. Just ten minutes."

❧11

𝒟𝑒𝑐𝑘𝑒𝑟 𝑝𝑢𝑙𝑙𝑒𝑑 𝑡ℎ𝑒 unmarked onto Sagebrush Canyon Road. Byron Howard sat shotgun, Marge stretched out in the back. From the corner of her eye, she noticed Howard staring at the Plymouth's in-dash computer, the radio transmitter and mike, all the little lights and dials. To him, it probably looked like NASA control.

They rode a half-mile without speaking. Finally, Marge asked Byron about the biker bar down the road.

The beekeeper waved his hand in the air. "Bunch of lazy bums over there. But they leave us in peace and keep out the niggers."

"Who owns the place?" Decker asked.

"Kid named Chip," Byron answered.

"Chip what?" Marge asked.

"Just Chip," Byron said.

Decker knew conversation was going to be one-way, but he tried anyway. "I hear your brother likes the pizza over there."

Byron answered yep, the pizza was good, and stared out the windshield.

The road bisected grainfields. Thousands of yellow stalks bowing in the wind, reflecting the fire of the sun. A stone grinding mill slowly came into view, sitting like an island in

145

a golden sea. The sky was freckled with blackbirds sliding through perfumed air.

Straight out of a Wyeth painting, Marge thought. She asked, "What're they growing here?"

"Looks like rape," Decker said.

Byron looked up from his lap. "It is rape."

"Rape?" Marge asked.

"It's a kind of corn—grain," Decker said. "My brother's first wife—no, his second—yeah, it was the second one. She was from Kansas, so that's where the wedding took place. Grain markets are big out there. Wheat, oats, rape, rye—"

"Just how many wives does your brother have?" Byron asked.

"Only one at the moment," Decker said. "She happens to be number three. Speaking of family, how many people live over at the Darcy farm?"

It took Byron a long time to respond. When he did, he spoke slowly, clicking off his fingers every time he mentioned a name. There was Pappy and Granny, Luke and Linda. Then there was Sue Beth and B.B., her husband.

Byron said, "Sue Beth is Luke's older sister."

He stopped talking. Decker asked if that was the entire family. Byron shook his head no.

"Who else?" Marge asked. She hoped she kept the frustrated tone out of her voice.

Well, there was Luke's younger sister, Carla, Byron went on to explain. And Earl, the youngest.

"He's not right in the head," Byron announced.

"In what way?" Decker asked.

"Just that," Byron said. "He's a retard. Nice boy, though. Does his chores without a complaint. Wish my boys were as polite as Earl."

"How old is he?" Decker asked.

"'Bout twenty-five," Byron answered.

Decker asked if there were any more people in the household, and Byron answered just the kids. Sue Beth had two, Linda had Katie. Decker added up the total mentally. Twelve people, but *nine* adults under one roof. And according to Annette Howard, tension between mother-in-law and daughter-in-law. Nine adults—nine opinions. A potential keg of dynamite.

"Know which of the Darcys went to the bee meeting in Fall Springs?" Marge asked.

Decker raised his eyebrows. Darlene must have told Marge about the Western Beekeepers Association. Margie had done a fine job of extracting information from Darlene. They'd compare notes later.

"I know Pappy and Granny D went down," Byron said. "And they musta took Earl, 'cause they don't leave him. I think everyone went except Luke, Linda, and Katie—and Carla. She don't go nowhere for the business. Girl has no sense of family."

Marge cleared her throat. A signal to Decker saying that statement could be significant, remember it because we can't write it at the moment. Decker coughed, and Marge sat back in her seat.

She asked, "What about Sue Beth's children? They go with the parents?"

"I reckon they would," Byron said. "I don't talk too much to the Darcys."

Decker sneaked a sidelong glance at Byron. His expression remained flat.

"Turn right there," Byron said, pointing to a dirt road.

Decker steered the Plymouth onto the path. It was lined with red-flowering bottlebrush trees and terminated at the entrance to a three-story whitewashed, wood-frame house. Next to the house was a red silo, the door open, grain spilling out like melted butter. The Darcys' residence, like the Howards', was located amid acres of blooming cloverfield. In the distance, behind the house, cows were grazing. The car had traveled about halfway to the residence when Byron told Decker to stop.

"What is it?" Marge asked.

Byron said, "Something's wrong."

"How can you tell, Mr. Howard?" asked Marge.

Byron swallowed hard. "Back up two trees, Mister Detective."

Decker put the car into reverse.

"Look to the right," Byron said. "The back branch of that bottlebrush tree."

Through the car window, Decker saw that the rear bough was coated with bees—like insulation around a duct.

"Ain't no way any of the Darcys would let a swarm like that just sit there on a tree," Byron said. "It's at least a day old, judging by the size of the comb." Byron looked at Marge. "Something's badly wrong."

"Sure you want to go in with us?" Decker asked.

"Yes, sir, I do," Byron answered. He dropped his voice a notch. "I do."

Decker shifted the transmission back to drive. He parked outside the house. As soon as he stepped out, the stench hit his nostrils. Something decaying. Bees were flying about his face, not nearly as heavy as the first swarm he'd experienced, but there were enough insects to create that ominous, low-pitched hum. He traded a wary glance with Marge.

Byron took a quick walk around the house. He came back and said, "All the cars are gone."

"What kind of cars do they drive?" Decker asked.

"Pappy D has a two-tone fifties Plymouth. B.B. has a full-sized Ford pickup," Byron answered. He covered his mouth. "Lord, it stinks."

"I'll get the gloves," she said.

"Gloves?" Byron asked.

"We don't want to destroy any evidence," Marge said. "Mr. Howard, I think it would be best if you waited outside."

"Well, I disagree."

Decker said, "Mr. Howard, I'm afraid I'm gonna have to insist that you wait outside."

Byron bit his lip, held back a mixture of anger and fear.

"I know you're concerned," Decker said. "I don't like what I'm smelling, either. But them's the rules, sir."

Byron turned away and muttered an obscenity.

Decker nodded to Marge, then turned the handle to the front door. As soon as it opened, a waft of hot, putrefying air blasted their faces.

"Jesus!" cried Decker, holding down a dry heave.

"Here," Marge said, handing him a jar of VapoRub. "Plug up."

Decker coated each nostril with the salve, then took out a handkerchief and placed it over his nose and mouth. Marge covered her face with her hands. The layout was similar to the Howards' place. A quaint country living room, but this one smelled as ripe as a slaughterhouse. Bees flitted through the air like confetti. The floors were peg-and-groove pine, and streaked with trails of red-brown crust. A path of footprints, stained the same color, led from the kitchen to the front door. Big feet—around a size eleven, followed by a smaller size—maybe seven or eight. Decker pointed it out to Marge, and she nodded and pulled out a notebook.

Decker took a good look around the room. Nothing overturned or uprooted. The furniture was upholstered in bright red and yellow florals, the material intact without rips or tears, the pillows decorator-arranged. The matching curtains were whole as well, the pleats hanging straight. Nothing yanked apart or pulled down. No overt signs of struggle here. Marge tapped him on the shoulder. She pointed to a dark, fuzzy line on the floor. The line moved, wriggled about like glitter, a queue of bees piled atop each other.

Decker cautiously stepped over the bees and neared the kitchen. The stench was unbearable, the air dense with bees droning out a requiem. Decker added more VapoRub to his nostrils and put the handkerchief back over his face. Marge coughed behind her hands.

The kitchen proved to be as large as the Howards' and equally as modern. Decker took a swift look around the room, forcing himself to study detail. The shiny sunlit steel appliances were splattered with caked blood. Puddles of curdled milk had collected on the countertops, and empty cans of formula were strewn about—on the stove, on the counters, on the floor. An open gallon jar of honey lay sideways, its contents now a plasmic glob on the floor. Hundreds of bees were wading in the cloudy brown pool, their forelegs and tongues eagerly gathering the pickings.

Finally, he allowed his eyes to rest on the center of the floor. First a quick peek, then he focused on the grisly sight.

In the middle were three bodies—one male and two females—all of them covered with a sticky coat of blood and honey, a nappy blanket of bees and flies, and rice-size maggots. The skin was bloated, the underlying fascia had been partially eaten away by bugs and decomposition. Though the insects were crawling over most of the flesh, it was possible to make out the remnants of faces—a light blue eye, a lip, a cleft chin. One female had a hand resting on her open bowel, the male had his right leg blown off. To the right, slumped against the metal door of a walk-in refrigerator, lay another male. His face had been a meal ticket for the bugs, and most of his innards had been exploded. His legs were nearly severed from his body. His body was attached to his limbs by only thin strings of tendons. A human marionette. Shotgun blasts all around. Decker shook his head.

As he stared at the piles of blood and infected meat, he felt a sudden, sharp pain on the back of his neck. Damn. One of the suckers had finally got him. He felt a warm swelling rise on his neck and looked around for Marge.

She'd left, but another had come to take her place. In the corner of the room stood Byron Howard, his eyes fixed upon the carnage. His shoulders sagged forward, his eyes and cheeks were wet with tears. His lips uttered one word over and over. *Linda, Linda, Linda . . .*

🙖12

Rina squeezed the Porsche into the garage and breathed a sigh of relief. She and the car were whole. Her head and neck ached from the tension of driving—God forbid she'd come home with a mark on the metal. Why were men like that about cars? To her, an automobile was nothing more than a way to get from one place to another. From now on, either she'd drive the Jeep or rent an old Volvo. Besides, she felt strange behind the wheel of a German car. Though it never bothered her parents—they'd driven Mercedes for years, and both of them were camp survivors—it bothered her. Carl Benz had been a war criminal, Ferdinand Porsche a star member of the SS.

She locked the car, closed the garage door, and heard banging coming from the backyard. Although the unmarked wasn't parked out front, Peter must be home. Maybe Marge had taken the Plymouth and dropped him off.

"Peter?" Rina shouted as she walked toward the barn. "Peter, I'm back. And the Porsche's still in one piece."

Rina entered the barn, then stopped suddenly. Her heart started pounding in her chest. A strange man. This one kneeling, bare-chested, wearing only corduroy shorts and sandals—one sandal, rather. His left leg was a prosthesis.

The handicap calmed her slightly—no doubt she could out-run him. Still, she reflexively pulled a .38 from her purse and gripped it in her hand.

"Who are you?" she asked.

The man eyed the pistol, then the woman.

"My name's Abel Atwater," he drawled. "I'm a friend of Sergeant Decker. I'm fixin' up his barn."

"Sergeant Decker never told me about any man he hired to fix up his barn," Rina said.

Abel kept staring at the gun. "Well, I don't think Pete wanted me here while you were here, ma'am. I just came back to get my tools, and I saw this warped board here. No one was around, so I thought I'd do a quick repair before I went home." Abel started to rise, then saw the woman's hand tighten around the butt of the revolver. "If you want to go into the house, lock the doors, and call him, I'll wait un-til he gets here. Or I'll just leave." He chuckled nervously. "Hey, I'll do anything you want."

Rina regarded him. Painfully thin, as if he had cancer . . . like Yitzchack in his final days. Only this one had normal coloring, wasn't ashen. . . .

She asked, "Where do you know Yitz—Where do you know Peter from?"

"We were in the army together—"

"Peter was in the army?" Rina interrupted.

"Yes, ma'am, he was."

Rina stared at him.

Abel said, "We did basic together—Fort Jackson, Polk for advanced training. Then overseas to Fulda and Nam—B Company, third squad. Later, they switched Pete from an A-gunner to a medic. He was too tall for footwork. . . ."

Rina said nothing.

Abel asked, "None of this sounds familiar?"

"No."

"Pete never talks about Nam, huh?"

Rina shook her head.

"That's old Doc for you—tight-lipped." Abel patted his prosthesis. "Uncle Sam's souvenir."

"I'm sorry," Rina said.

"Can I stand up, ma'am?" Abel said. "I'm frozen in an uncomfortable position, and that little piece of metal in your hand tells me I'd better ask permission before I move."

Rina nodded, backed away a foot, and kept her finger on the trigger. Abel stood.

"I've got a picture of him and me taken before we were shipped to the Southeast," Abel said. "It's in my wallet . . . in the back of my pants. Wanna see it?"

Rina didn't answer him. Abel slowly reached inside his pocket and pulled out his wallet.

"See, ma'am? Just a plain old wallet," Abel said. "Cheap. Not even real leather."

He fished out a color picture and tossed it to her. Rina bent down and retrieved the photograph, her eyes still upon Abel. Slowly, she stood and allowed herself to look at the snapshot.

It was definitely Peter—and the man who claimed his name to be Abel Atwater. Both were younger—kids, in fact. They were wearing camouflage hats, white T-shirts, and camouflage pants, and had machine guns strapped across their shoulders—Decker's left, Abel's right. They had their free arms looped around each other, and were smiling broadly. Abel had once been well built, broad shoulders and good height—judging from where he came up to Peter, around 6'. Looking at him now, he didn't seem much over 5'8".

But it was Peter who captured her attention—his grin so childlike, his face and skin so smooth . . . clean-shaven. She'd never seen him without a mustache, and was surprised at the Cupid's bow shape of his upper lip. But it was his eyes that kept her spellbound. They were the same color, the same shape . . . but they were different. It was the expression, the gleam of anticipation—eager eyes. Something she'd never witnessed in him even when he was at his happiest—when they made love, when he was with his daughter, when he played ball with her sons. Nothing, *nothing*, had ever lit up his eyes the way they shone in this shutter-snap of history. Sadly, she knew in her heart that nothing ever would.

"I have more," Abel whispered from behind her shoulder.

Rina jumped. The clopping of his prosthesis notwithstanding, she hadn't heard him move. He was a few inches from her, reeking of sweat. Immediately, she backed away.

Abel said, "I'm sorry if I scared you—"

"That's okay."

Abel's eyes went to the gun. "You know how to use that thing?"

"Very well," Rina said.

"'Cause it's dangerous if you don't."

"I do."

"Look . . ." Abel gave her a strained smile. "Why don't you just go in the house, and I'll get out of here. We'd both feel more comfortable that way. I'm really sorry about this intrusion. Tell Pete I'm sorry." He threw his hands in the air. "I'm always messing something up."

Rina didn't speak right away. Finally, she said, "You said you had more pictures."

"Yes," Abel said. "Yes, ma'am, I do. I carry my past in my pockets, what can I tell you?" He peered inside his wallet and pulled out some snapshots. "These were taken in Da Nang, whenever we had a few spare moments. Oftener than you'd think. Hours of mind-numbing boredom mixed with a few minutes of terror. Never could relax. When you did, you'd get caught with your pants down. Kind of like police work, don't you think?"

"I suppose."

Abel offered her the pictures. Rina took them. The tips of their fingers touched. Abel closed his eyes and swallowed dryly.

Rina said, "You can finish fixing up the board if you want."

Abel smiled. "Thank you, ma'am. I'll do just that." He walked back over to his tools, bent down, picked up a hammer, and put a couple of nails in his mouth.

Rina took a deep breath. Where do you draw the line between being cautious and being paranoid? The guy seemed straightforward, he and Peter were in that picture together. Yet he could be a psychopath, she had no way of judging him. Maybe the only thing that kept him from attacking her was the gun in her hand. Still, the trusting soul in her felt as if she should offer him something to drink. It was sweltering. But what if . . .

Rina turned her attention to the black-and-white photographs. The first one was a group picture—six boys—Peter smiling for the camera, his face grimed with mud. His eyes had changed, soured—the eyes she knew now. He was holding a machine gun in one hand, a bayonet in the other. Another picture showed him and Abel resting inside what looked to be a tent. They lay on separate cots, bare-chested, reading paperbacks. Did Peter's cover say *The Carpetbaggers*? Abel was reading Michener's *Hawaii*. Some sort of radio transmitter sat atop a pile of Coke cartons. The last picture showed Peter, Abel, and another boy boarding a helicopter. Still young, still smiling, but all of them with stale eyes.

Rina walked over to Abel and handed him back the photos. She held the earlier color photo and asked, "Do you have a copy of this one?"

Abel took the nails out of his mouth. "I don't. But you can keep it, if you want."

"I'll make a copy and send the original back to you," Rina said. "Is that all right?"

"You don't have to go to all that trouble, ma'am."

"It's no trouble." Rina paused, then said, "Can I bring you something to drink?"

"No thank you," Abel said. "All I want to do is fix this board and get out of here. I'm under specific instructions to be scarce while you're around."

"Peter's protective of me."

"He should be. Lots of nuts around town."

Rina asked, "What are you doing for him?"

"Rebuilding his barn, his stables." Abel placed a nail on the board and whacked it flush in one stroke. "They're in terrible shape."

"Well, nice meeting you," Rina said.

"Likewise."

As soon as she was gone, Abel placed the hammer down and felt hot tears well up inside his eyes. Though he knew it was a waste of time, he wondered what it might be like to be loved by someone like that—caressed by such perfect fingers, kissed by luscious lips. Her curves were edible, her face divine. But it was the hair—black and thick, as shiny as an oil slick. Man, he wanted her.

And she belonged to Doc. Pete had the badge and two whole legs as well. A part of Abel hated Decker with a consuming intensity. But another part loved him too much to let him go. And now it was Doc to the rescue, his only chance for getting out of the mess he was in. He wiped his eyes and slammed another nail into the floor.

Seeing Doc was painful, too painful. The prime reason why he'd never answered his letters after they'd moved to separate cities, why he'd never called him after he'd settled in L.A. Had he remained whole, Doc and he would have probably gone through Police Academy together. He was from Kentucky, Doc was from Florida. A century ago, they both had decided that the City of Angels held all the promises. Like the cowboys of old, they had made plans to head west. Abel would marry his Song, his Asian doll, Decker would be the best man. Together they'd off all the bad guys and make the streets safe again. But the dream disintegrated—his girl murdered, his leg gone.

And now this one shows up—with the same thick black hair. Doing things to his mind.

Gotta stop thinkin' about it.

Gotta stop.

Gotta stop.

He took a deep breath and tried to free his mind of pollution.

This time he was lucky, succeeded in letting go. He buried his mind in the minutiae of his work and didn't stop until he heard footsteps approaching the barn. He felt his face go hot.

"I brought you out some orange juice," Rina said. Ginger was at her side. She was carrying a tray on which she'd placed a carton of orange juice and a glass full of ice cubes. She stopped at the entrance to the barn and lowered the tray onto the ground. The gun was no longer in her hand.

"Thank you, ma'am," Abel said quietly.

"Are you almost done?" Rina said.

"Another five minutes maybe."

"Okay."

"I can leave now, if you want," Abel said. "I don't want to upset you."

"No," Rina said, backing away slowly. "It's okay."

"Well, I'll say good-bye then," Abel said. "It was nice to meet you. Pete told me that you and him have big plans. I wish you two lots of good fortune. He's a lucky man."

"Thank you."

"And thanks for the juice."

"Thanks for the picture," Rina said. "It means a lot to me. I'll get it back to you right away."

"Take your time," Abel said. He watched her walk away, the dog nuzzling against her hip. How he envied the four-legged bitch. He sighed and stroked his beard. "Take your time," Abel repeated, whispering it this time.

❧13

Slouched in the backseat of the unmarked, Decker smoked a cigarette. He'd removed his jacket and tie, and his shirtsleeves were rolled up to his elbows. His feet were propped over the driver's seat, all the windows of the Plymouth cranked open, the doors pushed out to the maximum. Hot tobacco air mixed with dry dust, and his mouth felt desert-arid. He eyeballed Marge outside, saw the sweat pouring off her forehead, and wondered if he should give her a break, whether she'd take offense at his offer. He shrugged and decided she'd ask for help if she needed it. She was talking to Byron Howard, calming him down, trying to get him inside the car so he wouldn't mess the ground if a grid search was needed. But the bald man wasn't heeding her advice, and paced as if he had something to hide.

Ten minutes later, Decker heard tires grinding against gravel. From the back windshield, he saw a black-and-white County Sheriff's car and a white crime-lab van park behind the Plymouth. The driver of the cruiser opened the door, stood, and stretched. He appeared to be in his sixties—a portly man with a pencil-thin mustache, pouches for cheeks, and a pale complexion. His hair was white and thin, combed to the side to cover an empty patch of pink scalp. He was dressed in typical detective fashion—a white short-

sleeved shirt, clip-on tie, navy slacks and black oxfords. He
sauntered over to the van, knocked on the window, and
waved the men from Forensic outside.

The techs were young—a crew-cut Asian and curly-
haired redhead splattered with acne and freckles, both
wearing long white coats and sweating in the heat. Slowly,
Decker swung his feet outside, stood up, and joined the
powwow.

Shaking Decker's hand, the sheriff detective introduced
himself as Ozzie Crandal. He said, "I was in the field when
the RTO patched the call through. Actually, I was on my
lunch break. It sounds like we've got a mess inside there."

Decker introduced himself and said "mess" was an un-
derstatement, explaining what they had was a quadruple
homicide.

Crandal bit his lip. "How'd LAPD field the call?"

"Case originated in my division just over the mountain. I
was doing follow-up when my partner and I stumbled onto
this one."

"Who's your partner?"

"Detective Dunn, the woman talking to the bald man."

Crandal touched the crown of his head and said, "Witness?"

"No, so far as I know. He's a neighbor—name's Byron
Howard." Decker turned to the techs. "Detective Dunn will
take you men in. It's ripe in there. Take along lots of VapoRub."

The Asian smiled, exposing large, square teeth. His name
tag said Tommy Chin. "I like challenge." He spoke in a
staccato voice. "Food for brain."

The redhead rolled his eyes, and pulled his partner by his
coat sleeve over to Marge. Decker watched the three of
them go inside the house, then asked Crandal if he wanted
to take a look at the murder victims.

Crandal ignored the question and said, "So you and your
partner are not technically with Homicide?"

"Nope," Decker said. "Juvey and Sex Crimes."

"But you found the kid in Foothill territory."

"Yes," Decker answered. "In the newest Manfred development just over the hill."

"Who's Manfred?" Crandal asked.

"Developer," Decker said. "Been building a lot in our division."

Crandal marked a line in the ground with the tip of his shoe. He said, "We can do a joint investigation, if you want—split the paperwork."

Bullshit, Decker thought. A joint investigation usually meant double paperwork on everything and people stepping all over each other's toes. But he paused only a moment before nodding yes. He couldn't get Katie's face out of his head, her tinkly laughter, her scrunched-nose smile. And Byron Howard sobbing *Linda, Linda, Linda* . . .

Dammit, one of those women was the little girl's mother.

Tommy, the Asian, came running out of the house, his mouth and nose hidden behind a kerchief. Wiping sweat off his brow, he came back to Decker and Crandal.

"We got a real problem in there."

"What?" Decker asked.

Tommy said, "Better if you see for yourself. Arnie's in there now. He try to figure out what to do. It's real bad. Especially bad if you are allergic." He let go with machine-gun laughter.

Decker removed his shoes, explaining to Crandal that there were two different shoe prints and the less mixup Forensics had, the better. He led Crandal into the house, offering him the VapoRub as they reached the front door. Then they stepped inside.

Time had done nothing to dampen the shock of the sight. Decker felt his stomach buck anew at the pile of bloated meat in the center, the legless man on the refrigerator. Pools of blood, layers of milk and honey. The bugs—especially the maggots—seemed to have multiplied in just a half hour.

The heat sped everything up. Marge was sketching the layout of the kitchen in her notepad, trying to draw, hold the tablet, and cover her nose at the same time. Arnie, the other lab man, was scraping some dried blood off a cabinet, transferring it to a glassine slide.

He said, "I can't keep this up much longer. Bee stings weren't part of the job description."

Tommy said, "I've seen bodies covered by beetles, ants, even worms. They like to lay eggs in the cavities—nose, eyes, ears. Never seen bees like this. I take a few for specimens, a few live ones, too. But the rest, they just background. They get mad when we try to do our job."

"And they're eating up the evidence," Arnie added.

"Give us a minute to decide how we want to handle this," Decker said. "In the meantime, can you take some blood samples from the bodies? I need to see if they match the blood found on a little girl's pajamas."

"Sure, I get you blood," Tommy answered. "How much you need? A tube? A pint? A gallon? They don't need any of it now." Again, the laughter.

"Whatever Forensics needs to run the tests, Tommy," Decker said.

"No problem." Tommy went back to work.

Arnie slapped his arm. "I can't work this way."

Decker said a minute, and waved Marge and Crandal outside. He then explained to Crandal that Byron Howard was a resident bee expert.

"Bet he can help us get rid of the critters," Decker said.

"Before he does that," Marge said, "he should look at the bodies and see how many he can ID. Who knows what those corpses will look like once we get all the insects off? With all the heat and bloat, we may be seeing the bodies at their peak."

"A gruesome thought," Crandal said.

Decker said, "Way Byron was moaning inside, one of the women should be Linda Darcy. The others?" He shrugged.

"Let's go ask Byron," Marge said.

Crandal wiped his forehead and said he was going to take a look around outside. When Marge asked him if he wanted his notepad, Crandal gave her a sour look and announced he was going to the car to get it. But Marge noticed he had been walking in the opposite direction.

As Decker and Marge approached Byron, Decker realized how slowly they were walking, how listless their movements had become. The sun was directly overhead, the sky cloudless and deep blue. The unrelenting heat, the rancid smells, everyone was being sapped of energy. Decker asked Byron how he felt. The bald man was ashen.

Byron said, "Kin I go home now?"

Decker said, "There's no legal reason why you can't. But we have a couple of favors to ask you."

"What?" Byron asked.

"First, someone should ID the bodies for us now—before any more decay sets in. . . ."

Byron didn't answer. Decker placed his hand on the beekeeper's thick shoulder, but Byron shrugged him off.

Marge said, "Mr. Howard, I know this is horrible stuff, but we need you to do this for us—"

"A couple of favors," Byron interrupted. He faced Decker. "You said a couple of favors. What's the other one?"

Decker fanned himself with the back of his hand and said, "None of us are used to working around bees. We have to get the bees off the bodies—"

"And wasps," Byron corrected. "Some are bees, but there're wasps too . . . they eat . . . bite . . . meat . . . I gotta sit down."

"Sure." Decker steered him to the unmarked, placed him down in the backseat. Decker and Marge sat on either side of the beekeeper, not too close but close enough to let Byron know what was expected of him.

Decker said, "Not feeling so hot?"

Byron shook his head. "I gotta get back to my own farm.

Darlene's gonna get fiery for me being out this long."

"Not once she hears the reason," Marge said.

"No, sir, Miss Detective. You don't know Darlene."

"Mr. Howard—" Decker said.

"You might as well call me Byron. This ain't no time to get formal."

"Byron, we need help," Decker said. "How do we get rid of those bees . . . wasps?"

"Smoke 'em, I reckon. Smoke confuses bees, makes them easy to handle. A few may still have a ornery disposition, but most you'll be able to brush aside, into a box or some supers. The wasps . . . smoke sometimes doesn't work. But it don't hurt to try."

"You have special suits for handling bees?" Marge asked. "Something our lab men can maybe borrow?"

"I've got some veils and gloves back at my farm. Take what you need. Then do me a favor and get out of my life." He shook his head again, this time with a "Dear God" escaping from his lips.

Marge said, "I'll drive you to your place. We'll pick up the veils, gloves, and the smokers, you show us how to use everything."

Byron didn't answer right away, but Decker pressed him, and the beekeeper eventually agreed. He added, "Darlene's gonna want to come."

"Let me handle your wife," Marge said. "You just handle the bees . . . and the identification of the bodies, Byron."

"The bodies first," Decker said. "I hate to do this to you, Byron, but . . . well, to put it bluntly, I don't want any further decomposition." Decker got out of the car, grasped Byron's shoulder, and gently led him in the direction of the house. "I know this is hard for you, but you can do it."

Byron wiped a thin sheen of perspiration off his nude scalp with his shirtsleeve. He coughed up a phlegm ball and spat. Great, Decker thought. Something else to confuse

Forensics. He'd remember to point it out to the lab boys later.

The beekeeper's steps toward the house were tentative, his breath sour and shallow. Decker felt sorry for him—he was shaking—but also reserved judgment on his guilt or innocence. He'd seen too many murderers crying bitterly at the sight of their victims floating in blood.

Once inside the Darcys' kitchen, Byron broke down—dry sobs coughed up from his chest, guttural groans emanating from his throat.

"It's . . . it's Linda Darcy, over there," Byron said. He pointed to the middle of the room, his lower lip trembling now. "Other one's . . . Dear God . . . other woman's Carla Darcy . . . the man on the Frigidaire is Luke . . . dear Jesus, have mercy on their souls."

"How about the other man?" Decker said softly.

"Huh?"

Byron seemed dazed. Decker spoke quickly. "The other man, Mr. Howard, in the pile with the women. Do you know him?"

Byron shook his head, his skin as gray as gunmetal. The Linda mantra tape was playing again, speaking her name as if he were in prayer. His eyes had begun to roll backward. Before the beekeeper went under, Decker escorted him outside and handed him to Marge, waiting by the unmarked. Byron allowed himself to be transferred as if he were a baby swaddled in bunting.

Decker pulled Marge aside and ID'd the bodies for her, explaining that there was still one unaccountable John Doe. Marge listened, then asked if Decker thought bee smoke would muck up evidence.

"I hadn't thought about that," Decker said. "You take Byron back to his farm, I'll ask the techs. Cameraman and the meat wagon should be here soon. Like to debug the bodies before we cart them down to the morgue."

"Be back in about a half hour," Marge said. She slid into the driver's seat of the unmarked, and was off.

Decker took the time to sort out the mess. Part of the Darcy family—Luke, his wife, Linda, and his sister, Carla—lay dead in the kitchen. Decker was curious about the part of the family that was missing. A set of parents, a sister named Sue Beth, and her husband and kids. Then there was the retarded brother named Earl.

According to Annette Howard, they were at a bee convention in Fall Springs. First thing to do was notify kinfolk and find out everyone's exact whereabouts for the last week.

Then, he thought, at least Katie has relatives.

Katie. The kid wasn't wandering around the Manfred development when all this went down. She was probably in the house, and someone couldn't stand the thought of her rotting with the others. Someone deliberately dropped her off at the Manfred development, hoping that she'd be found and cared for.

So what did that mean?

Decker tapped his pencil against the tablet, put aside his speculations for now. He began combing the outside area for evidence. In the front, he found dried spots of brown gook. Could be blood, could be anything. He swung around back. The rear side of the house faced a two-story redwood barn, weathered dusty gray. Next to the barn was a hundred feet worth of fenced corral, stacked bales of hay, and a 40' × 40' lot of yellowed weeds stained by oil and crushed by tire prints. Probably where the Darcys parked their cars. But it never hurt to have too much physical evidence. He'd point it out to Sheriff's Homicide, request a tire imprint and lab work on the oil.

Automatically, Decker pulled out a handkerchief, placed it over the knob, and tried the barn door. Locked, but at least no odor seemed to be coming from the threshold. He peeked through the window. Dark, the sun doing little to illuminate the interior, but Decker made out an empty cordoned-off area to the left, that portion of the ground covered with hay. The rest of the floor space was taken up with machinery—big metal cylinders, other pieces of brushed steel and chromium he couldn't identify.

He saw Tommy Chin come around back.

Chin said, "Arnie real mad about bees."

"Take a break," Decker said. "It shouldn't be much longer. I'm trying to get someone over here to get rid of the bugs. We're going to try to smoke them out. Will that ruin forensic evidence?"

Thinking a moment, Tommy rubbed his eye with his shoulder—his hands were gloved—then answered that the smoke might mix with some of the body gases, but the bees had to go. No one could work with thousands of things buzzing around. Arnie had already got stung on his hand right through the plastic glove. He was ready to claim disability. Decker asked him if Arnie was still inside.

"Arnie, he's a trouper," Tommy said. "We do as much as we can before you smoke the bugs. Scrapings, tissue samples, fluid samples . . . anything that might be affected by smoke. With the insects, I collect some maggots and put them in KAAD. I collect a few bees, ants, and beetles, too. And live bugs for control. Then that's all the bugs I need. You get rid of the rest, so we can work without getting stung."

Decker nodded. "Seen Detective Crandal around?"

Tommy said, "He was in the house, now he out of the house. Think now he's in the car."

Super, Decker thought. Just what he needed. A goldbrick on his team. He forced himself to jog over to Crandal's car. The old man was sitting in the driver's seat, windows rolled up, motor running. No doubt he had the air-conditioning on full blast. Decker knocked on the driver's window, the motor died, and Crandal came out of his cocoon.

"Just taking a break," Crandal explained.

Sure, Decker thought. He said, "Look, if we're going to be doing something joint, maybe we should talk about a division of labor?"

Crandal didn't answer.

Decker said, "I'll do the mop-up over here. I'll also handle all the background checks on the victims. We've still got one unidentified body. How about you going down to Fall Springs to notify and interview the surviving family? It would sure take a load off of my shoulders."

"Heaven forbid your shoulders should get too heavy," Crandal answered.

"Look, this isn't even my jurisdiction," Decker said. "It certainly ain't my idea of a good time. But I found the kid, I'd like to see this through, and it's what I'm paid to do." He calmed his nerves. "I'll tell Forensics to forward us both copies of what they found. You send me your notes, I'll send you mine."

Crandal sighed, then nodded agreement.

"I'll finish up on the outside," Decker said. "You do a grid search on the living room, I'll do the kitchen."

Crandal gave him an unhappy look, but went inside the house. The sheriff didn't seem too hepped up on working, but Decker went easy with the critical judgment. If it hadn't been for Katie, Decker would have passed on this one— would have been easy since he was in Sex Crimes, not Homicide, and had a truckload of back cases already crowding his desk. But for some reason, he felt obligated to the little girl. Change a diaper, the kid owns you for life, he laughed to himself. Ah, the hell with it, the kid deserved closure on her parents, facts she could tell the inevitable shrink when she was older. And Decker had done a six-year stint with Homicide way back when. It wasn't as though stiffs were foreign to him.

The sound of straining engines filled the static air.

Cars—Byron in a wood-sided Ford pickup, Marge in the unmarked. Inside the Ford's bed were three shopping bags, a 3′ × 3′ portable smoker leaking charcoal fumes, and over a dozen pine boxes. Decker instructed Marge to help Crandal out with the grid in the living room, and he'd help Byron unload the truck. The smoker was heavy and hot, Decker almost burned his arms. The bags were filled with protective garb and three steel bellows.

Decker said to Byron, "I noticed a bunch of machinery in the barn. What's all the stuff in there?"

Byron held up his hand and ticked off his fingers. "Extractors, drums, dry-heat cabinets, strainers—" He stopped himself. "Machinery for processing honey."

"Processing the honey *here*?"

"Yes, sir, we can do it all." Byron lifted a pine box from the bed. "Shame to let all them bees inside go to waste. Might as well hive them. I'll give them back to the Darcys, if they want 'em when they come back."

He looked at Decker, his skin shaded pea green. "They don't know, do they?"

"I haven't told them," Decker said. He asked Byron to give the directions on how to suit up. It took Byron a moment to regain his color, to find his voice. Finally, he explained the procedure and told Decker not to make any sudden moves. Bees get nervous, same as people, he lectured.

Wide-brimmed hat, long steel veil, thick gloves, rubber boots, Decker was drenched in sweat before he took a step. Looking through the wire mesh, he felt as if he were in jail.

Byron took the lead, Decker followed. Inside, Arnie was scraping blood off the living-room floor. Marge was scribbling in her notepad, Ozzie Crandal was examining a footprint on the floor.

"Did anyone order an impression of this?" he asked.

Decker said, "Not yet."

"Then I'll order an impression of it," Crandal said.

"Good idea," said Marge. She'd almost managed to keep the acerbic edge out of her voice, but Ozzie picked it up.

He added, "Someone was walking out of the scene, not in. The toe directed to the front."

Marge said, "How come there's only one print?"

Crandal seemed stumped. Decker said, "There's a bunch of prints in the kitchen. Maybe someone realized he was tracking blood into the living room and took his shoes off."

"That's the way I see it, too," Crandal added.

"Way I see it, too," Marge aped him.

Crandal said, "Look, lady—"

"Everyone cool it," Decker said. "I'm as hot as hell in this getup, and my patience is about to snap, too. So how about we all keep our mouths shut, okay?"

"Fine by me," Marge said, between clenched teeth.

Crandal muttered something, then went back to work.

Decker knew Crandal had done a lulu to unglue Marge, but now was not the time to ask her about it. Instead, he steered Byron toward the kitchen. Dressed in his work garb, doing what he knew best, Byron was no longer the broken-up man Decker had witnessed a half hour ago. He was the consummate professional, blowing soft puffs of smoke on sections of bees, then gently pushing them into his pine boxes with gloved hands. He worked slowly, and it took around an hour and a half, Decker constantly reminding him to watch his hands and feet so as not to mess up evidence. When Byron was done, almost all the bees and wasps were boxed, the corpses for the most part denuded of the winged creatures. Marge was right. With the bees gone, Decker could see the heinousness of the crime in all its glory—yards of bloodless entrails, open shotgun blasts in the abdominal and thoracic regions, half a heart dangling out of one of the women's chests. The faces had become blackened with exposure, maggots crawling out of noses and eye sockets.

Decker felt his head go light, and looked down for a moment. By the time he felt his breath coming back, Byron had left. Decker thought about running after him, questioning him on the spot, but squelched the notion. Unless he was prepared to grill him hard, use all the authoritative muscle he had, Byron would keep quiet. It seemed more logical to pry information from the loquacious women of the Howard household or catch the beekeeper when he was off-guard.

Decker kept on the hat, but removed the veil and thick gloves and stuffed them in his shoulder harness. He slipped on a pair of thin surgical gloves, then began the arduous search for evidence, scanning the dead for shotgun wadding, spent shells, evidence from any other weapons that might have been used. He pulled out evidence bags and slipped them over the corpses' hands—those that still had intact digits. He felt his insides kicking up, anger brewing and boiling deep within him. But his overwhelming emotion was sadness.

Poor, poor Katie.

14

At the top of the hill, just as the unmarked was about to descend into LAPD territory, Decker turned to Marge and said, "Are you going to tell me about Crandal, or are you still too pissed off to talk?"

Marge gripped the wheel, stared out the windshield, the late afternoon sun still a hot spot in the asphalt. The tar seemed to bake before her eyes, the mountains flanking the road quivering in the heat. A depressing fact since once the car hit bottom, the temperature would rise ten degrees. She'd turned off the air-conditioning twenty minutes ago; the car had begun to overheat as they had climbed out of Sagebrush Canyon. Hot wind blew across her face. Marge sighed, wished she'd called in sick this morning.

She said, "He addressed me as 'little lady.'"

"And that set you off?" Decker asked.

"I'm not little, Pete."

"And you certainly ain't no lady."

Marge laughed hollowly.

"Well, bless my soul," Decker said. "A seasoned detective like yourself. This one really got to you."

Marge didn't answer. A moment later, she said, "You know what pisses me off about cop films?"

"What?"

"Those cutesey ones where there's all this calm, witty banter around stiffs. Know which ones I'm talking about?"

Decker nodded. Marge threw the car out of low gear as the hillside inclines began to level. The overgrown canary shrubbery had thinned out, replaced by fields of crabgrass and dandelion weeds. Houses could be seen about five hundred yards up.

"Crandal was doing that," she said. "Making jokes. I didn't like it."

"Not that I'm sticking up for the guy, Marge, but he might have been doing that as a defense."

"Yeah," Marge said. "I know. And maybe I am acting a little weepy. But seeing it that close, that putrid. I don't know, I'm not used to working Homicide, and I didn't care for Crandal's attitude."

"Understandable," Decker said.

"So how'd you manage to live with corpses in your dreams for six years?"

"I thought I was managing just fine until Jan asked me for a divorce."

Marge laughed, genuinely this time. "So let me ask you this, Mr. Experienced Homicide Dick, what do you think? A family thing, or a burglary that went afoul?"

Decker didn't answer right away. Then he said, "I'll tell you what I don't think. I don't think it was a psycho case— another Manson gang hacking up the family and loving every minute of it. No smeared blood, no satanic signs. The homicides, as horrible as they were, seemed like an impulsive thing. Three in one pile, probably murdered where they stood. Luke pushed up against the fridge. Know what impressed me?"

"What?"

"All that spilt milk, the scattered bottles. Someone actually seemed to take time out to prepare bottles for Katie. Someone was planning on taking her, then changed his or her mind."

"Or maybe someone interrupted Linda when she was making bottles."

"Linda was trying to split with Katie and someone stopped her?" Decker asked.

"Just throwing out a thought," Marge said.

"Lots of possibilities with a family affair," Decker said. "Someone plugged them all, then impulsively decided to rescue Katie. *Or* someone saw what had happened, rescued the kid, and dropped her off at Manfred, not wanting to call the police. Family protecting one another."

"Or Byron Howard," Marge said. "I bet he'd be as protective as family. He doesn't cotton to strangers."

"Yeah," Decker said. "Think he was faking his reaction?"

"I think the reaction was real," Marge said. "But that doesn't mean anything. He could have done it in a fit of madness, then been truly shocked when he saw what he had actually done."

Decker nodded.

Marge passed six blocks of tract homes, then turned right onto Foothill Boulevard, back to civilization—fast-food stands, wholesale outlets, and shoddily built apartment housing, the plaster already cracking in the hot sun. Two blocks later, she hooked a right onto the 210 Freeway west, the traffic thick with rush-hour mob. They sat in silence, battling the stop-and-go rhythm for a quarter hour. As soon as traffic eased a bit, Marge asked, "What about Darlene as a suspect?"

"She certainly hated Linda."

"And if she did it," Marge said, "Byron would definitely be protective of her. Maybe even feel he caused Linda's murder indirectly because of his affair."

"The logic is there," said Decker. "The jealous-wife angle. But can you picture Darlene using a shotgun?"

"I've seen stranger things," Marge said.

So had Decker. He said, "Know what occurred to me a minute ago?"

"What?"

"Luke might have killed the others, then turned the gun on himself."

"No weapon was found at the scene, Pete. And we've got all these different bloody footprints in the kitchen. If everyone was dead, who made the footprints?"

"I don't know. Maybe somebody walked into the kitchen after the fact, and took the gun and Katie away."

"More than one person to justify all those footprints."

"Some of the footprints are bound to match some of the victims," Decker said. "Someone might have stepped in blood before he or she was gunned down."

Marge said, "Okay. So let's examine your theory. Luke killed the others, then himself. I could understand Luke being homicidal with Linda after hearing about her reputation. But why would Luke whack his sister and that other dude?"

"I don't know. I'm just thinking of the layout—Luke's on one side, the others huddled together in the middle. I see this big finger just pointing at Luke."

"What about the Kleenex fibers found on Katie?" Marge said. "Kid didn't wipe her own PJs."

"Obviously, someone took her away," Decker said. "Someone dumped her over the hill. The kid couldn't have walked it by herself."

"Pete," Marge said, "I just thought of something. The kid may have witnessed the whole thing."

"Think so?" Decker said. "She didn't seem traumatized. I'd have thought she might be, after seeing her mother and father murdered like that."

"Even so," Marge said, "don't you think we should consult someone?"

"Sure," Decker said. "Call up a local kiddy shrink. See what words of wisdom he has to impart to us."

"You don't like shrinks, do you?" Marge said.

"Fifth on that one," Decker said.

They rode for a minute in silence. Marge broke it.

"Our second-guessing isn't worth too much without all the evidence. Once Ozzie Crandal notifies the family, one of them will no doubt come by for Katie tomorrow. Prelim forensics will have come back by then, also. Crandal will interview the immediate family down there. By this time tomorrow, we should know a lot more than we know now."

"Good point, Detective," Decker said. "So the upshot is, I'm going to go home and try to forget about it until then."

"Let me know how successful you are."

Decker didn't answer. Instead, he thought of Rina. If anyone could temporarily obscure today's ugliness, it would be her.

He smelled the coals burning before he killed the Plymouth's motor.

Shit.

Rina was barbecuing.

Even though he was starved, the thought of red meat—*rare* red meat—made his stomach churn. All he wanted for dinner was a couple of bowls of cereal. Anything that didn't *bleed*. But he had to be nice, excited, enthusiastic that she'd taken the initiative to be domestic.

He parked the car in the driveway, got out, and shouted a hullo as he walked toward the back.

Rina turned around, her hair pinned up, covered by a kerchief, her face sooty from smoke residue. She looked so earthy, so *good*, he forgot about his growling stomach.

"I didn't know if your grill was *pareve* or *fleishig*, so I bought trout. You like trout, don't you?"

Fish, Decker thought. God bless her, barbecued trout didn't sound half bad.

"Trout is perfect." He walked over, gave her a short kiss on the lips, and regarded his supper. Five fillets. The fish had been butterflied, the heads removed. Sharing the grill with the fish were two potatoes, the skins baked crackling crisp. The smell activated his salivary glands. "It's too hot to eat meat anyway."

"That's what I figured."

She'd covered his slab redwood table with a white paper tablecloth, had set red-checkered paper dinnerware, matching napkins and cups, and plastic cutlery upon the cloth. Gracing the tabletop were a pint of coleslaw, a pint of macaroni salad, a basket of French rolls, and a platter of green grapes mixed with cut canteloupe and watermelon. In a bowl of melting ice were cans of diet cola for her, brown bottles of Dos Equis for him.

"I've died and gone to heaven," he said.

Rina smiled. "Doesn't take much to make you happy."

"You make me happy," he said. "I really needed this."

"You certainly couldn't have timed it better. It'll be ready in about two minutes. Take a shower, Peter, and put on something cooler. You can't be comfortable in those clothes."

He looked at his wilted brown suit and agreed. He showered quickly, then changed into a polo shirt and a pair of jeans. He would have preferred wearing a T-shirt and shorts, but he knew Rina wasn't wild about him wearing such informal clothing to a meal. A small sacrifice to make for a waiting meal and a willing woman. He pinned a yarmulke onto his hair and patted his stomach. His juices were flowing now, so much so that he almost managed to push aside the wretchedness of the day.

By the time he was outside, Rina was putting the trout on a serving plate.

"You can wash if you want," she said.

"I'll wait for you."

Rina put the trout on the table and wiped her hands on a napkin. "Okay."

They ritually washed their hands outside from a bucket of water that Rina had set up, then broke bread. Rina heaped three trout and mounds of salad and fruit on

Decker's paper plate as he sat there, a stupid grin on his face, thinking, I could get used to this. She poured him a beer, then served herself a half-piece of trout, half a baked potato, and fruit.

"Now I remember how you stay so thin," Decker remarked. He noticed his voice had a slight lecherous tone. He gobbled down his first trout in three bites, and went to work on number two. "But I'm not complaining," he continued. "More food for me. Although I wouldn't mind if you'd fatten up a bit."

"You think I'm too thin?" She opened up a can of soda.

"When I met you, you seemed a little more curvacious."

"I was ten pounds heavier."

"I didn't mind," Decker said. There it was. That same horny tone. He finished off half of his baked potato.

Rina smiled and speared a piece of watermelon. "Should I ask about your day?"

Decker shook his head.

Rina said, "Can I just ask if you found that little girl's parents?"

Decker winced. "Yeah, we found them all right."

His voice had tightened. Rina said, "Erase the tape. Forget I asked."

Decker took a swig of beer and asked, "You visit your parents?"

"Erase that tape, too," Rina said.

"So much for conversation," Decker said, laughing.

"Well, I've got something interesting to tell you," Rina said.

"What's that?"

"I met an old friend of yours, today."

"A friend of *mine*?"

"Abel Atwater," Rina said.

Decker's fork froze midair. He tried to keep his voice casual. "Really?"

"Yep, as you might say," Rina said.

"How'd you meet him?" Decker asked. He lowered his fork.

"He was working in your barn, fixing the flooring, I think. He said he was in the army with you. I didn't know you were in the army."

Decker didn't answer right away, rolled his tongue inside his cheeks. Then he said, "And how long did you talk to him?"

Rina stared at him quizzically. His eyes had gone hard. At first, Rina thought she detected jealousy, but a second later she decided it wasn't that at all. "Gee, I don't know . . . five, ten minutes. Is something wrong?"

"Well," Decker laughed, "I don't know. I just think it's kind of strange that you'd carry on a conversation with a man you've never seen before, given your previous experiences with men."

Rina was shocked into silence. Decker went on.

"I mean, really, honey, this guy could have been *anyone*."

"He mentioned your name before I did. . . ."

"So he knew my name. I'm a cop. Thousands of jackasses out there know my name, and any one of them could have had a personal reason for being here, and I don't know how in hell you talked to this guy—"

"Peter, I—"

"What you *should* have done the minute you saw some unknown jerk in the barn was rush into the house, lock the door, and call me. What the hell were you thinking when you talked to this dude? Rina, I have put a lot of *bad* men behind bars. Now, it's unlikely that one of them could have turned up for the big get-even, but it's a possibility. So unless you know who's who, you don't go around being Miss Congeniality."

"Peter—"

"I mean, let's face facts, honey. Your former friend-turned-rapist, your asshole brother-in-law, you seemed to have a knack for attracting weirdos."

Rina took her napkin off her lap and threw it down on her plate. "Doesn't say much for you, does it?"

She stormed into the house.

Decker sat there for a minute, calming down. It took him around a minute to realize that *he* had completely blown it. He heard Marge's voice: *So how do you manage . . .*

He rubbed his face, took another bite of trout, then stood up and headed for the house. He found her in his bedroom, sitting on his red-quilted bedcover, arms folded across her chest. She'd made the bed, polished his bedroom furniture—as if it were worth polishing. Just some knotty pine he'd slapped together for a dresser and a couple of nightstands. But she had told him how impressed she was, how talented he was. The afternoon sun was pouring through the window, casting a white spotlight upon the dresser. She'd polished the wood with care, rubbed it until it gleamed. He sat down beside her, his stomach in a knot.

"Sorry," he said.

She stood up and began to pace. She thought about what had happened to her, about a man she had thought was a friend who had tried to rape her. The horrible nights that had followed, how Peter had been there for her. His calming words, reassuring voice. Then, in a heated moment, he had unraveled her confidence like a run in a stocking.

"I don't believe you said those things," Rina choked out. "You spent almost an entire year convincing me that . . . that . . . that *incident* was not my fault, that it could have happened to anyone, that I did nothing to encourage you-know-who, nothing to lead him on . . . that the guy was a mental case. Now, you say I have a knack for attracting weirdos."

"I didn't say that."

"Yes, you did."

"Well, I didn't mean that."

"Then what did you mean?"

Decker thought a moment. His head had begun to throb.

"I meant you'd attract any man, weird or not, because you're so beautiful, and you shouldn't be talking to someone you don't know."

Rina paused, then asked, "Was Abel who he said he was?"

"Yes, but you didn't know that."

"Except I knew he knew you. He showed me pictures of the two of you together. You can't fake that."

"What kind of pictures?"

"Army photos. He let me keep this one." She fished it out of her pocket and handed it to him. "I told him I'd make a copy and give the original back to him."

Decker stared at the picture for a long time, his face as still as stone. Little Petie Decker, a dumb-ass grin plastered on his face, smiling as if he were about to go to a birthday party. Ready for *action*, ready for the *Big Times*. God, what a jerk he'd been. And to think he had enlisted, his dad had been so proud of him. . . . And Abel, looking just as stupid and a hell of a lot healthier. Decker wondered why he'd keep such a morbid reminder of a time gone forever.

Abruptly, he tossed the photo onto the bed.

"For all I care, you can burn it. I don't like living in the past."

He sat down and buried his face in his hands. A full-blown headache had seeped into his temples. Rina sat beside him, pocketed the picture, then slipped her arm around his shoulder.

"Now, we're both upset."

Decker was silent.

"Bad memories?" Rina whispered.

"Not as bad as Abel's," Decker said.

"Is he weird?"

Decker thought for a long time. What would be the point of telling her that she'd made chitchat with a possible rapist, making her feel even dumber than she probably felt already? She'd probably never see Abel again. Probably one of those flukey things. He just happened to show up, forgetting Decker's request to stay away. Abel was like that. Things went through him, although he could have a memory like an elephant when he wanted to. Decker would call him up tomorrow and remind him to get lost—again.

Finally, he said, "He's just one of those unfortunate vets who never made the adjustment back to civilian life." Decker wondered if *he'd* ever made the adjustment as well. After all, in police language there were two classes of people—cops and civilians. He looked at Rina and said, "I'm not comfortable with him, or any guy, hanging around you when I'm not around."

"Peter," Rina said, "you didn't give me a chance to explain. I wasn't as stupid as you thought—"

"I don't think you're stupid," Decker said. "Rina, I just love you so damn much, I get scared at the thought of anything happening to you."

"I'm still nervous myself, Peter. You don't have to convince me to be careful." She stopped speaking a moment, then said, "I had my gun with me."

Decker stared at her for a moment. "What?"

"My Colt thirty-eight Detective's Special. I've continued to take lessons in New York."

"It's against the law to carry a concealed weapon without a permit."

Rina's eyes widened. "So *arrest* me."

"You brought your *gun* with you from New York?"

"In my packed luggage."

"Why?"

"To *protect* myself. You speak as though it's an affront to your masculinity."

"Rina—"

"I'm just as scared about myself as you are. I thought you were in the barn, and when it wasn't you, I immediately reached in my purse and pulled a gun on this Abel Atwater.

And let me tell you something. It made me feel a lot more secure than running into the house and locking the door."

Decker lowered his head. Too much input in one day. He said, "I didn't know you were taking shooting lessons in New York."

"I didn't tell you because I knew you'd be upset. I know how you feel about guns, but frankly, I'm going to carry one. So why don't you be supportive of me and finally get me that carry permit I asked you for about a year ago?"

"It's not that simple."

"Oh, come on! You could pull strings if you wanted to."

"Honestly, Rina," Decker said, "I can't do it. Anyway, why do you need to be armed with me around?"

Rina said, "Witness this afternoon: You're not always around. And knowing your past schedule, you're not around a whole lot, period. But I'm not complaining. I don't mind being alone, I've been on my own for over three years now. Peter, I've got the boys to think about. I'm going to carry a gun whether I've got the permit or not, and you're not going to convince me otherwise."

"I can't get you a carry permit," Decker insisted. "I think the last civilian one was issued to Sammy Davis, Jr., back in the sixties."

"So I'll break the law," Rina said. "I can live with that."

Great, he thought. He couldn't control his own woman; how could he presume to control felons? Just drop the point. Pick it up on a better day. They sat in silence. Decker decided to ask, "So what did you and Abel talk about?"

"We agreed you were tight-lipped."

Decker said nothing.

"Like you're being right now," Rina said. "Peter, why didn't you ever tell me you were in the army?"

"I didn't consciously make a decision not to tell you, Rina. You never asked and I don't like to talk about it."

"Abel said you were a medic."

"Yes," Decker said. "What else do you want to know?"

Rina paused a moment, realizing how cruel it was to make him relive something so ugly just to satisfy her curiosity. She smiled and said, "Good. You can teach me CPR."

Decker picked his head up, his lips turning upward into a grin. "We can start right now, if you want."

Rina blushed. "What about the trout?"

"It's probably cold by now." Decker kicked off his shoes and said, "You shouldn't do CPR with your shoes on."

Rina said, "I never heard that one."

"Oh, it's true." He took off her kerchief and unpinned her hair. A sheet of black silk rippled down her back. "And it's very bad to do CPR with pins in your hair. Might fall into the victim's mouth."

"All sorts of little things to remember."

Decker fingered the kerchief and said, "I see you're covering your hair again."

"I'm feeling a little more religious."

Decker smiled. "That's good."

She smiled back. "I thought you didn't like me so religious."

"Rina, I love you just the way you are."

Rina felt her throat suddenly constrict. She touched his cheek, then looped her hand around his neck and lowered his mouth onto hers. He eased her into a supine position while kissing her, drinking her in.

"This isn't CPR," Decker said, a moment later.

Rina said, "I know."

🐿15

Decker walked into the squad room at 9:00 A.M., his phone ringing as soon as he crossed the threshold. He jogged over to his desk and, still standing, picked the receiver up. Marge was on the other end.

"Got a pencil?"

"Hold on, I just got in." He kicked his chair out and took a pen from his shirt pocket. "Let me find something to write on. Where are you?"

"Morgue. Been here for a while."

"Great way to start the day."

"At least no one here gives me lip."

Decker fished through his desk drawer and pulled out his notepad. Pen poised, he said, "Shoot."

"Prelim forensics," Marge said. "Rigor was gone, M.E. said the bodies were at least forty-eight hours old. That clicks with the maggot development. Entomologist found maggots in varying degrees of development—oldest eggs having been laid around two—three days ago. Mostly housefly, blowfly, and blue-bottle maggots, the latter two most common among bodies left outdoors. But the windows were left open, so those kind of flies had ready access to the bodies."

"Okay," Decker said. He was scribbling as fast as he could. "Got it."

Marge continued. "I spoke to Crandal this morning—woke the son of a bitch up at six in the morn—and he informed me that the Western Beekeepers Association Twentieth Annual Convention started three days ago, the Darcys showing up on the first day."

"How many people went down there?"

"Uh, I asked, I have to find it in my notes . . . here it is. Two hundred thirty-six registered, believe it or not. It's the big hoo-ha for professional and amateur apiarists."

Decker thought out loud to Marge. According to the time frame, the murders could have taken place before the convention started, or one of the family members could have driven back from Fall Springs, done the murders, and then returned before they were missed. None of the family really had an ironclad alibi.

"You're right about that," Marge said. "Anyway, family's been notified. Prelim interview, Crandal says nothing to write home about, everyone's shell-shocked. I just got off the phone with the sister who lives here—Sue Beth Litton—who was only semicoherent at best. The whole crew's staying down south until Sue Beth can—this I quote—'get this mess straightened up.' Fall Springs SD has them under watch."

"Sue Beth sound choked up?"

"Actually, she did," Marge said. "Stunned. First thing she asked about was Katie. Crandal must have told her that the kid was alive. Sue Beth seemed very anxious to get her out of the foster home. She said she could make it back up here around four, take the burden off her parents' shoulders. I told her I'd take her to Katie, but first she'd have to stop by here and formally identify the bodies. She was really upset about that, but agreed. I just looked at the corpses an hour ago. You can distinguish features, but they're in terrible condition due to all the bloat. I hope she doesn't freak out."

"You can handle it," Decker said.

"Thanks," Marge said. But her voice sounded unsure.

"You want to meet up at Sophi's, or is that going to be too late for your Sabbath?"

"No, four is fine." Decker thought, Thank the Lord for long summer days. Allowed you to finish all your paperwork before the Sabbath started. "I'll even do all the paperwork for Katie's release. But I want to talk to this Sue Beth before we give her the kid." He leaned back in his desk chair. "Anyone show the Darcys Polaroids of John Doe?"

"Believe it or not, Crandal had the good sense to take some pics of him and show them around. At this point in time, the family-by-blood was too hysterical to be of any help, and to be honest, John Doe's face is pretty bad. I spoke to Sue Beth's husband—Robert, whom they call Bobby Boy, or just B.B."

"Old B.B."

Marge said, "Well, B.B. said he might have seen our John Doe, but it was hard to tell since he looked like—I quote again—'a nigger, and I don't know no niggers.'"

"Did you explain to him that he was white, and death caused the skin to blacken?"

"Pete, we are not dealing with people loaded down with gray matter. I told him the man was white, he hesitated a moment, then said he might have looked like the kind of guy Carla might have gone out with. But according to B.B., Carla went out with a ton of guys—I quote once again—'niggers and other kinds and I have a real hard time keeping all the names straight.'"

"Seems Carla and Linda both liked men an awful lot."

"My thoughts exactly," Marge said. She excused herself for a sneeze, then came back on the phone. "The upshot is we still don't have an ID for John Doe. No one found any ID at the crime scene, that's for sure. His prints showed up negative at the local level; we're still waiting to hear from Sacramento to see if his fingers have been rolled at either the state or national level."

Decker paused a moment. "You recall what Mr. Doe was wearing?"

"All I can remember is a pile of rotten meat."

Decker pulled out his Investigate Checklist from the Darcy folder in his file drawer. Under clothing, he'd written for John Doe: *jeans—black or blue denim, black boots. Upper body's obscured by gun blast. Examine after all lab evidence has been collected.* He read it to Marge, then said, "Call the lab and see if JD had any upper-body clothes or if he was bare-chested. Also, ask the lab if they found anything identifiable on his pants or boots—a logo or brand name. The M.E. must have cleaned him up by now—gotten all the blood and gook off. Ask him if our man had any scars, birthmarks, tattoos—something."

"You've got it." Marge took a deep breath. "Now are you ready for the *Big News*?"

"There's more?"

"Oh man, you're gonna love this," Marge said. "All of them were full of pellets, no surprise. Wadding found was consistent with a twelve-gauger . . . which means that the sucker was pumped from ten feet or less. But listen to this! After Luke was cleansed of blood and maggots, Path laid him on the table yesterday evening and noticed these bullet holes in what was left of his head and neck."

Decker sat up in his chair. "Go on."

"The man's interest is piqued," Marge said. "I went back to the scene early this morning and found three thirty-eight bullets plugged into the fridge—"

"Why didn't you call me?"

"You were with your honey, Pete. I didn't think you'd appreciate the interruption."

She was right. Decker thanked her, and Marge continued.

"Luke's body and blood were blocking the fridge, so we missed them first time out. I scoured the place, but couldn't find bullet number six."

"Maybe there were only five in the chamber. Or we just

missed it. Whichever the case is, someone was angry and emptied the gun in him."

Marge said, "Unfortunately for us, we don't have the shotgun *or* the thirty-eight. Two weapons used, both of them gone."

"I'll call up gun registration," Decker said. "See if a thirty-eight was registered to anyone in the family."

Of course, he knew damn well how easy it was to obtain an unregistered handgun. Shotguns were even easier to buy, not even requiring a handgun's fifteen-day background check on the purchase. Legal gun purchases in California had increased by the millions. So what did that say about the illegal purchases? His mind focused on Rina. Last time he'd been to the range with her had been six months ago, when she'd come out on her first visit to L.A. since moving to New York. He'd even remarked on what a good shot she'd been considering she hadn't used a gun in six months. But now he knew she'd been taking lessons. And Rina had said nothing at the time. That disturbed him.

Decker said, "What was the make on the revolver?"

"Smith and Wesson," Marge said. "I had Path check the hands and clothes for residue, try to give us an angle on who fired the handgun. Nothing. Hands were just too fucked up from the shotgun blasts. Now, the big question. What is going on here?"

"A lot of things come to mind."

Marge said, "How about, Luke was the intended hit. The others were incidental, came in at the wrong time. Then someone got the brilliant idea of killing them all with a shotgun to make it seem like they were all murdered for the same purpose."

"No bullet holes were found on the others?"

"None," Marge said. "Then again, the shotgun blasts may have obscured the bullet holes. We're talking hamburger . . . bad, Pete. I feel really bad for Katie. That poor little girl."

"Yeah," Decker said softly. He allowed himself to think

about it for a moment, then snapped himself out of it. "My murder-suicide theory has just been shot to hell, no pun intended. Luke couldn't have blown off his legs and his head at the same time."

"This is true."

"This case is not going to be straightforward," Decker said. "Find out about the John Doe's clothing and marks ASAP, Margie."

"Right away."

Decker cut the line and walked over to the coffee machine. His mug was oversized, held sixteen ounces, and he filled it to the rim with the black mud that layered the bottom of the pot.

Two weapons, both of them gone.

Two murderers?

He sipped his coffee. Bitter as castor oil.

Mike Hollander lumbered into the squad room, joined Decker at the coffeepot with his C-cup boob mug. Today, Hollander wore black pants, white short-sleeved shirt, and a red paisley clip-on tie that stopped an inch above his navel.

He said, "You get a hickey from Rina?"

Decker said, "What are you talking about?"

"You got a big red bump right above your shirt collar. Keeeenkeeeee."

Decker's hand went to the nape of his neck. "That's a bee sting, Mike."

"Oh." Mike poured the last of the coffee into his cup. "I heard about that one. Listen, if you want to work on that shit, I can help you on your back cases. My own load's not too bad."

Decker thought about the offer. On the active file today: one morning court appearance at ten—testifying on a sexual assault, that one should be cut-and-dried because of all the physical evidence. Another court appearance at three, the rape survivor due to testify. He'd have to be there for that one. She was fragile and needed all the support she could get. At four, he'd have to meet Marge at Sophi's, talk to Sue Beth Litton.

"Thanks, but I'd better keep the ones I have," Decker said to Hollander. "I don't want any of the victims to think I'm abandoning them. If you could field my new calls, that would help."

Hollander said no problem and slurped coffee from his boob mug. Decker carried his java back to his desk and began Katie Darcy's paperwork. Stuffing a quadruplicate release form into his typewriter, he pecked away at the keyboard until he was interrupted by his phone. Marge again.

"John Doe's clothes," she said. "Or what was left of them. Half of a red bandanna—we probably didn't notice it because it mixed so nicely with the blood. Shreds of a leather vest, Levi 501 jeans. His boots were made by Wellington—heels coated with blood and grease. But get this. One arm was blown away, the other arm, once they got the blood off, had a tattoo—a babe wearing nothing but a helmet. J.D.'s ass was inked with the name Gretchen. Betcha anything John Doe owned a motorcycle."

"Any riding-club insignia anywhere?"

"Unfortunately, no," Marge said.

"Christ, Marge, the guy had a driver's license. Why would someone take away his ID? We're eventually going to find out who he is."

"Curiouser and curiouser," Marge said. "Sounds to me like it's amateur time. Who knows? Maybe he's the key. Maybe he shot Luke, then someone else shot the others."

"Anything's possible," Decker said. "Margie, how'd you like to join me for lunch?"

"What do you have in mind, big guy?"

"I was thinking about pizza and a beer at Hell's Heaven."

"You bring the car, I'll bring the Polaroids—a real appetite enhancer." Marge paused, then said, "I don't know how readily the motorcycle boys will talk to us."

"Well, we've got one thing in our favor."

Marge said, "What's that?"

Decker said, "We're white."

Quarter to eleven in the morning, and the outside temperature had already passed the 95-degree mercury mark. Decker stared out the window at the grassy fields of clover and grain. No breeze today, just stagnant air. The Plymouth's air-conditioning had frizzed out, and was sucking up the outside heat and blowing it inside. Decker flipped off the knob and opened the window. Marge followed suit, floored the pedal, and sped through the canyon. When the biker joint came into view, she slowed suddenly, then turned into the gravel lot, the tires kicking up dust. Forty full-sized choppers occupied the lot, chrome bouncing off dazzling rays of sun. Marge parked next to a customized cherry-red Harley, its winged logo painted Day-Glo purple and orange. The license plate was stamped HOG CHOW. Automatically, Decker felt for his service revolver.

He raised his eyes to Marge. "The hogs meet the pigs."

Marge laughed, but her eyes were wary.

The patio was three-quarters occupied, a cloud of tobacco and marijuana smoke hanging in the air. Decker paused a moment before climbing the steps up to the eating area, took a quick head count. Around thirty fat-assed chopper riders outside, must be another dozen or so inside. All of them held that ex-con look in their eye. They cradled their beers as they nursed them, looked over their shoulders as they talked. Some of them seemed more wary than confrontive, but a few looked defiant, aching for a brawl.

To hell with that noise. He wasn't out to prove himself.

Ten scrawny women decorated as many laps, another half-dozen were fetching beer for their men. No pizza on any of the tables. Two busty waitresses, wearing black sleeveless tops and shorts, were clearing away empty bottles and mugs. Decker thought he might be best off approaching the waitresses first. He looked at Marge, then the two of them climbed the stairs. Immediately, the entrance was blocked by a three-hundred-pound gorilla. Most of him was fat, but even so, that was a hell of a lot of bulk to contend with. His face was covered by a rabbi-sized beard, his body stank of sweat and alcohol. He wore a denim vest, and jeans ripped at the knees.

"You need some help, *Officer*?" he asked. He was smiling, teeth as soft and brown as rotten apples.

"As a matter of fact, I do," Decker said.

"Well, you just tell me how I can be of service."

Decker stiffened as he spoke. Asshole's breath was vile.

Decker said, "You can start by getting out of my way."

"Why don'tchu walk 'round me?" the biker challenged.

Decker said, "Look, buddy, I'm not here to give you shit, but if you want shit, I can give you a truckload. So why don't you get out of my way and let me do my business?"

"You ain't here to sling no shit, why the hell are you here, big city-boy cop?"

Calmly, Decker said, "Move your ass, buddy."

The biker's smile slowly faded. His eyes hardened, and the fat-lipped mouth was about to speak when it was interrupted by a deep male voice.

"Pig, just what the hell you think you're doin'? Get the fuck away from them."

The man who spoke was big, around two-fifty, and all muscle. He seemed to be about thirty-five, 6'1", had brown eyes, a Fu Manchu mustache, and buck teeth that were accentuated by a receding chin. He wore a red cook's apron over his bare chest and leather chaps, his hair pulled back in a ponytail. At first Decker thought the pig epithet had referred to him, but a moment later the muscle man punched the fat man in the shoulder.

"Can't you see that this dude and dudette are law? They ain't here to roust us none. Law's not crazy enough to roust us with just two people—one of them only a woman. Sheeeet. Use your head, Pig."

"Why's he here then?" Pig said.

"Move your fat ass and I'll find out." The muscled biker gave Pig a shove. "Get out of their fucking way, man."

Pig spat, muttered obscenities, but stepped aside.

"This way," the muscle man said. "I'm Chip. I own the place. We'll talk inside, in the back. It's about the Darcy thing, ain't it?"

"Yes," Decker said.

"Who are you two?"

Marge briefly explained their business, their connection to the Darcy murders.

Chip seemed satisfied. He led them inside—a dimly lit tavern/poolhall. Six green-felted tables—two of them in use—rested on straw-covered floors. Three fly fans were working overtime, whirling smoky air from one corner of the room to the other. The bar was U-shaped, occupying the two side and back walls. A dozen bikers were parked around the bar top, big leathery hands gripping beer bottles and whiskey glasses, drumming offbeat rhythms to ZZ Top.

Decker and Marge followed Chip through a door at the end of the back bar, into the well-lit kitchen, which reeked of ripe cheese and garlic. Swirls of flour had dusted the countertops and coated the floor. A rectangular butcher-block table sat in the middle, filled with pizza pans, stacks of cheese, and bowls of tomato sauce and toppings. A runt of a kid was spooning sauce onto pizza dough, his body junkie-thin. Two middle-aged Hispanics were cleaning the pizza oven and cooktop. A walk-in cooler spanned the back wall.

Chip stopped, leaned against the table and screamed at the kid. Something about the pizza sauce. The kid lifted up his head and nodded, his eyes hooded by drooping lids.

"Shit-for-brains," Chip muttered. He motioned them back toward the cooler. "He wastes half the sauce, splattering it all over the place. Goddam, it's hard to get good people." He surveyed the kitchen, told one of the Hispanics in fluent Spanish to bring more beer out front, explaining that the pizza wasn't served until noon, but the booze was served as soon as the doors opened.

Chip wiped his face on his apron, then said to Decker, "Pig's right in a way. You shouldn't be coming in here without warning. Some of them out there don't like the police."

"I take it Pig has had some prior trouble with the law," Decker said.

"Man, I don't want to go into that. Let's just say the police make Pig jumpy."

Decker said, "Right now, I'm not interested in anyone's past. I'm only interested in the Darcys."

Chip eyed Marge, then said to Decker, "You two ever fool around . . . like ball on your lunch hour?"

Marge broke into laughter.

Chip said to Decker, "What's so funny? You a fag or something?"

Decker said, "Is this where we talk about the Darcys?"

Chip said, "Darcys! Sheeeet! Byron was around here yesterday, telling us what the fuck went down. Or his version. Old man's face was green, man. Fucking *green*. Never saw By like that. Like he *needed* a drink. Gave him a beer on the house. You guys want a beer?"

Marge said, "I'll pass."

Decker said, "What did Byron tell you?"

"What a mess it was. That Linda, Luke, and Carla was whacked."

"I heard Byron had a thing with Linda," Marge said.

"Byron?" Chip exclaimed. "With *Linda*? You're shittin' me!"

"That's what I heard," Decker said.

"Well, Byron was upset, I'll tell you that much," Chip

said. "Old man usually talks in one-word sentences. But yesterday, man, he let it all hang out."

"What did he say specifically?" Marge asked.

"I remember him saying, 'Who woulda done it, who woulda done it,' over and over. Byron gets a whole sentence out, he likes to repeat himself."

Decker wrote in his notepad: *Byron upset! Too upset?*

"Remember him saying anything else?" Marge said.

Chip shook his head, paused a moment, then said, "Byron Howard and Linda Darcy." He shrugged. "I sure wouldna figured it, but who the fuck knows? Linda was rumored to have a thing with lots of people, but I never seen it. Never, ever. Boys 'round here like to wag their dicks, know what I mean?"

"What about Carla?" Marge said. "She was also rumored to have a lot of boyfriends."

"Carla'd fuck anyone in pants. Right out back—two, three in a row. In daylight. That lady was a rabbit. You ever see Carla?"

Only dead, Decker thought. He shook his head no.

"Man, she was ugly." Chip sniffed his nose in disgust. "I mean *ugly*—big ears, big nose, no tits, and an ass as flat as a pancake. And was she *stupid*. Used to be a rumor going round that she and Earl were twins. You know 'bout Earl, don't you?"

Marge nodded.

"'Course, it ain't true," Chip said. "Earl is retard stupid. Carla's just normal stupid. But she was nice enough. Nice fuck if there was no one else around. Linda was a different piece of ass altogether. Smart, sexy. Maybe a few of the guys were slipping it to her, but she kept it to herself."

Chip stopped and yelled another order to the sauce-splattering hype. Then he said, "I had the hots for Linda. Almost had her once. Think she was strung out, then."

"On what?"

"Mostly booze, but a little weed, maybe. I thought she

was giving me that hungry look, but it didn't work out." He frowned at the memory. "Best I got that evening was a blow job from Dawg's old lady. What a pisser!"

"Know anyone who didn't like the Darcys?" Marge asked.

Chip said, "Far as I know, the Darcys were cool. The old ones were a little cranky—Granny D's a Bible-thumper—full of fire and brimstone. Pappy D never had a problem telling you his opinion, whether you wanted to hear it or not. Man, the old fart really hates niggers and rich folk. Has a real hard-on for them developers—Man something."

"Manfred," Marge said.

"Thems the ones," Chip said. "Froths at the mouth when he talks 'bout them. But Luke and Linda and Carla . . . nothing. Used to come around here, eat my pizza, drink my beer, tip my ladies, shoot the shit. Carla would ball some of the guys. That's it. None of us knew the fuck what happened. Sheeeet, we knowed something was goin' down when all them cop cars started driving past. But till Byron came crawlin' in, we didn't know diddlysquat about details."

Marge pulled out the Polaroids. "Ever seen this guy, Chip?"

The biker took the snapshots, clucked his tongue. "Man, is he fucked up. Who's the nigger?"

"The man is white," Decker said.

"Can't be. Look at his skin."

"Skin does that when it's been left out in the elements," Marge said.

"But his lips are thick like nigger lips," Chip insisted.

"That's bloat," Decker said. "Take my word for it, Chip, he's white."

Marge said, "He had a tattoo of a naked lady in a helmet on his right arm, the name Gretchen tattooed on his rear end. Ring any bells?"

Chip stared at the picture. His eyes widened. "Goddam, is that Rolland?"

"Rolland who?" Decker asked.

"Sheeeet! Man, is that Rolland?" Chip asked.

Marge said, "We're asking you, Chip."

Chip said, "Rolland has a naked lady in a helmet on his right arm and Gretchen on his ass. Couldn't be two guys with those tattoos, huh?"

"Not likely, Chip," Decker said.

"Man-oh-man, did he ever get fucked in the ass." Chip muttered another "sheeeet." "I can sort of make him out now, but if you hadn't told me nothing about the tattoos, I never would have recognized him."

Marge said that was understandable. Decker asked if Rolland had a last name.

"Uh, yeah. Rolland Mason. Lives in your neck of the woods over the mountains. Bums off of his old lady. Think she hops tables in Saugus."

"Do you know his address?" Marge said.

"Not offhand. Try the book."

"What's his old lady's name?" Marge asked.

"Fuck was it? Betty or Betsy something. A real shit-for-brains."

"Know what his connection to the Darcys was?" Decker asked.

"No. He might have been ballin' Carla. But I can name four other guys swiggin' beer out there that was ballin' Carla as well."

"We'd like to talk to them," Marge said. "Would you tell us who they are?"

Chip thought a moment. "Why not? Maybe they know Rolland's connection to Carla. Anything, so shit like that doesn't happen here again. I'll introduce you. Tell them you're okay."

"Thanks," Marge said.

"Anything for you, honey," Chip said. "I like big women." He smiled at her. Marge smiled back, then rolled her eyes when he wasn't looking.

Decker said, "So you don't know of any other connection Rolland had with the Darcys other than his relationship with Carla?"

Chip smiled. "Relationship? You call being fucked belly down on a Harley a relationship?" He laughed. "Sheeeet, you don't know Carla. She don't have no relationships. Sure as shit don't know what Rolland was doin' at her house. Maybe he was putting the make on Linda. He's tried it before. Maybe he got lucky."

"Maybe Carla didn't like him getting lucky," Decker said out loud.

Chip thought a moment. "Not a bad point, Mr. Cop. Carla didn't like the attention that Linda got."

"Rivalry between the two?" Marge asked.

Chip asked, "You mean like did they fight?"

"Yes," Marge answered.

"Not in public," Chip said. "But Carla would get a mean look on her face when guys paid too much attention to Linda. Maybe she didn't like her sister-in-law stepping out on her brother, though she never said nothing to me about it."

"So you don't know if Linda was getting it on with Rolland?" Marge asked.

"Nope," Chip answered. "Ask Rolland's old lady. Woman used to watch Rolland like a hawk. That's why he stopped taking her here. I bet *she'd* know."

"Betty or Betsy something," Marge said. "A waitress in Saugus."

"Yeah, that's the one." Chip eyed the picture once again. "Man-oh-man, I sure don't want to sign off like this. He was found with Linda, Carla, and Luke?"

Decker said yes.

"Linda, Carla, and Luke look like this, too?" Chip said. "Like niggers?"

Decker nodded.

Chip said, "Sheeeet."

* * *

After jawing with a few inarticulate bikers, discovering
nothing of significance, Decker gave Marge the "Let's beat
it" look. They walked out to the parking lot, Decker offering to drive this time. As he slid into the driver's seat, he noticed Pig leaning against a chopper, glaring at the
unmarked. The son of a bitch looked mean as hell, but his
corpulent body language didn't suggest confrontation.
Decker shook his head. To think that this blob had once
been a baby bouncing in his crib. *What do we* do *to ourselves?* He gunned the motor and peeled off.

"What now?" Marge asked.

"Byron Howard," Decker said.

"Mister Chatterbox?" Marge said. "Guess we should
know where he was when all this went down."

"No doubt he was on his farm," Decker said. "And we
won't be able to prove or disprove it. But it won't hurt to
push him a little, see how he reacts. Also, maybe he knows
something about Rolland Mason."

Decker pushed the pedal to the floor and whizzed by the
idyllic landscape, his mind trying to picture Byron Howard
as the culprit. His extreme reaction: It could have been
guilt, or he still carried the torch for Linda. *Or* maybe they
were still seeing each other and no one knew about it. Then
Luke found out and bam . . . But how did Carla Darcy and
Rolland Mason fit into that scenario?

Witnesses?

Did Byron shoot everyone to get rid of witnesses?

Jigsaw-puzzle time. Can't force the pieces in, they just
have to fit.

Decker slowed when he reached the Howard Honey
Farm sign, then pulled the unmarked onto the gravel path
and parked next to the green shack-*cum*-business office. As
luck would have it, Byron was in, perched behind the metal
desk. And he'd thrown out the fly-studded pizza. The bee-

keeper said nothing as they walked in, but his eyes were anything but welcoming. Decker spoke first.

"We might have identified the other man who was murdered along with Luke, Linda, and Carla Darcy. Name Rolland Mason ring a bell?"

"No," Howard said.

"Never heard the name before?" Marge asked.

"No."

"He was a friend of Carla's, maybe a friend of Linda's too," Decker said.

"Don't know him," Byron said.

"He was a biker."

"Don't know him," Byron persisted. "Is that all?"

"No," Decker said. "I need to ask you some questions about your affair with Linda Darcy."

Byron turned deep red, but maintained eye contact with Decker. He said, "It was over afore it started, and it ain't none of your business."

Marge said, "It's our business if it has anything to do with the murders."

"It *don't*," Byron said.

"It was four years ago?" Decker asked.

Byron bit his lip. "About."

"And it was just one time?" Decker said.

Byron bit his lip, didn't answer right away. Finally, he said, "Yes."

"At the Sleepy-Bi Motel?"

"Goddam big-mouth women," Byron said. "I'm gonna kill both of them—"

"Like you killed Linda Darcy?" Decker said.

"*Whatchu* say, boy?" Byron coughed out.

Decker could almost see steam coming from his nostrils. "Just getting your attention, Byron. By the way, did you visit the Darcy farmhouse within the last week?"

"No," Byron said. His voice became soft and furious.

"No, I didn't. And I didn't have nothing to do with anything that happened over there. And I don't know where I was every single second of the past week, so if you got something to say, say it. If not, get out of here!"

Decker waited a beat, giving Byron a chance to cool off. He regarded the pinups in back of the desk. Byron, seeing Decker's stare go over his shoulder, glanced over his back and noticed the nude-women posters as if he'd seen them for the first time.

"Like your artwork," Decker said.

"My baby brother put them up," Byron said.

But you didn't take them down, Decker thought. "One more thing, Byron. Do the Darcys own a gun?"

Byron said everyone here owned a gun. Decker pressed him on it. What kind of firearms?

"Shotgun," Byron answered.

"What kind?"

"Browning Pump."

"What gauge?" Decker asked patiently.

"Twelve."

"Any handguns?" Decker asked.

"Don't know."

"We couldn't find anything there," Marge said. "Know where the Browning was kept?"

Byron squeezed his hands into fists and said, "Why don't you ask Pappy D these questions?"

Decker said he'd do just that.

🌀 16

Rolland Mason was not listed in the book. Nor did he have an unlisted number. But at least he wasn't a total cipher.

Marge reviewed her notes:

Rolland Mason, born in Macon, Ga. WM, 42, 6'1", 220, brown hair, blue eyes, no wants, no warrants, no priors, the last two words underlined with a bold pencil stroke—a real surprise. His prints had placed him in the USMC—a one-year tour in Nam in '67, obtaining his honorable discharge in '68. He returned home to Macon. Married Tammy Reebs a year later, *five* kids, worked as an electrician. Divorced 1983 after fourteen years of marriage, moved to California. Whereabouts unknown 1983–1985, no California driver's license, no taxes filed, no address, no phone number, no welfare, no nothing. In 1986, he did obtain a CDL, the address listed now a shopping mall. No info on him after that.

Marge took out the phone book and started calling coffee shops in Saugus, hoping that Chip's information wasn't pure bull. She hit pay dirt after twenty minutes of phoning. Betty Bidel who did the morning shift at Nicky's knew Rolland *very* well. Marge said she'd be right down, and Betty said good. The hour between ten and eleven was slow anyway.

Rolland's old lady was a stringy brunette with a pasty complexion. Hair packed into a net, Betty wore a starched white uniform, her name tag pinned above a breast-pocket handkerchief. She was manning the countertop, wiping coffee cups with a brown terry-cloth rag.

As soon as Marge identified herself, Betty said, "So the law finally caught up with him."

Marge smiled cryptically.

Betty cocked her head. "Knew it was only a matter of time. All that meth dealing. I didn't know nothing 'bout it. You got to believe me on that."

Marge said she did.

"Man, this *is* the final straw," Betty announced. "Even if he'd come back, I wouldn't take him. Not after the dealing. And what he did to me."

"What did he do to you?" Marge asked.

"Left me flat when I was three months pregnant," Betty said. "Asshole tells me to keep it 'cause he's gonna marry me, right? Then he just disappears. Come home one day and all his things're gone from my place. That was it! Hunnerd and fifty bucks out of *my* pocket to fix up *my* problem!" Betty folded the towel and began wiping the counter. "No more bikers for me, I can tell you that! Ever!"

"Any reason for his sudden departure?" Marge asked.

"'Nother woman, probably."

"Linda Darcy?"

Betty's eyes narrowed, her lips turned ghostly white. She let out a string of obscenities directed at Linda. What Marge finally learned was that Rolland was screwing many women, but Linda seemed to be a unique problem.

"He akchilly told me he loved her!" Betty cried out. "He wanted to marry her, can you believe that! Walks out on me after knocking me up to marry some fancy broad with fancy jeans and a fancy chest." She paused to catch her breath. "Fucking around is one thing. Guys just do that. Like I knowed Rolland was screwing Carla, but that was different. I mean, Carla was just a friendly girl. But Linda was above it all. Miss Perfect Princess. Tell Rolland he can drop dead if he wants bail money. Tell him to go ask Princess Linda for the money."

Then Marge broke the bad news.

Betty clutched her chest, leaned against the countertop for support. It took her around a minute before the tears came. She cried for her Rolland, wailed how she loved him. Marge hugged her, waited until her sobs turned to sniffs, then slowly exited the shop. Over her shoulder, Marge took a final look at Betty. She was still sniffing, her eyes moist and red. But grief hadn't interfered with her job. She did her chores swiftly, hopping from table to table, refilling salt shakers, muttering to herself as she worked.

Decker had an hour to kill before his three o'clock court appearance. He called home, but Rina didn't answer. He debated running out to the ranch to make sure everything was okay, but decided that was foolish. She'd probably gone over to the yeshiva to visit old friends. Or maybe she was shopping. Decker had left her the keys to the Porsche.

The hell with it, he thought. She could take care of herself. He'd have to trust her.

He decided to buy a carton of orange juice and read the paper in Van Nuys Park—his usual pit stop when he was tied up at court. He drove the unmarked out of the court complex, and hooked a left onto Van Nuys Boulevard. A minute later, he passed a block-long western-wear store, a string of iron-gated hock shops, several adult bookstores and a couple of dark, smoky taverns. As he headed south, the stores were replaced by acres of car lots displaying both new and used autos, their rock-bottom prices written in red on white placards placed inside the windshields

Van Nuys Boulevard. On a warm Wednesday night, it

was mecca for cruisers. The street was clogged with bumper-to-bumper cars containing youngsters, oldsters, anyone wanting to make that hormone connection. After his divorce, Decker had often traveled to the Boulevard, observed the pickup rituals and the souped-up cars. His biweekly treks had lasted about three years. He'd stood alone, hands in his pocket, people steering clear of him because he made no effort to disguise his cop demeanor. Once in a blue moon, a woman approached him. And once in a blue moon, he accepted her invitation, bought her a drink at one of the local bars.

Those days were long gone, and Decker felt no nostalgia for the lonely nights, some drunken cop groupie crying in her beer while groping him under the table. The very thought of it made him cringe.

Life do get bettah.

The car lots disappeared, replaced by high-rise medical and office buildings. A block before the Ventura Freeway, the name on one of the skyscrapers caught Decker's eye. Quickly, he jerked the unmarked into the right lane, and turned just as the light became red. Someone honked his car.

Decker smiled. He was honked at a lot and deserved every metallic blare he got. He drove like a jerk. But not when Rina was in the car.

He parked in an underground lot, and entered the Manfred Building from the back. The directory put the corporate offices on the top floor—the fourteenth, which was really the thirteenth, but the unlucky number had been eliminated from the list of elevator buttons. He shared the lift with a pin-striped suit with a runny nose and darting eyes. The suit got out on the seventh floor.

The elevator doors to number fourteen opened, and Decker found himself staring into the yawning portals of a paneled reception room. It was as big as a tennis court, as hushed as a library.

Badge in hand, he approached the receptionist—a plump young woman who wore her hair in a tight bun—and flashed her his ID. Her eyes reacted with surprise.

"Homicide investigation. I need to speak to the CEO."

The woman didn't answer.

"The chief executive officer," Decker explained.

"Who's in charge here?" Decker demanded. But his voice was soft.

"Uh, that would be Mr. Donaldson," she said. "But he's not the CEO. That would be Mr. Cartwright. And he's in Paris."

"Tell Mr. Donaldson that Detective Sergeant Decker from LAPD Homicide is here to speak with him."

"He's involved in a long-distance phone conference."

Decker didn't answer.

"I'll buzz his secretary," the woman said.

A minute later, Decker was sitting with a cup of coffee in the executive office of Mr. Creighton Donaldson—first vice president in charge of acquisition and development for Manfred and Associates. His secretary was around sixty, her gray tresses styled in a bouffant hairdo. A busty woman, she wore her glasses around her neck, the spectacles bouncing on her bosom whenever she walked. Mr. Donaldson would be right out, she informed Decker.

"Right out" was a half hour later. Decker was escorted into Donaldson's inner sanctum, full of rich, burnished leather and high-polished wood scented with lemon oil. Decker was motioned to sit in a brocade wingback while Donaldson took the chair behind a rosewood desk, its right corner covered by framed pictures of two little girls.

The vice president was much younger than Decker had expected—forty-five, tops. About 6' even, with a tennis player's build. Black hair, gray temples, sharp brown eyes, straight nose, and cleft chin. His white smile contrasted nicely against his deep tan. Suddenly, Decker felt scruffy.

"I apologize for the delay," Donaldson said. "How can I help you, Detective?"

Decker glanced at his watch. He was due back in court in thirty minutes. No time for niceties. Just cast the rod and see what you pull up.

"Name Linda Darcy ring a bell?" Decker asked.

Donaldson's eyebrows rose a millimeter. "Yes. What about her?"

"Tell me about your dealings with her," Decker said.

"They're business," Donaldson said. "And they're confidential."

"Not anymore, Mr. Donaldson," Decker said. "She's dead."

Donaldson immediately slumped into his desk chair, a seasick pallor washing over his skin. The man was sinking fast. Decker said, "If you want a drink, Mr. Donaldson, it's okay with me."

"Thank you." Donaldson stood and walked to a portable bar on the other side of the room. "Thank you, I will." He took out a cut-crystal tumbler and cleared his throat. "How about yourself? Or aren't you allowed to do that?"

Decker told him he didn't drink on duty, noticing the VP's hands were trembling. Donaldson poured himself something straight up.

"What was your connection to Linda Darcy?" Decker asked again.

Donaldson gulped down the first shot, poured himself another.

"It wasn't what you're thinking," he said. "Nothing sexual, although Linda was a very sexy lady . . . and it might have been nice." He turned to Decker. "Don't repeat that. I'm a married man, and I'm quite shaken. I'm not as controlled as I usually am."

"You didn't have an affair with her?" Decker asked. "It could be relevant to my investigation."

"No," Donaldson said. "No, I didn't. Our relationship was strictly business."

Decker paused a moment to let Donaldson know his statement was suspect. Then he said, "What kind of business?"

Donaldson ran his hands over his face. A diamond ring decorated his right ring finger, a gold band on his left. "My specialties are acquisition and development. Mrs. Darcy and I were . . . how should I say this? Her father-in-law owned a parcel of land that Manfred was potentially interested in acquiring. I had approached Pappy Darcy—as they call him—around two years ago, and our substantial offer was rebuffed. Which was fine. Around a week later, Mrs. Darcy . . . Linda approached me with the idea that perhaps given enough time and enough incentive, realizing the position for potential profit, that maybe if we were to present to Mr. Darcy the entire picture for gain on the upside, it might be possible using untried tactics—"

Decker interrupted. "You and Linda were scheming behind the old man's back."

"We weren't scheming," Donaldson said. He resettled into his desk chair, his breath smelling of scotch. "We were talking business contingencies."

"How to talk Pappy Darcy into selling off the land," Decker said.

Donaldson hesitated, then said, "Basically, yes."

"And?"

"And we tried several different approaches," Donaldson said. "None of them successful."

"When was the last time you tried an approach?" Decker asked.

"We came to him around a month ago. Not me personally, of course. A representative from my office."

Decker told him to go on. Donaldson said that Pappy Darcy wasn't interested. Nothing more was discussed be-

tween the two of them. But Decker read in his eyes that
there was more. He pressed Donaldson for details.

"Well," Donaldson said, "this was told to me secondhand,
but it was said that Pappy Darcy got quite irate—obscene in
his condemnation of the salesman, Manfred, and Linda—"

"Linda?" Decker asked.

"He seemed to feel that Linda was behind it all."

"She was, wasn't she?"

Donaldson paused, seemed to choose his words. "She
was instrumental in keeping our interest alive, but he accused her of masterminding the whole idea. That simply
was not the case."

"But she *was* keeping the whole idea alive," Decker said.

"She had a vested interest in Pappy Darcy selling the
land, true," Donaldson said. "Her husband had a third interest in the land. His share would have netted her a handsome
profit."

"How much?" Decker asked.

"Around one hundred and fifty thousand dollars. A lot of
money for a honey farmer."

A more than tidy sum for anyone breaking his back to
earn his keep, Decker thought. But something else came to
him. He asked Donaldson, "Who owned the other two
thirds of the land?"

Donaldson looked uncomfortable. Then he said, "Well,
it's public record anyway. Pappy Darcy of course, and
Luke's sister."

"Sue Beth Litton?" Decker asked.

"Yes."

"What about Luke's younger sister?" Decker asked.
"Carla Darcy?"

Donaldson shrugged. "I wasn't even aware that there was
another sister. Who is she?"

"Doesn't matter." Decker tried to sound casual. "She's
out of the picture." But in his notepad, he wrote, CARLA DIS-

INHERITED and underlined it three times. Decker steered the conversation back to Linda.

"So you and Linda were pestering Luke to keep after his father to sell."

"Not pestering," Donaldson said. "We were presenting him with options. We had several—one included giving Pappy Darcy free farming rights until such time as Manfred chose to develop the property. A very generous offer, but Pappy Darcy refused to hear us out."

"When was the last time you saw Linda Darcy?" Decker asked.

"At our last appointment—around two weeks ago. You can check with my secretary for the exact date."

Decker didn't say anything, just stared at the wall, then at Donaldson. The vice president seemed antsy under scrutiny. He got up and poured himself another scotch. Swirling the amber liquid, he asked, "How did she die?"

"In a very ugly way," Decker said.

"Was she by any chance . . ." Donaldson cleared his throat. "Was she murdered by gunshot?"

Lots of people were murdered by gunshot. But Decker wondered if Donaldson's question had been more an educated than lucky guess. He replied, "Why do you ask?"

"Because our representative . . . the last time he went out to the Darcy honey farm . . . Pappy Darcy had come out of his house holding a gun, claiming he was going to blow off the head of the next Manfred representative who trespassed upon his property." Donaldson slugged down the scotch. "He also mentioned something about blowing off Linda's head as part of the bargain—two for the price of one. Our representative was quite shaken by the threat."

"What kind of weapon was Pappy Darcy holding?" Decker asked.

"Just a big gun," Donaldson said. "I don't believe James, our representative, told us the make."

"What kind of big gun?"

"I seem to recall James saying that Pappy was holding a shotgun."

How convenient, thought Decker. He just happened to recall that bit of trivia. Decker said, "Can your representative tell a shotgun from a rifle?"

Donaldson drummed his finger. "Perhaps Pappy was holding a rifle. James said it was a *big* gun."

"But you recall him saying it was a shotgun."

"Maybe I'm mistaken."

"Can I speak to James?" Decker asked.

"He's away on business."

"And?"

"And he is unavailable for your questions."

Decker said, "You sent him to a place where there's no phone lines?"

Donaldson fidgeted a moment. Then he said, "Ask my secretary for his number."

"Great," Decker said. "You know, Mr. Donaldson, we're going to be investigating Linda thoroughly. Any illicit lunch dates, motel-room trysts . . . we're going to find out about them."

A slight blush rose behind Donaldson's ear. "I told you, Sergeant, our relationship was purely business."

"That's good." Decker handed him his card. "If you think of anything else, give me a call."

"I will," Donaldson said.

Decker turned to him before he crossed the threshold. "Would you mind if I took a look at the records concerning the property?"

Donaldson said, "I would very much."

"Why?"

"We have a lot of secret and valuable information contained in the Darcy file."

"What kind of information?"

"If I told you that, Sergeant, I wouldn't be what I am to-day—a trusted officer of the corporation."

"Fine," Decker said. "Have it your way. I'll get a court order."

"For what?"

"Material evidence for a homicide murder."

Donaldson looked aghast. "That's ridiculous."

Decker shrugged helplessly.

"Let me talk to Mr. Cartwright," Donaldson said. "I'll see what I can do."

Decker waited a beat, then thanked him again, telling him he'd been most helpful. Donaldson gave him a sour smile in return.

❦17

Marge spied Decker parked across the street and gave him a wave. She pulled her Honda into Sophi Rawlings's driveway and sneaked a sidelong glance at Sue Beth Litton. She'd been quiet in the morgue, completely mute on her ride over the hill—a woman shocked into silence.

But there were questions to be asked, and like it or not, Sue Beth needed to hear them.

Marge touched her hand, and Sue Beth jumped. The woman's face was drawn as pale and tight as a drumskin. In a different situation, she might have been labeled cute, with her thick auburn hair, green eyes, a freckled nose—somewhere in her bloodline was the name O'something. She had very big ears, though. Carla had had big ears. Carla had also had a big nose and flat chest. Sue Beth's nose was as small as a button; her chest, though not voluminous, was certainly not an ironing board.

Softly, Marge said, "I need to confer with my partner for a moment, Mrs. Litton. You can wait in the car."

Sue Beth nodded, her eyes directed in her lap.

Marge stepped out of the car and met Decker by the trunk of her Honda. They spoke in hushed tones.

Marge said, "I don't believe it. You beat us here."

"Defense asked for a recess for the weekend," Decker said.

"A new PD. Wants to familiarize himself with the case."

"What happened to the old PD?"

"Damned if I know. I told our woman that I'd be back Monday, giving her moral support. Hopefully, she'll return as well. One more delay, and I'm afraid she'll crack." Decker kicked the ground. "Enough of that. What did you find out?"

"Forensics first," Marge said. "Blood on Katie's PJs. Matches with her mother and Carla. The kid was obviously at the scene of the crime either during the shooting or after all the blood was spilled. My guess she wasn't there too long, otherwise she would have had blood from the others as well."

"Good."

"Rolland Mason. His sheet is clear, but that doesn't tell us the whole story. I found his ex-lady—a waitress in Saugus named Betty Bidel. Chip's tip panned out."

"That's good."

"Yeah, he was good for something. Anyway, from Betty I learned that Rolland was dealing in meth. She also told me that Rolland had left her and had plans to marry Linda."

Decker said, "Was Linda aware of his plans?"

"That I don't know. It might have been unrequited love."

"You know, Marge, we keep sticking Rolland with Carla like the two of them were an item. Maybe it was Rolland and Linda who were the happy duo, and they were confronting Luke about it. Tempers got hot, bam-bam."

"Then where does Carla fit in?"

"Funny you should ask," Decker said. "She may have had her own agenda. I visited Manfred and Associates today. I spoke to an associate."

Marge said, "Taking on the big guys again?"

Decker laughed. Last time he visited the head of a big corporation, he'd leaned too heavily on a well-connected CEO, and it almost lost him his job. Only his supportive captain had saved his neck. . . .

Decker whipped his thoughts back to the present and gave Marge a quick rundown of the conversation, including Carla's disinheritance. He said, "Suppose Linda thought she'd have an ally in Carla. Maybe Linda even offered Carla some money if she could get Luke to sell. So the two of them confronted Luke and were rebuffed. Then all hell broke loose."

Marge said, "And Rolland was attached to one of the women. His old lady said he loved Linda. But maybe when he found out that Carla stood to gain some bread, he decided to pair off with her because she was convenient."

"Sounds good to me," Decker said.

"Except for a couple of minor details," Marge said. "Even if Luke was willing to sell, he'd have to convince Pappy D and Sue Beth to sell before there was any money to be made. To me, Pappy chasing a Manfred representative off his property with a shotgun shows lack of interest."

Decker laughed. "I finally did get ahold of the representative. His full name's James Chatam, and his story jibes well with Donaldson's account *except* that he said Pappy Darcy had been carrying a *rifle*. When I asked him if it could have been a shotgun, Chatam said yeah, it could have been, he doesn't know the difference."

"But Donaldson used the word *shotgun* specifically?"

"Yep."

"Interesting that Donaldson would know the weapon and he wasn't even there," Marge said.

"Something to note," Decker said. "Although a lot of people use the terms interchangeably." He motioned his head toward the front of the car. "What about her?"

"She ID'd the bodies," Marge said. "Including Rolland."

"So Rolland wasn't a stranger to her."

"Apparently not."

"Press her on it?"

Marge said, "No, the timing wasn't right. But someone should before we give her Katie."

"You do it," Decker said. "She already knows you. And if you get into sensitive areas like who Linda or Carla was screwing, she might respond better to a woman."

"Fine." Marge checked her watch. "It's four-fifteen. You've got enough time before your Sabbath starts?"

"About three hours," Decker said. "After we get Katie squared away, I'm going to phone up Ozzie Crandal, get a feel for the parents and brother Earl."

"Having worked with Crandal, I think we should talk to the Darcys ourselves," Marge said.

"Agreed," Decker said. "But unless Crandal thinks they're going to bolt, it can wait until after the weekend."

"I'll set up something for next week then," Marge said. "By the way, I talked to a local kiddy shrink. Nice guy, spent an hour talking to me. He said yes, indeed, the kid should be seen. A, for the kid's sake—who knows what the hell she saw and how she has interpreted it? And B, things could come out that may be useful to us. But then he said since she was only twenty months, we shouldn't count on anything verbal."

"Then what kinds of things could come out?"

"Well, he said that if she saw the actual crime take place, a good shrink could get her to recreate her interpretation in something called play therapy—she'd play out the trauma with dolls or toys. If she didn't play it out, chances are she didn't witness anything. That in and of itself could be useful to us. Maybe she was sleeping in a crib when it happened. That could put the crime at night or during her nap time. Things like that. Like I said, we spoke for an hour. Anyway, I have his number if Sue Beth is so inclined."

Decker said, "And where is the woman of the hour?"

Marge said she'd get her. A moment later, they were all standing in the driveway. Marge made all the necessary introductions.

Decker said, "I'm sorry for your tragedy, Mrs. Litton."

Sue Beth didn't respond. But Decker could see her eyes

fill with moisture. The woman had an "ain't life a bitch" face. Weathered skin, green eyes as hard as jade. Her cheeks were high-boned, sharp and pale, her hair was pulled tightly back into a ponytail. Only her lips gave her visage a hint of softness—full and blood red. Perhaps they were the only part of her face that had ever known any tenderness. Decker said, "We have all the papers necessary for Katie's release—"

"When can I see her?" Sue Beth interrupted. Her voice was husky, strong.

"In a moment," Marge said. "After we've asked you a couple of questions."

"Here?" Sue Beth asked.

"Would you prefer to sit in the car?" Marge asked.

"Can't this be done another time?" Sue Beth protested.

Decker shook his head, then said, "I'll go check on Katie. Make sure everything is in order." He patted Sue Beth on the back. "This shouldn't take too long."

After Decker left, Marge said, "Again, I'm very sorry, Mrs. Litton. You've suffered a terrible tragedy."

Sue Beth said nothing, and Marge assayed the situation. Everyone had to be approached differently. Many grieving women reached out at a time like this. But this one was retreating, and Marge had to figure out how to reel her in. First, Marge tried empathy, how unreal this must feel. Then she expressed sympathy again, how sorry she was for the loss. But Sue Beth remained stoic and silent.

Then let's get down to business, Marge thought.

"I'm going to ask you some questions, Mrs. Litton," she said. "Some of the questions might seem odd, some personal, some like I'm trying to insinuate something. Believe me, I'm not. I'm just trying to get a total picture so we can solve this as quickly as possible."

"Go ahead," Sue Beth said. "Quicker you ask, the quicker I can get Katie and go home . . . or what's left of it. . . . Oh God, this is a real nightmare."

Marge agreed with her. Slipping out her notebook, she asked Sue Beth to go over the trip to Fall Springs. The woman spoke in a monotone as she recounted the past week. Four days ago, she, her husband, B.B., and their kids left for the Annual Western Beekeepers Association Convention at about eleven in the morning. Luke wasn't home when they left, but Carly and Linda were, and she said good-bye to them and everything seemed normal.

"Where were your parents?" Marge asked.

"Pappy and Granny were giving Carly and Linda last-minute instructions on how to take care of Earl. They were going to leave Earl at home for the first time in ages—Luke volunteered to watch after him. But at the last minute, they must have changed their minds and brought Earl along."

"Why do you think they changed their minds?" Marge asked.

"Most likely, Earl put up a fuss. He don't like being left out of things." She paused. "Did anyone explain about Earl to you?"

Marge said yes, someone did. She asked Sue Beth what time did she see her parents at the convention.

"They were there when we arrived," Sue Beth said.

"But you said you left before them," Marge said.

"Oh, I forgot. We all stopped off at a restaurant to eat. Nice one in La Mesa called Montequilla's. Sort of a family tradition when we go down to Fall Springs."

Marge said, "So your parents and Earl were at Fall Springs when you arrived."

"Yes, ma'am."

"You're sure about that?"

Sue Beth paused a moment. "Yes, ma'am."

Marge didn't know if the pause came from Sue Beth remembering something differently or an honest attempt to make sure she'd answered the question truthfully. Marge wrote down the reply and put in the word "pause" in the margin of her notes.

"What time did you arrive at Fall Springs?"

" 'Round two, two-thirty."

"How long does it take to get to there from your place?"

" 'Bout two hours."

"Okay," Marge said. "And everything was normal when you left?"

"Yes."

"And your parents seemed . . . just fine?"

Sue Beth frowned. " 'Course, they were fine. What are you trying to say?"

"Just trying to get a total picture of everything, Sue Beth."

Sue Beth still looked unhappy, but she didn't say anything.

Marge asked, "Your parents get along with Luke?"

"They worshiped him," Sue Beth said. "That man was the salt of the earth. . . ." Her lower lip began to tremble, and tears spilled onto her cheeks.

Marge pulled a clean tissue from her pants pocket and gave it to her. "I'm so sorry, Sue Beth."

She wiped her face, then nodded for Marge to continue. Casually, Marge asked, "Your parents get along well with Luke's wife?"

"Huh?"

"Your parents like Linda?" Marge repeated.

Sue Beth looked up, her features hardened. "As a matter of fact, they didn't. None of us did . . . 'cept . . . well, Linda was nice to Earl. I'll say that much for her."

"So your parents didn't like Linda."

"So what?" Sue Beth countered. "Lots of parents don't like their daughters-in-law."

Marge agreed with her. Then, she asked her about her sister, Carla. How did her parents relate to her? Sue Beth seemed pained.

"They thought Linda was a bad influence on her. She was, you know."

"What do you mean by bad influence?"

Sue Beth covered her mouth with her hands. "My sister was only fourteen when Luke married Linda. She was very—what's the word, impressed-like. . . ."

"Impressionable?"

"Yeah, that's it." Sue Beth went on to explain. Baby sister Carla was never a looker, very shy, and the boys didn't treat her too nice. Then Linda came along and showed Carla ways to attract the boys' attention.

Sue Beth shook her head. "'Course, it made my ma mad. Carla acting so common. And Linda. It especially weren't respectable for a married woman to act like."

"Was Linda playing around, Mrs. Litton?" Marge asked.

Sue Beth reddened. "Well, she said she wasn't, but my ma thought otherwise, I guess."

"And what did you think?"

"What did I think?" Sue Beth repeated. "Keep my nose out of it, that's what I thought."

Marge paused a moment. Linda and Carly. The "bad" girls. Getting Granny's dander up. Together in fun, together in death. She wondered if Sue Beth knew exactly where Rolland Mason fit in. At the mention of his name, Sue Beth stiffened. But Marge pressed her on it.

"What can you tell me about him?" she said.

"He was just a fellah that Carla knew."

Just a fellah? Marge said, "Were he and your sister a steady twosome?"

Sue Beth shook her head, explaining that Carla didn't have any steady fellahs, although she had lots of guys who liked her. Then Marge asked if Rolland had ever shown any interest in Linda.

Sue Beth stiffened again. "Lots of men showed interest in Linda."

"Rolland in specific?"

"Maybe."

"What did Carla think about that?"

"Like I said, Carla didn't have a special fellah. I don't think she cared who Rolland paid attention to. I barely knew Rolland myself."

"Yet you easily identified Rolland at the morgue."

Sue Beth blushed. After a pause, she admitted that maybe he'd been to the house once or twice. When Marge asked for what reason, Sue Beth slammed her hand down on the hood of Marge's Honda.

"Just what are you trying to say, Miss Detective!"

Marge didn't answer. Sue Beth began to cry.

"I'm sorry," she wept. "I'm sorry I lost my temper."

"Don't apologize," Marge said. "You're doing fine, Sue Beth. Great, under the circumstances. I know this is very hard for you."

Sue Beth sobbed. Marge put her notebook away and slipped her arm around her.

"I want to solve this thing. Give you and your parents some peace of mind. But I need help. I need to know all about Rolland Mason as well as your kinfolk. They were all murdered together."

Sue Beth continued to cry, but softer than before.

Marge said, "Think you can help me out?"

"It's just so *hard*!"

"I know it is." Marge got her another tissue. "You tell me when you're ready to talk again."

After a beat, Sue Beth said, "I'm ready now, I guess."

Marge took out her notebook. "We were talking about Rolland Mason."

"Yes?"

"Did he and Linda seem close?"

Sue Beth sighed. "Well, 'bout a month ago, Rolland started coming to the house . . . to see Linda, I think. Linda . . . she wouldn't do nothing with him at the house, wouldn't touch him, even talk to him while others were around. But sometimes, when they thought no one was

looking, they'd be whispering, planning to meet each other.
I tried not to listen, but couple times I couldn't help it.

"I'd get so angry. My blood would just boil. I'd be angry
at Linda, angry at my brother Luke, for not doing nothing
'bout his wife. But you can't go sticking your nose where it
don't belong, so I tried to act normal around her and Luke."

"Carla ever catch them whispering together?"

"Yeah, she knew 'bout it, too."

"She ever say anything about it to you?"

"Not really," Sue Beth said. But her voice was very hesitant. This time, Marge prodded her for more.

Sue Beth said, "Well, it's just that . . . I don't think Carly
liked the fact that Linda was seeing Rolland. Maybe she felt
bad for Luke, though she never said nothing before about it.
I think Carla was a little jealous, plain and simple. Linda
was twelve years older than her, but she had a way with the
boys. And she didn't have to act as . . . how should I put
this . . . act as . . . as wild as my sister did to get 'em."

Sue Beth shook her head.

"Things were sometimes bad, Miss Detective. Bad
'cause Linda was playing so close to home."

"Byron Howard?"

"I think that was the start of it."

Marge wondered about the beekeeper, if he figured into
all this. She asked Sue Beth how Linda and Byron got
started. Sue Beth shrugged and claimed ignorance. But she
did say that after the affair, Byron Howard kept to himself.
Never came over anymore unless it was absolutely necessary for him to talk to Pappy, B.B., or Luke.

"What about Linda after the affair?" Marge said. "She
didn't seem to keep to herself."

"Right about that," Sue Beth said. "Her thing with Byron
didn't change her wild ways one bit. She still acted up, going to Hell's Heaven, doing Lord knows what over there."

"I spoke to the owner of Hell's Heaven," Marge said.

"You spoke to Chip?"

Marge nodded. "He said Linda just used to drink there but didn't have a lot to do with the guys. Though quite a few seemed to be interested in her. What do you think about that?"

"Well, that's what Linda always said," Sue Beth answered. "She was just having fun, not doin' anything serious. But . . . but if I was a bettin' woman, I'd swear there was something going on between her and Rolland."

"Why Rolland?"

"I don't rightly know."

Marge asked. "What was Linda like as a mother?"

Sue Beth shut her eyes. "Her one saving grace. Linda was a very good mother to Katie."

Marge doodled cubes inside her notebook, thinking about Linda's duality. She might have been a madonna when it came to her kid, but to an old-fashioned couple like Pappy and Granny, she was nothing more than an evil whore, teaching her wicked ways to their younger daughter. Maybe Granny's rebuke had gone beyond verbal admonitions. But then where would Luke fit into all of this?

Marge dropped that train of thought, moved on to another motive—a stronger motive.

"One last routine question, Sue Beth," she said. "Do you know anyone who'd gain something from Luke's death?"

"Gain from Luke's death?" She shook her head. "Just Linda. But she's dead, too."

"Hmmm," Marge said. She continued drawing cubes. "What would Linda have gained from Luke's death?"

"His portion of the land, of course," Sue Beth said. "It's divided three ways between Luke, Pappy, and me—" She suddenly reddened, couldn't seem to find her voice.

Marge let her blush a moment, thinking, She knows what I'm getting at. Good! She said, "Three ways. What happened to Carla?"

Sue Beth was still scarlet. "Carla?"

"Yeah, Carla," Marge said. "She wasn't included in the inheritance?"

"When she married—if she married the right person—Pappy would have included—" Sue Beth had suddenly had enough. "What does *Carla* . . . or *Pappy* . . . or *me* have to do with anything? Lord knows, *I* was never interested in selling. And Pappy wasn't interested in selling. And Carla never said no words about it neither. The only one who was interested in selling was *Linda*!"

Marge said nothing.

"Well, you've already pried into all of our affairs," Sue Beth said. "What else do you want to know?"

Marge took Sue Beth's arm, stroked it gently. "I have to ask you these things, Sue Beth. I need to know everything if we're going to get anywhere."

Sue Beth suddenly seemed to shrink. Her face lost all its anger. Her lip began to tremble, her eyes watered.

"What else?" she choked out.

"That's all for the moment," Marge said. "You all right?"

"I don't know anymore," Sue Beth said.

"Would you like to see Katie now?" Marge asked. "Or do you want a moment to calm down?"

"No," Sue Beth said. "I want Katie. Let's get it over with."

Marge gently led her into Sophi Rawlings's living room. Decker and Sophi were drinking coffee, sitting on the sofa, kids scampering around them like bedbugs. They both rose when Sue Beth and Marge entered the room, and Sophi immediately offered them coffee. Both declined. Sue Beth was shaking, hugging herself. Sophi went over to her, threw her thick arm around Sue Beth's small shoulder.

"She's in the back," she said. "You want to go outside, or should I bring her here?"

Sue Beth mumbled something, realized no one understood her, then said loudly, "It doesn't matter."

"Then just sit down and make yourself comfortable, Mrs. Litton. I'll get you Sally." Sophi corrected herself. "I mean Katie. Whatever you call her, she's a fine little girl. Detective Decker and I were just talking what a sweetie pie she is. I'm so glad we found her kin."

"Thank you," Sue Beth said weakly. When Sophie left, Sue Beth muttered, "I'm so nervous."

"You'll be fine," Marge said. She patted her hand. It was ice-cold.

"It's not like Katie doesn't know me ... but ..." Her voice trailed off.

A moment later, Sophie came back carrying Katie in her arms. The toddler was dressed in a sleeveless white shirt and green shorts. Her feet were bare, her little toes wriggling and caked with mud. Her curls had turned even more blond. Her brown eyes widened with unabashed delight when she noticed Sue Beth. She reached out her arms to her aunt.

"Tatie Sooooo!" she shrieked. "Tatie Soo, Tatie Soo."

"Oh, baby," Sue Beth said. She scooped the toddler in her arms. "Oh, my poor, poor baby." She held her to her breast and began to cry.

"Mama?" Katie asked. "Mama? Mama?"

Sue Beth looked at Marge, panic etched into her face. "What do I tell her, Miss Detective? What *do* I tell her?"

Decker said, "As a matter of fact, Mrs. Litton, Detective Dunn has the name of a child psychologist who might be able to help you and Katie out."

Quickly, Marge reached in her coat pocket and offered Sue Beth a piece of paper. "His name is Dr. Germaine, his phone number is—"

Sue Beth looked up. "A *head doctor*?"

"For Katie's sake," Decker said. "They're used to dealing with crisis situations."

"Society for Victim's Rights will pay for the initial visit," Marge said. "Just try him out."

"Mama?" Katie said. She started to squirm in Sue Beth's arms. "Mama, Mama, Mama, Mama."

The child began to cry.

"Oh my Lord," Sue Beth said. "I feel sick to my stomach."

Again, Marge offered her the phone number.

Katie drooped helplessly in her aunt's arms, bleating out "Mama" like an injured lamb. Tears poured out of Sue Beth's eyes. Her skin had turned ashen and was damp with perspiration.

Slowly, she reached toward Marge's outstretched hand and took the piece of paper.

Ozzie Crandal said to Decker, "These people. They're a real piece of work."

"In what way?" Decker asked.

"Could I get a cup of coffee?" Crandal said. He loosened his tie. "I've been going seven hours straight without anything."

"If you can stand our squad-room brew," Decker said.

Crandal said he was used to axle-grease java, anything that didn't stick to the bottom of the mug seemed weak. Decker poured a cup from the squad-room urn, gave it to the thin-haired detective, and sat back down at his desk. Decker loosened his tie and regarded the sixty-year-old detective. Crandal seemed a little bit more alert today. Maybe because the room was cooler than the canyon had been. Heavy guy like him must melt in the heat. Crandal thanked Decker for the coffee, then pulled out sheaves of paper from a leather-scarred briefcase.

"This is your copy of my notes," he said. "Read them over, ask me any questions. Just don't ask me to reinterview them."

"Why?"

Crandal took another sip. "The old man is just so full of rage it makes you nervous. You wouldn't think it just by looking at him. I'd say he was about seventy. Squat guy with usual redneck face—tan and full of wrinkles. Got square shoulders for a man his age, back not stooped a whit. But when he talks." Crandal raised his eyebrows. "Get in his face and he'll blow you away."

"Think he blew his kids away?"

"No," Crandal said. "I don't think he did. First of all, he arrived at Fall Springs before the Littons did. Got at least a half-dozen people who'll verify that. So if anyone was suspect, I'd question Sue Beth. Find out if she had anything to gain by the deaths of her brother and sister."

Same point Marge had made, Decker thought. With Luke and Linda out of the way, Sue Beth stood to inherit everything when Pappy D died. Then he remembered the way she held Katie, taking the little girl into her arms, holding her so tightly, tears streaming down her face . . . and Linda was the *only* one who had ever approached Manfred with an interest in selling. Sue Beth just didn't seem like the type.

A gut feeling, Decker thought, not based on anything factual.

Crandal was talking, ". . . old guy was minimally cooperative when I asked him the 'who-what-where' questions. Actually started to choke up when he talked about his son. But when I attempted to ask him about anything personal that might have caused the murders, he started foaming at the mouth. Especially when he talked about the bloodsucking city slicks from Manfred Corp., and his wicked daughter-in-law."

"Yeah," Decker said. "Seems the family didn't like her too much."

"Old Pappy claimed she was driving them all to the poorhouse, and Manfred was waiting to swoop down like vultures when she did," Crandal said. "The old lady didn't have much to say about Manfred. Anytime I asked her a question, she'd defer to her husband, *except* when it came to her daughter-in-law. Old lady became livid, said all of it was *her* fault, because she was the Whore of Babylon."

Decker paused a moment. Linda driving them to the poorhouse? Linda's closet didn't seem overly stuffed. No cache of jewelry was found. It didn't make sense.

"What did Linda spend so much money on?"

"I asked Pappy D that very question," Crandal said. He took a giant swig of his coffee. "Granny answered for him. Seems the Whore of Babylon spent it all on wild living."

"Granny didn't get more specific?" Decker asked.

"You gotta picture the setup," Crandal said. "You got Pappy D, who was doing most of the talking, which wasn't too much to begin with. You got his mousy wife—an old broad with knockers down to her knees—standing about two inches behind him, head down, not saying nothing. *Except* every once in a while, she perked up, got this fire in her eyes like a woman possessed, and hurled a biblical insult at Linda. Then she retreated back into her shell."

"She doesn't sound too balanced."

"I don't think she is."

Decker said, "Think she could handle the kickback of a shotgun?"

"I think she could fire a cannon, if she had to," Crandal said. "But like I said, it seems they arrived before the Littons did. If the dynamic duo did it, they'd have to be very quick and breezy about it."

Murder took all of a moment, Decker thought. But what would they have done with Katie? Decker hadn't found her until one in the morning some ten hours later and one hundred miles away from Fall Springs.

Decker asked, "Anyone down in Fall Springs remember them having a toddler?"

"A toddler?" Crandal asked.

"Yeah," Decker said. "Pappy and Granny didn't have a kid with them, did they?"

"Just their retarded son, Earl," Crandal said.

"What was he like?"

"Huddled into a corner," Crandal said. "Every time I looked at him, he gave me a scared smile. Shaking like a dog that had just peed in the house. Every so often, one of Sue Beth's boys came over to him and started stroking his hair." Crandal broke into a smile. "Guess everyone needs a pet retard."

Decker didn't respond.

Crandal shrugged. "Kid seemed harmless enough."

"Did you talk to him at all?" Decker asked.

"Nope," Crandal said. "Pappy wouldn't let me near him. Just as well. I don't think I'd get much out of him other than one-word answers."

Like Byron Howard, Decker thought. He said, "So you have no indication that they were involved?"

"They seemed nutty enough to shoot," Crandal said. "But the time frame doesn't work out real well."

"Happen to ask Pappy if he owns a shotgun?"

"Yes, I did," Crandal said. "It's all in the notes. Yes, he owns one. A twelve-gauge Browning BPS Pump. He said he didn't bring it with him, of course, and as far as he knows, it's still back in the house. When I told him it wasn't, he said he had no idea where it was."

A Browning Pump, Decker thought. Byron's statement was on the money. And the wadding and spent shells found at the crime scene were consistent with that gauge.

He asked, "What about a thirty-eight?"

"Pappy claims he doesn't own one," Crandal said. "Of course, he could be lying."

Decker said, "Mind if I interview them when they come back up?"

Crandal hesitated a moment, then said, "Go ahead."

Decker opened his drawer and pulled out a copy of his notes for Crandal. "You can reinterview anyone I talked to, if you want. Just send me your notes."

Crandal stood, took the notes, stuffed them into his briefcase, and straightened his tie. He said he didn't see any reason to duplicate Decker's work at this point. He'd pass.

🐌18

At six-thirty, Decker pulled the unmarked in the driveway and shut the motor. As soon as he opened the door, he heard the steady blows of hammering and rebuked himself for forgetting to call Abel. He jogged over to the barn, and much to his surprise, Rina was standing at the threshold, an empty pitcher and glass in her hands. She was dressed in a long-sleeved blouse, a knee-length skirt, and her hair was covered. Sweat had moistened her brow, cheeks, and neck. Abel was kneeling ten feet away, banging a stud into the new piece of floorboard. He was bare-chested, his shorts cut at the knees, and he wore a tool belt around his waist. To his right was a pile of lumber, to his left were his portable bench saw and several boxes of nails.

"Get inside," Decker barked to Rina.

"Peter, I—"

"Get inside," Decker said. Louder this time.

"Will you let me—"

"Goddammit, Rina, stop arguing with me and get inside the fucking house right now!"

Rina glared at him with wet eyes, biting her bottom lip. With a single motion, she turned around and ran inside the back door. Decker noticed he was shaking, then saw Abel staring at him.

"What the fuck are you doing here?" Decker said. "I told you to keep away while Rina was in town. And don't tell me you forgot, because you just saw her here yesterday."

Abel continued to stare at him. "Little rough on her, don't you think?"

"You didn't answer my goddam question!" Decker said.

"I'm fixing your barn floor, Decker! What the hell does it look like I'm doing?"

Decker felt smothered by the heat, by his anxiety. It took him a second to catch his breath. "Just leave, okay? And don't come back. I'll call you in about a week."

Abel didn't move. "What's wrong, Pete? Afraid I did something nasty to her?"

Decker didn't answer, dammed back rage and guilt and cursed Abel's perceptiveness. Abel read his condemnation in Decker's eyes.

He rose slowly. Brushing off his shorts, he said, "I've had shit in my life and I've had shit. But, man, you've just given me enough shit to fill the sewers of America."

"Don't give me that wounded crap," Decker snapped. "I know goddam well, and *you* know goddam well, you came to see *her*!"

"I came because Bert's Lumberyard said they were delivering the lumber today, and I wanted to make sure I got what I paid for." Abel picked up his cane and twirled it. "No one was home, so I started to work. I didn't even know she came back until she brought me out a pitcher of juice."

"That's bullshit!" Decker said.

Abel balanced himself on his prosthesis and cane and slipped his foot into a huarache. He looked at his hands and realized he was shaking as hard as Decker. His face was probably as red as Decker's also. It felt burning hot.

"I busted my ass for you," Abel said.

"Hey, buddy, you've got it the other way around. I busted *my* ass for *you*!"

Abel hobbled past Decker and said, "Fuck you." He hopped on his motorcycle and gunned the engine.

Decker shouted after him, "Well, fuck you, too! Get another nursemaid to save your ass."

Abel took off in a cloud of dust.

"I'm not going to be there anymore for you, Atwater!" Decker screamed. "You fucked with me one time too many! Go on! Get twenty years in the cooler, for all I care." But even as he said it, Decker knew it was a lie. A second later, he mumbled, "Aw, fuck it!"

He stormed into the house. Rina was sitting in the dining area, her elbows on the table, head in her hands. She'd polished his cherrywood dinette set. Everywhere he looked, she'd polished or shined something. Place was beginning to look like a goddam museum. He stomped past her into the bedroom and changed into a pair of shorts and a T-shirt. Calling Ginger to follow him, Decker headed for the stable.

He still had an hour to go before Shabbos, enough time to exercise the animals and cool his rage. He ran the horses hard, galloping, jumping, stopping and starting on command, jerking the reins tighter than necessary. Each animal he rode broke into a sweat in a matter of minutes. Ginger panted furiously, but Decker drove her on. By the time he was done with the workout, his T-shirt was soaked, his hair as wet as if he'd dunked in a pool.

Afterward, he felt calmer, his anger now replaced by nervousness at having to face Rina. But screw that! He explicitly *told* her to stay away from Abel. How could she have been so stupid as to disobey him?

Disobey him.

As if she were a child.

Sometimes it felt that way.

By the time he was done grooming the animals, he barely had enough time to clean off before Shabbos. He

took a quick shower, shampooed his hair, and shaved while
drying off.

As he dressed, he wondered how to approach Rina. She
wasn't in the house when he came into the dining room, but
the Shabbos candles had been lit. The table had been covered with starched linen, the wine poured into a crystal de-
canter, the challah set under a velvet cloth. A vase of
wildflowers sat in the middle of the table. From the kitchen
wafted aromatic smells of fresh-cooked meat, spices, garlic, and onion.

Decker felt his head begin to pound. Placing a yarmulke
atop his head, he went back into the living room, took out a
siddur, and said the afternoon prayers, then *Kaballat Shab-
bat*—special prayers welcoming the Sabbath. It took him
about fifteen minutes, then he was forced to close the book
and deal with Rina.

He popped two aspirins into his mouth, then went into
the backyard. She was studying the sky, her hand shading
her eyes. She had changed into a white dress dotted with
gold, the fabric draped subtly to give a hint of her delicious
curves. Her head was covered with a white silk kerchief
trimmed with yellow fringes, the tassles running down her
back like drawn gold. The sun had gone down, but the western horizon was still bursting with reds and lilacs, the great
mountaintops gleaming like polished brass, the foothills
aglow with the last flickers of daylight.

He called her name, and when she didn't respond, he
walked over and hugged her from behind. At first, she neither accepted nor rejected the gesture, but eventually, she
nestled into Decker's arms. They stood for a long time, until dusk yielded to night, the mountains turning into deep
purple shadows, the sky an inky ocean glittering with sil-
very waves.

"You still mad at me?" Decker said.

Rina responded in a quiet voice, "*Shalom bayis.*"

Literally translated, it meant "peace in the house." But

Decker knew it meant, "*I'm still pissed as hell,* but I don't want to spoil Shabbos." Well, he could live with that for now. At least she was speaking to him. He said, "Let's make kiddush."

At the table, Decker made the blessing over wine, Rina responded with a lackluster amen at the appropriate intervals. After they washed and broke bread, Rina started to rise, but Decker put his hand on her forearm.

"Sit," he said. "I'll serve."

She nodded.

Decker said, "Before I do, you want to get it off your chest?"

"Are you going to listen?"

"Yeah, I'll listen."

"Fine, then I'll talk."

"Fine, go ahead."

"Okay." Rina took a deep breath. "It wasn't like you thought at all. I came home around three and realized he was here. First thing I did was call you. I called the station three times, Peter. Don't you ever pick up your messages?"

"If it's an emergency, they'd beep me."

"But this wasn't an emergency, Peter. It's not like the guy was a murderer or something. You just said to keep away from him. So I did. I cooked, I cleaned, I polished. I could have been the lead write-up in the *Journal of Balabustas.*"

Decker smiled.

"I'm not complaining," Rina continued. "I really like preparing for Shabbos. I'm old-fashioned that way. But I don't like feeling imprisoned. I kept waiting for you to call me. Then I thought, This is utterly ridiculous. I've lived by myself for two years at the yeshiva, a year in New York. I'm not going to start getting regressive just because you're around."

"It's not a matter of being regressive," Decker said. "I told you to stay away from him."

"What you told me is that you're uncomfortable about

him hanging around when you're not home. Not exactly a staunch warning that he's *verboten*. And I didn't *hang around* him at all. I didn't even see him for two hours. Then I went outside to take out the garbage and realized it was one hundred and two degrees at five o'clock. The guy had been working for God knows how many hours without water—unless he used the hose outside. So kill me! I took pity on the guy, *your* former friend, and brought him out a pitcher of orange juice. I even changed my clothes so he couldn't misinterpret anything. Know what happened?"

"What?"

"I scared him. I said, 'Abel?' And he jumped about fifty feet. He wasn't wearing his leg, he must have taken it off because it was so hot, and he tried to stand up and fell flat on his rear. Peter, the look on his face. He was so *embarrassed*. I just put down the pitcher and glass and ran into the house."

Decker didn't say anything.

Rina said, "An hour later, I came back to pick up the glass. Not more than five minutes before you came home. The guy turned beet red as soon as he saw me. He'd put on his leg, by the way. I tried to ease his discomfort. I told him about this guy I knew in the IDF who lost his leg—legs. And all the phantom-limb pain he had. I guess I was babbling until I heard you pull up the car. I said, 'Great, Peter's home.' Then you come roaring in like some crazed beast. What in the world came over you?"

Decker didn't answer.

They sat in silence for a minute.

Rina sighed, told herself to forget the whole thing. Peter looked so downtrodden, absolutely miserable. She squeezed his hand and said, "Sit, Peter. I'll serve."

"No, I said I would."

"I know. Relax. I'm sure I had a much easier day than you."

"Thanks, Rina." He gave her a weak smile.

"Boys send their regards," she said while in the kitchen.

Damn, Decker thought. He forgot to call them. He'd been lousy to Rina, lousy to Abel. He'd probably make a lousy father to her sons as well.

Rina came in carrying a three-divisioned platter—veal in the entrée section, potatoes with onions and peppers on one side, fresh asparagus topped with hollandaise on the other.

"I gave them your love as well," she said.

"I meant to call them."

"They understand, honey."

Sure they do. Decker put a slab of meat on his plate. "Rina, I did something very stupid. You asked me about Abel, and I didn't level with you."

Rina waited for more.

"I've known Abel for a long time," Decker said. "He's crazy, eccentric, but I've never known him to do anything even remotely violent. So I didn't want to sentence him before a jury did. But I should have told you this. I bailed him out of jail a few days ago. He'd been booked for sexual assault—rape."

Rina's mouth dropped open.

Decker said, "That's why I became unglued when I saw him with you."

Rina didn't answer, just stared at him. Decker threw up his hands.

"Go ahead and say it."

Rina said nothing.

"Okay, then I'll say it," Decker said. "How could I be so stupid? There, now you don't have to say it. Just give me some ears and a tail and send me off to Pleasure Island."

Rina cracked a smile. "Well, any man who knows about Pinocchio can't be all bad."

"Thanks."

She fidgeted a moment. "Did he do it?"

"I honestly don't know," Decker said. "I'd like to think he didn't, but there's some damning evidence against him. I'm supposed to be investigating the case for him, but I've been so preoccupied with my own work, I haven't had a spare moment. Abel was fixing up my place, working off the bail money I gave him, even though I told him he didn't have to pay me back . . . and then I forgot to call the boys." He stared at his plate. "I was way out of line when I spoke to you like that. And yes, I was an ass for not telling you. I don't know what goes through my head sometimes. Sorry."

"It's okay." She took his hand and kissed it. "Honestly."

"Thanks."

She withdrew her hand and started to eat. Though she smiled at him whenever their eyes met, Decker knew that Rina was still holding something back. Well, he wasn't open with his feelings, either. Often when work got him down, instead of complaining to Rina, he talked to himself. Rode his horses around and around while carrying on imaginary conversations. But Decker felt that with women it should be different. They were supposed to emote.

He said, "You're still mad, aren't you?"

"It's not that."

"Then what is it?"

"All right." Her voice was hesitant. She lowered her fork and said, "You scared me, Peter."

Decker was taken aback. "Scared you?"

"It wasn't what you said, or even how you said it." She paused and tried to find her words. "It was the look in your eyes. The absolute rage. I . . . I felt . . . forget it."

"Don't stop now," Decker said. He was trying to keep his voice calm.

"Put it this way," Rina said. "I was cognizant of the fact that you had a gun."

Decker was shocked. *"What?"*

"Well, you asked."

Decker covered his face with his hands. "Well, this is charming. You thought I was going to shoot you."

"I didn't say that. I was just thinking if the boys had been there—"

"I'd shoot the boys, too?"

"Forget it."

"No, no, no. Tell me. And you don't have to be afraid of anything, because I'm not packing."

"You're very hurt." Rina tried to take his hand, but he pulled it away. "I can't help your feelings, Peter. Maybe you don't realize how big and awesome you can be. And maybe you should realize it. Yitzchak was very soft-spoken, never raised his voice. I'm not telling you to be like him—I love you just the way you are—but I am telling you what the boys were used to. They've never seen a temper like that, and I'd like it to remain that way for *their* sake. They worship you. They'd be devastated if you . . . you glared at them like that. Especially Shmuli. You know how sensitive he is."

Decker pushed his plate aside, feeling tired and old. Rina had wounded him, but it wasn't the first time he'd been hit in that spot. Jan had told him the same thing once—a long time ago, right after they'd married. Afterward, he'd looked in the mirror. His eyes had been *murderous*. Decker supposed that look made him effective around the bad guys, but a hard person to deal with if you were on the right side.

"I'm sorry," Rina said quietly.

"Don't apologize," Decker said. "You didn't do anything wrong. Like you said, I asked."

"I love you, Peter."

"I love you, too."

"I know you do. And I know you'd never hurt me."

"I'd rather kill myself."

Rina got up and hugged him. "I know that. Dear God, I just want a little peace for the both of us. Okay?"

"Okay."

Decker pulled his plate back, picked at his food.

"You don't have to eat if you don't feel like it," Rina said. "I won't be offended."

"No." Decker sat up in his seat. "No, I'm going to eat and forget about work and Abel and losing my temper. I'm going to enjoy Shabbos and this wonderful dinner, because in a week you'll be gone and I'll be back to eating salami and crackers." Decker picked up a veal rib and chomped into the meat. *"Bon appétit."*

"Bon appétit," Rina echoed. She sat back down in her chair and picked up the other rib.

They sat for hours, talking, singing Sabbath songs, laughing, and eating until the roast was reduced to bones.

The Fifth Commandment deemed Sabbath a day of rest, an obligation that Decker chose to take literally. He spent most of Saturday afternoon in bed, sleeping or otherwise, depending on Rina's mood, and didn't think about work or Abel. Instead, he concentrated on renewing his bedraggled spirit and reached moderate success. He and Rina were all sweetness and light, stargazing lovers. They went out Saturday night, saw a terrible play at the Music Center, then indulged in triple-scoop ice-cream sundaes. Sunday morning, Decker called the boys in New York and sent them his love *directly*. Then Rina packed a lunch and they went on a three-hour horseback ride. By Sunday evening, Decker felt good about himself, good about Rina. His relaxed manner had a great effect on her. Her face radiated good cheer.

But Sunday night he slept restlessly, had disturbing dreams about Abel. Not Nam dreams, thank God, but nightmares nonetheless—Abel falling down a cliff, drowning in an ocean, sinking in sand. And Decker was always a minute too late.

He got up at five Monday morning, realizing he didn't have to be Freud to know what was going on. At six, he called County Hospital. The general operator wasn't on duty, so he phoned a special police line and found out that Myra Steele was still in the County Complex—Women's Hospital.

He dressed, showered, and said his morning prayers in a record twenty minutes. Right before he left, he gently shook Rina and told her he was going to work, his spare key ring was on the kitchen table. She could take the Jeep or the Porsche. She gave him a sleep-laced kiss, and pulled the covers over her head.

The sun had just risen, bad timing since he was heading eastward. Hot white light poured through the windshield, and Decker's eyes began to water. He slipped on his shades, yanked down the unmarked's sun visor, and sped down the Golden State Freeway and exited on Brooklyn Avenue in Boyle Heights.

East Los Angeles—Hollenbeck substation—had been Decker's first assignment after he'd joined the LAPD. He'd been directed there because at the time he'd been one of the few white boys whose Spanish had been fluent. After having worked with the Cubans in Miami, Decker had found the Hispanics in Boyle Heights a soft-spoken and compliant group. A long time ago, the area had been Jewish, but since Decker had moved to L.A. the only Jewish remnants he'd seen were a few languishing delis and the Breed Street Shul—a synagogue still gloriously beautiful, but falling apart because of lack of money and worshipers.

Seated on the apex of a hill, Los Angeles County Medical Center peered down upon the industrial sink of downtown L.A., the most prominent of its buildings a tiered wedding cake of faded yellow concrete, fronted by an asphalt parking lot. He entered the complex through Marengo Drive, drove past the psychiatric and pediatric units, and followed the inclined road to the top. This area of the center had patches of lawn and shade, looking more like a college campus than a hospital. In a sense, County General was a campus—USC Medical School trained its docs here. The day was turning hot, grass wilting as the minutes ticked on. Only the eucalyptus seemed unaffected. Easygoing trees, taking L.A.'s summer heat and smog in stride, always large and leafy, emitting the tangy smell of menthol. Decker glanced across the roadway and he saw a shaded pathway leading to Women's Hospital. Parking was around the corner.

He drove past the first group of structures, went around the block, passed the County Coroner's Office and parked in a pay lot. Across the street was an orange and blue Howard Johnson's resting in a deserted, weed-choked field.

Myra Steele had been placed in a semiprivate on the fourth floor. She and her roommate were sleeping, Myra closer to the door. The walls were institutional beige, the flooring new white tile. The room smelled of antiseptic spray and hummed with air-conditioning. A wooden file-holder was nailed onto the outside of the door, and in it was Myra's chart. Decker looked over his shoulder, then lifted the chart and quickly peered through the medical findings. Most of the jargon he didn't understand—technical terms for what had happened to her. He skimmed the pages for anything relevant.

Patient cooperates with procedures, meds, but refuses counseling at this time. Patient appears to be coping well, though still uncommunicative about the incident. Benefits of rape counseling explained several times to both patient and mother, but patient still refuses any psych treatment at this time. Mother may be an impediment.

Decker heard padded feet approaching and placed the chart in the holder before the nurse noticed him. He entered the room, found a chair, placed it next to Myra's bed, and pulled the privacy curtain around the bed and himself. The noise of the metal rings dragging across the rod woke her up. She jumped up, startled, but fell back on her bed a moment later.

"Great," she said. "Open my eyes and what do I see? Another cop. Leave me alone. I already sayed what I want to say."

Decker looked at the teenaged whore. Her right cheek had been bandaged where the knife wound was. The rest of her face was undeniably pretty. She was light-skinned, with amber almond-shaped eyes that slanted upward, giving her a hint of the Orient. Her jawline was long and sleek, her complexion smooth. Her lips were thick, her nose broad and poreless, her shoulder-length hair jet black, unruly and coarse, giving her a wild and sexy look. She had the sheet pulled up to her neck, until she noticed Decker's eyes upon her. She lowered it, allowing him to see her open hospital gown, see large mounds of coffee-colored breasts.

"Like brown sugar, honey?" Her voice was hoarse.

Decker didn't answer.

"Can always use more fuzz in my pocket," she said.

"How many of us do you have?"

Myra smiled. "Why don'tchu join the club and find out?"

"Amazing you're still going back to the trade after what happened to you."

Myra was silent. She covered herself.

"Your main man pressing you a little hard, Myra?" Decker said. "You don't work, it's fewer pennies in his pocket."

"Pennies?" Myra laughed. "Honey, I make more in a month than you do in a year."

"I don't doubt that," Decker said. "But everyone knows it's not what you get, it's what you keep."

Myra's smile disappeared. "Fuck off. I'm not gonna do it and that's that. So don't try to convince me no more, or I'm gonna get real pissed and drop the whole case."

Decker didn't say anything, just tried to assimilate what he'd just heard. *Drop the whole case?* Myra seemed to misunderstand his silence.

"Look," she said. "I sayed all this before, but I'll say it

again. Ain't the first time I've been cut up—been the worst time, but it ain't the first time. I go testify and 'spite all yo' double-talk about none of my past history comin' out, it's gonna come out."

Decker had to improvise. "The jury will be instructed to exclude any of your sexual history—"

"Shit, shit, and more shit," Myra said. She took out an emery board from her nightstand drawer. Her eyes glanced at the clock. "What the hell do you think you doin', botherin' me with your shit at six-thirty in the morning? I didn't even brush my teeth yet."

"I'm sorry about that."

"I bet," Myra said. She sawed her nail tips furiously. "Go away."

Decker said, "I just want—"

"You just want a big gold star on your record, and you don't give a shit what happens to me. Let me tell you this, Mister Policeman. My man and my lawyer are handling this. You just keep your big nose out of my face, and maybe you and your buddies'll get a itty-bitty gold star for putting the son of a bitch away for a couple of months."

"You're not worried about him coming back?"

Myra laughed. "They never come back. Just go on and carve up a new one. Hell, by then, I'm out of here."

"You don't seem too traumatized by the rape," Decker remarked.

Her eyes grew mean. "I don't need to cry and moan and weep like them weak bitches out there. But that don't mean it didn't happen to me."

Decker said, "I'm sorry about that, too."

"You just full of sorrys today."

Decker's brain moved fast, putting two and two together. Myra didn't want to testify because she didn't want her sexual conduct coming out in court. She was willing to plea-bargain the case down to a lesser count. But why? She seemed like a tough woman, could stand up against all the shit in court.

"Myra," Decker said, "I don't mean to sound blunt, but people know what you do. Why *are* you so anxious to keep it under wraps?"

"None of yo' business."

Decker thought hard. Who wouldn't she want to know her past. A boyfriend? Her parents? Or was she protecting her man by not testifying, afraid that she might give something away if she went on the stand?

All guesses. He recalled what he knew about her. She came from Detroit, but her three priors happened in L.A.

On a hunch, he said, "You called Mama when it happened, huh? And she came out to lick your wounds. She doesn't know about you, does she?"

Myra sucked in her breath, then let out a phlegmy cough.

Decker waited until she was done and said, "Can't blame you for not wanting her to know. What's your problem? Mama won't leave until the whole mess is settled? Meaning if this goes to trial, she's gonna hear everything about you?"

Myra said, "Man, if I'da knowed all this was gonna happen, I don't think I woulda said nothing."

"Mama's driving you crazy?"

"Mister Po-liceman, you don't know the half of it. Mama's fine in the clinch. And fine if you like tea parties with the preacher and happen to be sexual in the usual way. But since this girl never wanted no boys, no husband, and no *babies*, we just didn't get on real good, know what I'm sayin'?"

Decker nodded. "Can't get rid of her?"

"Like you said, not until this mess is cleared up," Myra said. "So you see why I don't want no trial. When I ran away, I wrote to Mama and told her I found a job. And she goes, 'Which job is that, honey? You don't got no education.' Well, then I told her I worked as a waitress during the

day and was studying to get my *high school diploma* at
night. Mama don't like bad girls. That kept her quiet. Now
she's back and asking me about when I'm gonna graduate. I
got to get her outta here before she finds out the truth."

"What would happen if she found out?" Decker asked.

Myra looked grave. "Mama has a bad temper for sinners.
Once she found out that my baby sister was chippin'. Mama
whopped her good. I mean, Mama's a good woman, but she
don't like no one giving her a bad name. So . . ."

Decker said, "Why don't you get your high school
diploma? Why are you doin' what you're doin'?"

Myra shrugged. "My man gives me a house, food, dope.
And I got lots of girlfriends in the trade. Guess I'm lazy.
And my man's got a mean temper. I quit now, he might just
get a little physical. But one day, I'll quit. Find me some fat
old fart with lots of bread. Get him to give me a *ring*. Let
the sucker fuck me while I whip him with cat-o'-nine-tails.
He'll hire me a cute little piece o' black ass that I can have
whenever I want. I got it all planned out."

"As long as Mama is out of the way."

Myra didn't answer. Decker stopped talking for a moment, let the silence cleanse his thoughts. Then he said, "If
your pimp didn't cut you up, why won't you give us his
name?"

"My man like to remain an-no-*mim*-no-mous. He says
publicity makes you fatheaded."

"I'd still like to talk with him," Decker said.

"Yeah, so would all of Vice." Myra laughed. "You is on
your own, mister."

"You say your pimp didn't cut you?"

"He didn't cut me."

"Then who did?"

"You *got* who did it," Myra cried out.

"Myra, there's some physical doubt that the man we ap-
prehended is the man who cut you." Decker sized up the
whore. She looked pained. "Way his lawyer figures it, the

man we have in custody had sex with you, but didn't cut you—"

"That's a lie!"

"We just don't want to play plea-bargain unless we have an ironclad case against him."

"He raped me!" Myra exclaimed. "Son of a bitch, bastard raped me and sliced me and beat me—"

"Okay, okay," Decker said, trying to calm her down. "I believe you. But I really need your man's name just to *clear* him. Just so I can go back to the district attorney and say, 'Hey, the woman's man definitely didn't wield the knife. It wasn't a domestic type of thing. Go ahead with the case as is.'"

"I won't give you his name," Myra said.

"Your man really has you spooked, huh?"

Myra said nothing.

"Your man a Santeria?" Decker asked.

The whore stiffened.

"A Palo Mayombero," Decker said. "Or maybe he has a *tía* who's a *bruja*. She'll put a hex on you—"

"Stop it!"

"You don't really believe that shit, do you?"

Myra didn't answer right away. Finally, she said, "I like to stay healthy, man. I like to stay healthy."

Decker regarded her. She looked anything but healthy, but the irony was lost.

"I want to help you, Myra," he said. "I want to make sure the guy is really guilty, so trial is out of the question, and we've got the goodies, so he'll be begging to bargain. But if you don't cooperate, give us your pimp's name, PD may get wind of what's going on, that his client has an out—your man. He'll insist on a trial. Then Mama may find out."

Myra broke her emery board in half. "You're bastards, all of you. Don't give a fuck what happens as long as you get your fucking gold star. So what if my mama finds out, if my man finds out? So what? Who gives a shit about Myra—the victim!" She laughed bitterly. "That's what I am. A fucking victim—twice."

Her eyes remained hard, but they were moist as well. Decker took a minute to think. He focused in on Abel, on all they'd gone through together. Yes, he had saved Abel's ass. But Decker couldn't count the number of times that Abel had saved him as well. It had been so common back then. Everyone saving everyone else's ass. Best thing you could have done was get along with everyone on your side. Because you never knew if someday that guy you called an asshole was the one to yank you down when enemy fire started, to jerk you away from stepping on a land mine, cover your body when a grenade exploded. Something you just did. Saved asses.

But that was then. Decker, the empathic rape cop of today, said, "You are a victim. And I'm sorry. Again, I'll find your man without your help."

"I bet," Myra said. She brushed tears away from her eyes and sunk under her covers. "My man finds out I talked to another cop, he's gonna fix me good."

"Myra . . ." Decker leaned in close. "Don't worry about your man. I can reverse whatever he puts on you." He closed his eyes, and murmured a Santeria chant he'd memorized from the old days. When he was done, he put his fingers to his lips and whispered, "All I need is a bag of chicken feathers and a roll of pennies."

Myra looked at him with a mixture of awe and dubiousness.

Decker nodded solemnly.

"You into that shit, too?" Myra whispered.

"Only for good," Decker said. "I can reverse spells, but not make them. Just my particular power. But you can't tell anyone."

"Oh no," Myra said.

"Good."

Decker paused a minute, found himself thinking as a

lawyer would. At least the prosecution was anxious to plea-bargain. Abel could milk that for all it was worth. Then again, if Abel held fast to his plea of innocence, she might even drop the charges rather than go to trial. But what if Mama had to leave suddenly? Then Myra might permit the case to go to trial. There was physical evidence against him, even if some was inconsistent—Abel might beat it. But then again, he might not. Should he cut his losses or go for the big one? Fuck it. He'd pass the info on to Abel's lawyer, screwing his compadres at Hollywood in the process. The last thought didn't set well with him.

Decker said, "I did something for you, Myra. Now, you have to do something for me."

Myra said nothing, regarded him with suspicion.

"Let's do us both a favor," he said. "Throw some attention away from yourself. Tell me the names of a few of the girls in your pimp's stable."

"Why?"

"I'll squeeze your pimp's name from them. Then you won't be the one who was talking too much, eh?"

Myra said, "Pass the buck?"

"Let's call it exchanging favors."

"How do I know you did whatchu said you did?"

"Are you doubting my power?" Decker said. "If you doubt the power, Oggun will get very angry—"

"I didn't say I doubted you."

"Good," Decker said. "C'mon, darlin'. Surely there's a bitch or two in the bunch that you can't stand. Someone who gets on your case all the time, rips off your stuff and junk and bad-talks you in front of the man."

Myra didn't answer.

"Just one name," Decker said. "Someone I can squeeze."

Myra finally said, "I don't know why I'm doing this, but I'm gonna do it 'cause I really hate this bitch. Too bad you can't hex, 'cause this bitch is worth hexing bad. Lotty's the first name, last name is spelled J-A-C-Q-U-E-S-O-N.

Thinks she's so fine, spellin' her name with a fancy Q-U in-stead of a K. Miss Fine and Fancy Bitch." She stuck out her tongue.

"Where can I find her?" Decker asked.

"In Hollywood, in an apartment right near Gower Gultch."

"You're a peach, Myra." Decker winked at her, retracted the curtain, and left, noticing her roommate was still fast asleep as he closed the door behind him.

ᕲ19

Refreshed from a weekend of relaxation, Marge was humming when she entered the squad room. She dropped her purse on her desk and asked Hollander what was shaking. He answered that she'd just missed all the action. Marge looked at him dubiously.

From his desk, Paul MacPherson eyed Marge, thinking, What a hunk of woman. He debated asking her out to the Shakespeare play again, but squelched the notion. Rejection wasn't palatable first thing Monday morning. "Actually, you did miss some excitement. Not a whole lot, but enough to make my blood pressure rise a notch."

"What happened?" Marge asked.

"A deuce was on the loose," Hollander said. "Somehow he escaped from downstairs booking, came up to the lobby, and started raising a ruckus."

"Slithery little guy," MacPherson said. "Turns out he was born without clavicles. Jailer claims he squeezed between the bars."

"Still say that's impossible," Hollander said.

"Took three of us to catch one of him," MacPherson said.

"Doesn't say much for our security," Marge said. "Or the physical condition of our officers."

Hollander took the comment personally. He patted his

belly and looked at Marge. "You ever see me when I was two hundred and rock-hard?"

"Since I've known you, Mike, you've always looked like you do now."

"Pity," Hollander said. He pushed his body out of his chair and grunted as he struggled to put on his coat. "I'm off to the nuthouse, Marge. Hear all the pleas of the bad little kiddies. 'Please don't send me to Judge Reilly!' "

"Who's Judge Reilly?" MacPherson asked.

"Juvey judge," Hollander said. "Real hard-ass, God bless him. You can get these kids to admit anything as long as you have Reilly hanging over their heads." He laughed fiendishly. "You field any new calls, Marge."

"Fine," she said.

After Hollander left, MacPherson said, "It's all a lie, you know."

"What?"

"Mike was never two hundred and rock-hard. But why ruin his nostalgic recollections with the truth?"

"Why ruin?" she repeated absently. She pulled out a current file, but her mind remained elsewhere.

A deuce on the loose.

Son of a bitch! *That* was where she'd seen that Douglas Miller—the asshole child-stealing father. He'd been booked here once as a 502, and a real mean drunk at that. They'd brought him in, cussing and fighting. She'd just happened to be downstairs. Must have been six months ago. Only he was definitely not using the name Miller. What the hell had they booked him under? Marge remembered hearing the name, but couldn't bring it up from the storage banks. She debated calling Benko, but decided to handle it herself. She stood up and said, "I'm going downstairs for a minute."

"Don't stay too long," Paul said. "Your sexual aura might make the incarcerated misfortunates horny."

*   *   *

Decker said to Marge, "Helping Clerical out?"

"Funny, Pete." Her eyes never wavered from her desk, which was covered with stacks of booking slips.

"Seriously," Decker said. "What are you doing?"

Marge checked her watch. "I could ask you the same thing. It's one-forty, and you haven't even logged in."

"I was at court."

"All this time?"

"I also had some personal business to attend to."

Marge smiled. "Man may not get it too often, but when he does, it's gourmet."

"I wish."

Marge raised her head. "You and Rina having problems?"

Decker laughed. "No. I didn't mean it that way. I just meant I wish that was what I was doing all morning."

"And what *were* you doing?"

"Chasing down a Marielito pimp who's into devil worship. He calls himself El Dorado."

"Like in the Cadillac?"

"The very one," Decker said. "Never found the golden man, but I don't need him anymore."

"What'd you need him for?"

"He's the pimp of the girl my alleged rape-o friend cut up. I figured he might have gotten mad at her, cut her up, and the girl was protecting him. I had to rule him out. And unfortunately for Abel, I did. Old El Dorado Juarez had a nice alibi."

"Which was?"

"I didn't talk to him directly, but I found out where he was when the assault went down—at a script meeting in the office of a major film producer. He was there the whole night with the producer and seven of his lackeys. Seems he—like everyone else in L.A.—has written a screenplay, and this producer bought it for six figures."

"Jesus."

"Producer's secretary says it's a . . . let me find my exact notes . . . here they are. Get this: 'a riveting firsthand account of his life—from the Mariel boat lift from Cuba where he was imprisoned as a political enemy . . . ' Guy actually ax-murdered his ex-girlfriend's brother—"

"Jesus!"

"Wait! There's more. Get this. ' . . . to his impoverished life in Miami, to his move to L.A. and his struggle to the top.' Studio thinks Juarez's a successful businessman. Seems he's done very well in the commodities market! 'Course we won't mention his undeclared income derived from illegal chemicals and women."

"Did you enlighten Miss Secretary?"

"I tried, Marge, but some people just don't want to be enlightened." Decker shook his head. "The upshot is, the scum's ass is covered, and my friend's head is still in the noose. So there you have it. Now I did Show and Tell. It's your turn."

"I'm looking through booking slips."

"I gathered that."

"Remember that child-stealer, Douglas Miller, the one Charlie Benko was looking for?"

"The father of the little girl we thought might have been Katie?"

"That's the one. Doug Miller was booked here about six months ago on a five-oh-two. Only he didn't use the name Doug Miller. I'm trying to . . . This is it!" She held up a slip. "I don't believe it. Rusty Duralt! This is the one, I swear it is! Man, will you look at this."

"What?" Decker asked.

"He was booked five months, three weeks, two days ago! I knew it was about six months. God, I'm great."

Decker smiled.

Marge said, "Rusty Duralt is a marked man." She looked at Decker. "Do me a favor. Call this number and find out if they have a little girl there named Heather—No, wait. That's no good. It'll make the wife suspicious."

"If the wife knew her husband kidnapped his daughter."

"But she might know."

Decker nodded. He thought a moment. According to the information, Heather Miller or whatever her name was now should be about two and a half. Could still be in diapers at that age. He said, "Give me the number."

Marge read off the digits, and Decker dialed the phone. A woman answered on the second ring. He explained he was doing a promotional for Pampers. Did they have any young children in the house? If they did, Proctor and Gamble would be happy to send them a free economy box of their newest line of disposable diapers. The woman answered him back, and Decker smiled.

"Uh-huh, two little girls," Decker said. "And what are their ages so I'll know what size to send them?"

Marge held her breath. A moment later, Decker gave her the thumbs-up sign.

"And you're still at the address . . ." Decker snapped his fingers, Marge shoved the booking slip under his nose. "Nine-five-five-six Pantella Way? Good. We'll send out those diapers right away."

Marge yanked on his arm, and scribbled furiously on a piece of paper.

"Or . . ." Decker spoke as he read, "better yet, we'll . . . have one . . . of our . . . field representatives bring out the diapers directly. Uh, I believe a woman named Marge does the route. . . . Okay . . . Okay. Just be sure you fill out the opinion slip for us, you hear? . . . Nice talking to you too, Mrs. Duralt. Bye now."

"Whoa!" Marge clapped her hands. "Pretty swift at the confidence game."

"Isn't that what we're supposed to do?" Decker said. "Inspire confidence?"

"In the abstract."

Decker said, "Time to turn on the charm, Detective."

"No problem," Marge said, smiling. "It's part of my makeup."

"By the way," Decker said, "I had a chance to check out Sue Beth Litton's account of the day of the murders. Seems three separate people remember talking to Pappy Darcy at least a half hour before the Littons arrived. And the Littons did stop at Montequilla's restaurant in La Mesa at about the time she said they did. Time frame works. Now the surviving family could have plugged the victims before they left, but it would take pretty good acting on everyone's part to go to a restaurant after doing something gruesome like that. I spoke to the waitress who served them. They said the family seemed to be having a great time, she served them second helpings of dessert." Decker shook his head. "I don't think murder is a good hors d'oeuvre."

Marge said, "What about Pappy and Granny?"

"According to Crandal," Decker said, "they arrived before the Littons did."

"That's according to Crandal," Marge said.

"Arrange an interview with the parents," Decker said. "They should be back at the farm by now."

Marge said she would.

Decker paused a moment. "No, no, no, I'm not ruling anyone out. But besides the family, we have Byron Howard, his wife, Darlene, a bunch of lunatic bikers, Rolland Mason's disgruntled girlfriend . . ." Decker frowned as he thought about it. "I've got a three o'clock appointment with Annette Howard. I talked her into meeting me in the city. *Alone.*" He raised his eyebrows.

Marge stood and gathered her piles of booking slips. She slung her purse over her shoulder and pinched Decker's cheek. "Turn on the charm, Sergeant."

He winked and answered, "Part of my makeup."

*   *   *

Decker was sitting at the counter, on his fourth cup of coffee, when he spotted Annette Howard. Thank goodness for small favors. He'd begun to think that she'd chickened out. She came over and started to sit, but Decker stood up.

"I've got us a booth in the back," he explained. "I was only sitting here so I'd be sure to see you."

"Counter's fine," Annette said. "I don't need anything fancy."

Decker smiled. "I like privacy when I'm with a pretty gal. This way."

He gently steered her to the back of the coffee shop. It wasn't the tackiest place he'd ever eaten in. The smell of grease wasn't too thick, and the flooring was clean. Someone had decorated it in earth tones rather than blaring pinks and oranges. The booths were whole—no stuffing leaking from the backs and seats—and clean, the bubble gum having been removed from under the tables. Even a few healthy ivy plants hung from the exposed ceiling beams.

"After you." Decker pointed to a corner booth. Annette seemed nervous. Jumpy walk, and flushed even though the place was air-conditioned. Decker also noticed she'd curled her hair and put on some makeup. She wore a dark crepe dress that complemented her fair complexion, pearl studs in each earlobe, a thin gold chain around her neck. Big day on the town, or was she telling him something? Decker handed her a menu and waited a minute while she studied it.

"What can I get you?" he said.

"Uh, hamburger's fine," she answered.

Her voice was timid. Decker said, "Anything else?"

"No, thank you."

"Okay, then I'll just signal the waitress—"

"Uh, french fries if it's okay."

"Sure." Decker paused. "Anything else?"

"No, that's fine."

"You're sure?"

"Well, coffee, if it's no bother."

Decker smiled. "How about coffee and a big piece of apple pie?"

Annette giggled and said, "Well, if you insist."

"I insist."

"Then all right."

Decker got the waitress's attention and ordered Annette her lunch and a refill of coffee for himself.

"You're not eating?" Annette asked.

"Wife's making a big dinner tonight. I don't want to spoil my appetite."

Decker examined her reaction. Her cheeks went a shade darker, and she lowered her head.

Life must be lonely in Sagebrush.

The waitress returned with Annette's coffee and refilled Decker's cup. After she left, he said, "Thanks for coming down to meet me, Annette."

"S' okay," she mumbled. She drowned the coffee in cream.

"How's Darlene doing?"

"All right, I suppose."

"Does she talk about what happened?"

"Sure. Everyone's talking about it."

"What about Byron?" Decker asked.

"Byron?" Annette answered. "No, Byron doesn't talk too much about anything, not even Linda's death. Darlene's got her ears open, and Byron knows it."

Decker pulled out his notepad and said, "Yeah, Byron's pretty quiet. Ever see him explode?"

Annette squirmed. "Maybe once or twice."

"What'd he do?" Decker asked.

"He didn't rant, if that's what you mean," Annette said. "Byron doesn't rant. He just sort of got all bug-eyed, turned red, and went for his shotgun. He didn't do nothing with it, but he got his point across."

I'll say, Decker thought. "What set him off?"

"Once it was Darlene's naggin'. Darl can be a terrible nag, and Byron don't like to be nagged."

Who liked to be nagged? But Decker knew that nagging took on a greater significance to this kind of man—just like the guys back home. Nagging represented an assault to their independence, a malevolent little birdie telling them they weren't perfect.

Get off my goddern back, woman.

Decker said, "When else did he lose his temper?"

Annette sighed. "Once with those Manfred boys. They kept coming around, and I guess Byron just got tired of saying no politely."

"What'd he do?" Decker asked.

"Took out his shotgun and told them to leave."

Suddenly, Decker kicked himself mentally. Byron Howard owned a *shotgun*, had fired it the day Marge and he had trod onto Howard's property. He wrote in his pad, *Check out BH shotgun. Own a .38, too?*

Casually, he asked, "What kind of shotgun does Byron own, Annette?"

The woman was not fooled one bit. She said, "Byron hunts."

"Skeet, too?" Decker said, smoothing his mustache.

"No." Annette relaxed a little. "Just hunts, and he don't do that so often anymore. He's got a Browning now, I think."

"Twelve gauge?"

"Twenty," Annette said.

Wrong gauge, but still worth checking out. Decker said, "I used to own an Ithaca deerslayer. My buddies and I used to hunt alligators with it, down in Florida. My uncle . . ." Decker smiled. "My uncle would get mad at us because we'd shoot the critter, and that's a big no-no for alligators. It makes 'em mean as junkyard dogs and ruins their hides."

He noticed Annette was hanging on to his words. Good.

"How do you kill alligators if you don't shoot them?" Annette asked.

"It's a whole procedure," Decker said. "First you bait them with a modified stick . . . it's a kind of a gaff. Once you have them biting, you tie them up, bind them completely. Then you insert this special type of gun in their mouths that shoots upward. It scrambles their brains without ruining the hides."

Annette stuck out her tongue to show displeasure.

"Sounds pretty bad," Decker said. "But if you don't keep the population under control, the buggers migrate and wind up in your swimming pool."

Decker smiled, Annette smiled back, looked like she was having a good time. He said, "I grew up in a family of independent folk, not unlike yourselves. We had lots of guns: rifles, shotguns, handguns. You carry a gun, Annette?"

"No, sir," she answered.

"How about your husband? Or Darlene or Byron?"

"Jeff has a rifle. Darlene and I know how to shoot, but we don't like guns, really."

"Byron carry anything smaller than a shotgun?"

"Byron don't like pistols," Annette said. "Says they're for killing people and not game. I've only seen him with his shotgun."

But something sounded off to Decker. He wrote himself a note to that effect and decided to change the conversation. Annette had become rigid, and he didn't want to lose her.

"Let's talk a little more about Linda," Decker said. "I've been asking around, found out that Linda had a reputation. What do you know about that?"

Annette didn't seem anxious to talk. She sipped her coffee, added two packs of sugar, and finally said, "Well, I heard things. But I didn't know for sure, so I didn't say anything. No sense spreading dirt."

Decker asked her what kind of things she heard. Annette

straightened up in her seat and explained that Linda and Carla were known as wild girls and some people talk.

"Like the people at Hell's Heaven?"

"Especially the people at the Heaven."

"Anyone in specific?"

"Carly had lots of boyfriends," Annette said. She added disapprovingly, "Too many to count. And Linda? I can't rightly say that I knew for sure if she was steppin' out, except with Byron, of course. But I knew there were problems with the marriage, so the rumors kinda made some sense."

"What kind of problems?"

"All sorts of problems."

"Like?"

Annette ticked them off. "Money problems, in-law problems, baby-making problems."

"Linda tell you all this?"

Annette nodded. "We used to talk, but not too often. After Byron, I . . . Darlene used to watch all of us, made me feel like a traitor if I talked to Linda. So I guess I just stopped. Family first . . ."

She seem burdened by that obligation.

Decker said, "Let's talk about the problems one by one. What kind of money problems?"

Annette told him that Linda had always wanted fancier things than what Sagebrush could give her. She wanted to sell the land for quick cash. Honey farming's a hard living unless you love it, and the land was probably worth more than the bees on it. But no way Pappy D would sell the land. He felt Linda was turning Luke against him.

She took another sip of coffee and said, "And it was sort of true. Everyone knew that Linda was trying to get Luke to sell out, move the cash into another business. Luke did a lot for Linda, things he might not of done for another girl, but he remained stubborn on the selling issue. Like Jeff and Byron, guess honey farming was in Luke's blood, too."

"Linda ever tell you how much she thought the land was worth?"

"No," Annette said. "I don't get involved in money affairs. Keeps me out of the family squabbles." She stopped talking for a moment. "Money and family squabbles do seem related. Guess I answered both problems one and two with that."

"Then let's move on to problem three," Decker said. "I'm assuming Linda had trouble getting pregnant."

Annette nodded.

"Was it just Linda who had the problem?"

"I think it was both." Annette turned scarlet, her voice dropped to a whisper. She leaned in close. "I think I recall Linda tellin' me that Luke wasn't really good in that department."

Decker whispered back, "He was a bad lover?"

"Oh no!" Annette protested. She sat up. "I didn't mean that at all. I mean, I don't *know* if he was a good lover or a bad lover. She never complained about that. I just meant that I don't think he was real fertile."

"But somehow she got pregnant and had Katie."

"Lord works in funny ways. Look at how long it took Rachel to have a baby."

Two years ago, Decker would have asked, Rachel who? But now he was well aware that she was referring to the biblical matriarch. He said, "Know if Linda or Luke was being treated for the problem?"

"She never said."

"Do you happen to know Linda's doctor?"

"Well, I know who delivered Katie."

"What's his name?" Decker asked.

"Doctor Stanford Meecham." She paused so he could write it down. "He practices in Sun Valley, and he's in the book."

"Great."

The waitress came with the hamburger and fries. She was about to refill Decker's cup a sixth time, but he placed his hand over the rim and shook his head.

The waitress said, deadpan, "I was wondering how much you could take."

Decker laughed. He waited until Annette had finished half her meal. Then he asked about Carla.

"What's there to say?" Annette answered.

"Know of anyone who'd want to hurt her? A jealous boyfriend?"

"Like I said, she had so many boyfriends, I lost track."

"Did her mother lose track?"

Annette looked confused.

Decker said, "Did her mother seem angry about Carla and Linda? Way I heard it, Granny D is a good Christian woman who doesn't cotton to sinners."

"That's true enough," Annette said. "Granny D didn't like Linda, everyone knew that. But you gotta understand Granny D. She was real close to Luke, and I don't think she would have liked his wife no matter who she was. Granny D is just that type of woman. Her family and no one else. She don't like B.B. either, you know."

"What did Granny D think about Carla's wild behavior?" Decker said.

"I'm sure she blamed it all on Linda," said Annette.

"And Pappy D?"

"I think Pappy was more upset about Linda talking to the Manfred boys."

Decker took a drink of ice water, then asked Annette about Byron, if he had any grudge against Luke.

"None I can recall," Annette said. "Lord, Byron felt guilty as sin for what he did."

"So Byron wasn't out to get Luke for Linda's sake?"

"Not that I know of."

No new information was turning up. Decker made small

talk until Annette finished the last of her pie. Putting his notebook away, he called the waitress over to settle the bill.

"You've been a great help, Annette—"

"You can call me Nettie. Everyone else does."

"Sure," Decker said. "And thank you for coming down and talking to me."

"Well, thank you for lunch," she said. "Only, I'm sorry you didn't eat anything."

Decker smiled. "I'm fine."

"Your wife a good cook?" Annette asked.

"Very good."

"Have a picture of her?"

Decker answered no, but he hesitated a fraction too long.

Annette said, "Yes, you do. I can tell you do. You just don't want anyone to know you carry it, 'cause you don't want to seem like the mushy type. Jeff's the same way."

"All right, I have one, then," Decker said.

"Well, let me see it."

"If you're really interested."

"'Course I am. Why else would I ask to see it?"

Groaning inwardly, he took out his wallet, knowing damn well what was going to happen. Reluctantly, he showed her a picture of Rina, and Annette's eyes immediately clouded. She studied the snapshot for a long time.

"She's very beautiful," she said quietly.

"Thank you."

"She looks young."

"She is young." Decker pocketed his wallet. "Not as young as she looks in the picture, but she's still in her twenties."

Annette wiped her mouth. "I think it's time to be going. What about you?"

"I think that's a great idea," Decker answered. He stood and thought, Good old Rina—always the showstopper.

❦20

The house sat on the eight hundred block of Whittier Drive in Beverly Hills, a two-story Spanish villa set back on a quarter-acre of front lawn. Usually, the courtyard gate was locked, but that was no problem for Abel Atwater. He had the key. He stared at the edifice, at the verandas dripping with bougainvilleas, the arched sashes, the stained-glass windows that broke the sunlight into thousands of colored droplets. The house could double for an old Mexican mission.

He gripped his toolbox, took a handkerchief out of his front overalls pocket, and wiped his face. The house would be cool inside, even without air-conditioning. Just the way those Spanish homes were designed—full of textured plaster that resisted the heat, and lots of windows for cross circulation.

This particular house also stayed cool because it was shaded by a dozen blue-leaf eucalyptus and Chinese elms. Full-sized trees, the best part of the property: to him, more impressive than the two acres in the rear with its designer rock pool and ivy-covered tennis court. The back grounds, though magnificent, were manicured, cut down and shaped by man instead of nature. But those dozen trees in the front . . . untrimmed, untamed.

Resigned to the task, Abel unlocked the gate and rang the bell that entoned deep, resonant chimes. A maid he'd never seen answered the door. This one was around forty, plump, with a broad nose and gold-rimmed front teeth. Lillian didn't like them young and pretty—for obvious reasons. Lil usually kept in her employ three housekeepers at a time, changing them as often as she did her lipstick color, finding tiny faults with each one. But at least she was nice to them while they worked for her.

"*¿La señora está en su casa?*" Abel asked.

"*Si. ¿Quién es?*" she answered.

"Plumber," Abel said, in English.

The big dark eyes scrutinized Abel. He was used to that. He remained impassive, waiting like hired help, as if time weren't money.

"*Un momento,*" she said.

The door closed in his face. It was a beautiful door. Paneled and carved, the lacquer sanded as sleek as fur. He'd done a fine job refinishing it. A half-minute later, Lillian reopened his handiwork.

"I didn't call any—"

Lillian stopped, a look of panic in her eyes.

Abel said, "You had a plumbing problem, ma'am?"

Her eyes darted from Abel to the maid. In rapid Spanish, she sent the maid away, then stepped outside and closed the door.

At fifty-eight, Lillian Sandler was fighting a losing battle with age. Abel had never seen her without makeup, and he felt embarrassed for her, catching her off-guard like this. Every single wrinkle and sag stood out like bas-relief, shouting that she was overdue for another lift. Her blue eyes were red and watery, her nose was puffy. Abel wondered whether she'd been hitting the sauce again. She was dressed in white sweats, looking a bit chunkier than he remembered, her hair wrapped in a terry-cloth towel.

"I made that call *five* months ago," she said. Her voice

was soft and furious. "I finally went and called a *real* plumber."

"So you have no need of my services. . . ."

"Cut the shit!" Lillian pulled a cigarette and a gold lighter out of her sweats. "You *look* like shit."

Abel could have said the same thing about her, but he didn't.

Lillian lit her cigarette and blew out a cloud of smoke. "So you come waltzing in here five months later and expect me to greet you with open arms. I left messages on your machine for a solid week. Couldn't you have picked up the goddam phone just once and returned my call?"

"I'm sorry about that."

"Sorry." Lillian smoked and tapped her foot. "I've heard that word enough times in my life."

"You want to stay out here and rant?" Abel asked. "It's fine if you do, Lil. I don't mind standing around while you let off some steam."

She didn't answer.

"You've got nine bathrooms in the house," Abel said. "Surely, one of the faucets has a drip I could fix."

Lillian's eyes began to water. "Why didn't you answer my calls?"

"I was in bad blue funk, Lillian," Abel said. "But I'm comin' out of it. I'm sorry that things aren't going well for you."

"Oh Jesus." She brushed tears away from her eyes. "I'm getting too goddam old for this."

"Up to you—"

"Stop it, Abel. . . . Just . . . stop it."

Abel put down his toolbox, waited for further instructions. Lillian smoked her cigarette down to the butt, then threw open the door.

She said, "There's a leak in the blue guest room's bathroom . . . in the tub. See what you can do about it."

"Yes, ma'am."

She stalked into the house, but left the door open for him. The same maid came back to show him to the bathroom. As if he needed help. He knew the house better than she did. But he dutifully followed her up the twisting oak-polished staircase, through mazelike rough-plastered hallways, floored with strain-grain strips of high-gloss mahogany and covered with genuine Navaho rugs. Lillian was remodeling again, the east side of the house this time. Endless money, endless time.

"Aquí," the maid said, bringing him into the blue guest room. *"En el baño."*

Abel nodded and closed the bedroom door. This chamber was one of the smallest bedrooms in the mansion, only 14'-by-14', and without a fireplace. It was done completely in blue and reminded Abel of an igloo. He walked into the bathroom and turned on the tub faucet. Small leak in the cold water tap. He opened his box, exposed the piping, re-fit the seat stopper, and, a minute later, the faucet was dripless. He stood and stripped naked, regarding himself in the mirror.

Lillian was right. He did look like shit. His shoulders drooped, and his ribs were stretching through his skin. Two years of grueling work—the pump-up exercises, the vitamins, the health food—blown to bits. Past six months he must have lost half of all his muscle mass. The depression had really hit hard this time. He'd stopped eating, exercising, working. Hadn't done anything but sleep—and sleepwalk. Waking up in all sorts of strange places, wondering how he got there.

Once they threw him in the drunk tank despite his protests that he wasn't drunk. But they didn't know what else to do with him, so there he remained while drunks puked on him.

Bad, he told himself. You gotta come out of it.

And he *was* getting better. His sex drive had even come back. Then this shit with the whore had to happen. Almost plunged him into another pit until Doc rescued him. Now

Doc had his own ideas about him. That Abel was *planning* to do something to his girl.

Abel shook his head with disgust. Oh man, what a girl! As if he could possibly hope to attain something so exquisite. Once he had . . . Yes, once he had.

Doc's girl. She reminded him of *his* girl. The way she spoke—a soft, soft voice. Then, him forgetting to refasten his leg when she called out to him, falling on his butt. Her going on about phantom-limb pain.

He wanted to scream, *Want to make me feel better? Suck my dick!* But of course he couldn't say that to her. She was no whore. All he could do was hold back, tell himself that she didn't know what she was doing to him, tell himself this was Doc's girl, so curb it.

Just curb it.

Then Doc walked in, red-faced, pissed as hell for no reason. But that time, Abel was pissed back. And at least that was better than being scum-sucking depressed.

He unclasped his leg, then peeled off the sock around the stump. Reaching in his toolbox, he found a carton of talc and powdered what had once been his left leg. The end of the stump was callused, a glob of white scar tissue that had once been pink with blood and flesh.

Gotta stop thinking about that. Gotta stop stop stop.

He hopped over to the bed, slithered under crisp sheets, and waited. Lillian arrived ten minutes later—done up as best she could on such short notice. She was wearing a long white silk robe, and as usual, didn't take it off until she was under the covers. Her body felt softer than usually, but it was home to Abel. He smiled at her; Lillian smiled back, afraid, a kid waiting for approval. And Abel knew it was his function to give it to her. He pinched her thighs.

"You've been a good girl," he said. "Been doin' Janie the Cong's workout every day?"

"You can tell?" she asked excitedly.

"What do you think?" Abel said. He stroked her, caressed

her. Like kneading a balloon partially filled with water, soft, rolling waves of fat. She closed her eyes and moaned under his touch. Began to massage his stump. That was how he knew she was ready.

He closed his eyes and did what he had to do.

Afterward, she slept, but Abel remained awake, thinking about how it had all started. A long time ago, he'd come to Lillian's house just to do plumbing. But he'd caught her crying, and Abel, ever the sucker for a woman in tears, had given her his shoulder. Somehow they'd ended up in bed. Maybe she'd felt comfortable with Abel because he hadn't been threatening, missing a leg and all. Whatever the reason had been, Abel had still been shocked when she'd tried to tip him with a hundred-dollar bill. It had been a pity fuck, and both of them knew it, but he hadn't expected to get paid for it.

He'd stalked off, offended.

She'd called him back that same day, let the phone ring, and ring and ring. Same thing had happened the next day, and the next. He had regarded her as a supreme pain in the ass. But a persistent pain. Maybe that had been why he'd agreed to see her again. Maybe a certain part of him admired her tenacity. Soon they had an arrangement, but the rules from the start had always been clear. Yes, she was paying him, but Abel was calling the shots. And she'd treated him with respect because of it.

He turned to his right, saw her head buried deeply in a down-filled pillow, her lips parted, snoring gently. He chuckled to himself. Good old Honest Abe Atwater, the one with cardiac muscle made of mush. It cost him his girl, his leg . . .

Lillian snorted, opened her eyes. Abel smiled.

"How was your beauty rest?" he asked.

"Good, thanks." Her face had softened, had become more

feminine. She took his hand and said, "Now that we have all this . . . business—"

"Plumbing business," Abel said.

Lillian laughed. "Plumbing taken care of . . . want to tell me why you came here?"

"Glad to," Abel said. "I need money, Lil."

Lillian nodded, her expression fixed. Abel gave her a lot of credit. She knew what they had, what this was all about, and didn't try to make it anything more. A minute passed, and she said, "I've got about two-fifty in my wallet. Will that tide you over?"

"I need fifteen hundred. Cash."

"Fifteen hundred?"

"Yes, ma'am."

"What for?"

"Bail money."

"*Bail* money?" Lillian laughed. "Got yourself in a little bind, did you?"

"A big bind."

"What did you do?"

"I didn't do anything," Abel said. "I fucked a whore. She accused me of raping her—"

"You're accused of raping a *whore*?"

"It isn't the rape part that's the problem," Abel said. "She was sliced up. They think I did that, too."

Lillian's mouth dropped open. She stared at him for a long time. "Did you?"

"Don't ask me that," he said. "It's insulting."

"Sorry," Lillian said. She took out a cigarette. "I'm very sorry. Of course you didn't."

Abel knew she wanted him to confirm her belief in his innocence. So he pleased her and did just that. Then he said, "Someone I know lent me the money. I've got to pay him back. I'll work it off for you, Lillian—plumbing, electricity, gardening, pool cleaning—"

"Abel, please."

"Save you lots of bucks. That should please Sy."

"The only things that please Sy are aged sixteen and under." She abruptly broke into tears.

Abel waited a minute, then said, "Been giving you a hard time again?"

"Oh, Abel, it's just more of the *same*!"

"I'm sorry."

She grabbed him. "Just hold me."

"For as long as you want," he answered, taking her in his arms.

A minute later, Lillian said, "When do you need the money?"

"As soon as possible."

"Let me get dressed." She broke away from his embrace. "We'll go to the bank, together."

"Thank you, Lillian."

She looked at him, stroked his long hair, then tucked it under his headband. "Why didn't you call me for the money in the first place?"

"I should have, Lil," he answered. "I should have."

It was Decker and six pregnant women. Every time the nurse called one of the ladies into the examining room, she cast a watchful eye upon Decker, a look that said, *Well, which one is your wife?*

An hour later, when all the women had filtered out, the same nurse came back in the waiting room. She put her hands on her generous hips and said, "You're still here?"

Decker always wondered how you answered a question like that without sounding stupid. Since he had no witty retort, he didn't respond. Instead, he said, "I'm waiting to see Dr. Meecham. He told me he could squeeze me in as soon as he was done with all his patients."

"He had an emergency C this morning," the nurse said. Threads of brown hair had come loose from her knot. She looked tired. "Throws everything else off-schedule. What's your name? I'll check the book."

"I'm not in the book," Decker said. "I called about an hour ago. Detective Sergeant Decker of the LAPD."

"Oh, *you're* the policeman. I would have brought you in right away. I thought you were an expectant father. You should have spoken up."

"And gone ahead of all those tired, gravid women?" Decker smiled. "I would have gotten lynched."

The nurse laughed—a pleasant laugh. "Not far from the truth. Come on. I'll show you to Dr. Meecham's office."

The fact of the matter was that Decker had enjoyed an hour of solitude. He'd brought with him some papers Rabbi Schulman had photocopied for him—sections of Talmud concerning capital crimes. The Rosh Yeshiva had taken the time to translate not only the Aramaic of the Talmud, but the commentaries as well. Decker had asked for them, then let them sit for over a month. Of course, a distingushed man like Rav Schulman would never say anything, but Decker knew the old man was waiting for Decker to bring up the subject. When opportunity strikes . . .

Decker folded the papers in his pocket, happy he'd gone through half of the material, and followed the sway of the nurse's hips.

Dr. Meecham was at his desk, talking on the phone. He motioned Decker down, and motioned the nurse out.

His desk was a mess—piles of papers, three Styrofoam cups, a half-eaten sandwich, an ashtray overflowing with cigarette butts. The whole room was a trash heap—a small cell crammed with junk. And this guy did internals all day? Must do his conferences with the women in the examining rooms.

The doctor himself struck a good appearance, the kind of older man who'd be soothing to younger women. He seemed to be around sixty, with a head full of white hair and a matching mustache. His face was long and lean, his skin craggy and tan. No telling how tall he was, but his shoulders and neck were wide. He wore a clean white coat over a white shirt and navy tie. He had a gold pen in his pocket, and a Gucci clip bisected the tie.

He hung up and looked at Decker. "You'd better be the cop."

Decker nodded.

"I don't know how many times I've told Joy not to bring people in here," Meecham said. "This room could give you the wrong impression."

Decker didn't say anything.

"Actually, I'm meticulous with my hygiene when I'm working," Meecham said. He took out a cigarette and lit up. "But I get careless now and then about myself. You smoke? You look like the kind of person who doesn't give a shit about what the Surgeon General says."

Decker took a cigarette just to make Meecham feel comfortable. They both puffed away for a moment, then Meecham said, "What gives?"

"It's about Linda and Luke Darcy."

"Yeah?" Meecham asked. "What about them?"

"They went to see you about fertility problems," Decker said, improvising. "What can you tell me about it?"

"Confidential." Meecham shrugged. "Sorry."

"Then you don't know."

"Know what?" Meecham asked.

"They're dead."

The cigarette fell out of Meecham's mouth. He quickly stubbed it out.

"Can I see their file now?" Decker asked.

"Is this some kind of joke?"

Decker answered the question by pulling out his badge, letting Meecham know he was for real. Neither one spoke for a minute.

Finally, Meecham said, "You coming down like this. I take it they didn't die in a car accident?"

"Murdered."

"Oh Jesus," Meecham said. "Oh God." He opened his desk drawer, took out a vial of pills, and swallowed one dry. "I've got to ask this: What about the kid?"

"Katie's fine."

"Thank God for small blessings." Meecham had turned green. "You didn't know how badly those two wanted a baby—especially Linda. Luke wanted one, too, but in infertility cases, it's usually the woman who brings the man. Jesus, after all those years, for her to get pregnant, just like that. Now, they're dead. That is *fucking awful*."

Decker waited for him to calm down. Watched him light up and smoke another cigarette. Then he took out his notebook and asked, "How long did you treat Linda for infertility?"

"Years," Meecham said. "Eight years, ten years. I was treating them both. Expensive, invasive procedures. But she was absolutely insistent. Both of them were very compliant, no problems as patients. Except whatever we did for them didn't work, dammit.

"Problems like that can really stress a marriage, Sergeant. Sex becomes mechanical, a woman becomes preoccupied with ovulation, with the acidity and temperature of her vagina, the man feels like he's nothing but a reservoir of sperm. But the two of them, they really stuck with it. *Together*. Then, about four years ago, Linda finally gave up." Meecham threw up his hands. "Just called one day and said, 'Stan, I can't take it anymore.' I talked to her for a long time, mostly listened to her cry. I told her to give it a rest. Try it again in another year or two. Then, boom, a year later, she's pregnant. Go figure."

"Then she wasn't under your treatment when she conceived?" Decker asked.

"Nope. She was still my patient, but I wasn't treating her for infertility."

"So she quit around four years ago," Decker said.

"More or less," Meecham said.

Same time as her affair with Byron Howard, Decker thought. He said, "You were surprised when she got pregnant?"

"Flabbergasted."

"What about Luke?" Decker asked. "What exactly was his problem?"

"Low sperm count, about half of his viable sperm were misshapen. Tails bent, so motility was compromised. Little suckers have to be able to swim to the egg. He had no anatomical reason for the low count—no varicoceles, his testicular temperature wasn't particularly high. Hot balls kill sperm. Just one of those guys who didn't have a lot of good jism."

"And Linda?"

"Endometriosis—her uterus was full of scar tissue. The etiology, or what caused it, was unknown. Could have happened in childhood—an infection masquerading as a bad stomach ache or a false appendicitis. One of those things that doesn't show up until the woman wants to have a baby. She starts trying for a year or so, then she suspects something is wrong. We do the tests, boom, life comes apart at the seams."

"But Linda got pregnant despite her endo—whatever you call it," Decker said.

"Sure did. Woman had one operable tube at the time, that one was twenty-five percent occluded, seventy percent scar tissue on her uterus, and a compromised husband fertility-wise. God is a better doctor than I."

"Let me ask you this," Decker said. "Do you think Linda might have gotten pregnant with another, more fertile man?"

"Either one of them had a better chance with other partners. But I'll tell you this much, Sergeant. Linda was already being inseminated with sperm other than her husband's."

Decker raised his eyebrows.

"No," Meecham said. "It's nothing like that. Luke knew about it and agreed to it. It's called a cocktail mixture, and it's pretty common these days. Husband's sperm is mixed with a bunch of healthy sperm from physically matched donors. Usually, the only way to know for sure is to do a blood test. The insemination is an expensive and painful procedure, the woman experiences a great deal of cramping, bleeding, the man is dehumanized, emasculated. His sperm isn't good enough. But Linda—and Luke—were willing to give it a try. That didn't work. And the sperm we used was as viable as any around."

Meecham finished a second cigarette. "That's what we were doing when Linda called it off. We tried the cocktail about a half-dozen times when she said she'd finally had enough."

"Did she say why she was quitting?"

"The whole gamut," Meecham said. "The physical pain, the anguish, the toll on the marriage, the expense, the hopelessness of it all . . . God, I was so happy for them when Katie was born. Luke's not the type to do anything like Lamaze—to him, birth was a woman's affair—so she did it all by herself. And Katie wasn't an easy delivery. Linda was thirty-eight, the labor was long. But she came through it like a trouper."

"How did Linda come to you as a patient?" Decker asked.

"Referral from a local GP in Saugus. Last of a vanishing breed. He refers me all of his OB cases, because the malpractice insurance is too high for him."

Meecham stopped a moment, seemed to collect his thoughts.

"Linda seemed a little bit more worldly than the other farmer gals I've seen. More at ease with city life. I don't know what her life experiences were, but I can tell you one thing. She wanted a baby. And now . . . she's . . . Jesus, I'm sorry, I can't talk about this anymore. It's really upsetting my psychic balance. I've had a stillborn this week and an anencephalic, and I can't take any more bad news. I'll be happy to talk with you later, Sergeant. But right now, I'd prefer to be alone."

Stanford Meecham was genuinely hurting. He looked as if he was going to do more pills or booze as soon as Decker walked out the door. Decker thought of Meecham's patients, those six pregnant women, a couple of them looking as though they were ready to drop any second.

"You on call tonight?" Decker asked.

"Yeah," Meecham answered. "Why?"

Decker did an impulsive thing. He stood up, went over to Meecham's side of the desk, and yanked open his drawer.

"What the hell are you doing!" Meecham screamed.

Decker pulled out a vial of pills—Valium—and a package of breath mints. Sure sign he had something more. He pocketed the pills and mints, and as long as he'd gone this far, he opened his bottom file and took out the expected metal flask.

Meecham regarded him, his face registering both anger and embarrassment. Finally, he said, "Yeah, you're right. Take it all. I can dope myself up tomorrow night, when no one's depending on me. My ladies and I thank you, Sergeant."

Decker told him, "Don't mention it."

~21

The fifteen hundred dollars were burning a hole in Abel's pocket. He thought of all the things he could do with it—new clothes, new set of wheels for his bike, food and lodging in Sin City itself—a quick trip to Lost Wages. He could book a room at the Palace, or maybe the MGM Grand—Monday nights were generally slow—and pick up a couple of whores. Some things were just meant to be done in groups of threes. Fifteen C's and he could purchase himself one truly unforgettable evening.

As he approached Decker's ranch, he reluctantly let go of his fantasies. He parked in the driveway, hoping that Doc would be home, so the girl wouldn't think that he was trying to make time with her. Of course, if he had to talk to the girl again, it wouldn't be the worst sentence in the world. The thought of her gave him goose bumps in 100-degree weather. Limping up to the door, he gave the rapper a hard knock and waited. His luck: The girl answered with a sweet "Who is it?" Abel drank in her voice.

"It's Abel Atwater, ma'am," he answered back. "You don't have to answer the door, but I'm leaving an envelope of money for Peter underneath your mat. I suggest you pick it up as soon as I leave, because there's fifteen hundred—"

The door opened. Those eyes looking at his, that *hair*—

shiny black, all loose and long. It made him weak-kneed. All he could choke out was a prepubescent hi.

"Hello," Rina answered. Poor guy. He was so nervous, he was blushing. Or maybe it was just the heat. He'd dressed up today; he was wearing a shirt. Still, as harmless as he appeared, Rina couldn't dismiss the fact that he was an alleged rapist. She decided to be civil and nothing more.

Abel said, "Uh, could you give this to Pete for me?"

He was offering her the envelope. Rina said, "You can give him the money yourself, Abel. He's out back with the horses."

"Well, you can take it for him," Abel said. "After all, you're like his wife."

"Your business is with Peter," Rina said. "Not with me."

"Yeeesss, ma'am," Abel said.

Rina relaxed, gave him a hint of a smile. "You can call me Rina, Abel. 'Ma'am' makes me feel sixty years old. Anyway, just go around back and flag him down. You can't miss him. He's wearing a hat."

Abel laughed, and she closed the door without another word. He slapped the envelope several times against his palm, then walked through the side pathway to the back acreage, suddenly noticing the banging of his heart.

He paused before he let Decker see him, watched Cowboy Pete, dressed in shorts, a T-shirt, and a Dos Equis cap, ride an Appaloosa around the corral. Doc always covered up with a T-shirt. Abel used to kid him about his fair complexion, used to call him lobster boy, he'd turn so red in the heat.

Abel stepped out into the open field, saw Decker's eyes fix in his direction. Decker immediately reversed directions and rode over to him, hopping off the horse before the animal came to a complete stop. He looped the reins over a post and threw his arm over Abel's bony shoulder.

"Come in the house," he said. "Let's grab a beer."

Abel stuffed the envelope in Decker's shorts pocket. "There," he said. "We're even."

Decker pulled the envelope, felt its contents, then pushed it back in Abel's hands. "I told you the money was a gift."

"And I told you I was gonna pay you back."

"But I don't want it back."

"Well, I don't rightly care about what you want." Abel tossed the package at Decker's feet. "You ain't got nothing on me now. And don't worry, Sergeant. The money's mine. I earned it. Fuck, did I earn it!"

Abel pivoted and started hobbling away as fast as he could.

"I fucking can't—" Decker picked up the envelope and ran after Abel. He grabbed his shoulder. "Hey, just stop for a moment, huh?"

"Get your hands off of me," Abel said.

"Just cool off—"

"I *said*, get your hands off of me."

"I will as soon as you calm down."

Abel whacked Decker's arm off his shoulder. Then sudden force and change of equilibrium threw Decker off balance. Abel backed up two feet and arched like a threatened feline. "When I say take your fucking hands off me, I mean *now*, pal. I may be a gimp, but I'm still your peer."

Decker turned red. "I just meant—"

"You just meant, you just meant," Abel mocked him.

"Oh, fuck off," Decker said. "I'll be damned if I'm going to defend my intentions. Yeah, you're a gimp, Abe. But worse than being a physical gimp, you're an emotional gimp—"

"Oh my God!" Abel waved his hands into the air. "You've given me sudden *insight*!"

Decker felt his body about to explode. Quietly, he said, "I'm sick of you, I'm sick of your mouth, I'm sick of your problems. Get some other sucker to bail you out. Just get out of my life." He slung the envelope against Abel's chest. "I don't need the bread. Go spend it on your goddam whores."

Abel let the money fall to the ground, stroked his beard, and let out a strange smile. He cocked his hip and said, "Now ain't that the pot calling the kettle black. Way I remember it, I was always the one draggin' *your* ass out of the hooches."

"That's because you were the one draggin' my ass *into* the hooches."

"I never heard you *complain* any, Decker."

"You were too busy sniffing for poontang to hear."

"Jealous of my rate of success?"

"Fuck off, Atwater," Decker said. "Just 'cause we toured together, don't start painting me with your brush."

"Hey, Decker, your memory gears need some oiling. I recall you having a right fine time in Bangkok—"

"Man, *I* didn't want to go to Bangkok. *You* wanted to go to Bangkok!" Decker was shouting now. "*I* wanted to go to Hawaii! All I wanted to do was sit on a beach without getting my ass blown off. Nuh-huh, that's not good enough for PFC Atwater. Honest Abe wants *excitement*. Nam's not exciting enough, mind you, he's got to have more. No fucking way was Bangkok *my* idea. Bangkok was *your* idea!"

"So if you wanted to go to Hawaii, why didn't you fucking well go to Hawaii?"

"You want me to tell you why?" Decker screamed.

"Yeah, tell me why!" Abel screamed back.

"I'll tell you why!"

"Fucking tell me why!"

"I went to Bangkok 'cause *you* wanted gash, and gash was cheaper in Bangkok!"

"Well, you didn't do so bad in the Bangkok gash department yourself!"

"How would you know what the fuck I was doing? You were too busy humping like a mutt in heat."

"Not too busy to notice you taking some slant slit up to your room. I seem to recall three days passing before you let the poor thing surface for air!"

Out of the corner of his eye, Decker saw Rina standing by the back door. Her hand was over her mouth, her eyes just staring at him.

How much *had* she heard?

He felt himself go feverish with shame, hot with rage. In a blind anger, he jumped Abel, both of them tumbling to the ground.

"You talk with respect around my woman!" Decker yelled, as he tried to pin Abel down. But Abel was stronger than he looked. He took his cane and rammed it into Decker's solar plexus. Decker doubled over, but managed to shove his own elbow full force into Abel's gut. The punch winded Abel, but it didn't dull his reflexes. He saw Decker come at him with his fist, rolled over, and heard Decker scream as his fingers hit dirt. He whacked Decker across the back with his cane at the same time that Decker grabbed his hair.

Decker picked Abel's head up by the roots of his hair, and was prepared to slam him against the ground when he felt light pummeling on his back—like a gentle rubdown. The fuck? he thought. Then he heard her—Rina screaming at him.

"Stop it!" she shrieked. "Stop it, both of you! Stop it right now!"

Decker let go of Abel's hair.

"Are you out of your mind, Peter!" Rina was hysterical. Decker felt her gripping his shirt. "Get off of him! Get . . . *off.*" She yanked his shirt so hard, it ripped, and she stumbled backward.

Abel burst into laughter, Decker tried to contain himself but was unsuccessful. He rolled onto his back and broke into loud guffaws.

Rina glared at them, a piece of fabric in her hands, huffing from the exertion. Two idiots, holding their stomachs

and howling with delight, squirming on the ground like infants. They *were* infants. No, infants had more sense. They
were little naughty boys, like *her* sons after they'd played a
trick on her.

Good old Mom. The butt of all the jokes. One part of her
wanted to stalk off, another part of her wanted to join in the
fun. Yet she knew from her own kids, it would spoil their little game if she laughed with them. She maintained her stern
expression.

"You two should be ashamed of yourselves," she said as
seriously as she could.

Just as Rina thought, they laughed harder. She shook her
head. "Absolutely ashamed at such outrageous, infantile behavior." She turned on her heels and waited until she was
inside before her scowl turned into a grin.

Abel's laughter had become so hard, tears were rolling
down his eyes. "Boy, are you in trouble!"

"Big trouble," Decker said.

"Real big trouble," Abel said. "As in: Forget about getting laid."

Decker frowned. "No. Not that much trouble."

"That's what you think," Abel said. "She was *pissed*."

"Yeah," Decker said. "She was." His laughter had sub-
sided now. "I think she was upset, but not *that* upset."

"That's 'cause you're deluding yourself that you've still
got a chance," Abel said.

Decker smiled.

They were quiet for a minute, the two of them on the
ground looking up at the hot bluebell sky, the sun cooking
their faces. Abel let out a small chuckle and said, "Hell, if I
lost a night with her, I'd be pretty upset, too." He faced
Decker and said, "She's a beautiful woman, Doc. Nice inside as well as out. Congratulations."

"Thanks," Decker said. He gave Abel another smile, but
this one lacked warmth.

"Scares the shit out of you, don't it?" Abel said.

"What do you mean?" Decker asked.

"I mean, you must keep asking yourself, 'What the fuck does she see in me?'"

Decker sighed. "You're a perceptive sucker, know that?"

"I just know how it is," Abel said. "It's scary when they're that beautiful . . . that smart. It's almost . . . a curse. 'Cause if you lose them, you're a goner."

"I try not to think in those terms," Decker answered.

Decker's voice held tension; Abel didn't respond. A minute of silence passed. Abel closed his eyes, let the heat nurture his aching heart. "Just do me one favor, huh, Doc?"

"What's that?"

"If Rina's ever interested in a cheap thrill," Abel said, "send her to me."

"I send her to you, Abe, she's gonna get spoiled."

Abel laughed.

Decker said, "So what gives, PFC Atwater? You going to join the human race, or what?"

"I'll stick it out as a what."

They both laughed.

"Keep the money," Abel said.

"I don't want the money," Decker said. "Buy yourself a good lawyer."

"They switched PDs on me," Abel said. "The new one I have isn't too bad, she's already talking about plea bargaining. Buy something nice for *your* woman. A bouquet of flowers can go a long way."

"I don't think Rina can be bought so easily."

"You'd be surprised," Abel said. "Tell you what, Doc, *I'll* buy her some flowers and you tell her it's from the both of us."

"Settled." Decker stood up, offered Abel his hand, then pulled him up. "Tell your PD to call me. At home."

"What gives?" Abel tried to keep the excitement out of his voice, but he could tell by the expression on Decker's face that he hadn't.

Calmly, Decker answered, "Abe, I'm in a precarious position, doing what I'm doing for you." Precarious wasn't the word for it. He was doing a fatal balancing act, playing cop to get dope for the defense. Pete the Mole. It didn't have a nice ring to it. He exhaled forcibly, then said, "The less you know, the better. Just have her call me, okay?"

"Whatever you say, Pete. And listen to me, don't get yourself in the shithole for my sake—"

"Stuff it, Atwater." Decker rubbed his shoulder. "You pack a mean wallop for a gimp."

"Know what I want to do right now?" Abel said.

"What?"

"Go one-on-one with you."

Decker burst into newfound laughter.

"I'm serious," Abel said.

"Come on, Abe—"

"Dead serious."

"Abe, we're over forty, and it's hot outside."

"Since when did you become an old fart?"

"Since I met Rina and realized I wanted to stick around a long time."

"I'll play you easy."

Neither one spoke for a moment.

"I'll tie a hand behind my back," Abel said. "One leg, one hand, can't get much easier than that, Decker."

"You really want to do this," Decker said.

"You bet your sweet ass I do."

"It's a macho thing?"

"Something like that."

"Okay." Decker wiped off the seat of his pants. "Okay. We'll drive down to MacGrady Park and rent a basketball. I don't keep any around anymore. Just let me brush down the horse and tell Rina what's going on."

"You report to your honey," Abel said. "I'll take care of the horse."

Decker nodded. As he walked to the house, he wondered

what Rina was going to say to him. He found her peeling potatoes at the kitchen sink. She put down the peeler, wiped her hands on her apron, and gave him a disapproving shake of her head.

"Are you pissed at me?" he asked.

Rina said, "Peter, he's a *cripple*, for godsake!"

"You don't have to worry about Abel," Decker said. "He can take care of himself."

"You acted completely childish. Both of you. You were talking as if those things happened yesterday instead of what, twenty years ago?"

"About," Decker said.

"Amazing."

"It's like this, Rina," Decker said. "No matter how old you are, the minute you step into your parents' home, you become their kid. And you play into it, too. Mom serves you, scolds you for putting your feet on the table. And no matter how independent you are, you sit there like a lump and take it all. That's how it is with Abel and me. We met each other as adolescents, and we act adolescent together."

She threw up her hands. "Is he gone?"

"No. He wants to play some basketball down at Mac-Grady Park—"

"You're kidding!"

"He thinks we're still twenty."

"You told him no, didn't you?" Rina said.

Decker smiled at her, asking for approval without asking her directly.

She let out a small laugh. "Have fun, boys."

Decker smoothed his mustache, tried to figure out how to say what was on his mind. "You know, as a kid I didn't always have the swiftest of judgment."

Rina didn't answer.

"Even our forefathers weren't immune," Decker continued. "The commentaries tell us that Joshua married Rahav the whore—"

"Oh, Peter, don't get *biblical* on me. You don't have to justify what you did." She laughed again. "You mean I wasn't the first?"

"Hate to tell you, kid," Decker said.

"And all this time, I thought Cindy was hatched parthenogenetically."

Decker said, "She was hatched just like your boys."

Rina smiled, lowered her head, her eyes suddenly drifting away.

Decker had seen the look before—sweet nostalgia for her late husband—and it bothered him. The first time he and Rina had slept together, she'd been extremely shy. Decker had known part of it was modesty, but he'd mistakenly thought that part of it had been innocence. After she'd become used to their nakedness, it had become painfully obvious to Decker that he had no new tricks to teach her. Suddenly, the roles had reversed, and now she was the one playing him like a virtuoso; all she'd needed had been a little practice to get her fingers nimble. As a matter of fact, he ranked Rina as one of his best, sharing the spot with such notables as a Vegas call girl and a twenty-five-year-old nympho named Candy he had once busted on a soliciting charge.

Rina's expertise *really* bothered him.

It also put her late husband, Yitzchak, in a completely different light. Until he and Rina had sex, Decker had always assumed that the soft-spoken Talmudic scholar had lived a boring, modest life. Now, Decker found himself wondering about the duality of the guy. A Jewish Superman—a studious *bochar* by day, a stud by night.

Rina certainly knew her way around a man's body. And Decker knew there had been only one other man in her life. He was dying to ask her what Yitzchak had been like, but knew that was just the old ego begging for reassurance.

Unsolicited, she had told Decker he was wonderful. But

everything he did she said was wonderful. Decker hoped his lovemaking wasn't as mediocre as his woodworking.

The faraway look still held fast in Rina's eyes. Decker'd had enough. He said, "You want to come with us?"

"Huh?" Rina answered.

"Yoo-hoo, space cadet." He waved his hand in front of her eyes. "Want to come with us to the park? It's not a great offer, but I bet it beats peeling potatoes."

Rina said, "Sure. Why not?"

It took Abel a shorter time to deal with the horse than it did for Decker to deal with Rina. Twenty minutes later, Abel saw Decker and Rina come out of the house. He was carrying two six-packs of beer, she was carrying the car keys. She had pinned her hair under a kerchief, but her face was still as radiant as ever. She stopped in front of Abel and gave him a feigned sour look. It was all he could do to keep from laughing.

"I'm coming for two reasons," Rina said.

"What's that, ma'am?" Abel said.

"One is Peter intends to consume beer, and I don't want him drinking and driving at the same time."

"Fair enough," Abel said. "And what's reason number two, ma'am?"

"Peter just taught me CPR," Rina said. "That means I'm still a novice, so don't test out my skill, please?"

"No, ma'am," Abel said. Meanwhile, all he could think about was her lips plastered to his, her breath filling his lungs. The image made him hard.

≈22

Opening the envelope, Decker frowned. Last Friday he'd requested all of Linda Darcy's credit-card receipts. Visa had been the first to respond, sending him photocopies taken off of microfilm. The print was small and smeared, and Decker knew it would take him the entire morning to sift through the list. He opened his desk drawer and pulled out a magnifying glass, unsure what he was looking for. But he trusted his intuition. If there was something of note, he'd note it.

After three hours of hunching and squinting, Decker stretched and poured himself a cup of coffee, wishing it were Friday instead of Tuesday. But at least something interesting had turned up.

Linda Darcy had paid for a room at the Sleepy-Bi Motel on Foothill Boulevard six times during the last year—the same motel she and Byron had gone to once upon a time. And a corollary pattern had become apparent. She had also purchased gas from the same service station—a Shell—on the same day she had paid for the motel room.

She'd paid for the room.

Let's hear it for women's lib.

Decker sipped his coffee, then dialed the Sleepy-Bi Motel. A desk clerk with a nasal voice answered. Decker introduced himself and his mission, described Linda, and gave Mr. Nose Voice the dates of the trysts. The desk clerk reported back that a Mr. and Mrs. Smith had checked in all the given days, in room 211.

Big surprise. Decker kept up the questioning.

"Do you remember what this Mr. and Mrs. Smith look like?"

"The missus sounds like the woman you described. Sexy little thing."

"And the man?"

The nasal clerk punted the question, saying that in his line of business he tried to forget faces rather than remember them.

Decker described Byron Howard, Rolland Mason. The clerk said he wasn't sure, but as best he remembered, both those men didn't sound like the man she was with. Decker thanked him and hung up.

A washout.

Ten minutes later, Decker dialed up the Shell station Linda had used. Maybe one of the pump boys remembered Linda and her anonymous beau. The man who answered the line identified himself as Grains. Decker started his pitch, mentioning Linda Darcy, and received an immediate unexpected reaction. Grains became defensive, dropped his voice to a whisper and asked, *What* about *Linda*?

Bingo!

Decker pressed on. Grains's voice became edgier and edgier. Finally, Decker announced he was coming down to pay Grains a visit. Grains pleaded for a half-hour delay. He owned the station, one of his men was out sick, and he was up to his neck in work. Decker agreed to the grace period, and they arranged to meet at the McDonald's across the street from the service station in thirty minutes.

Grains was sitting at a corner table when Decker walked in. The service-station owner had a long face, sparse blond hair, bulging blue eyes, and callused hands with nails full of grease. He seemed to be around forty, thin, with a prominent Adam's apple that bobbed whenever he swallowed. He was wearing a white short-sleeved shirt with the name Jim embroidered in red thread over the breast pocket. Decker sat down in the chair next to him. Grains didn't bother to look up.

"This is my only break." He was on his second Quarter-Pounder with Cheese. Besides the burgers were two salads, two helpings of fries, and a chocolate shake. "Let's get this over and done with."

"Get what over and done with?" Decker said.

Grains regarded Decker and sighed. He ran his hand over his face. "You're a real cop, right? Not some snoop from a private agency?"

Decker took out his badge and showed it to him. Grains seemed to relax a little. Decker said, "Why did you think I'm a private investigator?"

"I thought maybe my wife found out." Grains chomped on his sandwich. "Maybe I'm still a little paranoid. A lot paranoid. After all, I haven't seen Linda for over six months."

"How'd the affair start?" Decker asked.

"Linda had been having her car fixed at the station for six, seven, eight years, who the hell remembers. About a year ago, she started acting different toward me, real friendly." He popped a half-dozen french fries in his mouth. "My wife and I . . . we were going through some bad times. I fell for it, and I fell for her. Actually thought I loved the broad until she up and left me. I not only lost her, but I lost her business as well. Teach me to mix business and pleasure. I'm just lucky my wife never caught on. That's all I'd need. My wife's Mexican and comes from an old-fashioned Mexican family. Know what her brothers would do to me if they found out I was messin' around on her? God knows, if they didn't finish me off, a divorce would. Alimony and child support. I've got six kids. My wife is also a Catholic. I had to get dispensation to marry her. Jesus, don't ever mess around on a Mexican woman."

He spoke as if only Mexican women grew irate at their adulterous husbands. Decker said, "Let's go back to Linda Darcy." He pulled out his notebook. "What exactly did you mean by 'she started acting friendly'?"

"Well, for years she's all business. Lube the car, change the belts, flush out the radiator. Sometimes she drove the pickup, sometimes she drove the Dodge. That was a honey of a car. A two-tone job—"

"Jim, how did she act friendly?" Decker said.

"Well, she just changed. Smiled when she spoke to me, touched my shoulder as we looked inside the hood together. Then, out of the blue, she said she had a little time and suggested grabbing a cup of coffee at this very McDonald's. One thing led to another, next thing I know, we're in bed together." Grains paused. "But that's all in the past. What's this all about, anyway?"

"Linda Darcy's been murdered," Decker said.

Grain's eyes bugged out even farther, then he began to choke. Decker stood up and gave him a sharp rap between his shoulder blades. Grains coughed, spit out a mouthful of food into a napkin. Decker waited for him to settle down, but Grains kept uttering "goldam" over and over.

Decker finally said, "How long did you and Linda have the affair?"

"Goldam," Grains said. "Murdered? How?"

"Shot," Decker said. "How long did you and Linda—"

"You don't suspect *I* had anything to do with it!"

"Please answer the question, Jim," Decker said.

"You aren't going to tell my wife, are you?"

"How about we start with me asking the questions, and you answering them. How long had you and Linda had your affair?"

"Goldam," Grains said. "Six months."

"When did it start?"

"A year ago."

"And it lasted for six months?"

"Yes, sir, it did. Only saw her six times, actually. But man was she a tiger."

Decker thought, Six receipts from the motel. Six times. Made sense. He said, "And you haven't seen Linda since?"

"No, sir," Grains said. "Like I told you, lost her and her business when the affair ended."

"She give you any explanation why the affair ended?"

"Nope," Grains said. "That was the hardest thing to get over. She just said it was time to move on. Like I was nothing but a piece of cattle. Pissed me off. I asked her what she meant by that, and she didn't answer me. Just left the motel and I never saw her again."

"Did you try to contact her?"

"Hell, no," Grains said. "She paid for the motel room and for her gas, but I was giving her a ton of freebies—tires, oil, transmission and steering fluid, spare parts, belts that I think her husband was using on his machinery. A free spare gas tank filled with super unleaded gas. Man, she was costing me plenty. I guess at the time I thought it was worth it. I don't think so anymore today . . . like that matters now that she's . . . goldam, that's bad. Good goldam!"

Decker flipped his notebook closed and placed it in his suit pocket. He stood up. "Thank you, Mr. Grains."

"That's it?"

"That's it."

"You ain't gonna tell my wife, are you?"

"Don't see why I should have to," Decker said. "Unless, of course, you had something to do with Linda Darcy's demise."

"Shit no!" Grains said. "I don't know a goldam thing about it."

Decker said, "Just stick around for a while."

"I'll do anything you say," Grains said. "Just keep it from my wife."

Decker said he'd do the best he could.

"The good news is you got an envelope from Manfred," Hollander said to Decker as he entered the squad room.

"What's the bad news?" Decker asked.

"Your ex is on line two," Hollander said.

Decker scanned the room for a private corner. Nothing. He depressed the blinking light and said to Jan, "Can I call you back? I want to find a private phone."

"Private phone?" Jan answered. "This sounds ominous."

"Are you at home?"

"Yes."

Decker hung up. "Be back in a minute."

"Where're you going?" asked Marge.

"Upstairs," Decker said. "I need some space."

He was in luck. The locker-room phone was vacant, the place practically empty. The change of shift was still three hours away. Two uniforms—Hunter and Bailey—were bitching to each other, quieting when they saw Decker.

"Just came to use the phone," Decker said.

Hunter smiled widely. He was a strapping man of 6'2" with thick, swollen lips. His grin was conspiratorial.

Decker felt defensive. "Calling my ex, okay?"

"Whatever you say, Sergeant," Hunter said.

"Can I have a little privacy?" Decker said.

"A little?" Bailey said. "No problem."

Decker glared at them. They moved to the next aisle. He quickly dialed, waited for Jan to answer.

"What is it?" she asked.

"First, why'd you call?"

"I'll show you, if you show me?"

"Please, Jan."

She said, "Cindy called. She's in Paris. She's coming back to the States in two weeks. She said she'll probably stop off in New York for another couple of weeks. I thought Allen and I could meet her there. You're not planning a trip back East, are you?"

"I'm not planning one, no."

"Good," Jan said. "I know . . . I know you have business back there. I think it would be awkward if we were all there at the same time."

"No problem," Decker said. "Have fun."

"Okay," Jan said. "Now what's up with you?"

Decker said, "It's about that business you were referring to. I wanted you to hear it from me. Rina and I are getting married. I don't know exactly when, probably within the next couple of months. I just thought you should know."

Without missing a beat, Jan said, "Nothing like a young filly for breeding."

Decker felt his face go hot. "Well, thanks so much for your good wishes, Janet. I really appreciate them."

There was a rare silence on the other line. Finally, she managed to say, "You're right. That was awful."

Decker was aware of his heart beating. "Forget it," he said. Knowing the reason behind the barb, he meant it.

"No," Jan said. "I'm sorry. I hope you do have kids. Cindy could use another sib."

"Cindy is basically an adult," Decker said. "I think a sib would have little impact on her."

"No, I don't think so," Jan argued.

"Fine," Decker said. "We'll see . . . if it even happens—"

"What do you mean?"

Decker cursed his loose tongue. Then he thought, What the hell? Maybe it would soften Jan's opinion of Rina if she knew they had this sore point in common. He said, "We don't talk about it, but I know Rina has had several miscarriages."

A second of silence. Then Jan said, "But she's so *young*."

"You were young, too," Decker commented.

Another silence over the phone. This one full of palpable tension.

Cindy's conception. At that time, it had been a low point in his life. Four months past twenty-one, his mind still agog with bad memories, a rookie on the force. His first assignment had been the riot squad. In 1970, Nixon had sent U.S. forces into Cambodia. The protests had been hard and furious, had influenced even traditional party schools like the University of Florida at Gainesville.

Jan had been one of his first arrests.

The pregnancy had been a terrible accident.

Shit, she had said as she paced. *To be knocked up by a* pig. *I'm not going to keep it, that's for sure. I've already made an appointment with the doctor. I think you should pay for half, Pete.*

He had simply said, *You do anything to my kid, and I'll kill you.* His intensity had scared her into listening to him. Maybe he had reacted that way because he had been adopted. If his mother's pregnancy had occurred later in the century, he might have ended up a pickled fetus in someone's laboratory.

Four months after Jan's announcement, they were married, to everyone's displeasure.

Five more tries for children. One ended in a tubal pregnancy, three had been spontaneous miscarriages.

And one stillborn.

Seeing Jan being prepped for an emergency C-section. Him being whisked out of the labor room. An hour later, he stood there, listening impassively while a ghoul in a white coat told him the baby had died during birth. But the mother was fine, thank God.

Thank God, Decker had repeated. Then, his only words: *What was it?*

It was a boy, Mr. Decker.

Jan had again retreated into her shell. When she finally did speak, the first thing she stated was a willingness to start again.

Decker had blurted out, *Jan, give it a rest.*

She didn't speak to him for six months.

Now, her voice escorted him back into the present. "I was young, wasn't I?"

"Yeah," Decker said. "Look, I've got to get back—"

"I've often thought, Pete," Jan interrupted, "not to get too metaphysical, but I really think that the purpose of our marriage must have been Cindy."

"Probably was," Decker said.

"You know," Jan said, "your stoic, *goyish* manner used to really aggravate me—"

"Really now?"

Jan laughed. "But I'll say one nice thing for you. During all our most horrible, heated fights, you never threw my wanting to . . . my wanting to abort in my face."

"I could start now, if you want," Decker said.

"Schmuck," she said. "Never could take a compliment."

She hung up the phone.

Give it a rest. Linda Darcy's doctor had told her the same thing. Was that relevant to anything? If she had been anything like Jan, the need to have a child would have overpowered her, her husband, and their marriage.

He reentered the squad room, picked up the envelope from Manfred that was lying on his desk.

Marge stared at him and said, "Ex give you a rough time?"

"No," Decker said.

"I'll bet," Marge said. "What did you ask Manfred for?"

"Information file on the Darcy land." Decker took off his coat, slung it over his desk chair, and ripped open the glued-down flap. "Of course, I'm sure they deleted all the relevant facts and figures . . . but you never know what they might have left behind accidentally."

"What'd you find out from Mister Mechanic Jim Grains?"

Decker sat down and put his feet up. "He and Linda were definitely screwing."

"What's he like?" Marge asked.

"Nothing to write home about. Scared of his wife, just your average stiff. I punched him in the computer this morning, brought up his ten-forty and five-forty for last year. He's forty-two, and netted $34,862.38. Livable for his large family, but *no* room for leftover."

"So Linda wasn't after his money," Marge said.

"It doesn't seem so." Decker sipped cold morning coffee he'd left on his desk and scanned the Darcy papers for ten minutes. When he was done, he said, "Creighton Donaldson was consistent. Manfred had appraised the Darcy land at four hundred eighty-four thou, seven hundred for one hundred acres used for livestock grazing and bee farming."

"And?" Marge asked.

"And . . . that's all she wrote." Decker closed the file. "But reading *between* the lines, I'd say that maybe Manfred intended to use the land for things other than livestock and bee acreage."

"Such as?" Hollander asked.

"Developments?" Marge said.

"Oil and minerals," Decker said. "The file mentions several geologic evaluations done in conjunction with Eagle Petroleum with reference numbers and everything. But it neglects to include any of those evaluations. I'm going to have to ask old Creighton about that."

"Thar's oil in them thar hills," Marge said.

"I don't know if there's oil, but I have a hunch someone was doing some digging," Decker said.

"So what does that and the price of eggs have to do with the crime scene at the Darcy farm?" Hollander asked.

"Maybe nothing," Decker said. "But maybe Linda was pressing Luke to sell because the bucks suddenly swelled to mammoth proportions."

"Maybe someone felt she was pressing him a little too hard," Marge said.

Decker shrugged.

Marge said, "I called Sue Beth Litton, asked her about Katie. She didn't take the kid in to see the shrink."

"Big surprise," Decker said. "They think that kind of stuff is voodoo."

"But it wasn't a total loss," Marge said. "I arranged to interview her parents. They're back at the honey farm, trying to pick up the pieces. She was not happy about it. Said her parents had already been grilled by Ozzie Crandal and the Fall Springs crew. Pappy and Granny D had gone through enough. But I persisted. We've set something up day after tomorrow. Sue Beth says Granny's still a wreck. But her father will probably talk to us."

"You know, Margie, I've been thinking a lot about those two. I reread Crandal's initial interview with them, thought about what he said. Then I went over your notes. . . ."

"Yeah?"

"When you questioned Sue Beth Litton about her family being at the convention before she was, you marked a pause by her response."

"Yeah, I remember that."

"Why?"

"Without looking, I think I asked Sue Beth if she was sure they arrived before she did," Marge said. "And she hesitated and said she was sure."

Decker said, "Everyone I talked to at the beekeepers' convention remembers seeing Pappy D before the Littons showed up," Decker said. "But no one mentioned Granny D or Earl."

Marge thought a moment. "That's consistent with what

Sue Beth said. She saw her dad but didn't mention her mom or brother."

"Maybe that's why she paused when you asked if the whole family was up there when she arrived."

"Pretty sharp, Sergeant," Marge said.

"Only Crandal's notes say that Pappy, Granny, and Earl came up at the same time. I don't know if he assumed it or they actually claimed to come up at the same time."

Marge said, "I'll call up Sue Beth and check it out. She may tell me that she meant her whole family, but I'll listen for a hinky tone of voice."

"You're good at hinky tones," Decker said.

Hollander said to Decker, "You make a profile on all the guys Linda was balling? See if they have anything in common?"

"I did," Decker said. "They don't."

"Give it to me," Hollander said.

"Why not?" Decker tugged the Darcy file out of his drawer, pulled out the profile sheet, made a paper airplane out of it, and flew it to Hollander. "There're only three on the 'for sure' list—Byron Howard, Rolland Mason, and now this Jim Grains. Creighton Donaldson is a maybe. I don't have any proof on him."

Marge said to Decker, "I've been going over your interview with Linda's OB-GYN."

"And?"

"Is it possible that Linda and Byron had an ongoing affair and Katie is Byron's daughter?"

"I don't think she's Byron's, but I don't think she's Luke's, either," Decker said. "I think Linda's affair with Byron was discovered and *stopped* by Darlene before Linda could have become pregnant by him."

"So we've got a missing link somewhere," Marge said.

"Well, I don't know who the link is," Hollander said. "But I'll tell you something about him."

"What's that?" Decker asked.

"He's got a lot of kids," Hollander said.

Decker and Marge looked at each other.

Hollander said, "Rolland had five, Byron has five, Grains has six—"

"Oh Christ, talk about being right in front of my face!" Decker was disgusted with himself. "Of course! Linda stopped artificial insemination four years ago. Too much pain, too much cost . . . She never gave up! She was trying to impregnate herself using men with good track records!"

"It worked," Hollander said.

"You did good, Mike," Decker said. "I screwed up, but you did real good."

"Aw shucks," Hollander said. "Want to show your appreciation? Find out if your lady has a cousin."

"What about Donaldson?" Marge asked Hollander. "How many little buggers does he have?"

"Not written in his profile," Hollander said. "You're slipping, Pete."

Decker said, "I don't know for certain, but I remember several pictures of two little girls sitting on Donaldson's desk."

"Linda didn't screw him," Hollander said, matter-of-factly. "The dude hadn't proved fertile enough."

Decker was about to retort, but was interrupted by a flash in his gray matter. He bolted up and grabbed his coat.

"Where're you off to, Sherlock?" Marge asked.

"Off to find the missing link," Decker said.

He made it back to the Manfred development in a record seven minutes, jumping a few lights in the process. His overworked adrenals had caused him to break into a sweat, and his shirt needed a wringing by the time he reached Patty Bingham's house. When she answered the door, Decker didn't bother with the niceties. He said, "Where's your husband?"

Patty said, "He's not home."

Decker entered the house, paying no attention to Patty's high-pitched protests. The place was the same—a pigsty. The TV was blaring, laundry was scattered on the couch, a radio talk-show psychologist was blasting words of wisdom from the kitchen, kids were in various stages of dress. The boy was in his swimming trunks, one of the older girls was in shorts and tank top, the baby sat on the carpet, naked, examining herself.

Patty had on a bikini bra and a pair of cutoffs. Her skin had darkened to a bronze glow, but her nose was red and peeling. Her feet were bare, her toenails were long and sharp and painted bright red. They looked like bloody nail files.

"What the hell do you think you're doing, barging in like that?" Patty placed a hand on her hip and regarded his face. "The name was Decker, wasn't it?"

Decker nodded. "I need to talk to your husband, Mrs. Bingham."

"He's working."

"Find him for me."

"He's an electrician," Patty said. "He's out on jobs. What do you want with him? What's he done?"

"Call his office and have them page him on his beeper," Decker said.

"Mind telling me what this is all about?" Patty asked.

"The same thing I came here for last time. It's about a lost little girl. Only now I know her name. It's Katie Darcy. Name Darcy ring a bell?"

Decker saw it all in Patty's eyes. Her face crumbled, her lower lip began to tremble. Her eyes turned ugly. She turned to the kids and screamed at them to leave the room. They obeyed without question except for the baby, who began to cry. Patty swooped her up in her arms and comforted her with soft words and a kiss. It took Patty a moment to find her voice. When she did, it came out a whisper.

"Bastard knocked us both up at the same time. Otherwise, I would have left him."

"Why didn't you tell me this the first time I came here?"

"Why should I have?" Patty fired back. "*I* never seen the other kid. Didn't know for sure it was her. I never *wanted* to see her."

"But you knew when I showed you the picture."

"She had *my* baby's eyes. *His* eyes, the prick." She faced Decker, hate oozing from every pore. "So now you come over here and mess everything all up." She began to cry. "Make me suffer it all over again. Why, if you found out who the kid was . . . why in the hell did you come back here? To torture me?"

"Linda Darcy is dead," Decker said.

That snapped her out of her self-pity. "Dead?" Patty sank onto the couch. She sat there for a minute, then eventually said, "Jesus, you don't know how many times I wished her dead. God, do I feel weird."

"You ever act on your wish?" Decker asked.

"Oh God, no," Patty insisted. "No, no, *no!*"

Decker said nothing.

"God, I don't know a thing about this Linda Darcy, other than the fact that my husband had screwed her. I'd never even seen her 'cept in a pitchure. A pitchure my husband kept in his wallet, till I made him rip it up."

Decker said, "I need to talk to your husband."

"No, Sergeant." Patty Bingham was crying again. "No, you got it all wrong if you think Cliff had something to do with it. Cliff makes mistakes, he's not perfect. But he'd never, ever do something like . . ."

"Like what?"

"Like *murder!*" Patty shrieked. "Why? What for? He loved her, for godsake! The affair ended three years ago. As soon as she got knocked up. *She* was the one who broke it off. Said she didn't need him anymore. Cliff told me all about it six months later, cried on my shoulder, can you imagine such nerve? I was six months pregnant with this son of a bitch's kid, and he was bawling in his soup that his whore mistress didn't love him no more. Then he told me she was carrying his child." Patti wiped tears from her eyes. "I threw up all over him."

"What made him think it was his kid?"

"I don't know. I guess she told him it was his," Patti said. "I always thought that maybe she was lying until I saw that pitchure of that little kid. My gut knew who she was."

"I still need to talk to your husband, Mrs. Bingham."

Patty stared at Decker, a strange expression on her face. "You do that," she said. "You do that and tell him something else for me. Tell the bastard I'm out of here. Tell him I shipped his kids back to his ex, and I've gone back to Mama in Dallas. Tell the bastard I've *had* it up to here with him." She made a slash across her forehead. "I've had all that I could take. And I want no more part of it or him!"

Decker found a piece of scrap paper and a pen. He offered it to Patty and said, "Why don't you tell him yourself."

Patty pushed her hair out of her eyes and took the paper and pen. She sat the baby back on the floor and said, "Good idea. I'll do just that right this minute!"

Decker said, "You have your husband's work number?"

"Take one of his business cards," Patty said as she scribbled. "On the counter."

Decker pocketed the card and said, "Maybe I'll call him from the station."

"Whatever . . ." Patty paused a moment, then began her furious scrawling once again. "Whatever you want!" She punctuated the end of a sentence and broke through the paper with the pen point.

"Bye," Decker said.

Patty was on her second piece of paper. She didn't hear him leave.

❧23

The warrant had become wet with sweat. Marge dried her palm on her polyester-cotton pants and waited in the driver's seat of the unmarked for the positions to come over the TAC frequency. Charlie Benko occupied the passenger's seat, outwardly calm, but he kept shaking his leg up and down, the thing that teenage boys do when they're nervous or horny. Benko looked at her, gave her a thumbs-up sign, and Marge managed a tepid smile in return.

The block was dark and quiet. The house where Douglas Miller aka Rusty Duralt lived was texture-coat blue with white shutters, its front yard an unadorned square of straw-colored grass. A row of flowerless rosebushes had been planted in a side patch of dirt, an open trench for sprinklers bisecting the plot. A lone porch lamp cast a yellow circle on the cracked cement walkway. The shades in front and back were still drawn. Dawn was another thirty minutes away.

Everything taut, yet seemed to be going smoothly. Marge hoped it would remain that way. She'd obtained the arrest and search warrants at eleven-thirty last night, but Miller had been out for the evening. With a jumbo Thermos of coffee, she did her own stakeout, spotting Miller returning at three-thirty, soused to the gills. Rather than make the bust right there, taking a chance of him decking her or bolting, she called in for backup.

Marge remembered Duralt as having put up quite a fight that day in Booking, swinging his fists at whatever got in his way. Of course, he'd been really pickled that day. Then again, he might be nursing last night's hangover, no telling what kind of mood that would put him in. If he ran, the back and side doors and windows needed to be covered. If he should try to duke it out, she'd need plenty of men to control him fast.

And someone to get the kid.

"We gonna do something soon?" Benko finally asked her.

"Just waiting until we're sure everyone is in position," Marge answered.

"You know, Dotty wanted to come up to the door with us—"

"No."

"Yeah, that's what I told her. Doug's violent as hell, who knows what the sunnabitch may try? But she really wanted to do it. She wanted to spit in his face."

"Well, she'll just have to control herself," Marge said.

"You're sure he's in there?" Benko said.

"Positive," Marge said. "And so is Heather—you told Dotty they've renamed her Laurie, didn't you?"

"Yeah."

"The kids are the problem," Marge said. "We don't want him doing something crazy with either Heather or the baby—"

"I don't understand why you didn't just grab the kid when you saw it was her," Benko said. "That's what the sunnabitch did. Just grabbed the kid. You should have just grabbed her back."

"Mr. Benko—"

"I know, I know." Benko waved her off. "System doesn't work that way. You need papers, you need warrants, you need some asshole judge telling you, yeah, it's okay to do to the sunnabitch what the sunnabitch did to you. *You* couldn't have done it. But *I* could have. You should have called me as soon as you found out."

"I thought about that, Mr. Benko—"

"Charlie."

"I thought about it, Charlie, but I wanted to do this the right way, the legal way."

"You wanted a bust."

"That's a really low thing to say," Marge snapped.

Benko looked contrite. "Yeah, you're right. Guess I'm a little nervous for Dotty and all." He let out a jittery laugh. "Good scam you worked out, huh? Diapers for sale. I'm gonna use that."

Marge said, "Be my guest."

A crackling voice came through the police radio.

"What'd he say?" Benko asked.

"Shhh," Marge said. A moment later, she looked at Benko. "We're ready to roll."

"Finally."

"Sure you want to do this with me?" Marge said.

"Hell, I wanted to do this without you." Benko stuck out his hand. "Nice goin', Detective."

"Thanks." Marge shook his hand, pulled on the door handle, and pushed out the door. "Let's do it."

The two of them started up the pathway to the front door, their footsteps loud in the still of the night. The sky was charcoal dust, lightening to ash gray at the eastern horizon. Marge felt her heart race, glanced over at Benko. His face was slack and serious. She checked her watch. Five thirty-five.

They reached the front door. Marge knocked loudly. The Gestapo knock, she called it. They both stood at the side of the door frame, neither one expecting shooting, but neither one wanting to be taken by surprise.

No response.

"You *sure* he's in there?" Benko asked.

"Saw him go in myself."

"He could have slipped out the back if you was only watching the front."

"Could have," Marge admitted. "But I don't think so. More likely he's just sleeping soundly." She only had to knock one more time before she heard the rustle of activity inside.

"Someone's home," Benko whispered.

"Yeah?" a deep, husky voice asked from the other side.

"Police, Mr. Duralt!" Marge shouted. "Open up."

No response, then the scuffling of footsteps.

"God, he's gonna be a schmuck about it!" Marge swore.

"Let's break it down!" Benko said, getting ready to charge.

"Wait a second!" Marge held his arm, radioed the situation, then took a credit card and caught the lock. The door opened. Benko stared at her.

Marge said, "Sometimes the easy way works. Cover me."

The living room was dark and quiet.

"Where did the sunnabitch go?" Benko asked.

"We've got to get to the kids." Marge radioed in for backup through the front door, then said, "I'm going down the hallway, Charlie. You stay on my ass."

"Got it."

The center hallway was pitch-black. Marge groped the side of the wall for the light switch, found it, and flipped it up. She counted five closed doors that fed off the passageway.

She opened the first, found the light. A thousand Marges stared back at her. A mirrored room. In the center was Nautilus equipment, a weight rack filled with barbells and dumbbells and an Exercycle. She pushed back a sliding mirrored closet door. It was filled with sports paraphernalia—basketballs, handballs, rackets, fishing rods, baseball mitts, and bats.

No Duralt!

She closed the door to the room, then cocked her head in the direction of the next door.

A tiny bathroom illuminated by a night-light. She popped the main switch. The shadowed grays turned into blue foil wallpaper. The sudden whoosh of a ventilator fan. Empty.

On to the next door. When she turned on the lights this time, she saw a hump under the covers on a double mattress atop bare box springs. Marge looked at Benko, then walked over to the covers and pulled them back. The woman was huddled in a fetal position, wearing a pink shortie nightgown. Her dark hair was tied up, her skin riddled with goose bumps. Marge recognized her as Bonnie Duralt, the same woman she'd pulled the Pampers scam on.

Marge said, "Where is he, Mrs. Duralt?"

She answered, "He's not here."

"Where'd he go?" Marge fired back.

"I don't know."

"C'mon, lady, do better than that!" Benko yelled at her.

"I swear it!" Bonnie pleaded. "He just said, 'I gotta get out of here, Bonnie.' "

Marge felt her stomach churn. "He have a weapon on him?"

For the first time, Bonnie looked up. "You're the *Pampers* lady!"

"Well, now I'm a police detective, so answer my questions!" Marge ordered. "Does your husband have a gun, Bonnie?"

"I don't know."

"Cut the bullshit, Bonnie," Marge said. "Now, try again. Does your husband have a gun?"

Bonnie was shivering now. "He keeps one under the pillow."

Benko's hand went under the pillow. "It's not here."

Bonnie squeezed herself into a tighter ball, tears streaming down her cheeks. Two uniforms came into the bedroom—one was a Hispanic named Ramirez, the other a blond named Sutton.

Marge asked them, "Somebody guarding all the doors?"

"Yessir, ma'am, Detective," answered Sutton.

"Then the suspect has to be somewhere in the house. Consider him armed and dangerous." Marge focused in on Bonnie. "Get up, Bonnie. We're going to go get the girls."

"The baby's mine!" she cried out.

"I know," Marge said. "But we need the kids and you out of here—safe."

Bonnie blurted out, "It's his little girl, ya know."

"Not no more, lady," Benko snapped. He hoisted Bonnie up by her arm. "Let's go."

Marge gave him a "Cool the rough stuff" look, and followed Bonnie to the girls' room. It had been done in blocks-and-teddy-bear wallpaper—a homemade job, since the seams weren't aligned. The windows were draped with pink gingham curtains. Against the wall were two cribs, between them a white nightstand with a Humpty-Dumpty night-light. Marge peered inside the cribs. The children were sleeping undisturbed. At least Miller had the good sense to keep them out of it—for the time being. The baby was on her stomach, nose squashed against the crib's mattress. Heather was on her back, her face red with sleep, soft wisps of hair framing her face.

Up close, she looked quite different from Katie Darcy, her features more refined, a little older. Marge told Bonnie to take her baby, and Marge handed Heather over to Sutton. The child opened her eyes, looked at the patrolman, then slumped on his shoulder and went back to sleep. The baby continued sleeping in her mother's arms.

Marge said, "Ramirez, you, Benko, and I will cover the others until everyone's out of the house and into the car. Suspect may be watching, and we don't want any shots fired while we've got the kids in our hands."

"Got it," Ramirez said.

"Move with caution," Marge reiterated. "Apprehending the suspect isn't as important as the kids." She turned to Bonnie and said, "Don't try anything stupid with the baby in your arms, Bonnie. You're in enough trouble as is."

Bonnie didn't answer, but the frightened look in her eyes told Marge that she'd cooperate. Ramirez went first through the hallway, covered it from the front end. Marge and Benko stood at the threshold of the kids' room and covered the passageway from the back.

As soon as the children were out of the hallway, they were quickly escorted out of the house and into waiting patrol cars. Sighing with relief when the children were out of the way, Marge figured out her next move.

Miller hadn't been caught leaving the house. He must be hiding somewhere inside the dwelling.

Hiding somewhere.

Anywhere.

With a gun.

Marge told Benko to check the other rooms off the hallway, Ramirez to take the living and dining room, she'd take the kitchen and service porch.

The kitchen was compact, crowded. The countertops done in some sort of cheap terra-cotta tile, the grout cracked and grimy. An unopened jar of peanut butter, a dirty knife, and a trail of crumbs decorated the left side of the counter; the right side held three empty beer bottles. The sink was filled with dishes sitting in six inches of milky water. Above the sink was a greenhouse window, its shelves holding a half-dozen wilting plants. Behind her were the oven, the microwave, and the cooktop. Marge opened all the cabinets, the door to a walk-in pantry, and—just to be sure—the oven door.

Empty.

She went on to the laundry room right off of the kitchen. The washer and dryer were empty. She stood to the side and opened the broom closet.

Nothing.

But only for a moment.

In the abstract, she saw it all, the iron arcing down on her head. But it happened so fast, all she could do was ward off some of the impact and swear. She felt its weight crash into her forehead several times, felt herself go dizzy. A gush of blood streamed into her eyes.

"Shithead!" she screamed. She saw him race through the back door, heard the popping sound of gunshot. She staggered over to the back door, felt cool air fill her nostrils, but knew she was losing it. A moment later, Benko was helping her down.

"Chrissakes!" he was yelling. "Stay put, Detective."

"Did they get him?" Marge cried out.

"Got away," an officer told her. "He fired shots, Detective. They're after him—"

"Get him, Charlie!" Marge was sobbing, holding her palms against her head. Blood was oozing from her fingers, seeping out of her hands. "Get the fucker!"

"Just as soon as help—"

"Go *get* the fucker!" Marge demanded through tears. The pain was searing through her head. "Now!"

Benko ran outside.

Officers on foot scouring the block. Above came the crackle of helicopter blades—a giant flashlight from above. Dawn was adding color to the pepper-tinted sky. People were milling outside their houses, covering pajama-clad bodies with worn terry-cloth bathrobes, feet stuffed into slippers. Unshaven men with messy hair looked confused, the women gossiped. The approaching *wheeeee* of an ambulance cut through the early morning air as shrilly as an alarm clock.

Benko scratched his head and wondered in what direction Miller had taken off.

"Sunnabitch," he heard himself mutter.

A shriek came from his right. The front yard of the house

next door. "Over here!" yelled one of the officers.

Benko charged in that direction. "Where?" he asked.

"In the bushes," the officer said. He had his weapon drawn, but stood at a safe distance. "I thought I saw something move in the Eugenias."

"Careful, he's got a gun," Benko said.

"I know that," the uniformed officer said. His name tag said Van Horn.

Benko took a step forward, a big enough step to feel the wind of a bullet whiz by his temple. He hit the ground and swore. "It's over, Miller!" he shouted.

"The fuck you think!" a gravelly voice shouted back.

"Charlie!" screamed a feminine voice. "Charlie, are you okay?"

Benko picked his head up, saw the outline run toward him.

"Dotty, get the fuck down!" he hollered. "He's hidden in the bushes, and he's got a gun."

"You asshole!" Dotty stood, shrieking at the bushes.

Another pop of the revolver.

Benko cursed as he crawled toward her, tried to yank her down, but she pulled away.

"You fucking son of a bitch, bastard asshole!" Dotty jackrabbited forward, diving into the shrubbery.

"Nooooo!" Benko screamed, running after her.

Leaves burst into the overcast air, a cloud of foliage, as if someone had punched a hole into a feather pillow. Another pop, followed by high-pitched shrieks.

"Dotty!" Benko shouted.

"Son of a bitch!" Dotty screamed. "I'll kill you!"

A cluster of men volleyed into the shrubbery, bodies piling on top of one another. Benko felt some arms flail on his chest. Grabbing the limbs, he pulled them upward, saw what he'd fished out and grinned.

Grand-slam homer.

Miller struggling in his arms. Unshaven, his top dental plate out, his front teeth missing. His lip and forehead were cut, and his hands were empty. Bastard was a wiry thing, all sinews and tendons, wearing a pair of jockeys and nothing else. He seemed strong enough, but his eyes were terrified at the sight of Dotty.

"Keep her *offa* me," he pleaded to Benko.

Dotty sprang up, knee-dropped her ex, then battered him several times across the head with her purse. "Bastard! Fucking bastard!" She punctuated every syllable with a swing of her handbag. "What you put me through!" She kicked Miller in the shins, then kicked him in the scrotum.

Miller doubled over and sobbed. "Get her *offa* me! *Pl-ease!*" His nose had opened up and was spouting blood.

She kicked him in the testicles a third time. Miller threw up. Van Horn pulled Dotty away from her ex, another cop took Miller off Benko's hands.

"Bastard!" she panted.

"You got him good, ma'am," Van Horn said, trying to restrain her. "Just settle down now."

"Bastard, bastard, bastard!" Dotty cried.

Benko took her from Van Horn, held her tightly in his arms. "We got him, Dotty," he cooed. "We got him, and we got Heather. Let's all go home now."

"Bastard!" she sobbed.

"It's over," Benko said.

She buried herself in Benko's arms and cried.

Benko said, "Dotty, you shouldn't have gone after him like that. He had a gun."

"I know," she said. "But Doug was always a lousy shot. Never could do anything right."

Out of the corner of his eye, Benko saw a stretcher being loaded into the ambulance. "Wait here a minute, Dotty. I gotta do something."

But she followed him to the ambulance anyway. Benko

found Marge lying on the gurney, an attendant wrapping a bandage around her forehead.

"You okay?" Benko asked Marge.

"I've been better," Marge whispered.

"Did that bastard do that to you?" Dotty said. "I shoulda *killed* him, Charlie. I shoulda picked up his gun and *killed* him."

Benko took Dotty's hand and squeezed it. To Marge, he said, "You're one tough lady, know that?"

Marge thought, I don't feel so tough right now. She was enveloped in pain, dizzy, sick, shaky, and more than a little scared. "Do me a favor, will you, Charlie?"

"Anything."

"Call up the station. Talk to Sergeant Decker," Marge said. "Tell him . . . I can't interview Pappy D. He'll know . . . what I mean."

"Sure, honey," Benko said. "Whatever you say."

"Don't tell him why." Marge felt the contents of her stomach about to come up. "Don't want to worry . . . anyone."

"Okay," Benko answered.

But Marge knew he'd tell Decker why. Knowing Pete, he'd probably reach the hospital when she did. The thought made her feel a tiny bit better.

Marge opened her eyes, felt tubes running through her nose, things plastered onto her head. She was hooked up to machines, one of them beeping. Everything was out of focus.

But a wonderful familiar voice said, "What some people won't do to get a day off."

Marge didn't answer. Her head throbbed, her eyes held flashes of blinding light. Pete sounded like an echo. She lay back on her pillow and mumbled, "What do . . . I look like?"

"Beautiful," Decker said.

"Liar."

"You look alive. That's the only way you need to look right now."

"Feel like shit."

"I don't doubt that you do," Decker said. "You need anything? Something for the pain?"

Marge muttered no. She realized Decker was holding her hand, clasping it with both of his hands. God, for him to do that, she must look like death warmed over. She tried to zero in on his face. Two Deckers. Both of them looking worried as hell. Gotta reassure him, she thought. She croaked out, "Benko give you . . . my message . . . about Pappy D?"

Decker sighed. "Yes, he did. It's all taken care of. Forget about work."

A hammer was banging in her head. "Pete . . . Sue Beth sounded . . . hinky."

"Shhhh."

"Know . . . what I mean?"

Decker looked at her with newfound admiration, *The woman doesn't give up*. Like him. "You want me to ask Sue Beth if she remembers seeing her mother and brother at the convention when she arrived?"

Marge nodded. "Press her . . . Pappy D . . . when you do the interview."

Decker said yes, then discreetly pressed the nurse call button. But Marge caught it.

"Look that bad?"

"A little pale, that's all," Decker said.

A young Filipino nurse came in a moment later, studied her EEG readouts. "She okay," she announced to Decker.

"Sure, I'm . . . fine," Marge said. If a thousand hot pokers impaling your eyes meant fine, she was fine.

"You need something for the pain, Margie?"

The nurse said, "She not due for another dose until—"

"I don't give a fuck when she's due!" Decker exploded. "She's in pain! Get her out of pain, for chrissakes!"

Marge gave him a lopsided smile. She whispered, "Go . . . talk . . . Pappy D. Get out . . . my face."

The nurse smiled. "You heard her! Out!"

"Go." Marge gave Decker a light slap. "Now."

Decker didn't move.

"Go . . . please," Marge said.

Decker stood up. He said, "I'll be back in an hour, Marjorie. Like it or not."

Marge whispered, "Sure."

He left. She was glad. She didn't want him to see her cry.

Hollander grabbed Decker as soon as he stepped into the squad room.

"First, how is she?" Hollander asked.

"Messed up, but she'll be okay," Decker said. "Fucker cracked her skull. Doctor was amazed it didn't do her in, but thank God it didn't. They're monitoring her for pressure on the brain. But the doctor doesn't think she'll have any permanent damage except maybe the left corner of her head will be slightly caved in. So she'll change her hairdo."

"Bastard," Hollander said. "We put Miller with some real hard cases. Three Bee'ers—big, black, and been there before. Miller's got a nice tush. Ten-to-one his asshole's gonna be yawning before the day is through."

"It's not enough," Decker said.

"True, but it'll have to do for the time being," Hollander said. "Second, we got somebody waiting in one of the interview rooms. They wanted Marge, but told me you'll do if she's not around."

"Who?"

"Sue Beth Litton is there with her brother, Earl."

"What?"

"Seems Earl has a confession to make," Hollander said. "He's been Mirandized and everything. Don't want a lawyer, no, no, no. He and Sis are just waiting for you to put it all down in writing."

Decker stared at him. "Just like that?"

"Just like that."

"Marge asked Sue Beth if she remembers her mother and

brother being up there when she arrived," Decker said. "Now, suddenly, Earl, the *retarded* brother, mind you, has something to tell us."

Neither one spoke for a moment.

"Something stinks," Decker said.

"To high heaven," Hollander added.

☙24

The interview room was an 8' × 8' box toplit by two rows of fluorescent tubing. The acoustical wall tiles had recently been painted pale yellow and gave off an unhealthy glow under the harsh light. Through the door window, Decker could see Sue Beth sitting at the far end of the room, her eyes fixed upon her hands clasped and resting on the metal tabletop. Even though she'd donned a simple cotton dress, she'd made some attempt to doll up—eyeshadow, lipstick, hair curled. The makeup job seemed overdone. A silver charm bracelet dangled from her right wrist. Earl was positioned on her left side.

Though Decker knew Earl was twenty-five, it was hard to believe this male a man. His head was small for his soft body, his face round, with rosy cheeks. His eyes were coffee beans, close-set and filled with childlike fear—a boy caught with his hands in the cookie jar. His nose was flat, his chin held an extra layer of flab—not exactly a double chin, more like baby fat that never went away. His mouth was open—he seemed to be breathing through it—his teeth were yellow and small. A moment later, small, stubby fingers wiped his low-set brow. The only hint of his age was meager stubble over and under thick red lips.

Smoothing his mustache, Decker observed them for a

moment, waited to see if they interacted at all. They didn't. Decker entered the room, closed the door, and took a chair opposite Sue Beth and Earl. The cell was hot and humid and gave off a faint turpentine smell.

Decker pulled out a notebook and said, "Hello, Sue Beth."

She managed a nervous smile.

Decker's eyes shifted from her face to Earl's. He looked at him for a moment, then said, "Hello, Earl."

Earl looked down.

Sue Beth said, "Earl, answer the policeman."

"Hullo, Mister Policeman," he said. "How are you?"

"Don't get fresh," Sue Beth said.

"It's okay," Decker told her. "I'm fine, thank you, Earl." To Sue Beth, he said, "Detective Dunn is unavailable today. But Detective Hollander said you'd be willing to talk to me."

"That's what I told him."

"Detective Hollander also informed me that you've been advised of your rights, you understand them, and wish to have them waived. You signed a card to that effect, are you aware of that?"

"Yes."

"You also have declined the presence of an attorney."

"Yes."

"Sue Beth," Decker said, "I've requested an attorney be present for your questioning—"

"We don't need no lawyer," Sue Beth said. "My pappy was sure on that. No lawyers. Just let Earl tell the police what happened and get it over with."

"It's not that simple," Decker said.

"Well, why isn't it?" Sue Beth said. She seemed flustered.

Decker chose his words. "Earl can't waive his rights like you or I can because legally he's not considered a responsible adult."

"I'm responsible for him," Sue Beth said. "Have been for the last six years, when my mama got tired of seeing to his needs."

"You may see to his needs, but you may not be legally responsible for him."

"Doggone it!" Sue Beth blurted out. "I wanna do the Christian thing, and so does Earl. My baby brother wants to cleanse his soul and confess his sins, and *you* don't want to hear him."

"It's not that at all—"

"What in tarnation is wrong with this world?" Sue Beth ranted. Her made-up cheeks had gone from blush to bright red. "I thought that's what the police does. Listen to confessions."

Police and priests, Decker thought. "A lawyer should be with us momentarily. He'll advise us—"

"How long is momentarily?" Sue Beth said. "I'm not gonna wait here forever."

Decker saw a mulish streak in her eye. What she couldn't change with action, she'd impede with stubbornness. "Not too long, Sue Beth. Just hang on a second. Would you like something to drink in the meantime, a cup of coffee or tea or juice—"

"I like juice," Earl said.

"Don't be bratty, Earl," Sue Beth said. "Ask nicely."

Earl lowered his head and asked, "May I have juice, please?"

"Look at him when you talk," Sue Beth said.

Earl made eye contact with Decker and repeated the request. Decker said sure, and held himself back from tousling the grown-up boy's hair. As soon as Decker was out of the interview room, Hollander came up to him.

"I've contacted the PD's office," he said. "Someone should be over within a half hour."

"Couldn't get anyone sooner?"

"Half hour's the norm, Pete."

"Yeah," Decker said. "I know. I just don't want them to walk."

"Then take the confession," Hollander said.

"And have the whole thing tossed because the kid didn't know what he was signing?"

"But she supposedly knew what she was signing."

"But we don't know if she's legally responsible for the kid."

Hollander said. "The confession's probably BS anyway. Take what you can get."

"I will, if it comes to that," Decker said. "But if I can make it kosher, all the better. If there's any trace of truth in the kid's spiel, I don't want some asshole judge throwing all of it out on a technicality."

"*You* should be able to guard against that, Esquire."

"Nuh-uh," Decker said. "I start thinking I can do it all, I fuck up."

Hollander peered at Sue Beth through the window. "Our lady's gettin' antsy. You'd better think of something to keep her interest from flagging."

Decker said, "There's always your tap-dance routine."

Hollander laughed.

"Give Sue Beth more papers to fill out," Decker said. "That should buy us some time."

"What kind of papers? She filled out everything they had to."

"I don't know," Decker said. "Give her our health histories forms . . . and the car registrations triplicates. Anything that'll keep her occupied. I'll go get them refreshments."

"Righto."

Fifteen minutes later, Sue Beth had a hand cramp and was ready to walk out. Decker was just about to take Earl's "confession" when Hollander opened the door.

"Counselor's here, Sergeant."

Decker inwardly breathed a sigh of relief. He assured Sue Beth that they'd be ready any second now.

He left the room, waved hello to Louis Nixon, an old-timer. Twenty years in the Public Defender's Office, yet the guy was as mellow as fine wine. Nixon was a bespectacled, coffee-colored man of fifty, with a glint in his dark eyes, and a wide smile for any dirty joke. Over the years, coiled threads of silver had weaved into his close-cropped Afro.

Hollander said, "If I'm not needed, folks, I think I'll go down to the hospital."

"Let me know what's going on," Decker said.

"You bet."

After Hollander left, Nixon asked, "What's up, Pete?"

Decker said, "I've been working on a missing kid that turned into a quadruple homicide. Kid's okay, thank God. In the room are the sister and retarded brother of two of the victims. Seems the retarded brother is ready to confess."

"Confess to what?"

"I presume he's ready to confess to one or more of the homicides, but the kid doesn't want a lawyer. Actually, his sister doesn't want him to have a lawyer. And the brother will do whatever the sister tells him to do."

"How old's the brother?"

"Twenty-five."

"Who's his legal conservator?"

Decker smiled to himself. A legal conservator wasn't the type of detail these men would pay attention to. Not that farmers eschewed all urban life. Man, they could be wizards when it came to leveraging property or machinery for bank loans for expansion or modernization. But try getting them to make a will. He heard his father's voice ring through his ears.

What do I need a will for, Pete? I don't care what happens after the Good Lord sees fit to take me away.

Decker had tried to reason with him.

The estate would be thrown into probate, Dad. Your as-

sets would be frozen, and Mom would be strapped until the
funds were released. 'Course, Randy and I would take care
of her, but you know how independent she is. A will would
avoid all that mess.

Logic didn't change Lyle Decker's mind a whit.

Decker looked at Nixon and said, "I don't think they've
ever officially appointed a conservator for the kid. The
boy—rather, man—does have a mother and a father, but the
sister says she's the one who's been responsible for him for
the last six years."

Nixon said, "Let me talk to my clients."

"They may not be too happy to see you," Decker said. "I
sort of forced you on them. I want the confession, but I
want it done by the book."

"Give me a minute alone with them," Nixon said. Five
minutes later, he exited the interview room. His face had
become flat, his eyes had lost their sparkle.

"Everything okay, Lou?" Decker asked.

"You're right," Nixon said quietly. "They don't want a
lawyer. Especially a nigger lawyer."

"Oh shit, I forgot about that!" Decker said. "I didn't even
think about you being black. These people are backwoods,
have a thing against anything that's not white Baptist. I'm
sorry, Lou. I really am sorry."

Quietly, Nixon said, "It's okay. It happens."

"What do we do now?" Decker asked.

"Let me be there," Nixon said. "Let me advise them even
if they don't want it. Then, if they want to hang themselves . . . well, can't stop the world from turning, Pete."

Earl was slow to get started. He slurped his juice, looked at
his sister for approval; then, head down, spoke in a monotone.

"I did it."

"Did what?" Decker said.

"I advise you not to let your brother answer that, Mrs. Litton," Nixon said.

"Go ahead, Earl," Sue Beth said. "Don't pay no attention to . . . him. Just answer the policeman's questions."

Decker turned up the tape recorder and sneaked a sidelong glance at Nixon. His face was impassive. "What did you do, Earl?" Decker asked.

"Killed them."

"Killed who?"

"Don't answer that, Earl," Nixon said.

Earl closed his mouth. Sue Beth told him to keep talking.

"But the nigger hushed me up," Earl said.

"I don't want him in here," Sue Beth complained to Decker. "He's mixing up my brother."

Decker said, "You don't have to listen to your lawyer. But I want him here."

"Hear that, Earl," Sue Beth said. "You don't listen to the black man. Just answer the policeman's questions." She turned to Nixon and said, "And I'd thank you not to interrupt him."

"He's doing his job," Decker said. Then, quickly, he repeated his question, "Killed who, Earl?"

"Them."

"Who's them?"

"Don't answer that," Nixon said. But this time Earl didn't listen.

"Killed Linda," he said.

"Linda who?"

"My sister Linda."

"He means sister-in-law," Sue Beth said. She played with her charm bracelet. "He don't know the difference."

"I understand," Decker said. He spoke soothingly. "You killed your sister-in-law, Linda, Earl?"

"Yes."

"How?"

Nixon interjected, Earl spoke anyway.

"Shot her."

"Why'd you shoot Linda, Earl?" Decker asked.

"She was arguing."

"Arguing with who, Earl?"

"Luke."

"Luke was arguing with Linda?"

"Yes."

"What about?"

"Don't answer that, Earl," Sue Beth piped up. She looked at Decker. "It's personal."

"We need to know everything, Sue Beth," Decker said.

"I don't see why."

She was getting that stubborn look in her eye. Decker said, "It may be important to the case."

"He said he did it. Ain't that enough?"

Decker felt his chest tighten. "No, it's not enough. Look, you want this to be over with, let me do what I have to do."

"You don't have to answer anything you don't want to, Sue Beth," Nixon said. "Of course, now it's too late to pull your brother out. He's already confessed to one murder. But I advise you both not to say anything else incriminating."

"I just don't see it being important what they were arguing about," Sue Beth said to Decker. Her voice started to quaver.

"Were you there?" Decker said.

"Don't answer that," Nixon said.

"'Course not!" Sue Beth protested.

"So you don't know what's going on any more than I do," Decker said. "And you have no idea what is or isn't important. Look, Sue Beth, you're not in charge here. Furthermore, you can't bail out your brother anymore, because as Mr. Nixon explained, Earl's already confessed to a murder. So either you listen to your lawyer, or you let Earl answer my questions."

Sue Beth's lips began to tremble. "Nothing's ever simple, is it?"

Decker said to Earl, "What were they arguing about?"

Earl looked to his sister for permission to answer the question. Sue Beth nodded.

"Things," Earl said.

"What things, Earl?"

"Money."

"They were arguing about money?"

"Yes."

"Can you tell me more?" Decker asked.

"That Luke and Pappy was cheap."

"Who said Luke was cheap?"

"Linda."

"Linda called Luke and Pappy cheap?"

"Yes."

"Then what happened?"

"Luke got mad."

"How'd he get mad?"

"Started calling Linda names."

"What kind of names?"

Earl paused a moment, began to pick his nose. Sue Beth jerked his hand away.

"What kind of names?" Decker questioned again.

Earl said, "Sue Beth'll hit me if I say them."

"No, she won't," Decker said. He held the boy's hand. "You're just repeating the words that Luke said. What kind of names did Luke call Linda?"

"Whore, son of a bitch, pimp and the ef word."

Decker hesitated for several seconds, then said, "Luke called Linda a whore?"

"And a pimp and the ef word," Earl said.

"Luke called Linda a pimp?"

"Yes."

"Do you know what a pimp is, Earl?"

"No."

"Do you know what a whore is?"

"A bad girl," Earl said.

"And Luke called Linda a whore?"

"Yes."

"Why?"

"I don't know."

"And what did Linda say to Luke after he called her a whore?"

"Yelled."

"Yelled what?"

"She said the ef word."

"Sounds like Luke calling Linda a whore made her mad," Decker said.

Earl's eyes began to tear. "Yes. She started to cry."

"Linda started to cry?"

"Yes." Earl was crying now.

"Did that make you feel bad, Earl?"

"Yes."

"How did you feel about Linda?"

"This is stupid!" Sue Beth said.

Decker silenced her with a menacing look, and repeated the question.

"I liked Linda."

"You liked her."

"Yes."

"So you didn't like to see her arguing with Luke, did you?"

"No."

"And what did you do when you saw them arguing?"

"I shot him."

Decker paused a second. "Shot who?"

"Luke."

"You shot your brother, Luke?"

"Yes. He was making Linda cry."

"You shot Luke," Decker repeated.

"Yes."

"And you shot Linda, too, Earl?"

Sue Beth was about to speak, Decker held up his hand to

quiet her. Earl scrunched his eyebrows in concentration, then said, "I shot her. I shot them all."

"You're sure you shot Linda?"

"I shot them all."

"Who is all?" Decker asked.

"Linda, Luke, Carla, and Mr. Mason."

"You shot all of them?"

"Yes. With my shotgun."

First mention of the weapon.

"Okay, Earl," Decker said, "you're doing fine. Want to stop a moment, take a sip of juice?"

"Yes."

"Go ahead," Decker said.

Earl gulped down his second glass of orange juice. Decker offered him another.

"I'm hungry," Earl said.

"I'll feed you when we get home," Sue Beth said.

Decker thought, He ain't going nowhere, especially home. Arraignment, bail hearing. Not to mention all the prelims before the actual trial and sentencing. If the whole thing stuck in the first place. Earl's mental status made anything he said suspect. But it could take weeks before someone determined his capability. Sue Beth didn't know what she was in for.

He said, "Earl may be here for a while. I'll get someone to fetch him a candy bar, if that's okay with you."

"Please," Earl pleaded with his sister.

"Fine," Sue Beth said. "Just get it over with."

Decker summoned someone to bring food. After Earl gorged on four candy bars, three bags of chips, and a carton of milk, Decker resumed questioning.

"Earl? You said you killed them all with your shotgun?"

"Yes."

"Where's your gun?"

Earl burped. "S'cuse me."

"It's okay," Decker said. "Where's the shotgun that you killed everyone with?"

"It's gone."

"Where?" Decker asked. "Where did the gun go?"

"I had it," Earl said. "Then I lost it."

Decker tried to remain calm. "You lost the gun?"

"Yes."

"A shotgun's a big gun to just lose."

"Yes."

"Did you really lose the shotgun, Earl?"

"Yes."

Decker rubbed his hands over his face, then looked at Earl. The man/boy looked upset, scared that he'd done something wrong. Then Decker realized he'd picked up the slight nuance of disbelief in Decker's voice. Earl was keenly aware of how adults reacted to him, no doubt spent a lot of time worrying about displeasing the older folks. Decker smiled, took the small man's hand, and said, "How'd you lose the gun?"

"Don't remember."

"Can you think real hard and try to remember?"

Earl squeezed his eyes shut, then opened them and said, "Don't remember."

"Did you throw it away?" Decker asked.

"Yes."

Decker cursed himself. He knew the answer was worth zip. Leading questions. Just let Earl talk.

"So you don't remember what happened to the gun?" Decker backtracked.

"Threw it away," Earl said. "And the little one, too."

The .38 S and W. The boy had seen weapons. Did he use both of them as well? Decker said, "The little one?"

Earl nodded.

"Do you mean a little gun, Earl?"

"Yes."

"Was the little gun your gun, too?" Decker asked.

"No."

"That little one wasn't your gun?"

"No."

"Was it Pappy's?"

"Don't know."

"Granny's?"

"Don't know."

"Did the little gun belong to Linda or Luke?"

"Don't know."

Decker paused a moment. Slow it down. "Then where'd the little gun come from?"

"Don't know."

"Don't know?"

"No," Earl said. "But I threw that one away, too."

"Where?"

"Don't remember."

Chuck the guns for the moment. Decker said, "You said you shot Luke."

"Yes."

"Why?"

" 'Cause he made Linda cry."

"And you shot Linda."

Earl hesitated a moment. "Yes."

"Why?"

" 'Cause . . . 'cause he . . . she made Luke angry."

"How'd she make Luke angry?"

"She yelled at him. Called him cheap."

"And that made you angry?"

"Yes."

"How angry?"

"Just . . . angry."

"So what did you do?" Decker asked.

"I shot him."

"Shot Luke?"

"Yes." Earl added, "And Mr. Mason, too. I shot them all 'cause they were screaming and yelling and giving me a headache."

Maybe the boy just freaked out. Decker said, "Giving you a headache?"

"Yes," Earl said. "A bad headache. Mr. Mason called me a bad name."

"What did he call you?"

Earl began to rock in his seat. "A stupid, ef word retard."

"Okay," Decker said. "Mr. Mason called you a retard—"

"A stupid, ef word retard," Earl corrected. He was rocking hard by now. Sue Beth told him to sit still, and he put his hands in his lap, chastened.

"Excuse me, Earl." Decker's voice was soft. "Mr. Mason called you a stupid, ef word retard. Then what did you do?"

"Shot him."

"Who'd you shoot first?" Decker asked.

"Mr. Mason," Earl said.

"Why?"

"'Cause he called me a name."

Earl began to rock again. Sue Beth simply held his shoulder until he stopped.

"So you shot Mr. Mason first," Decker said.

"Yes."

"You're sure?"

"Yes."

"Was Mr. Mason yelling at Luke, at Linda?"

Earl didn't answer right away. Eventually, he said, "Yelling at Luke at first. Then Linda. He made her cry."

"Mr. Mason made Linda cry?"

"Yes. He yelled at her. And that made me mad."

"So what did you do?"

"I shot Mr. Mason."

"Then what happened?"

Earl paused, "I shot . . . I shot them all. They were giving me a headache."

Decker paused, carefully keeping his face neutral. "Where were your parents, Earl?" he asked.

"Parents?"

"Your mother and father?"

The boy looked confused.

Decker said, "Granny and Pappy D?"

Recognition in the boy's eyes.

"Where were they when you shot everybody?" Decker asked.

Earl said, "Away."

"Where was Sue Beth and B.B.?"

"Away."

"So who was taking care of you?" Decker asked.

"Linda."

"Linda?"

"Linda . . . and Luke . . . and Carly."

"Okay," Decker said. "Now you said you shot Linda and Luke and Carly."

"Yes."

"Weren't you worried that no one could take care of you?"

"No. I can take care of myself."

"Oh," Decker said.

"But," Earl said, "but I knowed I did something bad."

"You knew?"

"Yes."

"What did you do that was bad?" Decker said.

"I shot them all with my shotgun."

"Where?"

"In the kitchen. They were arguing in the kitchen."

"Who?"

"Mr. Mason and Luke."

"Anyone else?"

"Yes."

"Who?"

"Mr. Mason and Carly."

"Mr. Mason, Carly, and Luke were in the kitchen."

"And Linda," Earl added.

"Mr. Mason, Carly, Luke, and Linda were in the kitchen."

"Yes. Katie was taking a nap. I was in the dining room. Eating my sandwich. Baloney."

"And who was arguing?"

"Everyone."

"About what?"

"Money and Katie. And Linda being a whore. And Pappy being cheap like Luke."

"What did they say about Katie?"

Earl strained to remember. "Katie didn't belong with Linda."

"Why?"

" 'Cause Linda was a whore."

"Who said that?"

"Luke."

"And then what happened?"

"Linda started to cry."

"She started to cry," Decker said. "Go on, Earl. You're doing great."

"I got mad. I don't like to see Linda cry."

"So what did you do?"

"Got my gun." Earl's lower lip began to tremble. "I shot Luke and Mr. Mason."

"Shot Luke and Mr. Mason?"

"Yes."

Decker said, "Then what?"

"Shot the rest."

Decker asked, "Who did you shoot first, Earl?"

Earl thought for a moment, then said, "I think Mr. Mason."

"Are you sure it was Mr. Mason?"

"Maybe Luke," Earl said.

"Think real hard."

"Hard . . . I don't like to think about it."

"I know, Earl," Decker said. "And you're doing a great job. But you've got to try again. Who'd you shoot first?"

"Mr. Mason."

"Why?" Decker asked.

"'Cause he called me a stupid, ef word retard."

"What did you do after you shot Mr. Mason?"

"Shot the rest."

"Why, Earl?"

"They was givin' me a headache." Earl burst into tears. "Can I go home now? I feel very bad."

"A couple more questions, Earl," Decker said. "What did you do after you shot all of them?"

Earl wiped his nose on his sleeve. "I don't know."

"Try to remember, Earl."

"I . . . I just sat there."

"And what happened to Katie?"

"Katie?"

"Yes, Katie. You said she was taking a nap."

"Yes."

"Did she wake up?"

"Yes."

"Then what happened?"

"I . . . I don't remember."

"Did you take her out of her crib?"

"I don't remember."

"Where'd you go after you shot them all, Earl? You didn't stay at the house all the time your parents were away."

"No."

"So where'd you go?"

"Waited."

"Waited for what?"

"For Granny to call. She took me away. Up to Fall Springs."

"Granny D called you up?"

"Yes."

Earl seemed on certain ground now, answering the questions with no delay.

"Granny D called, and what did you tell her?"

"Told her I did something bad."

"And what happened to Katie?"

"Katie was crying."

"Okay," Decker said. "Granny called—"

"Granny D."

"Yes, Granny D called, and you told her you did something bad. Anything else?"

"Yes."

"What?"

"Told Granny D I shot them all."

"And what did Granny D do?"

"Came down and picked me up."

"What did she do with Katie?"

"Don't remember."

"Granny D didn't take Katie with her?"

"I think so. But I don't remember good."

"So Granny D picked you up?"

"I told you he was there at Fall Springs," Sue Beth said.

"Was he there when you arrived, Sue Beth?" Decker asked.

"I saw him for dinner," she answered. "That's all I remember."

"How 'bout your mother?" Decker asked. "Was she there when you arrived?"

Sue Beth ignored the question. She said, "I think Earl's talked enough. We'd like to go home now."

Decker said, "He can't go home, Sue Beth. He's under arrest."

Sue Beth looked at Decker. For the first time, he saw fear in her eyes.

"But he's not responsible for what he did," Sue Beth said. "He don't know nothin'."

"At the moment, that doesn't make any difference legally," Decker said. "I'll make sure he's placed in protective custody until you can post bail—"

"You can't put him in jail!" Sue Beth sounded horrified. "You just can't do that. I'll make sure he don't run away."

"I'm sorry, Sue Beth," Decker said, "but that's the way the law works. We're talking four counts of murder—"

"But the boy don't know what he did!"

"We're going to have to take him to Van Nuys to book him," Decker said. "We don't book homicide here."

"He'll die in jail!"

"No," Decker said, "he won't die."

"But . . . but . . ." Sue Beth was breathing hard. "He lies, Mister Policeman. What he said was all lies. . . ."

"I'm sorry, Sue Beth," Decker said. "It's too late for that. You might want to talk to your lawyer. He'll tell you what the procedure is, the fastest way to post bail."

"You can't just *leave* us like this!" Sue Beth exclaimed.

"Talk to your lawyer, Sue Beth," Decker said. "He's on your side."

"Up to you, Mrs. Litton," Nixon said. "I don't have to stick around."

Decker said, "By the way, Sue Beth. When you got up to Fall Springs, you're sure you saw your mother with your father?"

Sue Beth didn't answer. Decker repeated the question. Slowly, she said, "I didn't see my mama, but that don't mean she weren't there."

"But that doesn't mean she *was* there," Decker said.

"All I'm saying is, I don't remember seeing her right away."

"When did you see her?" Decker asked.

Sue Beth said nothing for a moment, then regarded Nixon. With halting speech, she asked him, "Do I have to answer any more questions?"

"No, ma'am, you don't," Nixon said.

"My lawyer says I don't have to answer any more questions," Sue Beth said to Decker.

"That's true," Decker said.

"Then I won't," she said.

❧25

Decker punched the "off" button of the portable tape recorder. It rested on the hospital night stand between a plastic pitcher of water and the nurse's call button. Marge's message to him through Hollander was: Bring the damn confession tape with you when you come, or don't come at all. Decker made it a point never to enrage a convalescing woman.

Even though Marge's color was pasty, her head still wrapped in yards of bandage, she was looking better. Her eyes remained red and swollen, but at least they were focused and alert. Instead of the dehumanizing hospital gown, she wore her own terry-cloth robe—pastel pink dotted with white fuzzy things.

"So, beautiful," Decker said, "what do you think?"

Marge had a lot of ideas, but it took her a while before she could verbalize them. They'd taken her off the monitoring equipment, unplugged her from the IV, but trauma and traces of Demerol slowed her agile wit. It took effort to think, even more energy to speak. When she did, her voice echoed in her head.

"I think," she said slowly, "that it's not total bullshit. That Earl was there when all the shooting went down."

"I agree," Decker said.

"But I really can't see Earl wasting Linda," Marge said.
"Ditto."

"The others . . ." She shrugged. "One thing sticks in my damaged brain, Pete."

"What's that?"

"Earl mentioned blowing them away with a shotgun," Marge said. "And he mentioned the little gun—no doubt the S and W. But Earl never mentioned *using* the handgun. And he didn't know who it belonged to."

"Where did the thirty-eight come from?" Decker said. "Big question mark in my notes. Know what else was odd? The kid seemed confused as to who he killed first. He kept saying Rolland Mason, but the way he talked made me think that he plugged Luke first. He kept on coming back to killing Luke."

"Yeah, but *we* know Luke was probably plugged by a .38 before he was hit with the pellets," Marge said. A tinny whistle sang through her head, then shut off as abruptly as it had come on. "I'm trying to visualize this scene . . . I don't know if it's water on the brain or what, but the whole thing seems screwy."

"One of those family tiffs that went haywire." Decker thought a moment. "Okay, let's try to reconstruct it. Luke, Linda, Carla, and Rolland are all in the kitchen. Linda, Rolland, Carla on one side, Luke on the other—a confrontational lineup. From what Earl said, Linda and Luke were the primary participants in this bout."

"Then why were Rolland and Carla there?"

"Good question," Decker said. "Maybe they were there for moral support for Linda, maybe Carla was after money from Luke and she wanted moral support *from* Linda, maybe Rolland was running away with one of the gals. A whole lot of reasons for involvement. But let's just concentrate on Luke and Linda for the moment."

"Okay."

"Something primal made mild-mannered Luke explode,"

Decker said. "In the past, Luke had tolerated his wife's wild ways. But suddenly harsh words were exchanged, and Luke blew up and called Linda a whore. Then Linda got upset and called Luke the ef word."

"What about Earl saying that Luke called Linda a pimp?" Marge asked.

"Well, that doesn't make any sense." Decker's eyes widened. "Unless . . . unless Luke called Linda a whore, then Linda turned around and called him a pimp."

"But—"

"Try this on," Decker interrupted. "Linda was fooling around, but we suspect she was really trying to get pregnant, right?"

"Right."

"So suppose . . . suppose, Linda stopped taking fertilization treatments because Luke refused to pay for them anymore. You know, I found out any kind of insemination procedure can cost thousands of dollars a shot."

"That much?"

"Yep," Decker said. "Eight years of treatment, figure two to three times a year. That can add up to *beaucoup* bucks. Now let's suppose with the cocktail mixture of other men's sperm, Luke figured that the likelihood of the kid being his was remote."

"Go on."

"Now take into consideration all those comments about Luke being cheap like his pappy."

Marge nodded for him to continue.

"Okay." Decker felt hot now. He suddenly saw Marge grab her head.

"What's wrong?"

"Nothing," Marge answered through gritted teeth. "I keep getting all these goddam flares of pain." She dropped her hands. "They come on suddenly, go away just as fast. But they're a real pain in the ass . . . or the head."

"You need something?"

"No more pain meds, Pete," Marge said. "They've already dulled whatever gray matter I have left."

"You shouldn't be working."

"Then what should I be doing? Moping around? Thinking about how I fucked up?"

"You didn't fuck up."

"Of course I did. I missed him, Pete. Asshole was right in front of my face, and I didn't see him."

"So now you know you don't have sonar," Decker said. "Margie, A: You didn't fuck up. And B: Even if you did, what can you do about it? No one except yourself got hurt, Detective Dunn. You'll get a commendation for an A-one collar—"

"But I know what happened."

Decker threw up his hands. "So beat your breasts and wrap yourself in sackcloth."

"Love your sensitivity, Pete."

"Kiddo, all my sensitivity is reserved for the rape survivors. Whatever's left goes to Rina." Decker thought a moment. "And she doesn't exactly get bushels full herself. You, being my partner and peer, get the standard male macho fuck-it-all-and-let's-tank-ourselves-into-oblivion speech."

Marge smiled.

"You up to doing this?" Decker said. "I could come back in an hour."

"Go ahead with your theory," Marge said. "I liked it."

"I lost my train of thought," Decker said.

"We were on Luke not paying for any more fertility treatments."

"Yeah, right," Decker said. "Okay, Luke said no more treatments, but Linda desperately wanted a kid. Luke told her, fine with him, go out and fuck somebody. Why should he pay for someone else's sperm when she can get gallons of it for free?"

"But then why would he call her a whore?" Marge said.

"Maybe he didn't think that she'd really take him up on

his offer," Decker said. "And when she did, maybe he brooded on it for a long time, then finally became unglued."

"And when he went beserk, so did she."

"Then," Decker went on, "Linda started crying, and that got Earl's attention away from his baloney sandwich. He saw what was going on and got his shotgun. But something else went down before Earl actually plugged anyone. Someone else shot Luke first."

"Linda," Marge said animatedly. Her head vibrated. She lowered her voice. "Had to be."

"Why?" Decker said. "Just because Luke called her a whore?"

"Nope," Marge said. "Remember Earl quoting Luke saying that Katie didn't belong to Linda?"

"But it should be just the opposite," Decker said.

"Bear with me," Marge said. "When you pressed Earl on that, he said that Katie didn't belong to Linda because she was a whore. Suppose Luke threatened to take Katie away because of Linda's affairs?"

"But the kid wasn't even his."

"That doesn't mean an irate guy like Luke wouldn't try to use it against her. Threaten to expose her."

"True."

"Now how far do you think Linda would go to keep her kid?" Marge said.

Decker held up his hand, made a gun with his fingers, then pulled the imaginary thumb-trigger.

"I think so, too," Marge said. "Now suppose Earl saw Linda killing his brother. Maybe he became irate enough to plug her."

"Possible, but . . ." Decker hesitated, "but picture this. Suppose Linda's pulling of the trigger was a big surprise to everyone, including Rolland Mason. Suppose he started to light into her—cussed her out. Remember, Earl said that he made Linda cry. Suppose Earl walked in at that moment, and Rolland started giving it to him—called him a stupid, ef word retard. Think of it through Earl's eyes. He saw Luke slumped over, Linda crying, and Rolland ranting. It's possible that Earl freaked out and wasted Rolland."

"And then Earl saw Luke lying there, and figured he must have killed Luke as well," Marge asked.

"Yes," Decker said.

"Of course, that doesn't explain why Earl would murder Linda and his own sister."

"Two things come to mind if the first scenario is correct," Decker said. "Earl went completely berserk and killed the girls. Or someone else finished off the girls and plugged Luke as well and tried to convince Earl that he did everything. Now it seems to me that only three people would have that kind of power over Earl—his mother, father, or Sue Beth."

"So the big question is, who was really there when the whole thing went down?"

"One of the bloody shoe prints we found corresponded to Earl's size—eight and a half men's. The other two were women's size 7—same size as Carla, Sue Beth, and Granny Darcy. Linda's foot was smaller. Could be Carla ran back and forth calling for help, but I'm betting the shoe print belonged to Sue Beth or ole Granny."

"Never found the matching shoe to the print?"

"No," Decker said.

"So who was there?" Marge asked.

"Well, Sue Beth went to Fall Springs with her family," Decker said. "Of that we're certain. The waitress will verify her presence at the restaurant where they stopped on the way. But that still doesn't clear her of the murder."

"I just remember talking to her the first time I broke the news, and later on when she picked up Katie." Marge shook her head. "Either she's a first-class actress or she was really in the dark about the whole mess."

"So we're back to Granny and Pappy Darcy," Decker said, "I'll try and talk to the parents. That's going to be hard, because I'm sure Nixon is telling the entire crew to keep the lid on. They're listening to Nixon now. Amazing how a 'nigger' becomes a lawyer when the family's in deep shit."

Marge smiled.

"Truthfully," Decker said, "we don't have a single thing on them. What we have is Earl's confession and physical evidence to tie him to the scene—his shoe print, his mentioning the shotgun—and the little gun. We've got *nothing* physical on Pappy, and just an anonymous shoe print the same size as Granny Darcy's. We're going to have to come up with something better if we want to solve this and make it stick."

Marge said, "Suppose it was like Sue Beth originally stated. That Earl was supposed to be left behind with Luke and Linda. But this mess went down. Granny sent Pappy up ahead of her to cover for them, and Granny stayed behind to clean up the mess."

"What about Katie?" Decker said.

"A *big* question mark."

"Look," Decker said. "If Granny did stay behind, how did she and Earl get up to Fall Springs by dinnertime?"

"Either Pappy took the bus up and left the car for Granny and Earl, or Pappy took the car, and Granny and Earl took the bus up."

"Agreed," Decker said. "Taxis are out of their league."

"Shouldn't be too hard to trace," Marge said. "Not too many buses go to Fall Springs. Seems to me a driver might notice a woman and her adult retarded son . . . unless Pappy took the bus."

Decker said he'd call the bus lines from headquarters.

Marge was silent for a moment. Then she said, "It just pisses me off that someone tried to pawn this all on Earl."

"Let's not be too hasty," Decker said. "Maybe he did do it all."

Marge looked doubtful.

"Yes, it stinks," Decker said. "But let's face it, Marge, hanging it on the kid makes a lot of sense. A judge would take one look at Earl and confine him to a home. Nice and neat."

"Blaming it on a retarded kid," Marge said.

"Despite what they say," Decker said, "the meek don't inherit too much."

Sitting at his dining-room table, Decker was on his fourth beer and his third cigarette by the time he heard Rina pull up. Quickly, he tossed the empty bottles and the stubbed-out butts in the garbage, sat back down, and brooded. Goddam bus system. No one who knew anything was ever in, the drivers were always out, and the goddam schedules were always changed at the last moment. Decker had wasted two hours, was expecting calls from at least a half-dozen people. But it was half past six and his phone had been silent.

Except for that one call from New York. A nervous voice on the other end.

Is Rina there?

No, she isn't. Can I take a message?

Just tell her to call home.

Where's home?

New York.

Is everything okay?

Yes.

Who's calling, please?

Just tell her to phone home.

Click.

Phone home. Like she was some fucking E.T. Treating him as if he were a venereal disease.

"Hi," Rina said. "You're home early."

Kiss on the forehead.

"Someone called from New York," Decker said, staring at piles of bus schedules. "She wants you to phone home."

Rina put the bag of groceries on the table. "What's wrong?"

Decker heard the panic in her voice and looked up.
"Don't worry. She said everything's fine."

"She?" Rina asked.

"She didn't identify herself," Decker said. "It sounded
like one of your sisters-in-law. Probably Shayna. She's the
one without the Brooklyn accent, right?"

"Yes." Rina started to unpack the food on the dining-
room table. "She give you a rough time?"

"Downright rude," Decker said. "Unusual for her. She's
always been the nice one."

"Maybe she was upset."

Decker tossed her a sour look.

"I'm really sorry," Rina said.

"Nah." Decker stood up and kissed her. "Just forget I said
anything. Not your fault. I had a frustrating day."

Rina hugged him. "Marge looks better."

"You visited her?"

"Brought her a cake," Rina said. "From the both of us."

Decker laughed. As if Marge would ever believe he'd
think to give her a cake. "You two girls have a nice chat?"

She smiled. "The way we both see you is amazingly
similar."

"How's that?"

"None of your business," Rina said. She went in to the
kitchen with an armful of produce and began to wash vegetables.

"Now that's not fair," Decker said, following her.

Rina handed him a head of lettuce. "You wash this, then
take a knife and cut it up into tiny pieces. Think you can
handle that?"

"Real men don't make salad."

"Try," Rina said. "Pretend . . . you're sifting through evidence. I've got to phone New York." She kissed his lips,
then wrinkled her nose. "And if we go anywhere tonight,
I'll drive. How many beers did you pack away?"

"Confession isn't part of my religion," Decker said. He turned the tap on full blast and doused his shirt as well as the lettuce. "Shit."

"Finesse, Peter," Rina said, laughing. "Finesse." Her face turned suddenly serious as she dialed.

"Shaynie, it's Rina . . . What? Calm down, I can't understand you . . ."

"What is it?" Decker asked.

"She's hysterical," Rina said. Her voice was quavering. She began to pace as far as the phone cord would let her. "Just calm down. Are my boys all right?"

"What?" Decker pressed.

Rina brought her hand to her chest and ignored him. "You're sure? Can I talk to them? . . . But they're okay . . . Is everyone okay? . . . You gave me a heart attack. . . ." She slumped against the wall. "Stop crying and tell me what's wrong." She was silent for a few moments, then said, "Oh no . . . oh God . . . how's Esther doing?"

"What is it?" Decker asked.

Rina put her hand over the phone receiver and whispered "Pessy."

Decker puffed out his cheeks and said, "*The* Pessy?"

Taking her hand off the receiver, Rina asked Shayna, "When did this happen? . . . Do you have a lawyer?"

Decker started to smile. "What happened to old Pessy?"

"Arrested," Rina whispered to him. "Don't use the Public Defender. You need a private lawyer, Shayna, someone who's done this kind of work . . . well, I know it's embarrassing, but—"

Decker started to laugh.

Rina told her sister-in-law to hold on. "Peter, stop it!"

"Don't tell me," Decker said. "Soliciting an undercover police officer."

"Worse," she said. "Picked up in a raid." To Shayna, she said, "Yes, I'm still here. . . . Shayna, he's standing right behind me. What do you want me to do, lie to him? . . . He is family. He's *my* family, okay? . . . All right . . . all right . . . stop crying. I'm sorry . . . yes, I know you're under terrible stress. . . . Where's Esther?"

Rina shook her head and sat down on the chair. Decker stifled more laughter.

"So who's watching her kids if she's tranquilized?" she asked. "*Eema* has mine plus Esther's? She can't handle seven kids! . . . Okay. Okay . . . I'll catch the first flight I can. . . . Well, how should I know when that will be?"

Rina rolled her eyes.

"Will you stop crying, Shayna? I'll be there, but it'll take me a little time to get organized . . . I'll try to make it in before Shabbos. Before tomorrow night. . . . No I don't think I can do it any sooner, but I won't know until I start calling the airlines. . . . I'll do the best I can. . . . Okay . . . okay. I love you, too. . . . Mendel? Sure, put him on, I'll hold."

"You're going back?" Decker asked.

"Pessy was arrested in a massage-parlor raid," Rina said, covering the mouthpiece with her hand. "Esther has fallen apart. My mother-in-law has Esther's five kids plus mine. I've got to help out, Peter. They haven't even hired a proper lawyer because they're too embarrassed to let this leak— Hi, Mendel."

"Why's Mendel talking to you?" Decker asked.

"Hold on." Rina turned to Decker. "I can't talk to two people at once!"

"I thought Mendel didn't talk to women."

"Well, he's talking to me right now, okay!" To Mendel, she said, "Yes, I'm still here. . . . Uh-huh, uh-huh . . . You've got to be kid— . . . Mendy, Peter doesn't know anybody in New York. . . ." She began to pace again. "Mendy . . . Mendy, every police department is different. Cops don't have reciprocity. . . ."

She listened to Mendel for a minute, then said, "You

know, this is truly unbelievable. All last year, you and Pessy gave him grief whenever he called. Now, you're asking for favors? . . . All right, all right . . . But don't expect . . . Okay. Hold on."

She held out the phone to Decker. He said, "I don't have any clout with the New York PD."

"Can't you do anything? Just a phone call to find out how serious the charges are? Surely there's some sort of network."

"Rina, a week ago you were ready to kill this man. Now, you want to get him off?"

"What can I do, Peter?" She looked so desperate. "He's family."

Decker ran his hand over his face. "Tell Mendel I can't do anything about it. Nothing! But between you and me, I'll call a few people, okay?"

Rina nodded, related the message, and hung up.

"At least horny Pessy's out in the open," Decker said. "Takes the heat off of you."

"One problem solved, another created." She sighed. "Dear Lord, I dread going back."

"Want me to come with you?"

"Can you?"

"I've got a couple of cases hanging over my neck," Decker said. "If I make headway on them, I'll join you for a few days."

Rina fell into Decker's arms. "I love you."

"Love you, too."

"Can you do anything for him?" Rina asked.

"Probably not," Decker said. "But as promised, I'll call around. It all depends on the charges, if there were drugs on the premises—"

Rina groaned, "I didn't even think of that."

"Think about it, honey."

"Then he's in deep trouble?"

"You kidding?" Decker laughed. "If it's the usual first offense, no drugs involved, a slap on the wrist. He'll be out
and back on the prowl before you fly home."

"I've got to get back."

"I'm not telling you not to," Decker said. "I'm just telling
you don't worry about it."

Rina sank into a chair. "Out of curiosity. Could you have
influenced people if this had happened in L.A.?"

"*Could* I have, or *would* I have?"

Rina didn't answer.

"Depends," Decker said. Then he smiled. "Why? You
have a parking ticket you want me to fix?"

"Oh, Peter!"

"What should I do with all this chopped-up lettuce?"

"Put it in a bowl."

"What do you want to do about dinner?"

"I'm not hungry," Rina said. "And I have to start calling
airlines. I hope I can catch a nonstop flight before Shabbos.
Shayna says come out *now*. Beam me up, Scotty. We live in
the jet-age world, but as of yet, travel isn't instantaneous."

The thought hit Decker as sudden as a gust of wind.

Travel isn't instantaneous.

As with the Darcy case, it was just a matter of putting the
horse before the cart. Had Granny Darcy come back to get
Earl, or had she been there all along? Thinking along those
lines, Myra Steele's case was the same damn thing.

*They took her to Hollywood Pres, but her mom insisted
she be moved to County, because she didn't have any insurance.*

The right ingredients, but he lacked *evidence*. But if luck
be a lady, he'd get a hold of something. Enough rope for the
hanging.

He said, "I'll call the airlines for you."

"You don't have to do that," Rina said. "My family has
caused you enough grief."

"It's no bother, Rina," Decker said.

"Honestly?"

"Honestly."

"Well, if you do that," she said, "the least I could do is throw together something."

"No," Decker said. "You lie down, read a book. After I call, I'll take you out to dinner at that Italian kosher restaurant on the other side of the mountain."

Rina smiled. "That sounds great!" She added, "I'll drive."

He wasn't the least bit tipsy, but thought it would be bad form to argue. "Fine, darlin'."

"Try to get me a United flight," Rina said. "I'm saving up for mileage with them."

"Fine."

As she started to walk away, Decker asked, "Honey, you ever been to Detroit?"

"Twice," Rina said. "Why?"

"What airline did you take?"

"Gosh, it was a long time ago." She paused. "It wasn't one of the biggies, that much I remember. I think it was Northern or Northeastern. It was Northeastern. As I recall, it was the only one that flew nonstop from L.A."

"Thanks," Decker said.

"Why?" Rina asked again.

Decker didn't answer. Rina didn't pursue it.

❧26

At nine the next morning, Decker called the Darcy residence. The phone rang twelve times before it was picked up. Decker identified himself and asked to speak to Pappy Darcy. The male voice on the other end was low and slow.

"He ain't home," the voice said.

"Know when he'll be back?"

"I ain't suppose to say nothin' to the po-lice," said the voice.

"Are you B.B. Litton?" Decker asked.

"I told you, I don't say nothin' without my niggerlawyer."

Decker swallowed back anger. "Is Sue Beth there?"

"Nope."

"Is she at the courthouse?" Decker asked.

Silence over the other end. Decker felt his frustration grow. "Tell Sue Beth I called, all right?"

"Maybe," the voice said. "Maybe I won't."

The line went dead.

Decker swore, then told himself to let it pass. He'd talk to Nixon later today and arrange the interview through him.

He picked up the receiver, dialed the Hollywood substation, and asked for George Andrick. A breathy female voice on the other end paused a moment, then said solemnly that

Andrick had died on Tuesday—just two days ago. Massive coronary.

"You want info on the funeral?" she asked.

It took Decker a moment to collect his thoughts. The woman on the other end said, "You still there?"

"Yeah," Decker said.

"You a friend of his or something?"

"No," Decker said. "No, I'm from Foothill substation. I'm sorry to hear about Andrick."

"Too bad, huh?"

"Yeah," Decker said. "Listen, I was working on one of his cases. Know who took them over?"

The woman said she didn't but transferred him to Medino—Andrick's supervising detective. Decker gave Medino a recap of the case. Medino paused, then started repeating the name Steele over and over, as if it were a religious chant. Finally, he admitted he had no idea who had the case.

Decker asked, "What about Torres and Hoersch? Are they out on patrol?"

Medino said he didn't know, then transferred Decker to the day-watch commander.

Ten minutes later, a Valley address in hand, Decker was on his way to see Officer William Hoersch.

The patrolman lived in Reseda. His house was in the middle of a quiet block, a faded green stucco ranch home with torn white awnings and a pocked-plaster walkway. The front lawn had been burnt-wheat-colored except for a round disk of grass that had been saved by the lacy boughs of an elm. Two dirt bikes rested against the trunk of the tree. The door to the garage was open, a restored '62 Vette was up on lifts, and two legs were sticking out from under its belly. Decker cleared his throat. A bare-chested man about thirty slid out. His face was clean-shaven and covered with grease, his eyes dirty green but sharp. They immediately sized Decker up as a cop. Hoersch stood, wiped his oily hands on his shorts, but didn't say anything.

"Hoersch?" Decker said.

"That's me."

"Talk to you for a moment?"

"Who are you?" Hoersch asked.

Decker flipped open his ID billfold. He said, "I'm not here on anything official."

"So why are you here?"

"About a week ago, you and Alfredo Torres answered a two-forty-one Hotshot over in Hollywood—a gimp involved in an ambulance cutting. Victim was a hooker, stopped the perp by hitting him over the head with a lamp."

"Yeah," Hoersch nodded. "I remember. What's Foothill's involvement?"

"Gimp's a friend of mine," Decker said.

Hoersch's eyes narrowed. He rocked on his bare feet. "So . . ."

Decker smiled, took off his jacket and draped it over his arm. "No tricks, Hoersch. I'm not out here to bribe you, trap you, or trip you up. And I'm not from IAD."

Hoersch scanned Decker's limp shirt, unpressed pants. "You don't look like someone from IAD," he added.

"Thanks for the compliment," Decker said. "I just want to ask you a few questions about the call."

A young woman wearing a bikini top and cutoff shorts came out the front door. She entered the garage but stopped when she saw Decker.

"Give him a break," she said. "He's still got a few hours before he reports in."

"Inside the house, Terry," Hoersch said.

"Andy's on the phone," Terry said.

"Tell him I'll call him back," Hoersch snapped.

"Geez, okay!" Terry's lips formed a pout. "Don't have to yell."

After she left, Decker said, "A few questions, then I'm out of here."

"Don't worry about her," Hoersch said.

Decker said, "When you answered the call, anybody with the woman?"

"I think a neighbor," Hoersch said.

"Know for sure she was a neighbor?"

"She said she was," Hoersch said. "I think she said she was the one who phoned it in. She was holding the victim's hand, crying that kind of gospel crying that blacks do in those old-fashioned movies. 'Lordy, Lordy.' That kind of shit. Victim was bleeding all over the place. Al—Officer Torres—immediately administered aid to the victim, took a towel and tried to stanch the bleeding. I went over to the perp and cuffed him."

"How'd you know who the perp was?"

"He was the only man in the room," Hoersch said. "Besides, the neighbor, in between her Lordies, kept pointing to him and saying, 'He did it! He did it!'"

"The neighbor made the accusation?"

"Yeah."

"How'd she know? Did she catch him in the act?"

"I think she did."

"Was this neighbor middle-aged?"

"Yeah."

"Do you remember her name?"

"Not offhand."

"Was it Leandra Walsh?"

"I think her first name was Leandra," Hoersch said. "Last name wasn't Walsh, though."

"Think you could ID her?" Decker asked.

"Yeah." Hoersch shifted his weight, cocked his hip. "Why?"

"What did the perp do while Leandra was shouting, 'He did it, he did it'?"

"He was dazed," Hoersch said. "Leandra had hit him over the head with a lamp."

"*Leandra* hit the perp over the head with a lamp?"

"Yeah," Hoersch said, nodding.

"Not the victim?"

"No way!" Hoersch said, laughing. "The victim was hanging on for dear life."

"Detective Andrick stated in his report that the victim knocked the perp over the head."

"Not the way I saw or heard it," Hoersch said. "'Course, they may have told Detective Andrick something different. You know how it is. People get mixed up all the time."

"Sure," Decker said. "When you talked to Leandra, what did she say happened?"

"Just that she'd heard screams," Hoersch said. "Came in through the victim's door—"

"Door was unlocked?"

"Must have been." Hoersch folded his arms across his chest. "You know, it's hard to remember without my notes in front of me."

Decker said, "You're doing better than I could. Besides, this is all off the record."

"This gimp really a buddy of yours?"

"Yep."

Hoersch raised his eyebrows.

Decker said, "So Leandra heard screams and rushed in the victim's door."

"Yeah," Hoersch said. "No . . . wait. I think it went like this. First, she said, she called the police. Then she rushed in and saw the perp attacking the victim. She conked him over the head with a lamp. He was still dazed by the time we got to him."

"She called nine-one-one first?"

"I think that's what she said. She heard screams and called the police. But the police were too slow, and she went in herself . . . something like that."

"A nine-one-one call was placed," Decker said, "But it was called from the victim's phone."

Hoersch paused. "I think she said she called the police from her apartment."

"Maybe her apartment was the same as the victim's," Decker said.

"I gotta look at my notes," Hoersch said. "I don't want to tell you anything wrong."

"But you'd be able to ID this Leandra?"

"Think so."

"What about Torres?"

"Yeah, he probably could, too. Or Andrick."

"Andrick is dead," Decker said. "Heart attack."

"No *shit*?" Hoersch whistled, shook his head. "Jesus. You see a guy . . . I've been off for three days. Went to Catalina to do a little diving . . . Shit, that's lousy."

"Can I look at your notes?"

Hoersch didn't answer. Decker repeated the question.

"Uh, guess that'd be okay." He paused a moment, then said, "How old you think Andrick was?"

"Mid-fifties."

"He was overweight, too." Hoersch patted his hard abdomen. "Man, when I'm that age, I'm gonna be fit. Body is only as good as the way you treat it."

Decker said, "When can I look at your notes?"

"I go on shift at three," Hoersch said. "Meet me at the station a half hour early."

"Thanks," Decker said. "I'll remember this, Hoersch."

Hoersch shifted on his feet again. "Don't worry about it, Sergeant." He smiled. "If you forget, I'll remind you."

Abel's motorcycle was lying in front of the garage door. Rina parked the Porsche in the driveway and entered the house, hearing steady banging out back as she closed the side door. As usual, Peter hadn't come home yet. As usual, she was left to her own devices.

She paced the living-room floor, deciding in a matter of minutes that she was not going to spend another afternoon with him working inside the barn and her imprisoned in the house. She'd have to approach him, tell him to leave. The idea made her jittery, but she was less afraid of Abel, having spent an afternoon watching him and Peter play basketball, seeing the friendship between them.

Still . . .

Anxiously, she felt at the bottom of her purse for the gun, checked it to make sure it was loaded.

It was.

She slung her purse over her shoulder and went outside. The barn door was wide open. Abel was working in the back, sifting through a pile of fresh lumber stacked against the hay bales. He wore a blue tank top and a pair of faded brown corduroy shorts. His hair was tied back into a ponytail, a red sweatband encircled his forehead. His natural foot and his prosthesis were housed in running shoes. Rina stood outside the door, called his name. Abel turned around, a smile spread across his face.

"You shouldn't be here," Rina said.

Abel's smile disappeared. "I'll go if you want."

"You know how Peter is . . ."

"Don't have to explain, ma'am."

"Stop calling me ma'am." Rina noticed an edge to her voice. "Look, I'm sorry. It's nothing personal. It's just the way Peter is, and I don't want to aggravate him."

Abel didn't say anything. Rina shrugged, then turned to walk away.

"Rina?" Abel called out.

"What?"

"Do me a favor. Toss me my cane while I clean up. It's leaning against the left wall."

"Sure," Rina said. By the time the cane was in her hand, Abel had moved so that he blocked the entrance to the barn.

It was as if the guy had floated through the air, he'd been that quiet.

Abel shut the door. Rina felt her heart begin to pound.

"What do you think you're doing?" she asked.

"Closing the door."

"Get away from the door."

Abel smiled again; this time it was eerie. "Why?" he asked.

So *innocent*.

"Why are you doing this to me?" Rina shouted out. "I know what you've been accused of doing . . ."

Abel shrugged.

"For godsake, Abel, I thought Peter was your best friend."

"He is."

"Then get away from the door!" Rina felt her throat tighten. "Please."

"No, ma'am."

"You know I have a gun in my purse."

"Yes, ma'am."

"I know how to use it," Rina said. Her voice sounded shakier than she'd hoped.

"Yes, ma'am." Abel started to walk toward her.

"Why are you doing this?" Rina said.

But he kept approaching her. Quickly, she reached inside her purse, pulled out her gun, and aimed it at his chest.

That stopped him for a moment. Rina found her voice. She said, "Just get out of here! Just leave and everything's forgotten."

Abel shrugged, started toward her once again. " 'Fraid I can't do that, Rina." He wiped his forehead. "No, I just can't do that at all."

Peter's voice rang in her ears. *A knack for attracting weirdos*. Then he'd soft-pedaled his indictment.

I meant you'd attract any man, weird or not, because you're so beautiful. . . .

Peter never knew how right he was. Men had always stared at her. Strange men, men she knew, her father's friends, the men in the community. It didn't matter. They always were smiling at her, speaking to her, or just plain ogling her. No matter what she did, how dowdily she dressed herself, how tired and drawn she appeared after a long day at work. When she sat in the subway, nose buried in a book, some jerk always came up to her, tried out some sort of asinine line. *What* was she doing to encourage them? Or was it just her looks, the looks she cursed at this moment. Sweat began to pour down her armpits.

"I'm going to shoot you!" Rina said.

"Yes, ma'am."

"I'll *kill* you, for godsake!"

"Yes, ma'am."

As he drew near her, she began to back up. Her feet felt like jelly, her stomach churned until she felt bile rise in her throat.

"Abel, I'm begging you to stop," she sobbed. *"Please!"*

"You've got two choices, Rina," he said. His steps were soundless, carefully measured. "Shoot me or don't shoot me. Now I'm betting that no matter how threatened you feel, you can't look me in the eye and pull the trigger. But if you do . . . hey, that's cool."

"Please," Rina whispered. The gun was shaking in her hands. Her palms were moist and hot. She felt as if she were about to faint, but willed herself the strength to do whatever she had to.

Abel waited until he'd backed her against the wall, then stopped around ten feet in front of her.

"You're sure you know how to use that?" he said.

So calm. Rina felt hot tears well up, spilling over her cheek.

"Yes," she managed to answer.

"Then you'd better use it," Abel said. "Or else I'm going to take it out of your hands."

"Oh God, please help me," Rina sobbed.

"Last chance, Rina," Abel said calmly.

Then, at once, he lunged at her. A second later, her hands were empty. Abel stood six inches in front of her, the gun resting in his hands. He smiled at her, shook his head sadly.

"You blew it, kid," Abel said. He twirled the gun like a slinger in an old Western. "If I were a rapist, you'd not only be up shit's creek without a paddle, you wouldn't even have a boat." He pointed the gun to her temple.

All Rina could see was the faces of her sons. She whispered, "I have children."

Abel said, "If I were a murderer, I'd say something like . . . you should have thought about them a second ago." He traced her jaw outline with the barrel of the snub nose. With his free hand, he pulled off her kerchief and loosened her hair. "You're a beautiful woman, know that?"

Rina didn't answer. Her boys. Orphans. Peter had no chance of getting them. . . . Her parents would fight for them. . . . Dear God, if not for her, for *them*. She began to recite the *Shema* to herself.

Abel moved the gun closer until the muzzle touched her forehead, held it that way for a moment, then let the trigger guard rotate around his finger until the barrel pointed downward. He stood that way for a second, two seconds, then three and four, until Rina finally realized he was offering the gun back to her. Slowly, her hand began to rise, until her fingertips touched the chamber. It was then that her feet gave way. She slid, back snaking down the wall, until she collapsed onto the floor and wept. Abel sat beside her, opened her purse, and slipped the gun inside.

"Shouldn't carry a gun unless you're prepared to use it, Rina," Abel said. "It's easy to kill a target, even fire off a couple of rounds at someone fleeing in the woods at night . . ."

Fleeing. Peter must have told him how she'd tried to shoot the rapist. Why would he have done that? To warn Abel off? It hadn't worked. She hated Peter for bringing this pervert into their lives.

"Yeah," Abel went on, "it's easy to shoot when you're not looking someone in the eye. Not too many people shoot face-to-face. Some can. Your husband-to-be can. But obviously you can't."

Rina couldn't answer. She was shaking too hard.

"Do yourself a favor," Abel said. "Toss the gun."

Whispering, Rina said, "You did this . . . to teach me a lesson?"

Staring straight ahead, Abel didn't answer her. Neither one spoke for a minute or so. Rina felt her strength returning. Anger began to smother the fear that had paralyzed her. When she spoke, her voice burned with hatred. "You sadistic bastard!"

Abel turned to her and smiled. But his eyes were disturbed. "You still have the gun, Rina. Maybe you'd like to use it now, eh?"

"You *wanted* me to kill you!" Rina cried out.

"No," Abel said. "No, I didn't want you to kill me. I really didn't. But I wouldn't have cared if you did." He took a cigarette out of his pocket and lit it. "When I was recovering in the VA on the amputee ward, we used to sneak guns in and play Russian roulette. Actually, they say there were some who played roulette in Nam. Like in the movie *Deer Hunter*—"

"I don't go to movies," Rina said. Then wondered why in the world she was answering this creep. She should bolt up and run away. But fright or its aftermath kept her rooted to the ground.

Abel went on, "Well, I never did see any grunts spin the gun while in Nam. Pete didn't, either. But I did do it on the ward. Few guys blew their brains out. But that was no big deal. Staff chalked it up to despondency—suicidal depression."

"It was suicide," Rina said. "It—" She stopped talking.

Abel waited for more, and when it didn't come, he said, "Yeah, I guess looking at it now, it was." He took a drag on his smoke. "But then, I never thought of it like that. Just something to do to feel your heart pumping. It's like this. You lose a leg, an arm . . ." A lover, he thought. "You lose something that was part of you, you go numb. And I wasn't the worst off, by any means. At least I was still a man, if you know what I mean. Others . . ." Abel felt perspiration drenching his sweatband. "Others weren't that lucky. So you're lying there trying to readjust, not doing it very well, you do anything to feel, even if the feeling's fear."

Rina said nothing.

He shook his head. "You couldn't possibly understand—"

"What I can't understand was how you could do such a horrible . . . cruel . . . monstrous thing to *me*!" Rina blurted out.

"I'm sorry—"

"Especially since I'm your best friend's fiancée."

Abel didn't respond. And in that moment of silence, Abel had said it all.

"It wasn't me personally, was it?" Rina said. "You like me."

"Honey, I more than like you."

"But you hate Peter more than you like me."

Abel laughed too loudly. "You are one bright lady."

Rina brushed away tears and said softly, "I was so *nice* to you."

"I'm sorry," Abel said. He realized how banal his apology was, but couldn't think of anything else to say.

"You set me up," Rina continued. "A payback for something Peter did to you. You *son* of a bitch!"

Abel nodded his head in agreement.

Rina tried to speak, but her voice was choked. She buried her head in her hands and wept.

"Know the worst part about it?" she finally said. "Peter must have told you what happened to me two years ago. About the attempted rape. Otherwise, you wouldn't have made that comment about me shooting at things fleeing in the woods."

"He did," Abel said.

"How could you do that to me—to anyone—knowing what I'd been through?" Rina dried her eyes on her shirt-sleeve. "What was Peter's crime? Surviving the war in one piece?"

"Saving my life," Abel said.

"Dear God . . ." Rina said a silent prayer, then ran her hands through her hair. "You're really sick, you know that?"

"I'm more than sick, Rina," Abel said. "For all intents and purposes, I'm dead. I died the day I lost my leg." He turned and faced her. "The key was quarter-turned in the ignition when I heard Pete screaming to get out of the Jeep. Didn't quite make it all the way out."

"And this is how you pay him back?"

"He should have let me die," Abel said. "My fiancée died that day. And *that* kinda left me addled. She was lovely, Rina, half Korean, half Vietnamese. A thoroughly beautiful woman, not unlike yourself. Her name was Song Duc Lu. Ask Pete about her. He knew her well, though not as well as he thought . . ." He looked down.

With shaky hands, Rina drew her purse onto her lap. She felt safe in an odd sort of way. He'd had his opportunity and didn't take it. Primitive thinking, but she held on to her logic as tightly as she clutched her purse.

"So you're angry at Peter for saving your life," Rina said. "For your girlfriend's death. You're crazy, Abel. You're crazy and you're right! Peter *should* have let you die."

Abel broke into a slow smile that spoke of his tortured soul. Rina was suddenly ashamed of herself. She stared at him, at this shell of a man consumed by the poison of untimely loss. Rina knew the feeling well. Once, she'd been as bitter as he. But time and God had calmed her soul. She knew some people who'd returned to God during troubled periods, but most did not find their ultimate salvation in religion. Time was a different animal. Most raging souls were soothed by the passing of years. Abel had been one of the exceptions, his war experience turning him into a ghost. There had to be more to his story, but she didn't want to engage him in any more conversation. Suddenly, the prospect of returning to New York didn't seem nearly as gloomy.

"Look," she said. "I . . . I'm sorry your fiancée died. But *I* didn't kill her."

Abel let out a bitter laugh. "True enough."

His presence was suffocating. She had to get out of there. She tried to stand, but didn't have the strength. In a clear voice, she said, "I'm a little shaky, Abel. Help me up."

Abel regarded her face for a moment. Full of anger, yet he knew she'd forgive him. She was that type of person, the exact opposite of himself. Even after all he had done to her, she couldn't sustain her hatred. He thought of her eyes as he'd threatened her. He'd known she couldn't pull the trigger.

He stood up, offered her his hand, then pulled her up, holding her hand a little longer than he should have. And she knew it, too. But she seemed too weary to pull away. He brought her hand to his lips and kissed the fingertips several times.

"You didn't do it, did you?" Rina said.

"No." Abel dropped her hand. "No, I didn't. I've got lots of bad qualities. You've just seen one of them, Rina—I can't let go of anything. But I don't hurt women—ever."

Don't hurt them physically, Rina thought. She turned on her heels and ran into the house without looking back. Ten minutes later, she heard the roar of the motorcycle's ignition. It spat and hissed, then faded until it dissipated into the hot summer air.

❧27

Cool and calm.

Decker had learned a lot over the years, two decades of police work had been an extended training course in control. Dispassionate inwardly, compassionate outwardly. Don't get overinvolved.

Except the bastard had put a gun to her head. Suddenly, nothing else mattered.

He parked the unmarked on a side street connecting Sunset and Hollywood—equidistant from the teenage prostitutes and the chickenhawks. The harsh noonday sun highlighted the ugliness. All around, neglected apartments. Buildings gray with grime and smog. Bungalows with rotted porches and rusted siding.

Abel lived in a two-story decaying structure called the Aloha. Its exterior was pink, but once it had been colored aqua, the old paint surfacing through in inkblot patterns. Decker jogged up a metal staircase coated with grit and walked down an outside hallway, heading toward the back. Abel's bachelor pad overlooked a pay parking lot. His door was open. Decker stepped inside.

The place was bare bones. Plaster walls painted yellow, a worn brown carpet as flat as packed dirt. His sofa had been gold and red brocade, but the fabric had thinned to surgical gauze. In front of the couch was a wood-grained Formica table resting on spindly black legs. A matching square table was shoved into the windowed corner, two orange plastic chairs pushed against it. The top was clean and clear except for a gooseneck lamp and an old toaster. A kitchenette was squeezed into a closet—a two-burner hot plate, a bar-sized fridge, and a small porcelain sink, its surface polished sparkling white. The room was stuffy and, as always, reeked with the smell of ammonia, bug spray, and disinfectant.

Abel was looking out the window, his hands resting on the sill, his shoulders hunched. His feet cleared the floor by six inches. He was shirtless, wearing a pair of gray shorts and a black-and-white checkered sweatband. His beard had been neatly trimmed, his hair washed and braided, the plait grazing the middle of his back.

"Ever think of hanging up a picture?" Decker said.

"There's beauty in simplicity," Abel answered.

Decker walked over to him, pushed him down until his feet touched the carpet. Abel turned to face him.

"Okay, buddy," Decker said. "Spit it out."

Abel didn't answer.

"Say it." Decker gave him a shove. "Say it! Say it, goddammit, say it!"

Decker pushed him backward. Abel stumbled but regained his balance by grabbing a kitchen chair. He said nothing.

Decker grabbed his shoulders, pulled him forward, and said, "She was *Cong*, you jerk! VC! Charlie! The enemy! The one who tried to blow your *balls* off, but had to settle for your leg!"

"I knew she was VC," Abel whispered.

"You *knew* she was VC?"

"She told me."

Decker felt his heart pounding. "You *knew* she was VC, and you went with her anyway?"

"She was being duped by her husband. . . ."

"You *knew* she was married?" Decker yelled. He let go of Abel with a shove and began to pace. "You took up with a married woman who you knew was enemy. I don't believe . . . You play with Charlie, you know what I say to you, buddy? You got everything you deserved!"

"You want to rant, or you want to listen?" Abel said.

Again, Decker grabbed his shoulders, but this time he shook him. "What I want to do is break your fucking neck for what you did to Rina! You got a beef with *me*, you don't go taking it out on *her*!"

"You're right. . . ."

"Friggin' maniac!" He pushed Abel away.

"I snapped, all right!" Abel said. "Man, I just . . . snapped. I saw Rina and she reminded me of Song—"

"Don't you ever mention Rina and that piece of shit in the same sentence!" Decker said.

Abel's eyes narrowed. "Don't you ever call Song a piece of shit!" He took a deep breath. "I *knew* she was Charlie, I *knew* she had a Charlie husband. I also knew that she was being beaten by the bastard, being pimped by him in Hanoi, then he took her down south as pussybait for us GI Joes—"

"And you never said a word of this to me or anyone."

"I *loved* her, Decker! And she loved me! You think she confessed to me for the hell of it? She trusted me! They would have *killed* her if they knew, because her husband was Cong."

"*She* was Cong!"

"She was *sixteen years old*, for chrissakes! Orphaned! Didn't know what the hell was going down, just did what she was told to do. Man, she never *killed* anyone. And she wasn't trying to waste me. It was a setup by her old man. He'd found out about us—"

"Bullshit!" Decker interrupted. "You jerk, if li'l Song was so innocent, why wasn't she in the Jeep with you when it blew up? Ever have the courage to ask yourself that?"

"She went back to get a necklace I gave her."

"You just don't see it, do you?" Decker said. "That's what they *do*, Atwater. They say, 'Let's go out for a ride, honey, and boom-boom in the jungle.' Then, as you get in the car, she says, 'Oops, forgot something. I'll be right back.' Second later, you're hamburger."

"No, *you* don't see it," Abel answered. "When Stiller dragged her out, she was wearing *my* necklace, Decker. You mean to say she went back into the hut, put on my necklace, and came back outside to watch me blow up?" There were tears in his eyes. His voice cracked. "Didn't you see the look of *horror* on her face!"

"That was *fear*, man!"

"You had a *gun* to her head!" Abel screamed. "How else should she feel!"

"What?" Decker said. "You want me to apologize for wasting her? Fuck you! I'd do the same thing all over, because if I didn't, she'd just go on and find another dumb sucker to off. And man, we were losing enough of us as it was. I saw it more than you, 'cause I was the jerk they'd call in to repair the damage."

There was a moment of stillness, the screams reverberating in the silence. Abel started to speak, but stopped himself. He limped over to the couch and sank into a lumpy cushion, running his hands over his face.

Finally, he said, "You never gave her—or me—a chance to explain." He wiped his wet eyes with the back of his hands. "I *begged* you not to, Pete. Through the morphine, the shock, through it *all*, I saw what was gonna go down, and I fucking *begged* you not to do it."

Decker didn't answer.

"Know what it's like . . . to see someone you love . . . explode?" Abel said.

Softly, Decker said, "All I saw was *you* exploding." He shook his head and tried to ward off demons. Felt a headache coming on. One that aspirin couldn't handle. "I lied a moment ago. If I had known then what I know now, I wouldn't have done it."

He exhaled forcibly, then sat beside Abel.

"But back then I . . . I don't know . . . I didn't have the presence of mind . . . the experience . . . I was just a stupid kid, Abe."

Abel threw up his hands. "We were all stupid . . . God were we *stupid* . . . I just wish . . ." He let his voice trail off.

Decker said, "You put a gun to Rina's head because . . . because you wanted to know what it felt like. You could have asked me directly, Atwater." His voice cracked. "Want me to tell you what it felt like? It felt like your worst friggin' nightmare. Think I don't remember her brains splattering my clothes, her blood spraying in my eyes—"

"Oh God!" Abel held back a dry heave.

"Everything . . ." Decker shook his head. "It just happened so goddam quickly. My first concern was you. It . . . I . . ." He tried to find his words. "I screamed to you about the booby trap—"

"I heard you," Abel said. "At least, I heard you screaming."

"Yeah," Decker said. "You looked up, came halfway out of the Jeep . . . Then it all came down. Boom! Chaos! I jumped out of the Jeep . . . Stiller, the Bagman, and DeMarcos had come with me . . . Stiller was driving . . . I rushed over to you . . ."

Decker stopped a moment, stared at his lap, and shook his head.

"God, it was a friggin' mess! So much smoke . . . my eyes were tearing like crazy, my nose was clogged from the stench of burning . . . rubber."

"Flesh," Abel said.

"Man, that, too . . . Your stump . . . gushing buckets . . . and you'd been diced by flying pieces of metal. Just . . . bleeding all over the place.

"I treated you while the others . . . Fuck, I don't know *what* the others were doing . . . I remember DeMarcos wanting to level the village. Man, I was tending to you and trying to prevent DeMarcos from making another My Lai. The village was supposed to be one full of friendlies . . . who the fuck knew . . . then Stiller came out of the blue, dragging out Song . . . talking about raping her—"

"I didn't hear that," Abel said.

"Man, you were so doped up, you didn't know what was flying. I must have shot you with . . . God, must have been three ampules of morph. A wonder you didn't OD on the spot . . . I was so friggin' scared. Your face, Abe . . . gone. Gray and cold. That look when you know they're one step away from the other side. I managed to control the bleeding, but shock had set in. . . ."

Decker pulled out a cigarette, lit it, and took a long drag. He felt sweat running down his neck and back; his body was hot and sticky.

"Stiller began yanking off Song's clothes. I told him don't . . . or stop. He started screaming at me, calling me . . . I don't know . . . a nip lover or something like that . . . saying I was as bad as you . . . just mouthing off garbage. Meanwhile, DeMarcos must have shoved a magazine into his sixteen. *He* started busting some caps . . . peeling off shots at the huts. Then Stiller . . . he must have dragged Song over to you and me. He put a Magnum to her head.

"God's honest truth, next thing I know the Magnum's in my hand . . . I remember feeling cold steel . . . I looked down . . ." Decker stared at his right hand as if he'd never seen it before. "I'm holding the fucking gun! Must have been the Bagman . . . must have been. *He* must have taken it out of Stiller's hand and put it in mine, 'cause as God is my witness, I didn't grab it or take it or anything like that. Then the Bagman . . . he says, 'You do it. Abe was your best buddy, man.' Past tense. They're talking about you like you're dead."

Decker stuffed the cigarette into his mouth and sucked on it so hard, the smoke singed his throat.

"By then I'm pumped up, completely wired. She's crying . . . pleading with me in Pidgin English, in Vietnamese. You're moaning like the wind. Abe, you may have thought you were screaming at me to save her. But I swear to God, you were just moaning—"

"You saying you didn't *hear* me begging?"

"I'm saying I saw a dying boy spitting up blood . . . babbling something I couldn't understand or didn't want to understand." Decker swallowed dryly. "Man, I looked Song squarely in the eye, and at that moment, I just saw . . . enemy. So, I plugged her. I . . . plugged her."

Decker covered his mouth with his fist. He felt winded, as if sucker-punched. Twenty years of repression surfacing as hideously as a bloated body. The heat of the room had become oppressive. He went over to the window, threw it open, and stuck his head outside. Street sounds filled his ears, obliterating the repulsive cries of memory.

But not totally. Decker had shocked himself. The clarity of the images, the details. A camera rolling at high speed but still capturing every moment. His brain wanting to forget, *begging* to forget an amoebic splotch of exploding flesh. But his memory was unforgiving. He gazed out the window for redemption, but all he saw was his guilt.

Five minutes later, he heard Abel hobble up behind him.

"Wanna beer?" Abel asked.

"Yeah."

Abel popped open two cans of Bud and placed them on his kitchen table. Decker sat down and emptied the can in four gulps. Abel gave him another, then joined him, sipping suds off the surface of the can.

"You didn't like her, did you?" he said.

"Wasn't her personally," Decker said. "I mean, she was nice enough. And she was beautiful. But she was a gook. Atwater, they were all gooks to me—the friendlies as well as the Cong. I couldn't get past the slanted eyes, not because I was prejudiced, but because out there I couldn't tell the good guys from the bad."

"I always thought you were jealous."

"Jealous of her, not you." Decker gained enough courage to look Abel in the eyes. "We were tight, then you met her and went all moony-eyed. That was bad enough—me being crapped out in paddyland and you walking on cloud nine. Then you stopped doing stuff for the kids. Well, who am I to talk, I never did a damn thing for any of them. So I kept my opinions to myself. What really got me and everyone else pissed as hell was your sudden conscientious-objector attitude. I remember once Tony the Wolf talking about gooks, saying something nasty, I don't recall his exact words. Then you piped in, 'You know the Vietnamese are people, too,' and stalked out of the hooch. Man, Tony was ready to waste you on the spot. I remember *physically* holding him back, and that was no easy task, 'cause Tony was built.

"I mean, we didn't have enough trouble from King Cong Janie telling us to put down our weapons, from people back home calling us baby-killers, from reporters asking us if we ever considered the moral consequences of our actions. Now, you're telling us that the enemy is human. Talk about demoralizing the troops. She was *getting* to you, Abel."

"We never talked politics."

"Bullshit!" Decker said. "You knew she was orphaned, you knew her husband pimped her. She told you something about her personal life. Something to evoke *pity* in you. To see the other side as 'people, too.' And they are people. But you can't think about that when you're shooting at them. Otherwise, you can't live with yourself."

Silence. Finally, Abel said, "Could be."

He finished his beer and squashed the can, thinking about Decker's words, about all the times he and Song had made love. Her arms and legs wrapped around him, her hair streaming in his face, in his eyes and mouth. Had her smooth limbs, her velvet tresses, been snares? Their loving had seemed so pure, felt so holy. But back then, Abel now knew, his soul had been starved, willing to accept any morsel. Her love. Had it been nothing more than poisonous bait? He knew Decker was right about one thing. VC had been indistinguishable from the friendlies.

He bit his lip, then said, "We'll never really know about Song, will we?"

"Not in this lifetime."

"Well, maybe that's good. Finding out the truth means one of us loses big."

"This way, we both just lose," Decker said.

"But not quite as big," Abel said. "We can both rationalize." He turned to Decker. "How'd you find out about her?"

"We captured her husband that morning. He had her picture in his pocket." Decker lit up another cigarette. "Same picture she gave you. My eyes almost dropped to the floor. Guy had no qualms about giving his wife away. Guess he figured if he gave her to us, we'd be lenient with him. Bad strategy—it left him dead. God, what an absolute friggin' *mess!*"

"And all this time, I thought it never bothered you."

"What did you think?" Decker said. "I was made out of stone?"

"I just remember the look on your face when you fired," Abel said. "You looked so happy."

"Dope," Decker said, "made everything look happy. No, I wasn't happy, Atwater. I was *terrified!*" He finished a second can of beer and dropped his half-smoked cigarette in the empty can. "Like I said, if I was given a second chance, I might have handled it differently." He stared at Abel. "But you still had no call to do what you did to Rina. She's forgiven me, even forgiven *you*. But man, she was shaken. Poor girl has really been through the wringer. Then you pull a stunt like this."

"It was low," Abel said.

"She could have shot you. I've got to tell you, I'm surprised she didn't."

"I'm not," Abel said. "I knew she couldn't do it."

"She should have."

"Yeah, I won't argue that."

"Jesus, what happened to you that you'd pull a suicide act like that?"

"Like I said, I guess I just went nuts. I was coming off a really bad time. Really bad one this time, Pete. Tons of blackouts, waking up in strange places, getting arrested for vagrancy, drunk and disorderlies."

"They're not on your rap sheet."

"They were in small towns—east and north of L.A. God only knows how I got there. You know, I can tell when I'm gonna have a low period. The memories start in my sleep. Then I start seeing things during the day, hearing gunshots every time a car backfires. My mind goes on strike until the memories start fading. Then I come out of it. And I was coming out of this one, too. But then this rape thing . . ."

Abel didn't continue his thought, and Decker didn't say anything. He'd almost made the case, but almost wasn't good enough. He waited for Abel to speak.

"You bailing me out." Abel spun the beer can on the tabletop. "Then, looking at me like I was a criminal . . . I thought to myself, Who are *you* to judge me? Then I saw Rina looking at me in the same way. Why'd you *tell* her?"

"I had to," Decker said.

"No, you didn't."

"Hey, I did what I thought was right."

"Even if it meant making me look like a jerk."

"Buddy, you did that to yourself."

"I didn't *rape* that whore."

"I'm not saying you did," Decker said. "But you fucked her. You want to stay out of trouble, you don't fuck whores."

"Thank you, Reverend Decker . . . uh, excuse me—Rabbi Decker."

"Abe, this is pointless."

"Truce," Abel said waving the gooseneck lamp. "Look, I know I shouldn't ask you to do this, but I wrote something to Rina. Can you give it to her for me?"

"She left for New York last night," Decker said. "Glad to get out of here."

"Did I mess things up between you?"

"We're okay. No thanks to you though."

"Can you mail the letter for me? I don't even want to know her address."

"What'd you write?"

"You can read it," Abel said. "No cheap excuses. Just a note of pure apology." He paused, then said, "You tell her what the deal was?"

Decker didn't answer right away. Finally, he said, "No . . . no, I just couldn't. I fudged. I told her we had a big blowout over a girl." Decker laughed hollowly. "Talk about a bad choice of words."

Abel said, "Why didn't you tell her?"

"I don't know." Decker cleared his throat. "It's too hard to talk about it. Like you said, Song was only sixteen, and I still think about that a lot. Of course, I was only nineteen— a war of teenagers. We were all so young and stupid. The scene repeats on me every once in a while."

"Our little secret," Abel said. "It's what we have between us." With his fingertips, he traced part of an imaginary barrier separating him and Decker. He said, "And it's what we have between us."

The door to the rabbi's study was open, inviting. The room was done in warm dark woods. Two walls were floor-to-ceiling bookshelves packed with tomes of Jewish law and commentary, volumes of Jewish history, sets of American jurisprudence, and secular works on philosophy. A third

wall was covered with display cases of antique Jewish arti-
facts and religious cbjects, including an old set of phylacteries made in Czarist Russia. They had been owned by
Decker's biological father—a religious man who had never
seen fit to marry, rather remarry. Decker had met him only
once. He'd looked up his adoption records and, after intro-
ducing himself to the old man by phone, took a quick trip
out to New York to meet him in person. They had nothing in
common except physical appearance, yet some kind of
bond must have formed in the old man's mind. All his religious articles had been willed to Decker.

The fourth wall was taken up by an oversized picture
window that framed a canyon view of towering eucalyptus
trees, shrubbery, wildflowers, and mountains. Rav Schulman's desk was in front of the window, placed away from
the wall so that chairs could be positioned on either side.
The rabbi sat with his back to the window, and when
Decker entered the room, he motioned him to the chair with
the view.

But Decker didn't sit right away. Instead, he studied his
father's phylacteries.

Rav Schulman regarded Decker's restlessness, had
known something was amiss when his student called him
immediately after the Sabbath requesting to learn. Schulman had told Decker to come to his study an hour after his
Saturday night lecture to his rabbinic students.

Decker shifted his gaze to Schulman. As usual, the rav
was dressed in his black silk suit, starched white shirt, black
tie, and high-polished oxfords. The old man met Decker's
stare with perceptive eyes. Though Decker had second
thoughts about being here, it was too late now. Schulman
knew he was troubled, so he might as well get it over with.

Decker spoke first, saying, "Rabbi, how much of our behavior do you think is inherited?"

Schulman shrugged. "I wouldn't even hazard a guess,
Akiva."

Calling Decker by his Jewish name. His name for over a year. But it still sounded foreign.

"My father"—Decker paused, then clarified—"my adopted father, my *real* father, I should say, is a very gentle man. Gruff outside but a sweetheart inside. I'm anything but gentle. I wonder if my biological father had a nasty temper."

The rav stood, his eyes pained by Decker's question. He twirled the tip of his silver beard around his finger. "What's really on your mind, Akiva?"

"I met an old friend of mine," Decker said. "We served in Vietnam together. He brought back memories—of myself—I'd just as soon forget. But it wasn't just him that made me aware of this. Once in a while, something will happen and I'll just lose control. I get this murderous look in my eye. Happened just the other day with Rina." Decker blushed. "You knew Rina had been in town, didn't you?"

"Of course," Schulman said. "We had several nice long talks."

The old man had to know they were sleeping together, but Decker couldn't read it in his face.

"I owe you a *mazel tov*, Akiva," Schulman said.

"Thank you," Decker said. "I've been waiting a long time for her to say yes." He cleared his throat. "I want to be a good husband to her, a good father to her boys. I want . . . I don't want them to be afraid of me. But sometimes it's as if I'm possessed. Something just takes control of me."

"Yetzer Harah," Rav Schulman said.

Decker considered his answer. The *Yetzer Harah*—the evil inclination. As good a description as any. He said, "It's not lust or gluttony or greed. It's just plain evil. Desire to destroy. What the he—what's *wrong* with me?"

"What do you do when your *Yetzer Harah* is strong in you?" Schulman asked.

"I usually manage to hold it in until I get off work,"

Decker said. "I work out the horse—too vigorously. I take potshots at my barn. If someone's around, I'll scream at them. Once, I kicked my dog. Funny thing is, these rages aren't necessarily brought on by anything big. It's just a feeling that overwhelms me."

"You seem to be controlling yourself pretty well," Schulman said. "Though we should be kind to animals of course. *Tzar ba'alei chaim.*"

"The only trouble is, now I live alone, and no one except maybe the dog and my horses know about my temper." Decker faced the old man. "But that will change. Rina saw me lose control once. I don't want her to see it again."

"Well," Schulman said, "it's nice to be able to be perfect, but we all lose our tempers—"

"But—"

"Wait," Schulman said holding an upright hand.

"Sorry."

"You get angry, I get angry, everyone gets angry. What you seem to be talking about"—The Rabbi spoke in a crisp, accented voice—"is extraordinary anger, which I suspect has something to do with your war experiences, otherwise why would you bring that up in the first place?"

Decker didn't answer.

The Rosh Yeshiva went over to his desk, pulled out a bottle of whiskey and two shot glasses. He poured a big one for himself, a smaller one for Decker, and said, "So, do you want to tell me about it?"

Decker held the glass, swirled the whiskey. "It's hard."

"Let me guess." Schulman downed the first shot. "You killed someone. You probably killed more than one person, but one specific person is sticking in your mind. Notice I used the word 'kill' and not 'murder.' A war situation, Akiva, you cannot consider yourself a murderer . . . unless the killing was gratuitous."

"I didn't think so at the time," Decker said. "I swear—"

"No *shevuah*, please," the old man said. "Swearing is serious business."

"I really thought that this girl—she was a sixteen-year-old girl—was enemy. I shot her at point-blank range. She . . . exploded all over me. Her blood was still warm . . . God, it was awful."

"Sit," Schulman demanded. Decker obeyed. The old man said, "Did you rape this girl before—"

"God no!"

"Just a question," the old man said. "You'd be surprised what kind of confessions have come through this office."

"I thought Jews don't confess."

"To God, we confess everyday," the rav said. "But confession to man is not a part of our religion. Unofficially, however, my *bochrim* have told me things. Believe me, you're not the first young man to tell me his dark secrets."

He poured himself another shot and urged Decker to drink. "Since this isn't confession in the Catholic sense—where a parishioner unburdens his soul and a priest listens and forgives in the name of God—I'm going to tell you one of *my* war stories."

"Please," Decker said.

"You know I was in the camps, *nu*?"

Decker nodded.

Schulman said, "I escaped in a very strange way. Only God could have fated such a rescue. I was young, but I came down with a very bad case of pneumonia. No use to the Nazis anymore. The Germans took a truckload of us out into the forest to be shot. Why out there, I don't know. The grounds around Auschwitz were piled high with dead bodies, maybe they were running out of room."

Decker winced, but Schulman was calm.

"So they drove us out for miles," the old man continued. "Deep into the forest until they found a clearing. They stripped us naked and commanded us to line up against a

row of trees. Oaks. That I remember, strangely enough—
the leaves, the bark . . . Anyway, the Nazis ordered us on
our knees, backs straight up, hands behind our heads—typical execution position. They had dogs with them in case
any of us decided to make a run for it. I thought, This is it. I
said *Shema*.

"But as we were lining up to be shot, I limped behind a
tree and tried to hide. I should have been spotted at any
moment—the tree trunk was narrow, minimum shield—
when suddenly, poof, I'm swallowed up by the earth."

Decker stared at him.

"Just like that!" Schulman snapped his fingers. "I went
straight down. I figured out later that I must have stepped
into some kind of animal trap. No one noticed my absence,
because who counted Jewish bodies? Piles of leaves and
mulch covered my head."

Schulman paused a moment and knitted his brow in concentration.

"I heard everything. The crying, the moaning, the shooting. Pop, pop, pop. One by one. All the while, I'm shaking,
thinking at any moment I will be discovered. I was petrified
I was going to sneeze or cough. But I went unnoticed."

"A miracle," Decker said.

"Truly," Schulman said. "A *ness*—a miracle from
Hashem. Now, to make a long story short—"

"No, please—" Decker said. "Don't cut it short for my
sake."

"I cut it short for my sake," Schulman said. "You don't
like your memories, I don't like mine."

Decker said nothing.

Schulman said, "I somehow survived my bout of pneumonia—*baruch Hashem* it was the summertime—and I became a very sturdy young man, living like an animal in the
forest for two years. Throughout my wanderings, I met very
few people. Hermits with beards down to their knees. Cra-

zies, feral, bestial people who lived by their instincts and wits. Maybe even a few of the crazies were escaped Jews like myself. But no one would let on, *nu*?"

Decker shook his head.

"Finally, I came upon a righteous Gentile couple who befriended me. Allowed me to live in their barn an entire winter. They provided me with blankets, hot coals, and coarse bread. This couple even dared to risk their lives by hiding me in their haystack when their SS son came on a surprise visit."

Schulman sipped his drink. "I tried to locate them after the war. I was unsuccessful."

He was silent for a moment.

"Their son's visit made me realize what a danger I was to these people. Without them asking, I went on my way. I lived—survived—eating berries and leaves, drinking water from streams. And I found a gun, several, in fact. Being kosher, I never attempted to hunt for meat. I don't have a *shochet*'s mentality, though theoretically I know how to ritually slaughter an animal. And I was able to sustain myself on the fruit of the forest. After such a *ness*, I was not able to transgress the laws of *kashruth* even if I had the excuse of *pekuah nefesh*—saving a life."

"I wish I had your faith," Decker said.

"You experience a *ness* like that, the faith just comes, Akiva," Schulman said.

He paused a moment, then went on. "Toward the end of the war—I didn't know it was the end of the war back then—I came across one of Hitler's elite wandering the forest. He was a young man—around eighteen, nineteen—dressed in a dirty uniform—and was roaming about half-dazed, his eyes glazed over. He must have become separated from his regiment. He saw me, snarled, and fired out one word at me. *Juden*. That triggered some . . . primal anger deep within me."

Schulman's eyes hardened.

"I became enraged, reached for my gun. Suddenly, I saw *fear* in the boy's eyes, Akiva. Imagine how that felt. A scrawny beaten-down Jew instilling a Nazi with terror. He started begging me for mercy, crying out his mother's name. I remained unmoved, thinking, *Gornish mein helfin*. Nothing would help him now. I knew if I let him go and he should be saved, I would be hunted down and shot. Or he'd just go on to murder other Jews. For my sake and the sake of *klal Yisrael*—the Jewish people—I . . . shot him."

He shrugged and looked Decker in the eye.

"Never any question as to the morality of what I did," Schulman said. "I knew I was correct. It didn't bother me then, it doesn't *really* bother me now. But every few years, I dream about that boy. I see the terror in his eyes. I wake up, say a *bracha* to God for delivering me. But then I ask myself . . ." He pointed his finger in the air and his voice took on a singsong cadence. "If I was so right, why does God allow me to see this child's terror as clearly as the day I shot him?"

"Do you have an answer?" Decker asked.

"I have postulations only," Schulman said. "My primary thought is that *Hashem* wanted me to experience the fragility of life. As that boy's life was in my hands, so am I in *Hakodosh Boroch Hu's* hands. That was the purpose of the biblical sacrifices. Do you think that *Hashem* needed us to give Him a goat or a ram for His ego?" The old man stuck his finger in the air. "Of course not!"

Decker smiled.

"*Hashem* wanted us to know how precarious is our hold on the thread of life. One minute that animal was alive, full of strength and vigor. A second later, it was dead. So it was with that boy. Those dreams come to keep me humble, Akiva. To make me understand that we are *mortal* creatures."

"Nothing like a war to make you feel mortal," Decker said.

Schulman patted his shoulder. "If I may interpret your pain, I'd say what you saw in that young girl's death was your own mortality. And it scared you. Witnessing death firsthand, taking a life—horrifying, frightful. You don't even realize how scared you are until after it's all over. First you're relieved to be out of that situation . . . then you become angry. Like discovering a practical joke had been played on you. The more scared you were, the more angry you are afterward. And the anger can stay with you a long time."

"You were angry?" Decker asked.

"Furious! Enraged! Crazed with vengeance!"

"So how did you get rid of it?" Decker asked.

"Who said I did?" the old man cried out. "I'm still an angry man! Sometimes I'll be reading an article in the paper about those *mamzers* from the *Historical Review*—the Nazi *mamzers* who say the Holocaust never happened. I read about the skinheads. I want to *kill* them. Ah, but I *don't*. And you may get angry, start shooting at the barn, but you don't murder, do you?"

"No," Decker said.

"Ask God for forgiveness, Akiva," Schulman said. "*Hakodosh Boroch Hu* is the only one who can give you solace. I've told you that before." He stood up, motioned Decker to do the same thing. The old man embraced him tightly, then looked him in the eye. Still holding him, he said, "Then, my boy, have the courage to forgive yourself." He broke away. "Enough of the past. Let's learn a little Talmud."

28

A weekend of dreaming in red, the images so realistic that even after Decker had awoken, he was disoriented. His heart raced, his skin was damp and sticky, his gut knotted with raw fear. Monday morning was especially bad, because he had to leave the confines of his bedroom and face the world. It took him a long time to shower and shave, to dress and say his morning prayers. He felt inanimate, removed from his flesh—a series of circuits programmed to follow a routine. It was as though he'd lost proprioception—his sense of self. He left for work without eating.

He knew the job would jolt him back to the present. With familiar people in familiar surroundings, he'd be okay, able to function. But the freeway ride over the mountains seemed surreal, the steamy hills melting into the asphalt, the cars' blurs of steel—futuristic cockroaches speeding away from burgeoning sunlight. Even the station house seemed an oddity—a dirty white stucco building planted in the middle of a burned-out field. A gag gift from some alien architect.

What brought Decker back to earth was the odor of Hollander's pipe.

"What tractor ran you over this morning?" Hollander asked.

387

Decker glanced at the clock—quarter to nine. "I think I'll call Marge."

"I just spoke to her, Pete. She sounds a lot better than you."

"She's okay?"

"Due to be released at ten. Her current flame is picking her up, and she sounded very pleased about that. You know, I think it was real lucky that she's dating a shrink. I mean, he's probably pretty good for her at a time like this."

"Probably."

"Building up her confidence," Hollander said. "That's the worst part. When you lose the confidence, start doubting yourself. Then things start looking pretty iffy out there."

Decker didn't answer.

"Something major happen to you, Rabbi?" Hollander said.

"I'm all right," Decker said. And at that moment, he decided he was. His memories were like old photo albums, to be stashed away in an attic trunk, opened only on the rainiest of days. "Really, I'm fine, Mike."

Hollander took a puff on his briar and blew out fruit-scented smoke. "Then you won't mind hearing that an hour ago they sprang our buddy Earl Darcy on his own recognizance."

Decker snapped to attention. "Who picked him up?"

"Sue Beth Litton," Hollander answered. "I didn't talk to her directly, but the jailer said she was pretty shaken by the whole thing."

"Sue Beth didn't have the foggiest notion of what she was in for when her brother confessed."

"That was the jailer's impression."

The two men looked at each other, Hollander fidgeting with his pipe, Decker smoothing his mustache. With all that had happened with Rina and Abel, Decker had put his cases on hold. Time to bury the personal life and take out the professional one. Time to work!

"Think they'll run?" Hollander asked.

"The thought crossed my mind," Decker said. "Honey farmers could live a long time in the wilds, raise bees almost anywhere there's cloverfield."

"They seemed attached to their land."

"I think they could reattach if they had to."

"Yeah," Hollander said. The stem of his pipe bobbed in his mouth. "Lots of cheap land outside of California, especially if they have Manfred money. Pick out some small town in Idaho or Montana. Continue where they left off. No one would ever be the wiser."

They were silent for a moment.

"Pay them a visit?" Hollander said.

"Absolutely," Decker said.

Hollander took the pipe out of his mouth and tamped down the tobacco. "You look better, Pete. Work agrees with you."

A mile into the ride, Decker realized how much he missed Marge. Hollander operated the unmarked as if it were an adversary, oversteering each turn, jamming on the brakes whenever he stopped. He grunted as he drove, sang snatches of tunes over the dispatchers' voices, making up lyrics as he went along. He had the decency not to smoke with the windows rolled up, but the pipe still leaked plumes of cheap tobacco. Decker sat rigid in his seat, his jaw so tightly clamped his teeth started to hurt.

Hollander started belting out off-key torch songs. Decker cranked up the police radio, hoping Mike could take a hint.

"Jesus!" Hollander said. He lowered the volume. "You trying to make us deaf, aiming for disability or something? What's *with* you today?"

"I'm on edge."

"I can see that."

"Exit here," Decker said, pointing to the ascending mountain road.

"Kinda steep," Hollander remarked.

"Want me to drive?"

"Yeah, why don't you?" Hollander pulled over onto the shoulder of the street. "You know the way."

Decker gunned the motor and burned rubber as he pulled out. He heard Hollander suck in his breath, but ignored him and kept accelerating the car.

A minute later, he said, "You take Granny Darcy, Mike. I'll take Pappy."

"O-kay."

"Keep the questions light. After all, we don't have anything to hold them on. Forensics hasn't released the bodies yet, so something still may come up. But as of right now, we've got zip—nothing to tie them to the crime scene. But they don't know that."

"O-kay."

"And don't smoke your pipe in front of her," Decker said. "From what I understand, she's a real fundamentalist. Probably thinks tobacco is an invention of the Devil." He inhaled a whiff of the odor in the car, then said, "Not far from the truth."

Hollander stuck his pipe in his jacket, leaned the passenger seat as far back as it would go, and closed his eyes. Decker shifted into low gear as he descended into the canyon, slowed as he hit the winding canyon road. Tawny grain fields glinted specks of sunlight, livestock grazed in the distance. An idyllic slice of Americana, discounting the butchery that had taken place. Sudden rage. It happened all the time. . . .

Abel's voice telling him: Who was he to judge?

Good point, Old Honest Abe. Very good point.

Decker heard Hollander snore. He'd known Mike for six years, never seen the man riled. Hollander was a good cop, not hard-driven, but his pacing had given him longevity in a job reknowned for burnout.

He passed Hell's Heaven, saw the rows of choppers, the

bikers armored with leather and denim. The same snapshot as a week ago. No doubt the same three weeks ago.

If four people died in the forest and no one noticed . . .

Decker shook Hollander's shoulder a mile before the Darcy farm. Hollander grunted, then woke. Decker slowed, turned right onto the gravel road that led to the house. The yellow crime-scene ribbon had been broken, but an end was still tied to the porch post. It lay lifeless on the ground like a used party streamer. Decker killed the motor, and he and Hollander exited the car. The air was warm and still, perfumed with hay and clover.

"Where's the welcoming party?" Hollander said.

"I wouldn't hold my breath waiting." Decker knocked on the door. Knocked again a minute later.

"We're too late," Hollander said.

Decker walked around back, Hollander followed. A fifties two-tone aqua-and-white Dodge was parked in the weed-choked lot. The windows were rolled down; stuffing leaked out of the tuck and roll. Decker tried the barn door—locked. He hooded his eyes with his hand and scanned the field. In the distance were the pine boxes—the beehives. A patch of blue gingham was moving between them. Decker walked about fifty feet forward, saw the outline of a stoop-shouldered woman wearing a veil and gloves. He continued forward.

Hollander said, "We should have brought some insect repellent."

Decker didn't answer.

Hollander struggled to keep up with Decker. "Think there's any merit to 'They won't bother you if you don't bother them'?"

"Not when there're thousands of the suckers," Decker said.

"Great."

The woman didn't raise her head as they approached. She was large-boned and big-bosomed. Her features were obscured by the veil, but Decker could see the ruddiness of her complexion. Her hair was straight and gray, cut to one length like the little Dutch boy. It fell to the nape of her neck and sparkled silver at the ends. Decker stopped when they were within speaking range.

"Mrs. Darcy?" he said.

There was no response. Decker spoke louder—maybe the old woman was hard of hearing, because she continued to ignore them.

Decker shouted, "We're police, ma'am! I want to tell you from the bottom of my heart how sorry we are for your loss."

No answer.

"I heard from all your neighbors what a fine boy Luke was. How much he loved you and his pappy. You must have done a right fine job of raising him."

She muttered something.

Decker said, "Excuse me, ma'am?"

The woman didn't respond.

"I know you raised him with the fear of God and the love of Jesus. A fine Christian soldier—"

"Not fine enough," Granny Darcy said.

"It wasn't Luke's fault," Decker said. "It was that she-devil."

Granny Darcy suddenly stiffened. She remained silent for a moment, then said, "You preach the word of the Gospel, but you ain't to be trusted." She faced them, then raised her veil. "Get off of my property."

Hollander shifted his weight. Decker said, "We need to talk, Granny—"

"I said, get off of my property!"

With surprising agility, she leaped from box to box, banging on the hives, liberating swarms of agitated bees. As the dark funnels coalesced, merged into a droning black cloud, she began to laugh.

Hollander and Decker started running, but the cloud was quicker. Soon they were enveloped, hard nodules of fuzzy sleet pelting their face and skin. Hollander swore, tried to bat them away, but it only riled the bees further. Decker felt one sting, then another, and another, His brain fired into overdrive, trying to find a way out.

Think like Byron Howard.

Smoke!

Decker found his cigarettes and began lighting them. He screamed to Hollander to light his pipe, explaining that smoke confused bees. Hollander reached into his pocket and held a match to the bowl of his briar. Immediately, a thick cloud of tobacco swirled around their faces. A minute later, the bees were still upon them, still surrounded them, obscuring their vision, but had slowed their attacks.

"Now what?" Hollander asked, puffing out smoke. He had to shout to be heard over the one-note dirge of the bees.

Decker coughed, dragging on five cigarettes at once, blowing out without inhaling. He yelled back, "We could try walking away . . . slowly." He heard more laughter in the background—Granny's laughter, he thought. But another voice was screaming as well. Words he couldn't understand. A moment later, a distinctly male voice shouted for them to stay in their tracks!

"I can't see a fucking thing!" Hollander screamed.

Decker reached for his snub nose, and told Hollander to draw his weapon. A bee flew in his mouth. Decker spat it out.

"I can't aim, if I can't see," Hollander cried out.

"Relax!" Decker yelled. But he was anything but calm.

Hollander quickly refilled his bowl and began puffing out steamy, scented smoke. He gripped his pipe and said, "I get out of this one, I'm gonna enshrine this sucker."

"Stay right there," the deep voice said. Less menacing tone this time. "I'll come fetch yeh."

The air suddenly thickened until they were engulfed by pillows of soot. Their eyes burned, overflowed tears, their throats were desiccated from smoke and heat. They coughed and sputtered, stoned by flying insects. Bees in their hair, under their clothes, on their hands, up their pant legs. Not biting now, just exploring, thready legs pricking skin as they crawled. The seconds dragged on as they stood choking in the inferno. Finally, two strong arms led them into open air and brushed them free of their live dust. Decker sucked in several deep breaths, coughing, clearing his lungs and mouth of the foul taste of ashy residue. Behind him were humming bellows of smoke rising and, thinning in the breeze, a cackle of crazed laughter.

The male voice said, "You men wait right here while I take care of them bees. And put away them guns. You won't need 'em here."

Through fuzzy vision, Decker made out the speaker. Not a large man, physically, but there was something about the way he carried himself. Independent. Straight back aligned perpendicular to a broad set of shoulders. A confident walk. He wore gloves but no veil. The hair atop his head was jet black.

Decker wiped his eyes. His neck was burning from bee stings. Despite the heat, he wore a jacket. So did Hollander. Thank God for long sleeves. He noticed thick welts on the back of Hollander's neck and hands. "You okay, Mike?"

"Yeah." Hollander winced with pain. "I'll live. They got you bad?"

"Back of my neck."

"Who's the savior? Pappy Darcy himself?"

"Probably." Decker watched the old man guide the bees back into the hives. Unlike Byron Howard, he worked quickly, effortlessly, ordering the old lady around as he needed her. The woman had transformed once again. No longer was she a possessed spirit. Now, she acted the perfect obedient wife, following her husband's commands with slavish duty.

The old man directed the bees onto wood-framed wire matrices filled with honeycomb. Once the insects latched on to their food, he dropped the frames one at a time lengthwise into one of the pine boxes. The man worked nonstop for a half hour. It took six frames to fill one of the pine boxes. There were enough bees to replenish four hives.

When he was finally done, he brushed off his pant legs, shot a quick glance at Decker, then stared at the ground. There had been surrender in the old man's eyes, a look that said nothing could hurt him anymore. He looped his arm around Granny Darcy's shoulders, guided her forward. Then, almost as an afterthought, waved for Decker and Hollander to follow him.

❧29

No one said a word until they were inside the house. The place was pungent with ammonia and lye soap. The floors had been mopped and polished, the yellow-and-red floral sofa and matching drapes had been cleaned. On the floor, Katie and Earl sat on a hand-loomed circular rug, playing building blocks. Earl was erecting a stacked tower, and Katie took extreme delight in his construction. An open cereal box lay on its side; its contents had spilled out in a heap. A trail of ants were working their way over to the brown sugary balls. Katie looked up when she saw the old couple enter, even smiled at Decker. But Earl stiffened. Only when Pappy D reassured his son that the policeman hadn't come to take him away did Earl relax and return his attention to the blocks.

"Knot down?" Katie asked.

"No, Katie, not yet," Earl answered. His tone was very serious. Carefully, he added another block to his tower. "*Now*, you kin knock it down."

"Knot down?"

"Yes." Earl turned to Hollander, giggling as he talked. "She likes to knock down."

The old man said to the old lady, "Take the two little ones in the other room, Granny."

396

"I wanna stay here, Pappy," Earl said.

The old man tousled the small man's head. "You kin come back in a minute or two, son."

Earl didn't move.

"Go on and git now. Don't make me say it twice, Earl."

Granny Darcy led the two "children" into a back room out of Decker's sight. Pappy Darcy motioned Decker and Hollander to the sofa. He stood, gazed out the window. A minute passed before he spoke. Finally, he said, "She ain't right in the head. My pardon for . . . for what happened out there."

"When did she start acting that way?" Decker asked. "After Luke's death?"

"Before. It started when Earl was born, got worse when Luke married. After Luke died . . ."

Pappy Darcy turned toward them. His face was long and tired, eyes bright blue but hooded with sadness, cheeks pitted and slack. A turkey wattle fell to his Adam's apple. He left them alone for a moment, came back with two napkins full of ice. Hollander placed his on his hand, Decker's went to the back of his neck.

"The baby-making thing," Pappy said. "When she found out that . . . that Linda's womb was being filled up with other men's seed. She went lunatic, believed in her heart that it was evil what Linda was doing. She thought Linda was the Devil."

"But Luke agreed to it," Decker said.

"'Cause Linda wanted it so bad," Pappy said. "She was driving my poor boy crazy. Driving *me* to the poorhouse." He shook his head. "Thirty thousand dollars I gave those two over six years. You have any idea how much money that was for me? Had to refinance my land, Manfred always on my back, waiting for me to default."

Hollander said, "A lot of effort for no results."

"You got it, mister," Pappy said fiercely. "I couldn't afford it no more. Misters, I tried for them. Tried for Luke's sake. I loved my son. But . . . but I got a daughter and two healthy grandchildren to think about. Not to mention Earl. All my money was goin' to Luke and Linda. It weren't fair, and I just couldn't do it no more."

The old man shook his head, reached in his pocket and lit up a cigarette.

"Then she started in on Luke, trying to get him to sell my *land*. Getting Carla all riled up 'cause she wasn't a partner in the land. Hell, why should she be? She didn't do no work for it. But the worst was when Linda started sending them rich builders over to pester me. The girl was plumb crazy with the idea of trying to get herself a baby. It made us all crazy. Specially Luke. Then one day he told Granny D what they were doin' to Linda, how the baby might not even be his . . . that drove Granny deep into her spells. Tell you the truth, mister, I didn't like the idea, either. I was spendin' all this money, and the baby weren't even gonna be my blood. I finally said, No more, Linda, No more."

Hollander transferred the napkin to the back of his neck. The pain from the stings on his hands had begun to subside. Decker said, "Linda didn't like being told no, did she?"

"You got it, mister," Pappy Darcy said. "She said she was gonna find her own way . . . then . . . dear Lord . . . it all fell to pieces. Just . . . fell to pieces."

"She had an affair with Byron Howard," Decker said.

"I was ready to throw her out on her butt," Pappy Darcy said. "My wife, too! But Luke . . . he felt bad. Like it was all his fault 'cause he couldn't make her a baby. And Linda was crying, carrying on so. So they stayed together. Luke said he was a believer in Jesus, and if the Lord could forgive, so would he. And he acted real nice and forgiving to Linda on the outside. But . . ."

"But what?" Decker said.

"But something changed him on the inside," Pappy knitted his brow. "And it brought out the worst in Granny. Luke and my wife . . . late at night. Talking and whispering . . . I tried to pretend that it weren't happenin'. But I knew in my heart it weren't no good no more."

"What were they talking about?" Decker asked.

Pappy Darcy shook his head. "It was wrong, what they was doing." He clenched his fist. "Just wrong."

"What were they doing?" Decker asked.

"They were makin' plans for Linda . . . the two of them."

"What plans?"

"Dear Lord." Pappy Darcy's eyes grew moist. "Who she'd sleep with so she could get a baby. Linda didn't want to do it. But Luke . . . like I said, mister, he'd changed. And my wife seemed to go deeper and deeper into her spells. They *made* her do it. Said she'd never be happy until she had her baby. Then Granny started tellin' her how much money we spent on her baby-makin', makin' her feel all guilty." He locked eyes with Decker. "But it was *wrong*!"

Hollander asked, "What'd they do specifically, Pappy?"

"Luke and Granny," Pappy Darcy said, "the two of them picked out men for Linda—men with lots of kids. If Linda would argue, my wife would bring up the affair with Byron, then the money again. Tell her she was lucky that she had Luke altogether." The old man wiped sweat from his forehead. "He'd question her afterward. All the dirty details, and she didn't want to talk about them. But he told her that she was his wife and he had to know. It was bad . . . mean-spirited."

"He pimped her," Hollander said.

Pappy D screwed up his face. "No, sir, no, no, no!" he exclaimed. "He didn't *sell* her, just . . . just told her who to sleep with to get a baby."

Decker tried to keep his face flat. But inwardly he wanted to take a shower. Luke degrading his wife, outwardly acting altruistic, inwardly gloating at his revenge on Linda for her affair with Byron. The whole thing was so smarmy. He said, "They were all chosen by Luke?"

"Luke and my wife," Pappy D said. "Like I said, this baby thing was making everyone crazy."

"Sue Beth know about this?" Decker said.

"No, sir."

"And Carla?"

"Carla . . ." The old man shook his head. "Poor dear daughter Carly." He stifled a deep sob. "She got real mad at Linda when she found out that Linda was steppin' out on Luke. Linda . . . she never told her the truth. Carly wouldn't have believed it anyway. Up until that time, Carly and Linda was drinkin' buddies. A little rowdy but harmless. But after Linda's affairs . . . Carly, she started gettin' real wild."

"And your wife permitted it?" Hollander said.

"She blamed it all on Linda."

"What happened after Katie was born?" Decker said. "Did they ease up on Linda?"

"No, sir," Pappy said. "They had a man waiting for her three months later. Linda wanted more time, but my wife . . . she said it had took her a long time to get pregnant with Katie. Gotta start right away for number two. Luke wanted five kids. That's what Granny told Linda, Luke wanted five kids, and Linda wasn't gettin' any younger."

Decker saw Hollander grimace. A moment later, Granny Darcy shuffled out, chin to her chest, hands rigidly at her side.

"Can I come out now?" she asked.

"No, ma'am," Pappy Darcy said.

"*Please*, Pappy," she pleaded.

"You go back in there right now, or I'll tan your hide."

The woman shuffled away. Pappy Darcy looked at Decker, then at Hollander. "She blamed herself for what happened."

"Want to tell me about it?" Decker asked.

"I guess I should."

"You were there when the murders took place?"

"Sort of."

Decker Mirandized Pappy before they went any further. But the old man still wanted to talk. Decker urged him to continue.

"The man they'd picked out," Pappy said. "Rolland Mason. Linda didn't want no kid by him, didn't want to sleep with him no more. It was the day we were supposed to leave for the beekeepers' convention in Fall Springs. Sue Beth had already left the house, matter of fact."

Decker nodded, told him to go on.

"Granny was out doing some last-minute chores for Earl. Me, I was packing clothes in the house. Well, Linda musta told what was going on to Rolland and Carly. 'Cause I heard Carly crying, cursing Luke, saying he was selling his wife and her out. Rolland was real angry at being used and said he was gonna tell Luke a thing or two. I met Luke when he pulled up in his truck, told him what I thought. Don't go into the house. Wait till they cooled off." Pappy shook his head. "He wouldn't listen. Said he was waiting for this moment. There was something not right in his eyes, misters. Something scary."

The old man crushed out his cigarette and lit another.

"I got fed up," Pappy Darcy said. "Damn fool of a kid not gonna listen to me, I ain't gonna stick around and hear all the dirt. Luke went inside the kitchen, I left the house, went to tend the supers."

"Then what happened?" Hollander asked.

"I don't rightly know," Pappy Darcy said. "Next thing I remembered were the pop of gunshots. I came rushing to the house. But . . ." Tears were running down the old man's cheeks. "It was all over by then."

There was a long stretch of silence. Pappy Darcy dried

his eyes and said, "My wife musta come home while I was out. She said she had to do it to protect Earl. As best as I worked it out, it seems that Linda had shot Luke 'cause Luke . . . this is Earl's words . . . was gonna take Katie away 'cause Linda was a whore. Then Rolland Mason started yelling at Linda for shooting Luke. Then Earl got scared and killed him. Granny . . . she saw all the shootin', said Linda was plum nuts by then, started screaming at Granny, waving the gun at her."

"What gun?" Hollander asked.

"Linda was holding a pistol, had her finger round the trigger. Lord knows where she got the gun. I never owned no pistol."

"Where's the gun now, Mr. Darcy?" Decker asked.

Pappy answered. "I threw it and my shotgun in the sea near Oceanside down South."

"So Linda was waving a pistol at your wife," Hollander said. "Then what went on?"

"Granny said that Linda'd gone lunatic, screaming at everyone, including Earl for shootin' Rolland. Called him all sorts of names. Earl started to cry, but that made Linda ever madder. My wife . . . she got real scared, 'cause Linda was saying some crazy things."

"What kind of crazy things?" Decker asked.

"That she was gonna shoot everyone, then herself." Pappy Darcy held back tears. "Earl didn't know nothing, didn't know what he was doin'. He thought Rolland hurt his brother, was gonna hurt Linda, too. So he thought he was saving her. And with my wife . . . you can see Granny used the shotgun in self-defense. Linda'd lost her head."

"What about Carly?" Decker said.

"Oh Lord forgive us all!" Pappy Darcy began to cry. "Granny D said it was an accident."

"You believe her?" Decker said.

"Yes, dear Jesus, I do."

Decker waited a beat, then said quietly, "But wasn't your wife angry at Carly for carrying on like she did?"

"It was an accident—"

"But your wife didn't like Carla's wild ways," Decker pressed on. "And then Carla started demanding her share of the land—"

"It was an accident!" Pappy Darcy insisted. "Granny shot Linda in self-defense, and Carly accidentally got in the way!"

Decker said, "Must have been hard for Granny, a good Christian woman, to see Carla acting so bad. . . ."

"It was an accident!" Pappy cried out. *"Sweet Jesus, haven't you ever had an accident in your life?"*

Pappy Darcy's cheeks were flushed, his hands were shaking. Decker backed off. He more than anyone knew what an accident felt like.

He waited a moment, then asked, "What happened with Luke? How'd his legs get blown off?"

"That . . ." Pappy Darcy's knees buckled. He sank into a chair. "I did that. Luke was dead anyway. I figured maybe I could make it look like . . . spare Earl and my wife . . . I don't know what I was thinkin'. I wasn't right in my head by that time, neither."

Hollander said, "You shot Luke?"

"After he was dead," Pappy Darcy whispered.

Decker asked, "Then what happened, Mr. Darcy?"

"The rest of us . . . we all left together. I took all the wallets . . . mebbe the police would think it was a robbery gone bad. Granny grabbed Katie out of her crib—"

"Katie's pajamas had blood all over them," Decker said. "How'd it get there?"

Pappy looked down and mumbled, "She followed my wife into the kitchen while Granny was makin' her bottle. Slipped on the floor. I took her out of there fast, I remember that. I didn't even realize that her nightie had blood on it until we was in the car. But Granny . . . she forgot to pack Katie some clothes, so we was stuck."

Didn't even bother to wash it off, Decker thought. Just wiped it off with a Kleenex. As if Granny hadn't cared anymore.

"Then what happened?" Hollander asked.

"We left." Pappy stopped to think. "But it was Katie. Halfway through our trip up, I remembered *Katie*. If Sue Beth saw Katie in bloody PJs with *us*, she'd know that something was wrong with Linda. So I left Granny, Earl, and Katie at a motel 'bout twenty miles away from Fall Springs. I told my wife to put Katie to bed early, then come with Earl and make like nothing happened. Like we decided to take Earl with us after all."

"That's when Sue Beth saw you all for dinner," Decker said.

"Yes, sir."

"You left a little kid alone in a motel?" Hollander said.

"She was sleeping," Pappy Darcy answered. "I told Granny to go back to Katie after she was done with dinner. And she did. Then, the next morning, she told me she fixed Katie up. That we didn't have to worry 'bout her no more. I asked Granny what she did, and she told me she left Katie with her father—her *real* father. I asked her what she meant, but she didn't say no further. Then, later on, after the police found Katie, I asked Granny what did she do with her. But my wife, she was completely gone by then."

Completely gone by *then*? The woman had been a certifiable lunatic for years. Pimping her daughter-in-law, murdering her, then killing her own daughter—accidentally or otherwise. Decker tried to reconstruct Granny Darcy's twisted logic. The old woman must have driven back to L.A., dropped Katie off in the Manfred development in the middle of the night. She probably left her in front of the Binghams' house—she knew who Katie's father was because she'd *chosen* him. Maybe the kid had been sleeping when she had left her alone. One thing Decker knew for certain was that sometime during the night, Katie had wandered away.

"Whose idea was it for Earl to confess?" Decker asked.

"Mine," Pappy Darcy admitted. "I didn't think the law would do no harm to the boy since he's not a full-thinkin' person. . . . I didn't see no other way. Sue Beth started askin' me if Granny and Earl was with me when I came up. I said, of course they was, but I knowed she didn't believe me. Then she told me the police were askin' her the same question. I got scared."

"So you had a long talk with Earl," Hollander said.

"Convinced him he was the murderer of his family," Decker said.

"I didn't mean it like that," Pappy Darcy pleaded. "At first, I just told him what to say. Told him to make pretend. But . . . but as I talked, I could see the boy thinkin' that he'd done *all* the shootin'. I . . . I just let him go on thinkin' it. I told him to tell Sue Beth what he told me . . . what he thought he told me. Then, natcherly, Sue Beth told me what Earl told her." Pappy Darcy bit his lip and held back tears. "I said, better take him to the po-lice afore they find out and come git him . . . Sue Beth, she don't know nothing 'bout this."

Decker nodded.

"Then they put Earl in jail." Pappy Darcy's lower lip began to tremble. "I didn't think they'd do that. I just couldn't take none of this no more. I told Sue Beth to go to Manfred, sell the damn land. I wasn't gonna run, no sir. But if'n we ever get out of this mess, I didn't want this farm anymore. Once it was the Promised Land for me, God's land of milk and honey. Not no more, misters. Not no more."

Pappy Darcy wept openly. Hollander stood, placed his hand on the old man's shoulder, then looked at Decker. Granny Darcy came out again, stared at her sobbing husband. Decker assured her he was fine, but the old woman couldn't take her eyes off of her mate. A minute passed before anyone spoke. Eventually, Pappy Darcy noticed his wife, beckoned her to him, and hugged her. She buried her face in his shirt.

"She ain't evil," Pappy Darcy said. "She's just not right in the head anymore."

"My trust is in my husband and the Lord Jesus," she said, looking up. "You can't do nothin' to us."

"Be polite, woman," Pappy Darcy scolded her quietly. Granny Darcy lowered her head and stared at her feet. The old man looked at Hollander and asked, "You gonna arrest her?"

Hollander nodded. Pappy Darcy turned his attention to Decker.

"You gonna arrest me, too?"

"Yes," Decker answered.

"And Earl?"

"It's best if you all come down to the station," Decker said. "Try and clear up the situation."

"What's gonna happen to us, Mister Policeman?" Pappy Darcy asked.

Decker didn't rightly know, and he told Pappy Darcy just that.

Byron Howard was tending his supers, pouring raw honey into a big ceramic vat. The sunlight bounced off the streams of molten gold, scattered onto the fields. A steady hum of apiarian activity punctuated the summer air. Byron worked slowly, taking his time. Dressed in veil and gloves, the bee-keeper didn't pay attention to the approaching steps, didn't bother turning around until he felt a firm hand on his shoulder. He pivoted, looked up, and locked eyes with Decker, waiting for the policeman to speak.

"It's all over for the Darcys," Decker said. "Want to know what happened?"

"None of my business," Byron said.

"You're sure about that?" Decker said.

Byron didn't answer.

"You know I had coffee with Annette last week," Decker said. "She told me you owned a twenty-gauge shotgun. A Browning, I think she said."

Decker could see the beekeeper tense. But he remained silent.

"Mind if I take a look at it?" Decker asked.

Byron didn't speak for a long time. Eventually, he said, "Go ahead. Darlene knows where I keep it."

"Thanks," Decker said. "Just one more thing. Annette told me you don't like handguns, that handguns were for shooting people and not animals."

Byron didn't answer.

"That true?" Decker asked.

"Yes."

"Yet your wife used to talk about pistol-whipping Linda—"

"Darlene had nothing to do with them murders!" Byron blurted out. Then he turned red-faced.

"Oh, I don't think for a moment she did," Decker said. "But it just got me thinking. That's a strange expression for a lady to use if she doesn't have a pistol. Now, nothing is registered to any Howards, but maybe, just maybe, you have an unregistered handgun around your place. . . ."

"Get off my property!" Byron screamed out.

"No, Byron, I don't want to," Decker said. "Now why don't you and I go into your house and take a look around?"

Byron didn't budge, but his hands dropped to his sides, his gaze sweeping over his feet.

"Byron?" Decker said.

"I kin give you my Browning," Byron hesitated, then said, "But I ain't got no pistol."

"Where is it?" Decker asked.

"I don't know."

"Would Darlene know where it was?" Decker asked.

"Darlene?" Byron jerked his head up. "I told you she don't know nothing about it."

"About what?"

Byron shook his head.

"What did you do with the gun, Byron?"

Suddenly, the old, leathery face crumpled. His lower lip began to tremble, his eyes dammed back pools of water.

"What'd you do with it?" Decker repeated.

"I gave it to Linda," Byron choked out. "She came to me about two weeks ago. Said . . . said that she was breaking it off with Luke." He heaved a deep sigh. "I was happy . . . Lord forgive me, but I was happy. Then . . ." Tears streamed down his face. "Then she asked if she could borrow Darlene's gun. I asked what she needed a gun for, and she told me she was afraid of Luke. I offered to come down with her when she told him it was over, but she said no. . . . Mule-headed woman, she said no."

"So you gave her the gun," Decker said.

"I didn't think nothing would happen."

"She asked you for the *gun*," Decker said. "You didn't think she might *shoot* Luke with it?"

"I didn't think she meant nothin' bad." His voice sounded like the bleat of a lamb.

"You didn't *care*!" Decker yelled. "All you wanted was Luke out of the way so you could have Linda."

"I *loved* her," Byron wailed out. Then he buried his head in his hands and sobbed.

"Right," Decker whispered to himself. What was the point of telling him that Linda had wanted only his sperm? That Linda probably went to him for the gun because she knew that if the gun were ever traced back to the Howards, old lovesick Byron would have gone to jail before condemning his former lover. People using other people. Decker tried to muster up some indignation, but his self-righteousness felt hollow and flat.

And in the background all Decker heard was the pathetic cry of *Linda, Linda, Linda*.

🙰30

Horses from Griffith Park had got loose, were galloping in and out of traffic. The Golden State Freeway was closed off until they could be rounded up and trailered. All lanes were being detoured to surface streets. Horns blared as cars, trucks, and semis ground to a halt. After a half hour, the unmarked's air-conditioning keeled over and died. Marge sneaked a sidelong glance at Decker. He seemed placid, but she still felt bad about dragging him out on his day off.

"Sorry about this," she said.

"Not your fault," Decker answered.

"Not a great way to spend your free time."

"You're right about that," Decker said. But his voice was light.

He was in a fine mood despite traffic. His last phone conversation with Rina had been wonderful. Once again, she assured him that Abel hadn't come between them, that she'd even forgiven Abel for what he'd done. Anybody that desperate doesn't deserve hatred, she'd remarked sadly. She'd also felt good about her judgment. Something deep inside had told her he hadn't any intention of hurting her. She'd been glad she'd listened to her intuition. Decker felt her resolution with Abel was gratifying, but what had been

410

most rewarding about the conversation was the love she'd expressed for him. They were destined for each other. It was *basheert*—fate. She'd known that the minute she had laid eyes on him. It had just taken her time to admit it to herself.

Just thinking of her words gave him a lump in his throat. He peered out the side window at the multicolored metal ribbon in front of him. "Screw this, Margie. Ride on the shoulder and let's get out of here."

She did just that until she was stopped by a Highway Patrol car. They flashed the CHP officer their gold badges and told him they'd just been patched to an emergency call. The chippy was a young buck, anxious to do a good job. With a very serious look on his face, he escorted them to the next available off-ramp.

After they'd exited, they both laughed.

"One of the few perks of this job, eh?" Marge said. "You know where we are? I always get lost around this area."

"We're not too far from the academy," Decker said. "Just go straight here, the road parallels the park. Do me a favor, Marge. As long as we had to exit, hang a right onto Los Feliz—I have some business in Hollywood I should take care of. You mind a half-hour delay?"

"Firing range ain't going nowhere," Marge said.

"Thanks," Decker said. But Marge's face looked tense. Decker told himself that she'd get over it, she was just a little anxious about getting back on the job. Had to prove herself. He hadn't realized how insecure she was until she had suggested a trip to the range. She'd tried to sound casual, but her voice had been saturated with uncertainty. Decker agreed to tag along.

Marge rode through the park's mountainous turns, past shaded picnic grounds and the old-fashioned pony ride—through acres of greenery until the winding lane merged into Los Feliz Boulevard. She drove westward, past rows of well-kept residential buildings. Behind, the hillside was stacked with split-level homes. As she crossed Vermont, the apartments yielded to stately mansions occupying acre lots on grassy knolls. On her left were gated communities where old Hollywood wealth used to reside. But now the area, resting in a smog-soaked basin of L.A., had lost some of its luster, fighting the aging process like an old-time movie queen.

"Where to, Jiggs?" Marge asked.

"Follow Los Feliz until it becomes Western," Decker said.

"What time's the Darcy arraignment?" Marge asked.

"Lou Nixon said some time in the late afternoon."

"We won't make it back on time," Marge said.

"Hollander will be there," Decker said.

"What's Lou shooting for?" Marge asked.

"Ultimately, probation for Pappy and Earl," Decker said. "And Earl and Katie to be placed with Sue Beth. As for ole Granny Darcy?" He shrugged. "Some sort of psych. eval. and treatment. Family's totally fucked up. The only one who gains anything at all is Manfred. Sue Beth told me the Howards sold out right after the Darcys. Manfred's already moving in the rigs. Seems they applied for drilling rights a long time ago, even before they owned the property. All the paperwork's in. Just waiting for the final stamp of approval."

"They could be protested."

"By whom?" Decker said. "There's no one left out there. Even Chip sold out to Manfred. And who could blame him? Not exactly a hoot slinging beers to hopped-up bikers. They've all taken the money and run."

Western Avenue was a succession of cheap motels, take-out joints, and liquor stores. The seediest part of Hollywood. A perfect place to live if you wanted to dwell in chronic depression. The unmarked weaved in and out of traffic.

Marge said, "Manfred moving in like that. It stinks."

"It's what they call in business an opportunistic situation," Decker said. "Turn right on Hollywood."

The unmarked whizzed by boarded buildings papered with movie posters, passed an empty arcade welcoming minors, boasting fun for all. Decker told Marge to slow down when they hit the Sunset overpass.

"Turn left at the next light, park in the lot, I'll pay."

Marge pulled the unmarked into an empty space, received a ticket from an Iranian attendant. She faced Decker and said, "Make it quick, huh? Your old buddy isn't a good influence on you."

Decker said, "You just don't want to burn your ass sitting in a hot car."

"That, too."

"Want to come up?"

Marge said, "And what would you do if I said yes?"

Decker smiled. "I'd be stuck."

They both got out of the car. Marge said, "Think I'll take a walk, buy a Coke. Can I get you anything?"

Decker shook his head. "Be careful out there."

Marge smiled, but it was a perturbed look. Decker said, "Just a phrase, Margie. You're quite capable of kicking ass if you want to."

"I don't know, Pete," Marge said.

Decker stopped her in her tracks. He placed his hands on her shoulder, looked her in the eye. She was a fine-looking woman, smart and sexy in all the right places. Often, he wondered why he had never made a move on her, and decided it was because he needed a friend more than a lover. Well, he certainly had a friend in Marge, and no way he was going to let some scumbag take her away from him.

"Trust me, Margie?"

"Look, Pete," she said, "I know you mean well, but I'm not in the mood for a pep talk—"

"Shut up," Decker said. "Just answer one question, okay? You trust me?"

"Not entirely."

"Good," Decker said. "Never trust anyone entirely. But

trust me on this one. You'll be all right." He pointed a finger at her. "You're going to take something out of this and come out better for it."

"And when do we get to the part where I save the entire city single-handedly?"

"You're not an easy person to console, Detective Dunn."

She shrugged. "Never bullshit a bullshitter."

He removed his hands from her shoulder, held them up in the air. "Go at it at your own pace. But as far as I'm concerned, you're still on my tag team."

Marge smiled. "Thanks. Now go make your peace with your ex-rape-o friend."

"Friend is good enough," Decker said.

Abel was staring out the window when Decker walked in. Still gazing outside, he asked Decker, "Who's the broad?"

"My partner."

"Nice-looking. Big. Even from up here, she looks big."

"She's big."

"A lot to hold on to," Abel said. "Think she'd be interested in fucking a gimp with a ten-incher?"

"I don't know," Decker said. "But she knows about your case. That might bias her against you."

"It should have gone to trial," Abel said.

"Myra dropped the charges," Decker said. "She wasn't about to accuse her own mother of assault. There was nothing left to try, Abe. The files got messed up after the primary field investigator died. Be grateful for what you have."

Abel turned to face Decker. "What I should have had was a declaration of innocence. That's not the same as having the charges dropped."

"You're not running for office, Abe. What difference does it make?"

"It makes a difference to your lady friend out there."

"She's a cop," Decker said. "She's suspicious of anyone who uses hookers."

Silence.

Decker said, "Want to know the giveaway?"

"What?"

"The old lady's airline ticket," Decker said. "Myra kept saying Mama came in after she was attacked, but her mother's ticket said she actually left for Detroit the night of the rape on a ten P.M. flight. She must have paid Myra a surprise visit in the wee hours of that fateful morn and didn't like what she saw. You just happened to be in the wrong place at the wrong time."

Abel shook his head. "Stupid bitch cuts up her own kid because she's turning tricks. And I'm the one who gets screwed." He hobbled over to his refrigerator and pulled out two ice-cold bottles of beer.

"At least you're a free man," Decker said.

"Yeah," Abel said. He placed the beer on the corner kitchen table. "Yeah, I am. Thanks, Doc. Thanks a lot."

"Don't mention it." Decker sat down and drank half a bottle. "Look . . . I keep thinking that one of us should have tried a little harder. That we let too much shit get in the way. What do you think?"

"I think, Doc, that we're like an old love affair." Abel sat down at the table. "Some good memories and a lot of bad ones. But with it all, there's still a little bit of macho male-pair bonding-type love, know what I'm saying?"

"Yep."

"So let's leave it at that," Abel said. "Your wife-to-be wrote me a gracious letter, returned my Nam picture. But she wrote about you and me in past tense—what kind of friends we *were*." Abel let out a small laugh. "Subtle but effective. To tell you the truth, I'm surprised she wrote to me at all."

"Rina's a very special lady."

"That's for sure."

There was more awkward silence.

Decker said, "You call me if you need anything, okay?"

"Always." Abel took his beer and returned to the window. They drank for several minutes, Decker at the table, Abel staring out the window. Decker wondered how many hours Abel spent looking at life passing him by.

Eventually, Abel said, "Your partner's back. Swinging some fine hips. What were you conferring about out there?"

"Business."

"Where're you guys off to?"

"Shooting range at the academy." Decker hesitated, then said, "She had some trouble a week ago. Some asshole tried to bash her head in. Her confidence needs a little bolstering. I was giving her a pep talk. I don't think she bought everything I was saying. But if she bought some of it, that's good enough."

Abel didn't answer right away. Eventually, he said, "That woman out there. Know what she is?"

"What?"

"She's your new macho love affair, Doc," Abel said. "Go out and create some memories with her. Leave the past behind."

"Sage words," Decker said. He stood from the table. "Maybe you should follow them."

"I should," Abel said. "But I won't."

They exchanged weak smiles.

Then they embraced.

The Joanna Brady Novels by
New York Times Bestselling Author

DESERT HEAT
0-380-76545-4/$7.50 US/$9.99 Can

TOMBSTONE COURAGE
0-380-76546-2/$6.99 US/$9.99 Can

SHOOT/DON'T SHOOT
0-380-76548-9/$6.50 US/$8.50 Can

DEAD TO RIGHTS
0-380-72432-4/$7.50 US/$9.99 Can

SKELETON CANYON
0-380-72433-2/$7.50 US/$9.99 Can

RATTLESNAKE CROSSING
0-380-79247-8/$6.99 US/$8.99 Can

OUTLAW MOUNTAIN
0-380-79248-6/$6.99 US/$9.99 Can

DEVIL'S CLAW
0-380-79249-4/$7.50 US/$9.99 Can

PARADISE LOST
0-380-80469-7/$7.99 US/$10.99 Can

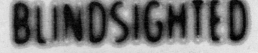